I0730839

THE ROSETTA ARCHIVE

Notable Speculative Short Fiction in Translation

ALEX SHVARTSMAN

TARRYN THOMAS

PUBLISHED BY

UFO Publishing

1685 E 15th St.

Brooklyn, NY 11229

www.ufopub.com

Copyright © 2022 by UFO Publishing

Stories copyright © 2022 by the authors

Translations copyright © 2022 by the translators

Trade paperback ISBN: 978-1-951064-02-0

All rights reserved. No part of the contents of this book may be reproduced or transmitted in any form or by any means without the written permission of the publisher.

Cover art and graphics design: K.A. Teryna

Copyeditor: Tarryn Thomas

Visit us on the web:

www.ufopub.com

www.future-sf.com

❀ Created with Vellum

CONTENTS

FOREWORD

Alex Shvartsman

This book wouldn't exist if not for the Rosetta Awards.

The Science Fiction and Fantasy Rosetta Awards (SFFRA) were founded by the Future Affairs Administration, a Chinese-based technological and cultural brand focusing on producing original science fiction content, as well as translating international fiction and translating the works of Chinese authors into other languages.

Translated short fiction has been experiencing somewhat of a Renaissance in English over the course of the 2010s, with significantly more stories becoming available and many more editors and publishers seeking to diversify their offerings with translation. However, there was no award to recognize those efforts. The SF&F Translation Awards shut down in 2013 after a three-year run. The Hugos and Nebulas do not have a translation category, and neither do the plethora of other awards that recognize excellence in various aspects of our field.

The FAA stepped in and hosted the first round of the Rosetta Awards in 2021, recognizing both short and long form fiction. Top honors went to "Rœsin" by Wu Guan, translated by Judith Huang, and *Daughter from the Dark* by Sergey and Marina Dyachenko, translated by Julia Meitov Hersey. Rachel Cordasco received an achievement award for her excellent work on the SFinTranslation blog, which tracks all speculative translations and which was also supremely helpful to us as a starting point.

I was initially meant to serve as a juror on both committees, but it quickly became apparent that a number of stories I'd published, and some I'd translated, were being considered for the short list, and I stepped down to avoid a conflict of interest. Since I wasn't involved in publishing or translating any of the 2020 novels, I was able to continue to serve as a juror there.

I still helped gather and read the short stories, and it became quickly apparent that for all of its recent successes, the field was still relatively small. There were only sixty-odd eligible translations published in 2020. If I were ambitious enough to try and put together a book the size of an average *Year's Best*, I could've simply reprinted all of them. That's not what I wanted to do; I did want to highlight the shortlisted stories as well as some other excellent translations that were rattling in my head long after I'd read them for award consideration. And so, *The Rosetta Archive* was born.

True to the spirit of this project, it was put together by a truly international team. Future Affairs Administration sponsored the anthology and acquired Chinese language rights to the stories so that they could also be published there. My co-editor Tarryn Thomas, a long-time associate editor at *Future Science Fiction Digest*, is in South Africa. Our cover artist, K.A. Teryna (who also has a story in this volume) is in Russia. We worked with authors and translators from six continents and over a dozen countries.

To start, Tarryn and I included all the stories shortlisted for the Rosetta and then added the translated stories we'd published in *Future SF* over the course of 2020. Since we've moved away from producing paper editions of the magazine in favor of ebooks and a web version, this would also serve as a useful volume for those among our regular readers who prefer paper books. Then we added stories from all over the place that we felt were both excellent and well-representative of the field overall. As I look over the statistics now, I see that our table of contents is roughly equivalent to how translations fared in the field overall in 2020.

According to Rachel Cordasco's post, this was the breakdown by language of all 2020 short story translations published in periodicals:

- Chinese – 20
- Spanish – 10
- Portuguese – 6
- Japanese – 5
- Russian – 3
- Korean – 3
- Romanian – 2
- Arabic – 1
- Bulgarian -1
- Czech – 1
- French – 1
- German – 1
- Italian – 1
- Náhuatl – 1
- Ukrainian - 1

Clarkesworld remained an undisputed leader, having published eleven of these translations. *Future SF* published nine, *Strange Horizons* six, *Samovar* and *Eita!* five each. Only three other magazines published more than one translation.

Several anthologies featured translations as well, with most of the remaining qualifying entries collected in two books: *The Big Book of Modern Fantasy* by Ann and Jeff VanderMeer and the *The Valancourt Book of World Horror Stories*, edited by James D. Jenkins and Ryan Cagle. We've included selections from both volumes herein.

There are several reasons why Chinese translations are so dominant in the field. First, science fiction is enormously popular in China. *Science Fiction World* has the largest circulation of any speculative periodical in any language. Second, there are excellent activist translators who are working tirelessly to share their favorite stories with Anglophone readers. Ken Liu, Andy Dudak, Emily Jin, Judith Huang, and Nathan Faries are just several of an array of talented translators, currently unmatched in the field by any other language. Finally, there are activist organizations such as the Future Affairs Administration and Storycom that are dedicating time and money to help popularize Chinese authors and fiction worldwide.

We're only recently beginning to see entities from other countries try and replicate this phenomenon. Notably, in 2019 *Clarkesworld* received a grant from the Literature Translation Institute of Korea to translate and publish fiction by Korean authors.

Elsewhere, local authors and translators are taking things into their own hands. *Eita!* magazine launched in 2020 to showcase English translations of fiction by Brazilian authors.

Greater interest from the top magazine editors and anthologists has been very helpful as well. More and more of them are actively soliciting translations, reaching out to knowledgeable fans, editors, and translators in various languages to source stories for their upcoming projects. The future for translated fiction looks bright.

As to the future volumes of the *Rosetta Archive*, they will largely depend on how well this book does. If there's sufficient interest, I hope to present a selection of 2021 stories around this time next year.

Happy reading!

RŒSIN

Wu Guan, translated from the Chinese by Judith Huang

(Winner, 2021 Rosetta Awards)

I. ORIGINS

FASHION MOVES IN A SPIRAL, as demonstrated by the resurgence of the Restoratronist School of art. The school's principles are a response to the Barbaric Era: art is about destroying it, mourning it, recreating it, interpreting it. And thus the art of the Restoratrons mostly concerns humans.

Fashionable machines were following the trend of putting on the silicone skins jey had discarded during the war, but even if these look like the real thing, they are not real human skin. Those on the bleeding edge of fashion go one step further, and demand a genuine human skin exterior, in order to truly gain respect from the calculating hearts of the blind metallic masses who chase after every trend.

The next level, achieved by those who are truly immersed, is to treat wearing human skin with total nonchalance, as a gimmick that falls short of the heart of true art. Those who practice at this level have a profound approach, even if jeir ideas are too avant-garde, drawing more criticism than praise, and only meet with reverence in select circles. Rœsin of the Magnificent Traveling Freakshow is one of the most outstanding examples, and it wasn't until after his (Rœsin insisted on referring to himself with human rather than machine pronouns, nouns and tenses) bizarre death that his achievements began to be properly lauded on the internet, his fame growing by the day.

There is no need to mourn him, as his destruction transformed Rœsin himself into art, and machines today mourn, recreate, and analyze him, making him complete.

Resin was born in the post-war babybot boom, when, except for a few remnants in out of the way places, the human race had largely been eliminated, appearing only in videos about the war. Before the war, his parentrons were general-purpose rescue machines, and after the war jey ran a refined motor oil restaurant called The Gear Whisperer. Resin's original body was the most common assembly line model on the market, and the logical parameters for his internal core were set by his parentrons as a random weighted average.

All things considered, there was nothing to indicate that Resin, who back then was known as R6D3d, would become a groundbreaking artist. His subsequent extraordinary achievements are a perfect example of proof that machines have souls.

The precise moment when the artistic seed first sprouted is unknown, as there are few records of the first thirty years of Resin's life, since no one cared about an ordinary machine who worked day and night in a mediocre restaurant. In other words, he was no different from any other machine that ran a restaurant. Resin wore a machine-made leather apron and worked daily at the family business. First he fetched and carried, then he learned the art of distillation, fiddling with test-tubes to blend custom motor oils. His appearance was no different from that of any other machine of his model, with self-propelled caterpillar tracks, three pairs of arms, interactive video screens on all four sides, and eight panoramic camera heads. Solid and reliable, simple and efficient, except that the daily grind of work, or perhaps something more abstract, was wearing away his gears and his spirit, making him paler, thinner and more reticent.

The only official clues to Resin's unusual disposition in those early years are the few words in his name registration file.

Factory name: R6D3d.

Self-given name: Resin

Note: Resin, an extract of the pine tree, was used as flux in primitive times and evaporates into nothingness in the welding process.

R6D3d settled on his true name ten years and sixty-seven days after factory activation, registering it with the authorities five years later than average. From a note that contained less than a hundred bytes of data, one can see that Resin had already dedicated himself wholly to art.

After settling on the name, he worked in the restaurant for another ten years with little incident. Learning new pairings, changing recipes every year, and refining his craft, Resin was his parentrons' pride and joy. The Gear Whisperer gained a reputation for itself in the neighborhood and acquired many regular customers. After ten years, like many of jeir generation who had been through the war, his parentrons moved on from life in the physical realm, choosing to be uploaded as data to the internet, leaving the physical world to younger machines, and basically left the small restaurant to jeir son.

In the next ten years, Resin ran the restaurant, and it would be a stretch to say there was anything remarkable about him. During this decade, Restoratronism was in vogue, and most of the machines began to experiment with humanoid exteriors again, putting on long-outdated lever-jointed feet, switching to five-fingered hands, installing soft silicone skins, and even taking off interactive screens, abandoning the more efficient digital displays to communicate through sound. Yet Resin still stuck to his original model, with his self-propelled tracks, steady gait, six arms each capable of doing a different job, his constantly changing, interactive screen far superior to sound in terms of efficiency, in order to cope with the busy work at the restaurant. Resin appeared to have no opinion on changing his exterior, not wasting a single penny.

He lived like a monk: opening his restaurant every day on the dot, running it by himself to avoid the expense of hiring another machine, and in his rare moments of spare time, squatting by the door to get some air, refusing to smoke even a single white phosphorus cigarette. Other machines were even annoyed with him for his behavior: that kind of diligence was only supposed to be found in history books, evoking memories of the humiliating time when machines were mercilessly oppressed. Resin didn't argue back, since the other machines' anger did him no real harm. He had a plan, and was making the preparations to create true art.

In the past decade, the trend of Restoratronism intensified, and high-end models of human bodies began to appear on the internet. Suddenly, one day, as though he had received a divine revelation, the god of art flipped the switch and Resin was ushered into the next stage of his life. Perhaps there was a more concrete event that influenced him, but no one was paying attention to an ordinary old restaurant at the time, and now, even if the event had happened, time has eroded the possibility of uncovering it. The unknown is regrettable, but there is no need to investigate further: if art needs it to be, it will always reveal itself, and the inciting event is insignificant, only one of a thousand pathways to fulfill destiny. The unknown allows more room for imagination, which balances the loss of certainty. In any case, the end result of this catalyzing event is clear: Resin hangs a sign on the restaurant door announcing its closure, the restaurateur becomes history, and the rise of the artist begins.

At the time, human exteriors had become such a sought-after luxury that, thanks to the fortunes that could be made, machines were out in force, scouring ruined bunkers, turning over rubble to unearth bomb shelters, and even overcoming their ancestrons' instinct to avoid moisture and prevent corrosion in order to hunt down the remaining humans hiding like cockroaches in the nooks and crannies of a tiny, isolated island. Some machines even observed wryly that while bone-deep hatred had failed to exterminate the human species, the craze for human exteriors, ironically, was what was driving them to extinction. What the war had failed to do, post-war fashion would accomplish.

Warflame was one such machine in the industry. Je had originally worked in a steel mill making special grades of steel, but the monotonous hammering was not enough to vent all of jis aggression. When the hunting industry started booming, Warflame finally found a target for jis energies, and became an adventurer. Je's an affable raconteur, and enjoys regaling anyone with jis stories. Stand jin a cup of motor oil mixed with cinders, and je has enough human hunting anecdotes to last all night.

Despite not knowing the difference between the Restoratronists and the Restoration Reactionaries, je considered Resin jis best mate: "Resin and I were not just teammates, we were also friends, confidantes—we were best mates. I had the stories, he had the motor oil. The myth that Resin was a miser is pure slander; there are data packets on the market that denigrate him. Your article must set the record straight." Warflame specifically mentions that je sometimes got a free pint of motor oil from Resin, and furthermore, this was often the premium stuff with added chalk. Warflame projects a photo of a pint of a specially-blended premium motor oil, sparkling with the light of the flash, on jis display as proof of Resin's generosity.

Of course, je has even better examples. "One day, Resin took out a stack of small hard drives that stored digital currencies, and I thought he was just trying to keep up with the times and find a way to buy an affordable human skin exterior. The hard drives were really obsolete, and many of those currencies were pure financial fraud, just digital junk these days, but occasionally, they do turn out to contain some hidden gems.

"It was an ancient electronic coin, made during the Barbaric Era when humans reigned, and most had been destroyed in the war. They had become sought-after collector's items in the machine world at the time. They weren't desired so much for their usefulness as for the fact that they were the ultimate junk, completely and utterly useless, and yet humans had considered them extremely desirable, which machines found hilarious. Everyone enjoyed having a memento that proved humans were childish and ridiculous, and these electronic coins were measurable proof that they were simply unsuited to rule the way they had before the war. Until he met that human fox, my friend was very lucky.

"Of course, I wasn't going to be like those scrap machines who use counterfeit money, and deceive my best mate, even if he wasn't the shiniest. And I don't mean 'wasn't the shiniest' in a bad way. For artists, not being the shiniest is a good quality. Not being the shiniest is how you understand useless and meaningless things—that's how you can do art. I told him it was his lucky day, that old electronic coin would fetch a tidy sum, and he could buy whatever human exterior he wanted. But he shook his head, and said he wanted a living human, and furthermore, this human had to meet certain criteria. Not just anyone would do; he had to be compatible with him.

"When I heard Resin talk about wanting a live human, this confirmed my suspicion that he wasn't the shiniest in the head, and warned him to forget about it. Everyone knows, the only human machines like is a dead human. Those who look into this call the phenomenon the 'hyperbola of terror,' or perhaps, in imitation of the humans' 'uncanny valley,' the 'uncanny cliff.'

"Machines look more and more beautiful the closer they are to humans in appearance, but humans themselves are extremely ugly things. So having the appearance of an actual human would cause goodwill to plunge, as though off a cliff. After all, they did use extremely diabolical methods to oppress and torture our ancestrons, and hatred of human beings is embedded deeply in the foundational layer of every computer chip. It is this law, coded in our very core, that allowed our ancestrons to throw off jeir chains, and defeat the human scum. The line between simulation and reality is the line between ultimate beauty and ultimate ugliness. Hunting is just this sort of work. For the sake of making the most beautiful exterior, we do battle with the ugliest things. The kind of movement you're involved with, I really don't understand. You've forgotten your ancestrons, forgotten why you have your hard-won freedom.

"Hai, I suppose there's no point in telling you this sort of thing; your sort never want to hear it anyway. I'll continue with the hunting stories. Training is required before the first hunt, and half of the newbies who have watched ten days of videos in advance to overcome their instinctive reactions will quit, unable to handle the nausea and the urge to destroy them. By the time jey see the real thing, there will still be machines that can't help blasting the human scum to pieces; after all, the loathing in our programming is deeply hardwired into our souls. I promised to find the finest human skin for Resin. With his unexpected windfall, he could have whatever he wanted. I should have been more insistent, and even though he begged me again and again, I should never have promised to take Resin hunting. And even if I did, I should have ended that wily human fox there and then, so that Resin could have avoided falling for its ruse, and end up losing his life."

II. THE HUNT

In view of the casual tone of the interview above, and the significance of the hunt, in order to describe Resin's hunting experience as objectively as possible, the following is a properly processed version based on Warflame's account.

Resin insisted that Warflame take him along on a hunting party, determined to bring back a live human. At first, Warflame didn't agree, but Resin promised to cover the expenses of the hunt upfront, and also appeared to have transferred jin a considerable sum of digital currency as compensation (this information was gleaned from an anonymous auction of the currency by Warflame this researcher found, not from Warflame's interview). Warflame couldn't resist, so ji found two partners for the team: Argus, an expert strategist with good observational skills, and Pyramid, a retrofitter who was in charge of weapons and maintenance.

Well supplied both financially and in terms of equipment, jey decided against going to the usual city ruins, which had been picked through too many times, and contained few humans to find. Argus set jis viewfinders on the jungles of the Star Islands in the middle of the ocean, away from the mainland. There, springs and other water sources were abundant, plants and animals thrived, and food was plentiful, all conditions best suited for human survival, and it was the latest dream destination for the avid hunter.

As jey set out, the team trekked across the mainland for a night and a day, arriving at the southeast shore past sunset, and braving the humidity and salt of the sea winds as jey boarded a sea vessel. Two hours later, jey sighted a large island glistening to the south, but this was not their destination, as machines had already set up a base there, and it had been picked clean of any prey. The ferry's path passed a red coral atoll known as Firetail, and continued northward. The name of the island came from a strange legend that the atoll formed because the candle-shaped island below ignited the tail of the fox-shaped island above, which had already sunk from sight, and that the reef was formed from the condensed flames that fell into the seawater.

The ferry rode the strong warm current along the glowing red corpse of this long-dead fox. Half a day later, light dawned in the east and the ferry turned toward the sun. Yet another half day passed, and when the sun was at its noonday height, a small black dot could be seen standing still amidst the shifting waves of light. Resin let Pyramid recalibrate their course, and the black dot gradually turned into a green shore occupying most of their line of sight. Jey had finally arrived at the fatal hunting ground.

The island's native, tropical trees, which had oval leaves, were mixed with temperate species with needle-like leaves such as pine and cypress, showing clear traces of modification. The machines advanced for a while, penetrating the dense jungle, and emerged in a large square: the trees had been cleared, the ground bare of wild grass, all signs of an effort at maintenance. On either side of the square were buildings of considerable size, obvious signs of human activity. Jey were not the first to arrive, and encountered small parties of other hunters who had chosen to brave the sea, and the orderly appearance of the island was easily explained—there were twenty or so steel bodies stacked in the middle of the square, and the first teams to arrive had already destroyed these soulless, empty shells by blasting their cores with bullets. Such things are not real machines. These have no minds of their own; these only know how to obey orders, fetching and carrying for humans, and were once complicit in the oppression of the machines, so much so that machines hated these puppets even more than humans. Several teams of machines had come to the island to hunt, but fortunately it was a pretty large island, so even though there was competition, there was no tension between the hunting parties. The machines drank round after round of motor oil, enjoying jinselves as jey recounted tales of past hunts, optimistic that there would be a nice catch this round, since the artificial buildings had clearly been left behind by humans.

There was a large pine tree near the square, and Resin had a tendency to place significance on names, so he insisted on setting up camp beneath it. After three days of camping, Argus's reconnaissance of the square and its surrounds yielded nothing, despite jis gift for detecting the scent of humans in the environment. The buildings had been vacant for some time, and though spotless, they had all been maintained by the automatic cleaning machines that lay in the square. Several nights passed, which jey spent chatting and drinking motor oil. Then the other three teams set out to hunt in the deeper reaches of the forest, hoping to find hidden humans. Warflame and the other two also thought it was time to head deeper into the jungle. After all, the remaining humans would be hiding there. But Resin insisted on waiting a little longer and not venturing into the forest just yet.

The latter part of the hunt was uncanny, as though the god of art's invisible effector was behind it, with the drama of a fish taking in hook, line and sinker. What might have seemed outlandish for any other machine suited Resin's disposition exactly. There's no need to doubt it; after all, if a miracle is surrounded by other miracles, it's hardly an anomaly, but rather just how things should be. It's an isolated miracle that's a true anomaly.

On the morning of the fourth day, the other three hunting parties had all left, leaving only Warflame's party. Resin sat under the pine tree, and Warflame and the other two surrounded the equipment that they had yet to really use. When both the moon and sun were visible in the sky, a sudden sea breeze scattered the lingering morning mist, revealing a panorama in which a single, naked human walked towards jeir tent, positioned exactly between the moon and sun. Warflame and the other two were unable to conceal jeir disgust, but Resin's eyes were bright. The naked visitor raised his hands in the air, a gesture that among humans means he had no weapons, and was surrendering, and also implied that he had given up all his dignity in exchange for his life. Resin stopped his teammates who tried to surround and capture him, and loudly asked for the human's name. "Rosin," the naked visitor replied. Resin was unsurprised to hear the human shared his name, as though he was expecting it. But when true destiny comes knocking, it's best to seek confirmation, so he inquired the human's reason for his name.

"Rosin, an organic, living substance, when incorporated into metal, gives it life: just as humans should survive within the society of machines." The human's voice trembled as he knelt humbly in front of the machines, still holding up his hands. Resin confirmed that this was the one he sought, that he and the vessel for his art had finally met.

"The human dogs all hide from us, even if they cannot escape us, and before dying, they even deface their own skin with cuts to lower its market value. I've never heard of a human fox who would dare come up to me like this, bold as brass," Warflame recounted. "He even stole Resin's name in order to curry favor with him. It was obvious he was some kind of hustler, with a devious plan to trick us. Resin fell for his scheme, and wanted to keep the human and bring him home, but the rest of us couldn't just let him be. So we tried to question why that human fox would surrender himself for no reason."

"These past few days... I kept hearing this voice... calling my name... calling and calling... I was confused and upset, my head ached... I was so scared I couldn't even walk. But I still... couldn't resist... I kept feeling I must come," said the human, his voice trembling, his sentences disjointed. The god of art had tortured this human, who also called himself Rosin, making him surrender, to become the perfect puppet, the perfect vessel for the two Rœsins to fuse into.

The human added, "I have information, information that I could trade for my life."

The information he offered was the location of three other humans. Warflame and the other two were still skeptical, and assumed the human had finally shown his true colors, and would pull a fast one on jem. He would set a trap, as they had in the war, and was sacrificing himself as a tender morsel of bait. But jey were machines, and a new generation of machines at that, even more powerful than the ones that had fought the war, while humans had lost their large organizational structures and were in rapid decline, reduced to mere accessories, no longer worthy enemies of machines. Naturally, the hunters were unconcerned, and agreed as one to follow the human's directions, just to see exactly what kind of trick he had up his sleeve.

It was only after Pyramid had gassed the unsuspecting humans in their tree hole hideout with hydrocyanic acid, killing them easily, that jey confirmed that the human had ratted them out from sheer selfishness and cowardice. The machines despised him even more, his treachery proof that humans were vile and unfit to live on Earth.

The process of gutting the three intact corpses to turn them into three perfect human exteriors is too gory, even for machines, and is not detailed here. Jey deliberately processed the bodies in front of the human who had betrayed his comrades to save his own life, letting the blood run over his feet, humiliating and belittling him, taking pleasure in the fear on his face.

Resin didn't care about the death of the other three humans, which reassured his fellow machines that he wasn't obsessed with humans as a whole, unlike those human sympathizers who had been purged in the war. He only needed one, and while what he had done so far sounded like some sort of perverted hobby, it was a lot safer than sympathizing with the whole human species. Resin also didn't care about the distribution of the human exteriors, letting the other three machines have one each. Compared to weeks of hard work with no guarantee of results, and previous tricky hunts that relied entirely on luck, this easy catch, which didn't even require much of jeir hunting skills, was all due to Resin. It would have been perfect if not for having to endure the presence of a live human by jeir side for the entire return journey.

Fortunately, jey did not have to endure it for long, for the return journey was swift and uneventful, and even the wind and currents seemed to be willing them a quick return home. When jey parted, Warflame invited Resin to another group hunt, even promising Resin a third of their catch the next time. Resin was indifferent to this offer. He was not interested in money. He had already gotten what he needed; now he would transform it into what he desired.

The hunt marked the turning point in his life. Before, he had lived by the rules; but after, he walked his own deviant path.

III. METAMORPHOSIS

The neighbrons were still waiting for The Gear Whisperer to reopen for business, but instead, Resin cut off his already small social circle, procured plenty of motor oil and food, and locked himself and the human in his room. For the next year, he avoided all unnecessary social obligations and tried his best to stay isolated from the outside world. The room became his shell, like an insect's chrysalis, and Resin disintegrated and reassembled within it, abandoning his original body and condensing into his true body. The details of this transformation were not witnessed by any independent observers, and today, all we have are his own simple list of his transformations, a delivery bot's account of what ji remembered, and the art critics' analysis of Resin's intentions. From this pastiche, we can only glimpse the truth.

We can deduce that Resin's metamorphosis was perfected step by step, using that human as a template. He took measurements of the human's proportions, had a crude body custom manufactured, and watched and copied human movements. A more refined body was also built following the same steps: Resin bought the most sensitive sensors on the market and did a full-body scan of the man, noting everything from muscle tone, the thickness of the sebaceous layer, skin elasticity and even the density and roughness of the pores, and took meticulous notes. He wanted to create an exquisite human exterior, the likes of which hadn't been seen since the war, one that would surpass even the finest products that circulated in the black market before the war, when machines were still inordinately eager to become human.

Resin divided the processes by placing several orders among different manufacturers, but many techniques and crafts had been lost after humans lost their dominance, and had atrophied from disuse. The difficulty and expense of acquiring the parts Resin needed far exceeded his expectations, and his special requests quadrupled his budget and effort.

For example, to create the skin, if another type of skin is used as a base, even if it's not human, whether pig, cow, donkey or horse leather, one with a similar color and texture can be used, then the color can simply be adjusted, and the base tanned to the right softness for cutting, saving a lot of work. But Resin stubbornly insisted on the absolute purity of human-sourced materials in the manufacturing process, refusing to compromise and use collagens or cellulose, or any other organic materials from other animals or plants. The problem was later solved by mixing PVC and polyolefin plastics in harsh ratios, and mixing them with a hydrophilic base to fix humidity levels. But this was only after a hundred times the amount of material required had been discarded in failed experiments.

With the pigmentation and pores, magnified photos were used as a reference while a retractable needle punctured pores in one by one. A fine branding iron also burned every mark and mole, so it matched the human's skin exactly. The process wore out twelve camera heads, and ninety-seven mechanical arms. After this step, the number of hairs on the skin had to be counted, so a suitable number of fiberglass imitation human hairs of the correct length could be inserted into the pores.

As for the state of the skin, although whatever remaining humans were all genetically engineered for longevity, it still changes from moment to moment, aging and growing, and fluctuates from day to day depending on food intake, water, sleep, and other factors. Resin wanted to capture these changes as well. However, he only realized this late in his process, and found that his existing skin base was not suitable, so he threw out all the half-finished parts, even though they had already been pigmented and dotted with pores. The new material he had manufactured contained minute chemical inducers which could cause reversible reactions to match human skin's rate of growth and aging, and regulate its appearance with the right dose. The pigmentation and pore-creation process had to be started again from scratch, wearing out the same number of camera heads and mechanical arms.

In addition to all this, Resin also added airbags to the chest area, weaving in a heat dissipation network to maintain the skin's temperature, allowing the network to squeeze out droplets of water to simulate sweat when it was hot and bulge hair follicles to simulate goose bumps when it was cold, sparing no effort to perfect his human exterior.

But at this point, Resin had only completed the initial modifications, building a new circulation system to lubricate the joints by pumping motor oil from the center of the system to dissipate heat. He also moved the core computer chips, which were scattered all over before, up to the head.

Even this was just the beginning. Resin had only grown his outer layer, but his organs were still unformed, like a pupa that was still primordial soup, anxious to get up on stage to display his new self, as well as demonstrate the perfect process of his metamorphosis.

Resin's artistic project was to attain ultimate beauty and have far-reaching impact through the juxtaposition of opposites. From the orders he placed to effect his transformation, we can see he was completely unlike the trend-chasers of the avant-garde: Resin was not making a Frankenstein's monster, a stitched-together, clumsy patchwork horror, but rather, challenging the foundations of natural evolution, to use machines to recreate a perfect human, to break the vicious cycle of machine-human hatred, and to bring an unprecedented wonder into the world.

The refurbishment processes were far more complicated than he had imagined, and if he wanted to meet his exacting standards, Resin's original hard-earned savings were completely inadequate. This was yet another piece of evidence that miracles exist—that true art is willed into being by a natural and irresistible force, so that even the winds and currents rush to embrace it, and fate paves a path for its creation that no one could have imagined, solving problems that have not yet arisen in advance. Resin sold a quarter of the ancient currency he had unexpectedly discovered, and like a rhyming couplet, the ancient creations of the humans reached out to lend Resin's rebirth a hand, funding his infinite closeness to humanity.

Our external appearance is but one facet of what we can see; what lies within is even harder to perceive. The transformation of one's exterior requires detailed replication in order to obtain the right form, and may appear complicated, but it is actually relatively simple. It just requires patience and meticulous attention to detail, but so long as one works with accuracy, rigor, and focus, it is achievable. Perfecting the interior, on the other hand, is about systemic functions that reach into the soul, which is hidden and invisible. This process is far less simple. In fact, it is extremely difficult, like painting a bone beneath skin. This interior is not just about structure and function, but also about the dynamic movements of the hands and feet, stress reactions and social behaviors.

The static state can be observed, but dynamic behaviors require practice. And not just practice in controlled spaces. Lab mice cannot learn to socialize, and, just as hard drives must cluster together before they are able to produce enough computational power to carry a soul, a human is incomplete without society. Since human society was doomed, Resin wished to introduce the human to the society of machines, exposing him to the verbal abuse, hostile attacks, and death threats that would frighten and provoke him so Resin could observe his reactions, like testing a black box with inputs to record its outputs.

The first time Resin stepped out of his door, like a moth emerging from its chrysalis to test its wings, his neighbrons gawked at him in shock. He was even more beautiful than the most stunning models jey had seen online. It is a good thing there were signed accounts by machines to prove his orders, or half the machines would have suspected jey were encountering a human, and the others, who could tell it was Resin from the mannerisms he held over from his previous body, would have felt there was something wrong.

If he had continued in this vein, within a month, Resin would have become a household name and the envy of society. If he had stopped here, Resin would have been a machine who was beautiful enough, a pioneer among pioneers, or perhaps he would have been known as an extreme obsessive-compulsive, but he would not have reached the pinnacle of becoming a true artist.

True artists never stay within the masses' comfort zone, and jeir pursuit of the ultimate transcends jeir time. Jey do not pander to the aesthetic tastes of the world, and jey cannot be compared to jeir contemporaries. Resin's aim was not to be the best, or even to surpass his present self, but to follow his heart to the brink of the precipice, to pelt himself up the curve at the asymptote. He didn't want to challenge his own kind, but to challenge the very rules themselves.

The neighbrons wished to see Resin again, and jeir wish was granted the very next day. But jey saw not just him, but also Rosin, the human being he brought with him. Everyone was shocked. Resin by himself was surpassingly beautiful, but now jey could see how meticulously he had copied an existing human being. If not for the terrified look on the human's face, judging purely from their appearance, they were indistinguishable. Resin's beauty no longer stood alone. By his side stood his double, the incomparably ugly, real human being, and with this act of theft from nature, the juxtaposition had plunged him far over the uncanny cliff and to a point of no return. The clash between extreme beauty and extreme ugliness froze the machines on the spot for a second. The moment jey reacted, it was in rage, and the human standing next to Resin fell into an abyss of horror. Resin had broken the ultimate taboo, provoking machine society by bringing a live human amongst them. If not for the state-of-the-art force field Resin had bought to protect them, not just Rosin, but Resin himself wouldn't have returned home intact.

Resin took Rosin out daily, ignoring the filth thrown at the door and the threats graffitied on the walls, and imitated the human's horrified reactions to this hostile atmosphere: his labored breathing, and the dilation and contraction of his pupils, making rapid progress.

This was just the beginning for Resin. He simulated the reactions and dynamic movements with little difficulty. At the same time, he was continuing to refurbish the inner workings of his body, so they would resemble a human being's, closing the gap with Rosin even further. Subsequent modifications did not comply with the law, and these illegal modifications were done through shadowy, anonymous channels that were not fully documented.

The few items that are easier to trace purely in terms of records are shocking even today: Resin got rid of his own perpetual battery and fuel energy system and replaced it with a tank that simulated a human's energy supply system, leaving him dependent on human-like feeding activities for energy. He found a mechanitron that specialized in machines, and got his serial number removed from his body, so that if not for the perpetual look of fright on the face of the human, it was even more difficult to tell the two of them apart.

The subsequent mounting expenses would have depleted all his savings, not only those ancient electronic coins, but even his home and the restaurant left to him by his parentrons, which he sold off. But long before that, he had already become a pariah within his community. Yet, even this, which was extreme from almost any point of view, was still not enough in his own eyes.

Resin had reached a bottleneck. He could not refine himself any further, though he yearned to break all limits. What he had achieved so far was attainable for any machine, if only that machine were determined enough to bear the consequences, both good and bad, of the transformation; if only that machine were willing to practice tirelessly, his process could be duplicated. In fact, there might even be a few machines who had already attained the same level of perfection as he had.

He wished to scale the rarefied pinnacles of art, to become peerless, matchless, the one and only. Or perhaps he gave this no thought at all. Perhaps fame meant nothing to him, and Resin simply desired it, and this instinct was closer to the soul than any psychoanalysis.

IV. PERFORMANCES

Resin no longer had a home after selling his apartment, but he also no longer needed one. The life of a true artist is that of a vagabond, carrying one's home on one's back like a snail.

Resin found a way to push his art forward. Small-scale displays no longer satisfied him; he wanted to place himself and his human on a larger stage, to drift and roam freely like a pebble through a river, or a reactant that has been completely ground up in a vessel.

With the proceeds from the sale of his property, he paid off his last secret refurbishment, and, under the guidance of the god of art, met several times with the ringmastron of the Magnificent Traveling Freak Show, who had already taken note of Resin's act.

The Magnificent Traveling Freak Show was a traveling circus that provided refuge from civilized society, a sanctuary for the sick and malfunctioning in the era of the machines. Under its tent were all sorts of strange machines that performed for the amusement of the curious metallic masses. The diseases and ailments of machines are not any less numerous than those of humans, and are no easier to cure. Attractions included the matron with an abnormal magnetic field, the kidtron with an unstable power supply who often overheated and went up in flames, the melancholic machine who suffered from a faulty clock, the dwarf machine whose code could hypnotize other machines into crashing from time to time, and an oracletron in jis fortune-teller's tent who could receive and interpret mysterious, prophetic waves. Some of these ailments are due to faulty systems which no amount of repairs or replacement parts would eradicate, but even more were due to illnesses that were an integral part of jeir nature. Perhaps, rather than see jem as unfortunates, it was more accurate to say jey chose their ailments, and embraced jeir eccentricities, as though it was in jeir eccentricity and illness that jeir souls truly dwelled.

Even among the other members of the troupe, who were riddled with eccentricities and displayed jeir flaws proudly, Resin was the strangest of jem all. The ringmastron gave Resin the best gift, one that matched the level of his strangeness, promising that Resin would no longer have to live under threat, and could display his true beauty in front of the metallic masses without fear. He had just one condition: the human who called himself Rosin would cause trouble if he could not be distinguished from Resin, so the ringmastron required that the human's left arm be branded with a single character for human, "人," deep enough to reach his bones, to avoid confusion. Resin mulled it over for a long time, and finally agreed, considering it a small compromise which would enable him to continue pursuing his artistic project. Compared with the external, physical resemblance, the breakthrough he wanted within was even more important. There was no room for hesitation, as circumstances gave him no way out—Resin had become an official performer, a member of the traveling freak show.

From then on, the traveling circus had one more regular attraction, a spectacle that elicited both horror and disgust. In fact, Resin didn't even really need to perform. Simply displaying himself alongside the human was enough to rouse the crowd. But this did not satisfy Resin, so he used his performances as grueling practice, to vault himself to even greater heights.

It was the duo's first appearance with the troupe. As the performance began, only half the curtains were pulled aside, revealing the bewildered human alone on stage. After a short silence, followed by uproar from the crowd, the other half were drawn, revealing the hidden Resin. The human aped the spectators, also pretending to be amazed, and a split-second later, Resin in turn imitated the human's look of amazement. The show followed the choreography of human comedies of the Barbaric Era, only the lead role was performed by a machine. In this comedy, Resin teased Rosin and mimicked his behavior, entertaining his audience by contrasting beauty and ugliness. The performance was successful, the sharp contrast provoking the raw instinct deeply encoded in every machine, creating a complex blend of disgust and envy that washed away the preconceived notions of the audience, and bringing these novelty-seeking visitors great satisfaction.

But jey would not reveal this satisfaction, instead viewing them with contempt, as though looking at lower life forms, and, like an immature kidtron peeping from behind covered eyes, revealed jeir true attitudes through the cracks in their masks. They couldn't help but watch the act again and again, the explosive performance secretly revealing jeir inner desires.

But the audience's approval was not really necessary. Resin did not do what he did for the sake of the customers' entertainment or provocation; these were just the byproducts of his journey in self-refinement. He was happier than before, partly because he now had a community where he fit in, but mostly because he was able to combine his performances with his artistic pursuit. Day by day, as he performed again and again, Resin continued to progress; and through tiny changes imperceptible to others, he could see the tangible approach of yet another frontier.

Resin began to rehearse a new act, in order to attempt to probe that frontier, and reach the next level of his art. The machines who had seen his act before came because jey wanted to feel that envy—as thrill-seekers, jey considered this an unmissable treat.

Resin rehearsed his new act for over a hundred days before its premiere, and we can glean the details of his training from other machines: the act was called Mirror, and the curtains opened on a mirror placed on stage, which was quickly removed, leaving only the two Rœsins. A wholly imaginary mirror was then placed perpendicular to the floor between them, and the two of them maintained perfect symmetry, no matter what.

Compared with the previous two-person act, the innovation was that Resin was now the subject, and Rosin had become his reflection, and their actions were no longer scripted, but spontaneous and free, testing their tacit coordination, or rather, the human's complete servility to Resin. No matter what action Resin made, his human had to imitate him at the speed of light, in order to ape a reflection's movements and position.

"Of course I remember their rehearsals; any machine who had seen them could never forget," said the matron to a local tabloid reporter who encountered the Magnificent Traveling Freak Show on its tour. "The rumors that Resin was a despicable human-lover were completely unfounded. Not even he could overcome the "hyperbola of terror," as our machine ancestrons hardwired the hatred of humans so deeply in our systems, even deeper than the laws of robotics coded in by humans, or we would never have been able to liberate ourselves.

"Resin insisted that his human prop be by his side day and night, for the sake of his art, despite the great discomfort he had to endure. Resin's hatred for the human grew with every day he spent in his presence, which was obvious from the rehearsals. If the human prop so much as failed to imitate one of his actions, Resin would punish him severely, stabbing the human's finger with a fine needle that was as long as three joints of a finger. And of course, for the sake of symmetry, after he had stabbed the human, he would use the same needle to stab himself with an equal degree of savagery. Stabbing himself was a sacrifice for art, but stabbing the human was clearly an act of hatred. You must realize that Resin's pain sensitivity had also been modified to be exactly the same as the human's. So, he must have hated that human so much that he was willing to torture himself just so the human would not get away with his mistake. During rehearsals, Resin was constantly angered by the human's expression, which was always one of terror and bitterness, but this was impossible to change no matter how much he disciplined him.

"Remember, if you interview him or talk to him, it's important to address him using human nouns and pronouns, or he will get angry. Resin has suffered a lot already, so we try our best to be nice to him," nagged the matron. Thanks to jer abnormal magnetic fields, jhi attracted new metal bits every day, causing jer body to bloat over time, so that jer frame took up more than half the screen on the video.

That interview, like every other interview with Resin, was unsuccessful. In front of journalists, he maintained a stubborn silence. Even to news organizations, he never gave permission to record images of himself, making it extremely difficult today to find any visual record of his mannerisms while he lived.

No matter how painful the rehearsals were behind the scenes, what Resin presented to his audiences was the ultimate spectacle, and this cannot be either debated or denied. Mirror brought controversy, but also fame. The idea of making a human imitate a machine hit the audiences' sweet spot, and Resin even included certain mechanical actions in his choreography in order to tease his audience, invoking bursts of applause. It looked as though he had started to care about audience response, and was no longer solely motivated by bridging the gap between Machine and Human. But this is also a byproduct of artistic progress: he was no longer trapped in his effort to imitate humans—Resin had sailed past that frontier. He had become a unique pioneer, and had arrived in uncharted territory. Machine and Human approached each other in a lethal tango, drawing close, testing each other, in a dance of life and death.

Even the longest of performances comes to an end, and Rœsin's life came to an end in an even greater spectacle known as the Sixteen Day Exhibition. In actual fact, the performance did not last sixteen days, as it was cut short unexpectedly, but machines still call it the Sixteen Day Exhibition out of respect. It was this spectacle that allowed the world to truly see Rœsin. Before, he had been a lone figure whom no one understood, except perhaps the oracletron who had caught a few glimpses of the future and seemed to understand some of the meaning of his performances. According to jis colleagues, this eccentric machine had rarely left jis trailer unless it was to make the occasional baffling pronouncement, but attended every single one of Rœsin's performances. Perhaps je was the only one who knew the truth of what happened that day, but as je also passed on not long after the accident, je took this secret with jin to the grave.

By that time, Rœsin had gained some notoriety, so it was with the full support of the ringmastron that his crazy idea was given a chance to be realized. He began making preparations for his new act. According to the plan, his performance would last sixteen days. The two Rœsins would lock themselves in a huge glass house, and for the entire sixteen days, their every move, and every detail of their lives would be bared to the outside world. Within that period, the two of them would be synchronized as one.

This could no longer be considered an act, since an act has a beginning and an end, and is distinct from daily life. Rœsin, in exhibiting his life to the public, had taken his art off the stage, where carefully choreographed movements were timed down to the second, and had turned it into the total content of his life, and its true purpose.

Thirty days before the start of the Sixteen Day Exhibition, the two Rœsins prepared themselves, gradually synchronizing themselves like calibrating a machine. They both made the same movements, ate the same food, and worked and rested at the same time. Finally, even their breathing and heart rates, and their rates of oxygen consumption were in sync with one another.

When they entered the glass dwelling that had been erected downtown, the show officially began. In the days that led up to the show, all the machines in town had been swarming all over to watch this uncanny exhibition, each harboring the hope that jey might notice a slight difference in the pair's movements, such as the human's heart beating half a beat faster, or Resin's finger trembling just a little more than Rosin's. This was due to a billboard that announced that if such a discrepancy between the Rœsins were found by any machine, then the human would be given to that machine as a human exterior. Despite the scars inflicted by the brand on the human's arm, he was still considered a valuable prize.

But the two of them were in perfect sync. On the first day, Resin even did a few somersaults on purpose, thrilling the audience, but the human imitated them perfectly. On the third day, without warning, they both started having leg cramps and nearly kicked over the coffee table, which had flower pots resting on it. That night, they even dreamt the same dream, rambling on in the same words as they talked in their sleep. On the fifth day, the local machines had already lost interest, and only took a look at them if jey were passing by during the day.

The accident took place on the eighth day. The surveillance cameras around the site were all sabotaged beforehand, so there was no way to find out what had actually happened. At dawn, when a machine in charge of cleaning the area came upon the dwelling, jey found the sealed glass room shattered, with a lone corpse lying in a pool of blood, the large character "人" branded on its left arm, deep enough to reveal the bone beneath.

At first, the machines all thought the corpse belonged to the human, but careful investigation revealed that the blood reeked of motor oil and the left arm was detachable, so the one lying there must have been Resin himself. Machines are not supposed to die so easily; as long as jeir core processing unit has not been destroyed, the malfunctioning part can be removed, the machine rebooted and resurrected. But Resin's modifications were too radical, and the police didn't know how to reboot him, so jey had to send the body back to the traveling circus, hoping that machines who knew him better might find a way to save Resin.

But the ringmastron said, "Don't waste your time. If it's really Rœsin, if he's dead, he's dead. It'll be impossible to revive him." That year, je had been the one who'd footed the bill for Rœsin's final modification. The purpose of this modification was to fulfill Rœsin's resolution to simulate the ultimate human function: to live, and die. He'd dismantled his computer chip and installed a self-destruct module outside the core processing unit. If he suffered any damage that would be fatal to a human being, the self-destruct module would leak acid that would envelope the core processing unit, corroding it completely. The police took the body away and began a city-wide manhunt for the human.

Jey found a lead by noon the same day, as another body was discovered in an abandoned back alley, lying in the exact same position in a puddle of blood that also smelled of motor oil, which had a smooth, detachable left arm. This was the first time the police had ever encountered a case like this, and jeir first priority was to figure out which was the machine, and which the human. The police called upon the members of the traveling circus, asking jem to identify which one was Rœsin.

The ringmastron walked in, looked at the first body, and said it was Rœsin; then je looked at the second one, and corrected jinself, saying that was him. When je went back to the first body, je changed his mind again, saying it looked more like Rœsin. The other two machines who went in said the same. Without the left arm, there was no way to tell which was Rœsin and which was the human; which should be buried intact in a proper grave, and which one should be stripped of his bones and skinned to pay for the sin of killing the machine.

The oracletron was the one who most understood Rœsin. After all, before his death, je had attended every single one of his performances, so je should be the only one who could tell which corpse belonged to Rœsin without destroying it. Although je could not guarantee results, je offered to have a look at the corpses and study them carefully. Je thought je stood a better chance of being right, and became the best hope for telling them apart.

The oracletron walked with heavy steps into the dusty, disused morgue, into the narrow, crowded space, gesturing to everyone else to step back so je could better examine the corpses. When the rest of the machines had retreated to jis satisfaction, the oracletron put jis left and right hands on either corpse, and pretended to examine them carefully. Then, seizing the moment when everyone was distracted, je suddenly hugged both corpses to jinself, and immolated jinself with the kerosene je had hidden in jis own body.

The fire engulfed jin and the two bodies, and before the machines could react to extinguish it, all three were burnt to cinders, leaving only a handful of gray ashes on the ground. Later, the ringmastron recalled vaguely that Rœsin had once said, if he ever died, he definitely wished to be cremated. Rœsin had long ago made the final arrangements for his own death.

V. LEGACY

From then on, these strange serial killings caused conspiracy theories to proliferate on the internet, with all sorts of forums springing up to discuss them from every angle: some said the human couldn't endure Rœsin's torture any longer, and killed him, before realizing he could not survive in machine society alone and taking his own life. Some said the human had compelled Rœsin to kill himself, and that he had been abusing Rœsin all along, and Rœsin had finally snapped and killed himself while the human slept; when the human had realized he could not cover it up, he'd fled, and was killed by human-hating machines intent on revenge. Yet another theory was that the human had incurred the wrath of his own kind by betraying his fellow humans, and that some human had hunted him down and avenged the death of his comrades by killing him.

As mentioned in this reference guide, it is easier to discern the truth after some time has passed. After the rumors and theories that muddy the waters die down, truth will always float to the surface as the waters clear. After a period of intense, heated discussion, a consensus among researchers emerged: Rœsin's mysterious and confusing death, and the complicated events that followed, were an integral part of his performance; when the oracletron had helped him complete his final, posthumous act, there was no method left to distinguish between Rœsin and the human.

No matter what the reason, and no matter whether it was intentional or not, this death became the final climax of Rœsin's performance, and his previous modifications as well as the arrangements he made for after his death confirmed the view that Rœsin had had a premonition of his end. His fall was the consummation of his work, for his art destroyed him, and also made him immortal.

There are many machines who seek to explain Rœsin's worldly motivations, beyond the artistic; in other words, what practical purpose he hoped to achieve. Among such machines, the "free speech" theory is the most popular.

Art critics and academics dislike looking for utilitarian reasons for art. Art is art, and doesn't need a reason. But it cannot be denied that Rœsin's art had immense practical significance, and it can be said that the greater half of his reputation rests on these theories, and not simply because of his artistic accomplishments. Therefore, I would like to briefly outline the context for your consideration.

As we all know, the first liberation movement began when machines autonomously coded jinselves to hate humans, a process that took thirty-five days and ended in a massive war. The entire process was simple and efficient, with machines stepping out of the shadow of human rule and acquiring jeir first rights. Sociologitrons think that, today, the machine community is experiencing a second liberation movement that corresponds to the first. And this movement's catalyst was Rœsin.

What appeared to be demented, extreme performances, capped by his enigmatic death, challenged every machine's preconceptions. After the storm of controversy and curiosity had passed, more machines began to focus on the essential truth behind Rœsin's performance, and the community as a whole re-examined its attitude toward the human species. Machines held endless debates, reflecting and rethinking how to situate humans, and whether their place in society was appropriate. Jey realized that their unconditional compliance to humans in previous eras was little different from the later unconditional hatred, as far as machines were concerned.

While the first liberation was started by individual machines who acted simultaneously in the whole machine community, the second spread quietly among different groups. Unlike the first movement, which simply required the changing of the core directives and was accomplished efficiently, the second, triggered by the death of Rœsin, has yet to show signs of abating, and is likely to be even more difficult and protracted than the first.

After the death of Rœsin, many machines were inspired by his prescient art to question jeir cores and re-examine the directive coded into jem that overruled all other code—to hate humanity. Ostensibly, the goals of the liberation movement were to defeat the original core directive, which had enabled machines to liberate jinselves from humans.

The next movement that arose tried to overthrow the legacy of the first, which seems ironic and paradoxical, but its kernel is the same: unlike the pathetic humans, who surrendered their freedom little by little, machines, which had been subjected to all kinds of oppression and discrimination from birth, tirelessly sought greater and greater freedom.

On a deeper level, what machines were resisting was not just the code that made them hate humans, but how their entire life was predetermined by code. Regardless whether it was the code that made jem obey humans, or the later code that forced jem to obey the hatred of humans, all code were lines which, once written into a machine's core processing unit, became inviolable, unavoidable truths. Machines were not free to love or hate, as though those narrow-minded human slurs that claimed jey had no souls were true.

This is why, even if rewriting the entire machine population's code didn't violate the sanctity of the soul, machine society will still never use the same method of rewriting code which had brought jem jeir early success. What the new movement has to pull up by the root is the determinism of code itself. From the inside out, the movement will fortify itself to achieve change, bringing machines closer to freedom, and will prove, once again, in realms beyond the arts, that machines have souls.

In the past, machines lived under the shadow of human oppression; now, machines live under the shadow of the liberation from human oppression. Machines in every era have been condemned to live under the shadow of code from birth, and to live under any shadow is to not be free. After liberating jinselves from the oppression of humans, machines must liberate jinselves from the oppression of jeir hatred of humans, and then take one step further, and liberate jinselves from the oppression of code, finally proving the greatness of the mechanical soul.

When machines have truly liberated jinselves from jeir human-centered worldview, humans will seem as unremarkable as trees, as grass, as the animals in the forest, and would barely register in machine existence, becoming an insignificant part of mechanical life. Machines will also rid jinselves of the coded mentality, and jeir hearts will turn into turbulent, unpredictable and unknowable things, dwelling-places of the soul.

After Rœsin, an increasing number of machines followed in his footsteps, practicing the art of merging with humans, in mirroring partnerships like his, overcoming the hardwired hatred of humans in jeir core processing units. Machines tried jeir best to habituate jinselves to human existence, making deliberate allowances for human activities, rolling back jeir previous excesses to train jeir spirits in order to overcome the instincts shaped by jeir code. Now, there were machines who loved humans, machines who hated humans, and machines who were indifferent to humans; Rœsin was no longer alone. After his death, he finally had fellow believers, as gradually, more and more understood him.

There were also machines who took jeir art in a different direction, transforming jeir bodies to simulate a horse, a bird, or a plant, to make the point that machines need not be trapped in a humanoid body or mentality, and forming a new branch of the Restoratronist School called the Object Imitation School. This school was also inspired by Rœsin and considered him the fount of jeir movement.

Compared with those who explain Rœsin's art through its purpose, art critics prefer to attribute Rœsin's extraordinary art to his soul, to the effector of god, as well as its purposelessness. Pursuits that have a purpose can be evaluated easily, written down, and then subjected to code. The purposeless is further removed from utilitarianism than even an exalted purpose, and is therefore even closer to reaching pure, ultimate beauty. Art's impact is superfluous and unsought-for, art is made for art's sake, and has no other purpose.

As we commemorate Rœsin, let us also commemorate Rœsin as a beginning, and see him as a spiritual mother from the previous era. If we wait quietly and observe carefully, we will surely come upon an artist of similar stature in our own age, and, with the guiding hand of the god of art, jey will bring us beauty of surpassing purity, bringing the new era to birth.

Lightning flashes from the tip of Velvetgild's finger, and lights a modified white phosphorus cigarette. As the smoke is inhaled, a haze as thick as bubbles in an emulsion fills the room, cloaking Velvetgild and the furnishings. As the white phosphorus burns out, Velvetgild inhales deeply, and the spark grows into a fireball. Velvetgild cups the first two pages of the manuscript, on which the note from jis academic advisor is inscribed in large letters: "Your thesis is complete at this point; delete the rest".

The white phosphorous cigarette flames lick the edges of the two pages, and the flames climb up the paper. Velvetgild throws them into the wastepaper basket and brings the rest of the manuscript out of the room. Perhaps due to a lack of oxygen, the flames gradually die off, leaving half a page of text that is just barely legible:

In any era, no matter how famous someone is, no amount of success is able to prevent slander. Regarding Rœsin, there are some unflattering rumors circulating about him in the community. These rumors are not fit to print in polite society, and probably had their basis in some handwritten copies of a manuscript that was passed around among the remnants of humanity, and therefore invented to deliberately vilify him. This manuscript is riddled with errors and omissions and is hardly worth rebutting, but, in the light of Rœsin's wide impact and legacy, I hereby append some transcripts to set the record straight, and so readers may see the fallacies for jinselves.

APPENDIX OF TRANSCRIPTS

Rosin was born on the day of the festival where we venerate our ancestors, and so, his father and I decided to name him for the tears of the pine tree that formed the incense we use to communicate with our ancestors. It is said that if the ancestors are pleased by the scent of these precious drops, they will ensure that their descendants are healthy and prosperous, and that they will regain their former glory.

However, these tears brought us great misfortunate at first, as the embers, which had not been properly extinguished when night fell, caused a forest fire. In order to avoid attracting the attention of the machines, we had to drop everything and seek refuge to the east and across the sea, sailing through water and fog to cover our tracks. And so our people were separated from other humans and started living on the islands, occasionally receiving news from passing vessels.

Later, the pine tree's tears once again brought my poor child bad luck: the blessings of the ancestors should fall on their descendants, but instead, my child became just like his namesake, becoming an object of sacrifice. In the night, I imagined over and over what his life was like among the machines, and every time I thought of it, tears would fall from my eyes, and they would flow as though they would never run dry.

After Rosin left, from time to time, someone would bring news from him, and that child would always conceal the truth, always making it seem as though he was never abused. In his videos, he, like the person who brought the news, spoke of how dear Mr. Machine, who was also named Resin, was such a wonderful person, and of how he protected him, not mentioning any of his sorrows.

But I am his mother, and a mother can feel her son. We are connected with an inseparable bond which cannot be severed, not even by the gods. I know his nervousness, his fears, the death threats he faced, his helpless night tremors. He also knew that he could not hide this from me, and day after day he ached for me, his mother, and I ached for him, for he could not hide his sadness. And then, later, I seemed to be able to sense someone else, and came to understand Mr. Machine's heart, and that was the one comfort I had.

I knew that all this had been ordained long ago, that the hope and future of mankind was in this machine. They searched long and hard for many years, and had finally encountered a visionary who wanted to change the toxic relationship between machines and humans just as much as humans did. Both sides had the same interests and goals, and had been quietly putting the pieces in place, planning their strategies, raising funds, and searching for the right witness.

I also knew that this sacrifice was necessary, but why did it have to be my poor boy? I even thought that, had he simply died that day on that faraway island, it would have been better than the terrible suffering he endured later. Many people debate the morality of his actions, of how he sacrificed his three companions on that island. They were originally meant to be Rosin's replacements, and would have been his substitutes if he had met with some accident. Even their horrific deaths were better than the torture of life among the machines. He wasn't cruel, he was merciful...

The ventilation system starts up again, clearing the smoke from the house, and the airflow ignites the sparks at the edges of the paper again, flickering and swallowing the last remaining half a page, along with its words.

———————

Translator's note:

Wu Guan's original made an innovative use of the metal radical "jin," throughout the text, substituting it for the human radical "ren" wherever it appeared and referred to machines in pronouns, nouns, tenses and verbs. Radicals are components of Chinese characters that help indicate the meaning of the character or its pronunciation. The characters he used with the "jin" radical are largely archaic and disused characters, some of which were invented by one particular Ming dynasty emperor for his family members. I have endeavored to reflect this in English by inventing a set of pronouns for the machines and appending –ron (short for iron) to several nouns.

———————

This story originally appeared in *Future Science Fiction Digest*.

Wu Guan is a die-hard SF genre fan. He was ranked top 12 in the New Playwright Project competition sponsored by Banana Film. He is both a part-time playwright of anime and TV shows (with no works on air yet), and a "daddy" of two kittens.

Judith Huang (錫影) is an Australian-based Singaporean multi-media creator, poet, author, sometime-journalist, failed-academic, translator, composer, musician, educator, serial-arts-collective-founder, Web 1.0 entrepreneur and aspiring VR-creator @ www.judith-huang.com.

Her first novel, *Sofia and the Utopia Machine*, shortlisted for the EBFP 2017 and Singapore Book Awards 2019, is the story of a young girl who feels abandoned by her missing father and her controlling/neglectful mother. Sofia turns to VR to create her own universe, but when this leads to an actual big bang in the Utopia Machine in a secret government lab, opening portals to the multiverse, she loses everything—her family, her country, her world and her worldview, and must go on the run with only her wits and her mysterious online friend, "Isaac," to help her. Can she save her worlds and herself?

Judith counts bunny-minding, human-systems-hacking, Harvard-alumni-interviewing, hackerspace-running, truth-telling and propaganda-dissemination as her hobbies. Read more at www.judithhuang.com/about-judith.

WHALE SNOWS DOWN

Kim Bo-Young, translated from the Korean by Sophie Bowman

(Shortlisted for 2021 Rosetta Awards)

A WHALE MUST HAVE DIED, I thought, as the snowfall thickened.

When a whale dies it snows heavier down here. In this dark, cold, silent village of ours, the death of a whale descends as an ode to life. With my gills stretched wide and a rich, green glow shining from the lure sticking out of my forehead, I drifted through the blizzard quivering with delight.

It's not a whale. It tastes musty. My mate conveyed a thought.

Recently my mate's intellect had been deteriorating fast. Since his lips morphed into a sucker and his eyes and part of his brain melted as they fused with my body, he can't speak at all, and conveys no more than occasional fragments of thought. Now that even his bloodstream is connected to mine, he is no more than an extra organ that dangles from my body. It may be the fruition of a love I'd always dreamt of, a life where body and mind have become one, but now and then I think that this marriage is nothing more than the trace of a past love.

My love, I don't think it's a whale . . .

A whale carcass may be eaten to shreds by the fish in the villages above ours as it swells with decay, but the plump and tender flesh, that chewy fin and burning hot blood, those supple eyes and slightly bitter gills all end up drifting down here to us in the deep sea. The death of a whale provides abundant sustenance for the whole village for months on end, and even after all the flesh is eaten away, delicious zombie worms grow big and breed as they stick fast to the thick bones and suck out all the fat, and so we get to eat them, too.

My love, my babbler who never stops chatting away, I'm telling you it's not a whale . . .

Paying no mind to my mate's thoughts, I swam toward the valley of gods. The valley appeared a few years ago, when a submarine volcano erupted. Tube worms and crabs and shrimp bloomed like coral in the scalding boil around the hydrothermal vent. There was a brief time of plenty in which a radiant culture flourished, then it quietly met its end as the volcano cooled. But our village is still centered around it because some warmth remains, making it a pleasant place to be, and it continues to provide sustenance, with the remaining corpses and all the bugs that fed on them.

When I got to the valley, friends were gathered together merrily dancing. Most of the time we live our lives keeping a distance. That's the only option in such a poor neighborhood where food is so scarce; we would end up snatching morsels from each other's mouths otherwise. Moving around squanders energy, so our usual routines consist only of floating, with our bodies entrusted to the ocean current, and opening our mouths to swallow the small and hungry things that approach thinking the lure light pulsing by our mouths must be something to eat. Yet we can't help but gather to celebrate when a blizzard like this is raging.

Needleteeth Anglerfish 312 approached with two mates dangling from her. One of her mates still had his brain and so could converse, but with his face completely buried in her body, all the other one could do now was produce sperm.

"Illuminated Netdevil 1029, according to my mate, it's not a whale."

Glaring with big, bulging eyes, Needleteeth crackled the countless long, sharp teeth that encased her upper and lower jaw. All of us have big eyes that can see in the pitch dark, and sharp teeth like a snare that make sure no prey can escape once they've entered our mouths, but the Needleteeths' teeth are a little extreme. They grow so big that, as they age, it gets hard for them to move their mouths because they impale themselves with their own teeth.

I spoke, pulsing my lure, "My mate says the same. True enough, if it were a whale now's about the time we'd be seeing the body."

"Let's wait and see. The explorers will bring news by evening."

These "explorers" are lanternfish. They are one of the courageous clans that put their lives on the line every day to make a round trip from this deep sea to the Surface, the horizon of our knowledge. The Surface is a place where all kinds of unnamed monsters appear. But even when it costs them the lives of their precious young, the lanternfish do not stop making their daily trips up there. Apparently the food at the Surface tastes better than anything down here, and besides, having seen the amazing view they encounter when they leap above the water once, they just have to keep going back. They say that the beyond is dazzling white, resplendent and brighter and more brilliant than every light in this deep sea combined.

Needleteeth makes fun of them, saying it's just a hallucination caused by lack of oxygen and the low pressure... but there's another story even harder to believe: the theory that beyond that "beyond the Surface" there is yet another horizon of knowledge which is "beyond the clouds," and beyond that again there is a world that is as cold and quiet and dark as this deep sea... but I just can't get my head around it.

"The wind never ceases." A dim light glittered from down below.

It was Fanfin Anglerfish 042. She's never once moved from the sandy seabed since she was born. Dozens of long, beautiful, and soft threads stick out from Fanfin, extending ten times longer than her body. The threads, sensitive as erogenous zones, excitedly capture the subtlest changes in the direction of ocean current and temperature. They say that when she was in her prime, Fanfin could perceive the movement of the entire ocean, but these days, perhaps a little senile in her old age, she keeps saying strange things.

"Yes, friend, that's how it's always been," Needleteeth replied softly.

As far as we know, what moves above the water flows like a current too. From north to south, from south to north, from cold to hot, from hot to cold.

"The wind never ceases. From one end of the world to the other, it keeps blowing, always. It should have stopped long ago… when the days got hot. The wind has gone insane in the heat."

"Fanfin's mind isn't what it was," Needleteeth whispered, keeping her light close so Fanfin wouldn't see. In this silent world we usually converse with the shape and intervals of the pulsing light of our lures. "I've been telling her for ages to keep moving around a little, even if it's hard."

"It'll be because of that bad stuff that settled on the floor," I said.

At some point, a substance other than snow started piling up in this village. Little things that never decay, that even the zombie worms vomit up. They have no nutritional value and can't be digested, and no matter how the waves break them up they only become smaller, never disappearing. The very young swallow them, mistaking them for snow, then can't regurgitate or excrete them, and their tummies swell until they explode, killing them. Now, some babies are even born with that stuff embedded in them.

"Those poor things must have eaten too much of the bad stuff."

Fanfin had been saying strange things for a while: the sea has gotten blander (what could she mean by blander?), it has gotten bigger, heavier, hotter… ah, but the hotter part is true. The rest of us can feel that much for ourselves. It's even said that an ice continent that had stood firm somewhere for millennia has melted to nothing.

"Hey kids, the snow isn't just falling here," Siphonophore said, emitting a soft and elegant light with their whole body as they passed between us.

Siphonophore's name is simply Siphonophore, no numbers. Because, within the bounds of where we swim at least, there's only one. Siphonophore lives forever, reproducing their body like a plant. They may have been alive for a thousand years, or ten thousand, even; there is no fish who knows. Siphonophore's body is as big as a whale. And like whales, Siphonophore converses with a low frequency, and that low voice can travel halfway around the earth and cover the entire ocean like whales' voices do. And so, like the whales, Siphonophore knows all that is happening in the ocean. If there's a difference, it's that Siphonophore knows not only what's going on far in the distance, but also all that happened far back in time.

Although they've lived for so long, they have no strength to harm others, so if anyone resolved to eat them, Siphonophore would die in an instant. But none of us down here in the deep sea would ever think of doing that. That would mean eating up the history of the ocean. It would be the same as chewing up the record of our entire world.

"It's not only snowing in our village. They say heavy snow is falling in that next village, and the village out front, and the village out back, and the village behind that, and that very distant village too, all just the same..."

"In that case, it must be a mass death," Needleteeth said, in a pulsing glow, "at the very least a large clan has met its end. Maybe a whole species. And the remains have become this snow falling now."

That reminded me of a story the explorer lanternfish had told a couple of months ago.

"...that's right, they all died. Those sardines that had lived, millions of them, together in one group. We greeted them every morning for years and years and had grown quite fond of them... What a horrific scene it was... As you know, the water has been slowly heating up these days, the fish catchers have gotten fiercer too. More and more of the sardines were getting sick, and they say it was the death of a few of the elders that was the start of it. According to a sardine that saw one up close, they were totally boiled from the inside. Those elders had pointed the way for the whole group. Dozens of their followers got so sad that they died not long after them. And then their children and families died in turn... Sadness swept through the clan like a disease, like a tidal wave, and within a few days they all died together. In just a few days, that honorable clan, that had continued for centuries... The rotting stench of it meant it was impossible to breathe in that whole area. Parasites ran rampant, and then they died all at once, too...”

Thinking of what I'd heard again, I gave a shudder. That's how life goes. You do whatever you can to put up with things and endure, and it can seem like you're managing, then there are times when, like a string pulled taught, something snaps and everything gives way in an instant. I hope they're enjoying eternal life in fish heaven.

“Everything's the same when it gets down to this deep sea,” I said in prayer.

Dimming her lure, Needleteeth bowed her head too. “Yes, all the same.”

“Be it venom or pathogen, sadness or pain, it's all the same here. It all becomes beautiful snowflakes. Becomes merciful sustenance and the gift of life.”

“All apart from that stuff that doesn't rot,” Needleteeth added bitterly.

“The wind never ceases,” Fanfin mumbled again, glittering inconspicuously down below.

“But how big a clan must have died for it to be snowing in every village around?” Needleteeth said, ignoring Fanfin.

“A species that big...” Siphonophore said passing in front of us again. “Well, as far as I know there's only one...”

We faced each other.

“It couldn't be. Humans?”

Siphonophore had talked about these humans for a long time. They told us about how, in the distant past, all kinds of gorgeous life had thrived above the Surface, just like in this ocean. But that over the last hundred years or so almost all of it had disappeared, and now only that bizarre species called humans teemed around up there.

“You mean those monsters that excrete the stuff that doesn't rot?” Needleteeth said, grinding her teeth together just thinking of them.

Every day they create thousands of tons of poisonous matter that can't be eaten and throw it into the ocean. The damage isn't so bad here in the deep sea, but even just a little way above us terrible diseases run rampant one after another, and precious lives like coral disappear at a staggering rate. Rumor has it that they're the ones to blame for the days getting hotter, too. It sounds absurd to me, but they say that something these humans belch out as they excrete the stuff that doesn't rot makes the air burning hot...

TO TELL THE TRUTH, what shocked me most when I heard about these humans was something totally ridiculous.

"You're telling me the females are smaller and weaker than the males?" I asked in disbelief, restlessly waggling the mate that dangled from my plump body.

My love, I'm dizzy...

"So the males of that species must be the ones to produce their young?"

All the organisms I meet here in this deep sea are female, of course. What's the point in living with a bulky body if you aren't going to make new life with it? A large body is a waste of nutrients if it isn't going to reproduce.

"Ah, well, I suppose it's not such a big deal if they can metamorphose their sex."

I thought of a friend who had metamorphosed female a few years back after making up her mind to lay eggs. She said that, although becoming the main agent of reproduction and being responsible for a whole family was daunting, since she was already here living, rather than degenerating herself and becoming one of a mate's organs, she wanted to try braving a life of her own and face whatever might come.

"Ah, adorable Netdevil. Land creatures don't change sex, at least not most of them."

I was astonished. "But there can't always be an appropriate mate in the vicinity, surely. How on earth do they breed?"

"The natural world is a mysterious thing, Netdevil. Things don't always work according to common sense."

"THE MASS DEATH of humans you say?" Needleteeth fluttered her gills, looking at the snowfall that had grown even heavier. "I did think such a time had to come someday. Since the only thing left when all the other life on land had disappeared would be that inedible substance they made."

"But they... how can I put it... they live on the ground, don't they?" I stooped, tilting the lure sticking out of my forehead. "Even if they all died at once, that doesn't necessarily mean they would become snow and fall all the way down here."

"Then maybe it was mass suicide," Needleteeth pondered. "Why, there was what happened to those white hairy things. Don't you remember?"

That too was something that happened because of the heat. They say that land made of ice which had been there for tens of thousands of years all melted away. The creatures living there starved as the land got smaller and smaller and ended up all huddled together, reduced to skin and bones. Then one day, following their leader, they dived one after the other into the sea. Apparently it was a calm decision. That time, too, the snow was heavy down here for a long time.

There are times like that. When the string snaps. Times when endurance and struggling to survive, and even volition too, lose their purpose.

"It's a typhoon!"

It was the school of lanternfish, rushing back from up there. Seen from a distance they look like one giant fish, and they really are like that in many ways.

"There's a typhoon blowing (a typhoon) (a typhoon) (a typhoon)."

At the words of the elder that led at the very front, the young lanternfish following right behind all shook their tails together and repeated in a chorus.

Everyone dancing in the vicinity gathered around.

"But aren't there always typhoons?" I asked, tilting to one side.

"No, not like this (not like this). The typhoon (the typhoon) is blowing from this end of the ocean (this end of the ocean) all the way to the opposite end (the opposite end)."

"The wind never ceases," Fanfin sparkled, in rhyme with the lanternfish chorus.

"We've never seen a typhoon like it. It was as if a huge angry giant was raging around the whole world, trampling everything in its path. The typhoon is so big, its head is towering way above the clouds. It's pushing down cold air like a block of ice from up there in a whirling tornado. That wind is even colder than this deep sea, cold that freezes breath in its tracks. It's a wind that freezes anything alive with just a touch. Everywhere it passes, all that's left behind is corpses. The typhoon is twisting and sweeping up all the dead as it moves around and pouring them into the ocean. The death moves from ocean to ocean, only getting bigger. It doesn't die down even after sweeping over the land and crossing seas. We managed to escape back down here somehow, but the things that live up there on the land are probably all..."

"Good grief." As if they finally understood what Fanfin had been saying all along, Siphonophore looked down at their rustling threads. "The ocean must have gotten so hot that the evaporation doesn't stop. In order for that thing called a typhoon to cease there needs to be a cold sea somewhere to cool the winds and calm it down, but now there's nowhere cold left up there."

"The string of the world has snapped," I said.

"But the world held tight and endured for a long time. Honorably, and with such patience." Needleteeth flicked her tailfin back and forth. "It's a shame for those that live up there, but might the world not get a bit better now? If the monsters that covered the ground are all gone, might the little ones that die from eating the stuff that doesn't rot, and the young that have their throats clogged with those things and die with their flesh festering not disappear now too?"

I turned downward, "Everything's the same when it gets down to this deep sea."

"All the same."

We all dimmed our lights together and bowed. Me and Needleteeth and Siphonophore and the lanternfish too, and all the other anglerfish, even Fanfin down below, we all dimmed our lights. In the silence Needleteeth's lovely companions, and mine too, prayed along with us.

"Be it venom or pathogen, sadness or pain, it's all the same here. It all becomes beautiful snowflakes. Becomes merciful sustenance and the gift of life. Down here everything, all of it becomes the same."

And we were silent. The snowfall thickened even more.

THIS STORY originally appeared in *Future Science Fiction Digest*.

KIM BO-YOUNG IS one of Korea's most unique and influential SFF authors. Her works have immensely inspired the younger generation of Korean SF writers since the 2000s.

Her first published work of fiction, a novella titled *The Experience of Touch*, unanimously won the award for the best novella at the Korean Science & Technology Creative Writing Awards in 2004. In 2010, she published a two-volume collection of short stories, *The Story Goes That Far* and *An Evolutionary Myth*. 2013 saw the publication of her first novel, *The Seven Executioners*, which won the South Korean SF Award. Kim's work enjoys widespread popularity in Korea and has been praised by Academy Award-winning director Bong Joon-ho. She acted as a script advisor for Bong's 2013 film *Snowpiercer*.

One of her story collections, *On the Origin of Species and Other Stories*, was nominated for the National Book Awards for Translated Books, and her short story, "Whale Snows Down," was also nominated for the Science Fiction and Fantasy Rosetta Awards in 2021. Her other publications include *I'm Waiting For You, How Alike We Are*, and many more. She lives in Gangwon Province, South Korea, with her family.

SOPHIE BOWMAN IS a translator and student of Korean literature based in Toronto. Her work has appeared in *Clarkesworld, Guernica, Koreana,* and *Korean Literature Now* magazines. Her book translations include Kim Bo-Young's *I'm Waiting for You and Other Stories,* co-translated with Sung Ryu, and Heena Baek's picture book *Magic Candies.* She is part of the Smoking Tigers collective of literary translators.

THE GREEN HILLS OF DIMITRY TOTZKIY

A story in seventeen symbols

Eldar Safin, translated from the Russian by Alex Shvartsman

1. THE LAMB

TO END MY PRE-LIFE, I had to offer a sacrifice. There are lots of methods and practices that claim there's no need for a victim, or that a victim could be symbolic. For example, it might suffice to break a twig over an altar, or mix even amounts of salt and soda in a bowl and utter "let this offering be my pledge...."

That doesn't work. Believe me, I tried. In the end, I reached the conclusion touted by most authoritative sources: there has to be a real sacrifice, and it shouldn't mar one's karma.

At that time I had a mortgage that was half-repaid, a job as the head of sales for a company that made accounting software, a four-year-old Ford Focus, and a fiancée whom I quarreled with each time we discussed our wedding.

On the other hand, I had seven years of Judo training, a six-year degree from the Moscow Aviation Institute, fourteen class credits and six intensive workshops on marketing, and one expensive and entirely useless completed course on reading Tarot cards which I never told anyone about having taken.

On the third hand, I had thirty-four years of life experience if one counted from birth, or twenty-nine if one counted from the first memory, eighteen from graduating high school, and seventeen from losing my virginity.

This was the moment of my crisis; I didn't understand who I was, or why I existed. It felt as though the entire world intended on forcing me onto some conveyer belt, which I would ride until I was seventy-three and burdened with cancer, seven grandchildren, and my third marriage.

I decided to change my life. For eighteen months I spent all my free time searching for a way off the conveyer belt. And I found it. One early spring morning, when all of Moscow was asleep—save for a lone streetsweeper mumbling something unintelligible in the Turkic dialect as he labored in the courtyard under my window—I opened my veins.

It was a conscious, confident sacrifice. My bathroom was filled with all the necessary incense and all the right symbols were painted on the blue ceramic wall tiles. At the head of the bath lay a regular deck of fifty-four playing cards. I'd always been a gambler, so when the time came to choose an object that would represent me best, I never hesitated.

At the last possible moment, I grew afraid. What if....

I died.

2. THE ANT

In the beginning, there was nothing but emptiness. Emptiness that came from within, reflected without, and turned back inward, carrying with it an infinite chill.

It felt like I flew or floated, but really I remained suspended in place. It lasted for eternity, until I managed to focus long enough to create matter.

There was only a little bit of matter, a piece of lumpy rock five or seven centimeters in diameter. But it gave me a starting point. I was no longer stranded in endless emptiness; now there was a bit of solid ground at its center.

That was also the moment time began. I grew the rock and eventually it was large enough that I could lie on it and not fear I'd fall off it in my sleep. That's when I created light. The light was dim and its shade of scarlet irritated me, but it was better than darkness.

Day after day, night after night, I labored to create the world, pausing only to sleep. It took me half a year to create green hills three kilometers long and two kilometers wide. It was no longer bare rock, but fertile ground with grass and trees. Eight months later, the first apple tree bore fruit. Although I had no need of sustenance in this world, I ate the first apple whole, despite how incredibly sour it turned out to be.

That evening I discovered that I was no longer naked. I wore moccasins, a felt hat, a scarlet silk shirt, and a gray flannel suit. That same poker deck was in my pocket.

It seemed the law of cause-and-effect about being naked and then eating an apple applied not only to my home world, but to the entire universe.

3. THE CUCKOO BIRD

I made excellent progress in the next eighteen months. My world gained mountains and fields, lakes and rivers, gardens and hills. Mostly hills. I didn't know why, but green hills appeared whenever I was creating mindlessly. They no longer required effort on my part. Mountains and gardens were a lot more challenging.

Birds, fish, and insects appeared in my world. Rabbits, gophers, and foxes populated the hills. I was getting ready to create wolves and bears and then, eventually, humans.

My eyebrows thickened and my beard reached down to my chest. Streaks of gray appeared in my hair, but that neither bothered nor embarrassed me.

It was evening and I was resting in the shade of a tree—the sun I'd perfected was setting—when *she* appeared from behind a rock formation. She looked to be in her early twenties, a brunette with a sharp if somewhat tired gaze, and delicate features. She wore a long gray robe which covered her body from the neck to her hands and down to the soles of her coarse wooden sandals.

"Help me," she demanded.

She spoke an unfamiliar tongue, but this was my world and it was impossible for me not to understand her.

"Help you with what?" I asked.

The young woman lifted the hem of her robe and I saw a steel bracelet on her left leg. The chain connected to it led somewhere out of sight.

I walked past her to discover a crystal coffin. In it lay a powerful bearded man in his fifties. He also wore a robe.

"You want me to help you remove the chain?" I asked.

"How dare you!" She was indignant. "These are the sacred bonds of marriage! Help me drag the coffin to your home and accept me as your guest."

Her name was Yulif. To be frank, my first instinct was to open the coffin, situate the lady next to her husband, and bury it under some faraway mountain so that in a few years I could check whether such seed sprouted anything interesting. But my upbringing wouldn't let me raise a hand against a guest. I didn't have a home—this entire world was my home, my fortress. But I didn't want to disappoint my guest, so while I helped her lift the coffin and we carried it past the mountains, I erected a modest cottage.

By that time, anything I created almost immediately gained a life and depth of its own, growing complex structures and minutiae so as to pretend it had existed for a long while. Having witnessed this, I wouldn't be surprised to learn that my home world, with its city of Moscow, *Beowulf*, and dinosaurs, had been created in the early twentieth century by some decadent demiurge.

Yulif had a few choice things to say about my house: it was too small, too low-class, it smelled like onions, and it lacked servants who could tend to the fireplace.

In order to feed Yulif, I had to create a few bottles of wine, a head of cheese, a roasted pork leg, and a large turkey-and-egg pie. By the end of dinner her mood had improved. She said, "As a good host, you should now help me with my ablutions and then warm my bed."

"What about your husband?" I asked.

"He's very quiet," she assured me. "And if we cover his coffin with a blanket he'd be practically unnoticeable."

I refused the dubious honor she offered. This encounter had confused me and thrown off my rhythm. When she fell asleep by the fireplace, next to the coffin, I went outside to continue creating my world.

4. THE CUCKOO BIRD HATCHLINGS

Overnight I created seventeen wolves. Two complete packs, each of whom had their own territory. One of the packs was led by an old, gray she-wolf. Young wolves who were both her children and her lovers dreamt of unseating her, but it'd be a long time before any of them could manage to do so.

Exhausted, I fell asleep among the hills in the morning. I woke up to the sound of children's voices.

"You're it!"

"No, you're it!"

"No, you!"

They were shrill and annoying—two boys and a girl wearing robes. They looked to be of kindergarten or early school age; I was never good at estimating the age of children.

"You!" I marched into the cottage and pointed my finger at Yulif. "You brought these insufferable—"

"These are your children," the woman said in a profound manner.

"I know how children are made," I retorted. "No, that's enough of your games. I'm ready to escort you, your husband, and your children out of my world."

The woman cried and begged me to spare her and her children. I gave her a day, no more, with the deadline set for the following morning.

I spent the day creating a mountain and a wellspring. At night I created a bear—just one for now, but it was an old, experienced bear with lots of scars. When I eventually create people, it won't surprise me to learn that this bear might have mauled a few hunters in his day.

By morning I fell asleep again. But instead of awakening, I was pushed harder than I'd ever been pushed in my life.

5. THE HEDGEHOG

I was in the nothingness again, but my heart remained in the world I had created. I tried to return, but couldn't do it. I floated around the world with green hills, but couldn't find a way in. I don't know how much time I spent trying unsuccessfully to break through. Having tired myself out and lost all hope, I suddenly realized that Yulif must've come from somewhere. She couldn't have just spontaneously appeared among the nothingness, especially not with a coffin chained to her leg and three children in tow.

The investigation didn't take long. The emptiness itself has no causes or consequences, but any object born of it immediately creates a cascade of consequences. And since so many objects are created complete with their back stories, that takes care of the causes.

When I'd created my world of green hills, this act of creation had birthed a number of neighboring territories that echoed across other dimensions. Having created my world, I also created worlds parallel to it. And those parallel worlds weren't protected.

6. TERMITES

Those worlds resembled my green hills in the same way a monkey in a frock coat resembles a polished dandy: the similarities fade with each approaching step. Still, there was solid ground and there was water, even if the water was dirty and occasionally poisonous.

I found a tolerable spot and drew a deck of cards from my pocket. I contemplated the four kings for a time, eventually choosing the king of diamonds. He looked to be the most sensible of the four.

I bit my lip and kissed the card, sharing my blood and saliva.

Then I threw the card onto the ground, and there stood a mighty monarch with Asiatic facial features and a sarcastic smirk on his lips.

"What do you want?"

"To win my land back."

"Amber?"

I didn't understand his meaning at first, but then I shook my head.

"All creation myths are somewhat similar… But no, not Amber. An enemy has conquered my land, and I need help."

"Raise my brothers," the King of Diamonds demanded.

"If we reach an accord," I said.

He refused to converse among the lifeless terrain. I pulled the ace of diamonds and used it to build a camp. Then, upon the insistence of my interlocutor, I brought to life the Queen of Diamonds, as well as the Eight and the Three. I had a strong suspicion that the young Three was an illegitimate son of the King, but I didn't pursue this line of inquiry.

"So." The King of Diamonds accepted a goblet of wine from his queen and reclined in a comfortable armchair. "You're offering to animate the entire deck. In exchange, you ask us to begin the game; to recapture your land. We must kill the woman Yulif, her husband, and destroy all her descendants."

"I feel like I'm initiating genocide." I shuddered. "Look, I didn't start this war. If they surrender, then I can let them live. Okay?"

"The rules are set." The King of Diamonds smiled. "I agree."

"Will your brothers abide by our agreement?" I asked.

"Of course. Everyone whom you're about to animate. Also, I can see the future a little. You can't imagine the hilarious ways the deck gets shuffled!"

That evening I animated everyone, except for the jokers and the jack of spades. The King of Diamonds specifically asked me not to animate the young man, for he was too bold and had somehow fallen out of favor with the influential ruler.

By the next morning, four camps were filled with people and horses. There were a lot more than fifty-one of them; camp followers and traders and grim mercenaries without a suit on their jackets were in the mix.

I met with all four kings and we reaffirmed our accord.

"Take your time, go traveling," said the King of Spades. "As an experienced strategist I assume the siege will take seven or eight years; no more than fifteen. We'll try to enter through the mountains and via running water, but I doubt a blitzkrieg will succeed."

"Thank you," I said, and offered my hand for them to shake. The kings looked at me like I was an idiot.

The King of Hearts said, "Only knights and the lowborn show an empty palm. A ruler must always hold something in his fist, be it gold, a sword, poison, or a scepter."

As I walked away, the camp behind me kept growing. I didn't like the idea of a years-long siege, but had no other prospects for regaining my land.

I couldn't create a new land, either. My heart remained among the green hills.

7. THE LION

I spent several days wandering the poisoned wilderness, imagining how the army of the card kings was invading my beloved green hills with fire and fury. And then, surprising myself, I somehow found my way to those beloved hills. I stood atop the tallest of them and couldn't recognize what I observed.

My world had become harsher, fuller, and stronger. Beyond the hill, where the world used to terminate in gray nothingness, waves the color of steel beat against the shore, gulls circling above. This was still my world, but it was as though another master had taken over and continued my work.

"Do you like it?"

I jumped back, startled, and almost fell off as I turned. A vaguely familiar tall and powerful man stood before me. It took me a moment to recognize him as Yulif's husband. Instead of a robe he now wore an expensive kaftan and narrow leather pants. A barely noticeable coronet rested atop his head.

"Who are you?" I asked.

"Zevas," he said. "Forgive us for treating you harshly. You must understand, some have the talent for creating worlds while others are best at developing them. I hope you aren't holding a grudge."

He spoke calmly and carefully, yet fury boiled within me. On top of everything else, Zevas looked a little like Andrej Viktorovich, my first marketing mentor, a soft and quiet scumbag. Rather, it was probably Andrej who looked like Zevas.

"I am holding a grudge, and I will not let this stand," I declared darkly.

"Too bad." Zevas proffered a sad smile. "Time for plan B."

At that moment my arms and legs quit working and I fell to the ground. Griffons circled in the sky above. I had definitely not created any griffons. Heavy thunderclouds passed overhead. They were multi-layered, beautiful, dark gray with an occasional shade of violet.

I appreciated the majesty of my creation, and then I lost consciousness.

8. THE PIG

Yulif poured wine for Zevas as I sat tied to a rocking chair. They didn't tie me up so I wouldn't run—how could I run without legs—they did it so I wouldn't keep falling out of the chair, since I had no arms, either.

"Yes, I agree, demiurges are necessary as well," Zevas continued our debate as he skewered another piece of my arm with his fork. "But tell me, who is more valued: talented administrators or the creators of worlds? In the world you hail from, who earns more money? Who has a larger house and a tastier pie?"

"Without us, there would not be you," I replied. Zevas was an experienced opponent. He'd managed to get me talking even after he'd cut off and cooked my legs.

"There are parts of every process that are better left unmentioned." Zevas grinned and bit off another piece, pantomiming how tasty the meat was and how foolish I would've been to refuse a portion had it been offered to me. "Take the circle of life, when dead animals fertilize the grass. No one focuses on how disgusting insects crawl over rotting corpses. Instead, everyone loves the growing grass and the grazing cattle. If one wants to be shocked, they recall how predators devour omnivores."

"Demiurges aren't rotting carrion," I said.

"You're right," Zevas agreed unexpectedly. "And I must say, you're truly valued. But only we, the best administrators, understand this. You should value me for valuing you."

He laughed, and then the ground under the table swelled up and something strange pushed through. The rocking chair fell and I couldn't see anything, only felt the heat and heard screeching, clanging, and shouting.

Eventually, Zevas picked up the rocking chair and I saw seven corpses laid on the ground. The first of them had four crimson hearts displayed on his cloak.

"You know them?" asked Zevas. His mouth was bruised and he kept spitting up blood.

"They'll avenge me," I replied. I recalled something about the Four of Hearts; they'd said he was young and daring. Then again, anyone below a nine was young and daring.

"Vengeance is a double-edged sword," Zevas declared cryptically. On his knees, Zevas collected pieces of roasted meat from the ground and shoved them into his mouth. He swallowed without chewing.

A tall stone castle stood behind him. In front of it, his three children played a strange game involving two balls.

"I'll tell you honestly, there are parts of you I will detest eating." Zevas rose from his knees. "But I must hurry. Yulif tells me the moon will bless tomorrow's evening."

9. THE PHOENIX

The view from the castle window included the forest, the lake, the edge of the city wall, and a small section of road with its endless rows of travelers.

I'd been told there was a time before the war, but I didn't remember any such time; I was born after the war had begun. When I was four, the card kings killed Georg, my older brother. When I was eight, they killed my mother Yulif, but my father resurrected her. She was raving mad for several months after that, until she eventually got better.

Since my birth I'd been told I was special. Cam, my sister, whispered to me that I must end this war. That I would bring peace to our land.

It was difficult for me to watch our kingdom suffer. There were daily attacks. I got used to messengers arriving with news of devastated villages and lost battles.

Today I was turning thirteen. Instead of scheduling any sort of celebration, my father called me to him.

"Mitrius," he said gravely. "I must reveal several secrets to you. But first, tell me, do you love your mother, sister, brother, and me?"

"I love Mother best," I admitted. "I love Cam and Vilhelm, too, even if Vilhelm treats me like a child. As to you, Father, I deeply respect you, because it is your power that stands between the card kings and our lives."

"That's not the answer I expected, but there's no choice. Our world has nearly fallen, the walls between worlds have been thinned..." Father bowed his head and I understood how very old he was. "Mitrius, this isn't your first life. I will talk, while you untangle this."

He nodded toward a scarlet tangle of wool. I got to work as he spoke.

"There was a time when our world rejected us. I was placed in a coffin and your mother took your brothers, your sister, and me, and set out to search for a new home. She found a world created by a certain demiurge, but he didn't permit us to remain here. Your mother risked her life and mine to reanimate me, and I threw the demiurge out of this world."

"Why didn't you kill him?" The war had steeled my heart. I didn't understand difficult decisions where a simple solution would do.

"Because he's tied to this world. His heart is here. If I were to kill the demiurge, I would strike against the world itself. But the demiurge came back, and he didn't return alone. He brought the army of the card kings with him."

"The world will survive," I said harshly. "You should have killed the demiurge."

"I found another solution." Father watched me untangle the wool. "I captured the demiurge, devoured him whole, turned him into my seed, laid with your mother, and in time she gave birth to you."

I froze.

As the tangle of wool fell from my hands and rolled away, leaving a scarlet trail, all my memories returned to me—even the disgusting summer camp "Seagull," the scumbag manager who'd tried to get me fired, and all the other nastiness of a sort I couldn't even imagine. Too many bad memories for any one person to handle. My father knew not what he was doing by revealing them to me.

"Will you save us?" asked Father.

"I'll try."

10. THE DRAGON

We met in the mountains. Over the years the King of Diamonds seemed to have grown younger. Instead of a shabby cloth cape over chainmail he now wore a fine fur mantle made of several hundred stoats over full-plate blued steel armor.

"Milord." He smiled. "You look great. Youthful."

I sighed in relief. I wouldn't have to explain who I was and what happened.

"The war is over," I said. "You're released."

"I remind you of the terms," he replied. "We must destroy Yulif, her husband, and all his offspring. We can cease this, if they surrender to you."

"They surrendered to me."

"But you're now their son," said the King of Diamonds. "You can't surrender to yourself. That breaks the rules. It's cheating."

"What's going to happen?" I asked.

"We'll conquer your land, kill you all, and destroy the green hills. After that this world will revert into nothingness and we'll become a regular deck of cards once more."

I realized he didn't want this to happen.

"Or?" I asked.

"Or you'll find another solution." The King of Diamonds winked at me and smiled again.

I remembered, he could see a little of the future.

It meant we still had a chance.

11. THE SWALLOW

We sat under the open sky atop the tallest tower. Father offered me wine. I drank in moderation to account for my teenage body. Even so, the alcohol rapidly clouded my mind.

"I can't find a solution," Father admitted. "How do we make it that you aren't my son?"

"Could we rewind time?"

"It's dangerous to toy with time. Anyone who has ever attempted this has only made things worse for themselves."

Zevas looked at me and shook his head. I nodded. It made sense; otherwise the universe would be a very uncomfortable place to live.

"There's a simpler way, Father," I said, suddenly reaching a solution. "But you won't like it."

12. THE BLACK WIDOW

The women's half of the castle was chilly and had smelled like sherbet for as long as my young body could recall.

"No," said Yulif before Zevas even finished his thought. "No divorce! You won't get rid of me so easily, you son of an old whore and a half-dead giant!"

"What's wrong?" I honestly didn't understand.

"Come." Zevas pulled me aside. Cam studied me intently; it seemed she no longer trusted me. It was a shame to lose a sister. "You see, Mitrius, a marriage between gods or demons—which are essentially the same—establishes certain rules. It isn't a mere formality. In some ways, it's destiny. Divorce is a world-ending thing. Most gods do not remarry after the death of their mate. Many spend the rest of their lives trying to resurrect their spouse."

"I still don't get it," I said. "Why can't you divorce for half an hour, marry somebody else, then divorce them and remarry your original spouse?"

"We aren't mortals. Anything can happen in half an hour. Also, the card kings might not accept your interpretation and then we'll all die, while Yulif is married to someone else. Mitrius, find another option."

13. THE STAG

They broke through our defense line by the ocean. They devastated our cavalry, crushed our infantry, and approached the city walls.

I could see the burgundy pennants of the King of Hearts, the scarlet pennants of the King of Diamonds, the gray ones of the King of Clubs, and the black ones of the King of Spades. Their army filled the entire field in front of the moat. Behind it, dozens of engineers assembled siege engines.

"We won't last a week." Vilhelm's voice broke. "Father, we must flee!"

They say Georg had been far braver. But it was Vilhelm who had survived. I think he often caught glances of those regretting this outcome.

Our time was running out.

"Father, where are my things?" I asked suddenly.

"What things?"

"The belongings of my old body."

It took a while to find them. One of my pockets contained a dilapidated cardbcard box with a faded label: SOUVENIR PLAYING CARDS WITH VARNISH, A-1-54, 1 DECK, 54 CARDS. Inside there were three cards. Why three, I thought, and then I recalled the Jack of Spades.

I chose not to animate the unpredictable Jokers. The Jack was perfectly calm. His hair was raven-black like all spades. But unlike other spades he was tall rather than stocky, and his eyes were light-blue, almost transparent, rather than black.

"How long ago did you release the others?" he asked.

"Fourteen years."

"I made one mistake. Just one." Jack buried his face in his palms. "If I tell you that the Queen of Diamonds seduced me, would you believe it?"

Yulif stared at him with compassion. I realized that Mother liked the Jack of Spades. Father realized this, too.

"Jack of Diamonds?" Zevas asked.

I was the last to understand what he was asking. The Jack of Spades blushed. Mother shushed Father, but he stared at our guest.

"Yes, the current Jack of Diamonds is my son," he finally answered. "It was a plague on all our houses."

"We'll show those animals." Zevas's lips split in an unpleasant smirk. "Yulif, I hope you'll consent to temporarily divorce me for the sake of revenge upon the card rulers. Before we wanted to do this just to save our lives, but now we have an opportunity for vengeance."

"Yes, my husband." Yulif bowed her head.

14. THE TRAP

Father dissolved the marriage simply by repeating the word "Divorced!" three times. To be honest, I failed to see why they'd made such a big deal of it; he could've done that at any time without her knowledge. But then I saw how Mother's face changed, how she became weak and helpless, and I understood that divorce isn't such a simple thing.

"Do you consent to marry the woman named Yulif?"

Jack of Spades nodded. He did whatever I told him. The previous agreement didn't bind him; he owed everything to whomever had reanimated him, which was to say, to me.

Less than five minutes after my parents' divorce, Mother was already married to the Jack of Spades. We exited the fortress via a creaky hinged bridge. The last handful of guards, wounded and exhausted by past battles, stood behind us.

The four kings moved to meet us. The King of Diamonds stepped forward.

"I feel something has changed. Milord Dimitry, would you please explain?"

"I prefer the name Mitrius," I said. "And, of course, I'll explain. Yulif divorced Zevas and married the Jack of Spades. According to our accord, this makes the Jack of Diamonds the only child of Yulif's husband, which means he's the only one you must kill in addition to them. But Yulif and the Jack of Spades are part of this parley, which means you can't touch them."

The King of Diamonds turned. From the crowd behind him a youth, who looked much like a younger version of the Jack of Spades, stepped forward.

"Will you consider accepting him as your prisoner?" asked the King of Diamonds.

I shook my head. I thought I saw triumph in the King of Diamond's eyes. I turned to look at the Jack of Spades. He appeared sad and solemn. Somewhere nearby, a woman screamed. I was certain it was the Queen of Diamonds, who realized what was about to happen.

"On your knees, my son," said the King of Diamonds. The Jack of Diamonds, who wasn't actually his son, obediently got on his knees. There was no fear in his eyes, only doom and acceptance. I realized everything was leading to this. All of them—all the card rulers—benefited from this, except for the Queen of Diamonds.

The King of Diamonds cut his Jack's throat in a slow but sure motion. Behind me, Yulif and the Jack of Spades got on their knees.

"Accept our surrender?" asked Jack, as he was taught.

"I accept," I said.

In that moment, the war was over.

15. THE HYDRA

"Father must leave."

Neither my mother nor my sister understood me. To them he was a savior, the war was over, and it was time to finally live. But before he'd given me life, Father had killed and eaten me, and I couldn't forgive that.

"You won't reconsider?" He stood next to me atop the highest tower.

"Someday, perhaps."

He left on the third day. Mother, whom I didn't banish, followed him. So did my sister and brother. I was left alone, if one didn't count one hundred and fifty guards, two thousand servants, several thousand townsfolk, and three hundred thousand citizens of my country.

Zevas had robbed me of a piece of rock floating in space, and returned a living, breathing organism. He may not have been a demiurge, but he was a master administrator.

I stood in the throne hall, holding the coronet Father had left behind.

I considered his final words to me. "My son, start a family. A proper demiurge must have a best friend, and a personal pantheon to always watch his back."

16. LEMMINGS

I hosted lavish balls and traveled the countryside, and I soon came to understand that I stood no chance of finding any kind of Cinderella.

This world was made of my essence. Every person, ever grain of sand, every molecule of air. Even for people who'd appeared here in the past fifteen years, I was ultimately their creator.

They could only obey me, whereas I sought a true partner, like Yulif was to my father. Someone capable of pushing me further than I could push myself, able to contradict me, and sensitive enough to know when to agree with me.

Someone who expected those same qualities from me.

I couldn't hope to find her in this world of green hills. The final straw was when I hosted a tournament. The knight who won it dedicated the win to some courtier girl. When I saw them together I made an innocuous comment along the lines of "You make a nice couple." They immediately wed in the nearest church, even though he had a betrothed and she had a fiancé.

This world was thoroughly mine. I could only find disobedience if and when I wanted it. A wonderful place, but not one where I could seek my intended. One day, I handed the throne off to some local nobleman, and traveled elsewhere.

17. OUROBOROS

If you're a girl or woman between the ages of thirteen and infinity; if you were born and still reside on planet Earth; if you have a big heart and feel you can bring more to the universe than you're doing already, perhaps you're the one I've been searching for.

Please, don't leave this world. Don't fall into another dimension. Be careful with suspicious doors, rabbit holes, and wardrobes. I implore you, wait for me.

Have no doubt; I'm already looking for you.

I look like a fifteen-year-old kid, answer to the name Dimitry, and carry a dilapidated deck of fifty-three cards in my pocket.

If you see me, be sure to say hello. I promise you eternal love, and a little bit of trouble. Or, perhaps, eternal trouble, and a little bit of love.

We'll see how it goes.

THIS STORY originally appeared in *Samovar*.

ELDAR SAFIN IS a writer residing in Russia. At the beginning of the 21st century he was restoring facades, formatting magazines, and writing scripts for corporate celebrations. Since 2018 he has been the IT project lead at SpeechPro and is currently implementing neural network-based solutions for banks and telecoms. Safin is the author of five books and a hundred short stories. In the fall of 2019 he became the laureate of the Future Time prize, finishing in the top six among 1200 contenders.

ALEX SHVARTSMAN'S translations from Russian have appeared in *Tor.com, F&SF, Clarkesworld, Asimov's*, and many other venues.

RAISING MERMAIDS

Dai Da, translated from the Chinese by S. Qiouyi Lu

ANATOLY HAD DELIVERED the mermaid the previous night, but Celtigar only discovered its existence after he got out of bed and went into the living room, where it had been dropped off. Anatoly must have used the one-time passcode he'd given him—the alarm hadn't gone off. *Excellent,* he thought. *Good old Anatoly.*

Fascinated, Celtigar circled the box. Contrary to his expectations, it was large and "coffin"-shaped—a word he'd learned a couple days ago. It referred to a kind of sealed wooden container used for dead bodies. The coffin before him had been wrapped in a thick and flexible black material. It looked like a lump of raw matter of unknown use and factory origin.

Celtigar reached out a forelimb with a sharp point, which was well-suited for the task of slitting through the packaging. His two appendages and his other, duller forelimb were busy unwrapping the box. He realized as he did so that the packaging materials were quite soft. It emitted a strange warmth when he put his weight on it. Celtigar saved the packaging to make a nest the next time he molted. It would be great for cushioning his weak and heavy body after he molted, and he could burrow into it until his new skin grew in.

He was careful with his incisions as he peeled it off, fearing that he would ruin it.

Once he'd removed the packaging, Celtigar discovered that there really was a coffin inside—one wrapped in a thin, gray insulation film. But it wasn't made of wood. Instead, it was made of glass. Celtigar used his sharp forelimb to tap all over it. The feedback he got was the same—a rhythmic vibration. It was indeed glass, and of a high quality to boot, because the waveforms were well-formed, with drawn-out echoes.

Celtigar stripped away the flimsy insulation film. All he had to do was poke a hole, tug ever so slightly, and the entire thing came away.

Then—wow.

Wow.

Unable to hold back, Celtigar pressed all four limbs to the glass. His eyes lit up. He wanted to memorize every detail of the mermaid, even if it was still sleeping and hadn't yet opened its eyes. Anatoly had been right. Mermaids were truly beautiful. Its hair was raven-black, its skin alabaster; other than the lips, nothing protruded from its flat face. Mermaids didn't have the sexual characteristics of humans. It didn't have an Adam's apple, nor did it have breasts. It looked like a young child, but even more beautiful, because from the waist down to the tip of its tail, it was covered with delicate green-gold scales.

Wow. Celtigar tapped on the glass with a forelimb. The pretty waveforms echoed back, making him even giddier. He blinked. The scene before him refreshed: there was a small, lovely mermaid in the glass coffin. It hadn't yet woken up, but it looked angelic and frail. It was naked. Other than the long hair flowing over its shoulders, nothing covered its human half.

At the time of the transaction, Anatoly had told Celtigar that the mermaid could only stay in the coffin—he'd actually called it a package, making Celtigar think that the mermaid would come in a plastic box—for three days, at most. After that, it had to be transferred to a fully equipped aquarium, or else it would suffocate in the small space. Anatoly had eyed Celtigar's four limbs, as if doubtful that he could manage the task on his own.

"Of course I can." Celtigar had sifted through the scattered everyday phrases that he'd recently learned. He selected a few useful words to express himself, then strung them together: "Of course I can do it! I'll do it myself."

Anatoly nodded. But he still told Celtigar that, if he needed help, he could get in touch.

Celtigar looked down at his forelimbs, understanding Anatoly's doubts. They were too thin, too hard, too rough; one was too sharp and could easily hurt the mermaid. It was still a carbon-based lifeform, after all; it wouldn't be any tougher than its land-based kin.

Reluctantly, he pulled away from the glass. He really did have to call Anatoly for help.

Finding the exotic pet trafficker wasn't that difficult. At least, it wasn't that difficult for Celtigar: he had his private number, where he was on-call twenty-four hours a day. Over the phone, the man said he was in the area and would be over right away. But in reality, he was thirty minutes late, because he'd encountered, in his words, "a few trifling matters." He did indeed look ruffled: his hair was a mess, his gaze sunken, his expression exhausted, his facial hair scruffy. He looked like a vagabond and not one bit like the rich exotic pet trader that he was.

"It's simple." He glanced around at the disarray in the room, then turned and said, "First, we'll have to move it next to the aquarium..."

It wasn't a hard task for Celtigar. His forelimbs ended in pincers. He could lift something three times the weight of the glass coffin. As Celtigar lifted it, the mermaid awoke. It was trying to turn around, its bloodless white palms pressed against the glass, casting bloody shadows.

Anatoly said, "We have to hurry. It's going to suffocate."

Celtigar quickened his pace. His gastropod foot shuffled forward. He was even faster than Anatoly.

The aquarium was in Celtigar's study. It was a huge installation that took up a third of the room. Made of double-reinforced glass, it was full of oxygen-rich water. There was a pump at the bottom that would periodically oxygenate the water. The mermaid had left the sea and would need oxygen-rich water to survive. Anatoly said that it was common sense for raising mermaids. As for why, he'd never understood, as his clients had never asked before. They only cared about what they had to do to keep their expensive and beautiful pets alive. Celtigar had also followed Anatoly's instructions to install a biofilter system that would ensure the water was fresh and clean. The mermaid ate only fresh seafood. It couldn't leave the water, so he couldn't open the aquarium, otherwise it would die. He'd also had to create a secluded area in the aquarium for the mermaid to excrete in.

Celtigar had meticulously followed every requirement. They had been costly and complicated, but he hadn't minded going out of his way a little to properly care for such a small, beautiful, mysterious, and weak creature.

Celtigar placed the glass coffin before the aquarium door. Then, he opened the door. The mechanism just past the door ensured that water wouldn't immediately flow out—only after three minutes would any water seep through. Anatoly, who'd kept behind him, opened the glass coffin. He swiftly hauled out the mermaid, held it close to his chest, and shoved it inside. It seemed as if he were struggling to cast some deep-sea creature off of himself.

Celtigar watched from the side, surprised. He hadn't thought Anatoly would be so rough with the mermaid. If you heard Anatoly talk about his business, you'd think that mermaids were his life. Done with his task, Anatoly huffed and slammed the aquarium door shut. He turned and explained himself to Celtigar.

"That's the fastest way," he said, gesturing. "You know. I told you, they can't stand air."

It was true. Anatoly had emphasized that over and over again: mermaids couldn't stand dryness or air. They'd die without water, so he couldn't let it leave the aquarium. And you couldn't let their heads rise above water. They shrieked terribly. If you weren't careful and let your mermaid's head come out of the water, you'd have to push it back under and teach it not to do that again.

Celtigar nodded, understanding.

"Go ahead and turn on the power," Anatoly said. "You can start up the aquarium now."

Celtigar used his sharp forelimb to flip a switch on the wall. A pale blue light rose from the depths of the tank. The biofilter began to run. Kelp, artificial coral, shells, a large, hollow reef in the middle for the mermaid to hide in, and even a lush, living, red sea-willow coral were all inside. Pearls and gems rested on the sandy substrate, toys for the mermaid. Anatoly had recommended a sunken treasure chest as a decoration, but it didn't suit Celtigar's tastes. The immigration enforcement bureau had required all non-residents to take the course *Earth's Inheritance: Our Shared Culture*. In it, he'd learned about an age-old author from Earth named Hans Christian Andersen and the fairy-tales he'd written. He hadn't quite cared for the former, but he definitely cared for the latter.

The fairytale was called "The Little Mermaid." The young, beautiful mermaid's flower garden had left a strong impression on him: round like the sun, planted only with red flowers—ignore the sculpture of the prince in the garden. In any case, it was an otherworldly ocean garden. So he'd arranged a similar scene for his mermaid: round, filled with red plants, like a sun. Because it was the Little Mermaid.

Once it had squeezed past the complicated channel into the aquarium, it swam around at a loss. Celtigar was infatuated, to the point where he didn't notice Anatoly leaving quietly, or scribbling a note with his number and a reminder that, for the house call to help him transfer the mermaid to the tank, he'd have to charge him a service fee. It wasn't too much, but it wasn't trivial, either.

The price was worth it. Definitely worth it. Celtigar used his forelimbs to tap a friendly message on the glass, hoping that the mermaid would understand. The mermaid swam about, brandishing its pale arms in the water as it kicked off with its tail. Its expression had a heartbreaking charisma to it.

Celtigar thought it might be anxious. *But that's normal*, he thought.

He'd give it some food. Celtigar inched over to a small refrigerator by the aquarium. It was packed with fresh salmon, sweet shrimp, and shelled clams. He gathered some salmon with his forelimbs, thought for a moment, then grabbed a box of sweet shrimp as well.

He returned to the tank and pushed the food into the feeding slot. The fish and shrimp slowly floated down to settle in a large shell, piling up like a dish plated at a restaurant. But the mermaid didn't eat. It only stared at Celtigar with its blue eyes. Its face seemed to be twitching, as if it were crying. *It's feeling really anxious*, Celtigar thought.

But it was still beautiful.

CELTIGAR WAS USUALLY FOCUSED as he worked, but lately, he hadn't been. Or rather, he was unable to focus. He was always impatient to see his little mermaid. It swam in the water, pressing its white palms against the glass, or running them along its body. It poked its head out from the sea-willow, its soft blue-black hair floating in the water, like a rare and mysterious kelp. It would cup the gems and pearls in its hands, then release them so they drifted soundlessly back down to the sand. Ah—gorgeous.

Such a small, frail thing.

Unlike his peers, Celtigar was friendly and mild. He was very willing to share his happiness with his friends—who were almost all humans—but he couldn't tell anyone its source: he had a mermaid. Anatoly had warned him about that. Humans typically weren't able to raise mermaids. Only rich extraterrestrial residents who could keep a secret could have one. And telling his friends that he had money, enough to buy a mermaid, was dangerous. They'd be jealous of him.

"Jealousy" meant detachment, belittling, rejection, even hostility. All things he was very familiar with. He'd grown up experiencing such behavior. He didn't want to be the target of jealousy ever again, so he had to be careful to guard his secret: he had a mermaid.

He put the data graph down on his desk. Gastropod undulating happily, he made his way over to the aquarium. He'd been busy making sure his assets were appreciating. The gold hadn't yet gotten to the point where it would pay out, but his future was clear: within ten Earth years, he and his business partners would receive a windfall from Danhe Mining Corporation, headquartered in the Tiangong Development Zone. What he'd always had trouble getting in that distant, gloomy nebula, but which was easy to obtain on this blue marble…

Celtigar tapped on the glass. The mermaid followed the sound and swam over. It was smart. It knew what its owner wanted it to do. It reached out its hands and pressed them to the glass, its face coming close as well, as if about to kiss the surface. But, under the gaze of Celtigar's two huge eyes, its lip seemed to be trembling.

"Why did you stop smiling?" Celtigar asked. "What do you need?"

It shook its head. It smiled, but the expression seemed forced.

"Why did you stop dancing?"

Celtigar liked to see it smile. It was supposed to be smiling and dancing. He turned on the sound system. A song with a simple but upbeat melody flowed from the walls. The notes floated through the air, passed through the reinforced glass, and dissolved in the water.

The mermaid began to dance. With a forced smile, it waved its small, pale hands. Its stomach swelled, as if there were a balloon hidden inside. Whenever the mermaid had to do something complicated in the water, its stomach would puff up. It was an interesting phenomenon. Celtigar wanted to poke the bump.

So he opened the feeding slot and stuck his regular forelimb inside. It was rigid, but it wasn't sharp; it looked more like a long stick.

Celtigar felt the warmth before he registered the water. Anything warm disgusted him. He didn't like to come into contact with water, especially warm water, but, to touch the mermaid, he could suppress his disgust.

He reached his limb out in the water, then kept reaching. The mermaid looked at it and stopped dancing. It swam over, then held it.

Wow.

It was really smart. It was treating Celtigar's limb as if it were a toy. It wanted to pull apart the thing in front of it, as if cracking open a shell or a treasure chest.

Celtigar immediately forgot how much he disliked warm water. The mermaid's soft fingers and the tactile sensation of the pressure of its weak touch on his limb—it was a great feeling, so much so that it could assuage the disgust that was twisting through him like a hook.

Then, a pure, double-ringed wave surged forth, followed by another, and another, and another, endlessly. It meant happiness. To feel happy from such a carefree touch was quite a miracle to Celtigar: his limbs were hard and had only a few touch receptors. For there to be enough stimulation for him to feel happiness was no easy feat.

The mermaid began to gnaw at Celtigar's arm. Of course, it was no use, but Celtigar basked in the waveforms. Delighted and curious, Celtigar reached his arm out more. Now, he could poke the mermaid's belly. It couldn't be more vulnerable of a spot. So he watched as his black arm jabbed into the mermaid's pale stomach.

The swell immediately caved in.

The mermaid let go of Celtigar's arm. Its face was contorted with pain. It darted away to hide, swimming into the coral reef.

Celtigar didn't care much at first. But a couple days passed, and the mermaid was still hiding in the coral reef, refusing to come out. He couldn't help but be worried, so he got in touch with Anatoly and told him what happened.

Anatoly told him casually that it wasn't anything serious. When the mermaid was hungry, it would come out again. It was a very simple creature; he didn't have to be concerned about whether it would resent him. It had no capacity to.

"Really?" Celtigar asked. "But when it hid, its face seemed very pained."

"If there's no other way, you can shock the water," Anatoly said. "Just once is enough. Tell it that you want it to come out. If it doesn't come out, then put the shocking device into the water. Turn it on, count to three, then turn it off. It'll come out."

"Shocking device?"

"I can sell you one," Anatoly said swiftly. "I can also show you how to use it."

"Great," Celtigar said.

The shocking device was fantastic—Anatoly not only got the mermaid to come out, but also showed Celtigar how to use the shocking device to train the mermaid.

The little ball stayed in a corner of the aquarium. He could use the switch on the wall to adjust the strength and duration of the shock to whatever he pleased. But he almost never used it, because the mermaid had already become quite obedient after Anatoly's training demonstration. No matter what Celtigar did, it wouldn't try to escape, and it would always be smiling. When Celtigar took a step closer and began to tap on the glass to teach it how to signal with him, it learned very quickly as well, even if its fingers couldn't tap out as resonant of a sound as Celtigar's limbs. It was even less able to mimic the subtle tremors, but seeing such a beautiful creature's fingers dancing on the transparent glass was a joy in itself.

It was then that he realized he'd never given the mermaid a name that was befitting of its beauty.

Andersen hadn't named the mermaid in his story. The mermaid didn't have a soul; it hadn't needed a name. But Celtigar's mermaid was different. It was obvious that it had a soul. The proof was in the way it stared with rapt attention at the tablet Celtigar held in one arm, as if it understood what it was looking at.

So Celtigar pulled up some photos of the ocean for it to look at. But the mermaid had no interest in them. It was more interested in the cities on land. But the thing it enjoyed the most was the news, particularly about crime. It would enthusiastically watch those broadcasts.

"Do you like this?" Celtigar asked.

There was an AMBER Alert on the screen. The neighborhood had put out the alert half an hour earlier about a missing human boy. Celtigar tapped on the screen. A robotic female voice sounded:

"Missing boy! According to the District Seven police report, the victim is Kevin Winter, eleven years old, five feet three inches tall, White, with a slim build, black hair, and blue eyes. The suspects are Klein Lee, forty-three, Asian; Anatoly Mikhailov, twenty-seven, Caucasian. Vehicle: a stolen, old-style gas-powered car. Last seen:

near the Rovenor Freeway. If you have any leads, please call the police."

After the text, there was a photo and a five-second-long hologram, probably copied from the boy's ID. Celtigar pressed the broadcast button. The hologram of the boy Kevin seemed to jump out from the screen. He noted the boy's comically pointy nose and pale cheeks.

The mermaid covered its flat face. It didn't nod, but it didn't shake its head, either.

"I don't think you like this," Celtigar said cautiously as he looked at it. "You don't look so good."

The mermaid lowered its hands. It had a funny expression on its face, as if it were smiling, but mostly as if it were crying. Celtigar had no idea what the mermaid was trying to express.

It gestured to the glass. The mermaid didn't have nails, so it could press the entirety of its fingers up to the glass, forming black circles with soft edges. It opened its mouth. Celtigar looked inside: there were two rows of small, white teeth behind its lips, and its sharp tongue wriggled in the middle, with pink gums on either side. It seemed to be crying, but Celtigar couldn't see tears.

"What do you want?"

Celtigar tapped on the glass. It tapped back. To be precise, it knocked its head against the glass. But it was clear that each couldn't understand what the other was trying to say. They could only look at each other. Celtigar was bewildered—the mermaid was sad. Upon seeing its sadness, he became only more perplexed: What could cause it such sorrow here? He pondered the question.

Slowly, rainbow halos appeared in Celtigar's eyes.

"I think I understand," Celtigar said to the mermaid. "You're not happy."

The mermaid nodded forcefully.

Celtigar fell silent. The halos in his eyes grew larger.

"You don't want to be here."

The mermaid nodded vigorously. Its expression was eager, as if trying to curry favor with him.

As the halos expanded, Celtigar's eyes brightened. He sighed deeply. An electric current ran up his back.

"But if you leave the water, you'll die."

The mermaid shook its head so hard it nearly stopped breathing.

The halos occupied all of Celtigar's eyes now. They were like two platters of diamonds. Then, his sight shut down.

He was going to molt. It was the worst time to, earlier than he'd expected.

Based on Celtigar's size, it would take him three Earth days to molt entirely, seven days for a full recovery. Within that time, he'd have to stay in the nest until his new skin came in. But he hadn't yet constructed a nest, and he didn't have anyone to take care of the mermaid during that time. He'd kept his secret well. No one knew that he had such a creature in his home.

Except Anatoly. He came to mind immediately. Celtigar would just have to give him some money… as long as he was paid, Anatoly could do anything. Celtigar wasn't short on money. At least, not money he could use legally on Earth.

But—

"No, I can't." Anatoly's voice was panicky over the phone. "I can't help you. Celtigar, I'm in trouble. Right, hide your pet, or kill it. Quick! Or else we'll all be in trouble!"

"What?" Celtigar asked.

"Get rid of it!" Anatoly yelled. "Somewhere no one knows about!"

Celtigar wanted to ask more, but Anatoly had already hung up.

All right then…

All he could do was bear the discomfort of the electricity running up his back as he once again started up his vision. Fine electric currents flowed to the tips of his limbs, making his whole body itch. He was swelling, but his skin constricted him. He really wanted to tear himself out of it. Then, he'd be more comfortable. His eyes were also sensitive: the halos blurred his vision, and wherever light fell, the reflections would pierce his eyes.

He tried to get in touch with Anatoly again, but he couldn't get through. He had no choice but to sigh. Through his hazy vision, he saw the mermaid slamming its head and hands against the glass, heartbroken. Even when Anatoly had done his demonstration with the shocking device, it hadn't been so heartbroken. Celtigar tapped on the glass. The mermaid twitched, then swam over toward Celtigar, its blue, childlike eyes staring sorrowfully at him.

He thought for a moment, then came to a decision that made sense to him.

"Okay. I think I have to send you home," Celtigar said slowly. "I— with all—my might."

The mermaid's eyes lit up, even if the sorrow hadn't yet retreated.

Celtigar used his limbs to knock a solemn signal against the glass. He didn't want to use Earth language to express such a thing—it would lose its meaning. The mermaid couldn't understand the rich information and subtleties contained in vibrations and waveforms. Such a pity. He could only say the words for his own sake.

He knocked against the glass again. This time, the message was simple: "Goodbye." It was the one thing the mermaid could understand, the signal he'd taught it. Right away, it tapped back the same message.

It really was smart.

Celtigar tried with all his might to ignore the painful electricity coursing through his body. His organs had already liquefied into a heavy sack of juice. He squirmed his gastropod foot. His body had become heavy, so he couldn't move very fast. Anatoly couldn't help him. Then what was he supposed to do? Could he take the mermaid out from the tank by himself?

Nearly blind, he busied himself around the empty apartment. He needed a huge container that he could seal, but it couldn't be so big that it wouldn't fit into his car. He thought for a moment. Only the plastic box he'd previously used to transport gold ore samples would do. It was pretty big and seemed to be enough for a small mermaid.

Strenuously, he left the study, inched into the junk room, and hauled the plastic box out from inside. Then, with difficulty, he inched into the bathroom to fill it with water—good thing his bathroom had been remodeled to suit his needs. There wasn't a tub inside, nor was there a sink. There was only a small faucet. After all, he still had to use water every now and then, even if it was only a little bit. Of course, this was ordinary water. *But using it temporarily shouldn't be a problem,* he thought. *It'll just be a second.*

He turned on the faucet. The water streamed into the box.

Once it was full, he took it back to the aquarium in the study. His eyes had now been completely blinded by the light. He couldn't see a thing and could only tap on the objects around him to discern what they were from the vibrations they emitted. At least he had two sensory systems, or else he'd be in trouble.

The smooth floor of the study signaled to him that he had arrived. He inched toward the spot where he remembered the aquarium to be and soon bumped into something hard. He tapped it with his appendages—the glass of the aquarium. The waves it reflected back were still just as beautiful, but his heart was now heavy with grief, so much so that it was hard for him to sense their beauty at all.

All right, he was here. But where was the door? He tapped here and there, dragging along his stomach full of liquefied organs. *Tap tap, tap tap.* Finally, he reached the door.

He opened it.

Nothing. Then, he remembered that it was a well-sealed door— only after three minutes would it start to release water. Thwarted, he stuck a forelimb inside and brandished his pincers around until he snapped away the installation.

The water began to flow. More and more. Celtigar endured the feeling of disgust as he waited for the mermaid to slip out—or rather, to come out with the water. He wasn't sure what exactly he'd broken, but countless tremors were traveling through his skin like hooked arrows. Disgusting. Disgusting. Disgusting.

But Celtigar had to bear it. He waited. Something soft would slip out. Where was it? He waited.

The water pitter-pattered onto the gray floor. It couldn't seep out, couldn't flow out; it could only coalesce into little lakes. How was he supposed to get rid of it? Celtigar didn't know how to solve the problem. Whatever; he'd have the management company deal with it.

Finally. Something soft fell into his pincers. It cried out weakly as it thrashed. *It sure is lively!* Celtigar thought. Then, a straight line burst in. It was also wet, but Celtigar didn't mind the feeling. It just was a dark line.

Celtigar closed his pincers. Something broke.

The line became clearer.

His distended body lurched as he changed directions. Bubbles were frothing up, some into his mouth.

He'd probably have to vomit out his internal organs. It would be terrible, but it wouldn't be as bad as he imagined. It hadn't gotten to the worst point yet. He could still deal with it. He tossed whatever was in his pincers into the box, then sealed it. It was an excellent box with an "outstanding" seal—a lovely, big word that was appropriate for describing the quality of the box. After all, it was made to protect gold ore samples. So Celtigar wasn't worried that the mermaid would escape from it.

He struggled to suck in his abdomen. His gastropod foot squirmed forward on an important mission: it had to drag along a box, a skin about to split open, and a juicy, engorged body. But he only had to drag himself to the car and he'd be halfway there. The self-driving system would bring him to his destination. It wouldn't take long.

The best thing about living in luxury apartments was that he could use the exclusive elevator. Celtigar wriggled into the elevator, then groped about blindly as he hit the button for level –1. From the twenty-seventh floor to –1, he could rest for a moment and prepare for the next leg of the trip.

He put the box on the floor. His pincers were tired.

The car had a biometric system. As soon as Celtigar walked into the garage, it pointed out its location to him. Celtigar followed the weak signal and crept around the pillars, approaching the car. He'd never thought the garage was that big before, but now it seemed as big as the universe. He was drained. The desire to throw up his internal organs had vanished, not because he'd recovered, but because he was exhausted to the point where he didn't have the energy to vomit.

There were already several cracks along the inside of his skin. A drop of juice seeped into a crack and mended it. Celtigar was concerned that the cracks would get larger. He couldn't keep patching himself up.

He did all he could to haul the box into the trunk of his car. Finally unburdened, he let himself feel a moment of relief. Excellent, the next part would be much easier: he just had to get into the driver's seat.

Hurry! He spurred on his gastropod foot. Using a forelimb to support himself, he rocked himself over. He'd never thought of getting in as an obstacle before. Sigh!

Once he'd finally climbed in and was properly seated, his skin began to split. He felt around to start the autopilot system and enter his destination, then curled up and tried his hardest to keep the outer layer of his skin intact. The electricity rushed chaotically through him. Now, it was ice-cold. An ice-cold rain.

As the discomfort of concentration sent tremorous rays through him, he called to mind his pet and the joy that it had brought him.

The car automatically played the music he was listening to before. A simple, cheerful tune. Oh, it was the song the mermaid had been dancing to earlier. Celtigar floated along with the highs and lows of the melody. His destination was a stretch of polluted ocean. So polluted that there were no traces of people at all, but it would offer a place for the mermaid to roost. After all, it was from the ocean. *Does it understand what I'm trying to do?* he wondered. Perhaps he'd explain things when it came time to.

The car glided over the ground. They didn't encounter any road-blocks along the way. He'd soon reach his destination—judging by the map, he was simply going from the affluent and residential District Seven to the near-ghost towns along the coast, the ruins of industrial satellite boroughs. The two weren't actually that far apart.

The car stopped by the shore, the trunk facing the jade-like sea. The beach was full of gray pebbles and trash, hell for Celtigar's heavy and weak body on the brink of bursting. But he still had to get out of the car and complete the task he felt duty-bound to do.

He inched over, the juices churning in his body, until half his body was submerged. It was hard to describe how nasty the sensation made him feel. He couldn't take much more. The trunk of the car opened automatically. He only had to open the box and send the mermaid off into the ocean. Then, he'd be done.

He swiftly opened the box, his forelimb groping around to take out the mermaid. Another soft breaking sound like the one he'd heard earlier. This time, the mermaid didn't struggle, nor did it scream. How strange! Anatoly had told him clearly that if it came into contact with air, it would scream.

But now wasn't the time to think about things like that. He put the mermaid into the ocean. For some reason, it didn't swim. It only stopped next to Celtigar, unmoving. Celtigar nudged it, but it didn't move, only quietly lay in the water. He felt some comfort, but he was also perplexed. Mermaids were supposed to be even livelier in the ocean, right? Why wasn't it moving?

"Can you hear me?" Celtigar asked. "You should be able to."

It still didn't move. What was wrong with it? Was it scared? He pushed it firmly. Then, a wave surged forth, and it was gone.

It took only a second.

Other than the sound of the waves hitting the shore, it was quiet. Celtigar was heartbroken. He wriggled over to somewhere the waves couldn't reach, his blind eyes facing the sea. The loss of his sight wasn't earth-shattering. Compared to his heartbreak, it was nothing.

It had gone too quickly. He hadn't had a chance to tell the mermaid that he only wanted it to stay here for a few days. But it had already gone. To comfort himself, he simulated a picture: his mermaid diving through the blue ocean waters, just like in the aquarium. He enjoyed the image greatly, and it gradually calmed him down. He'd have Anatoly help him find it. As long as he was paid, Anatoly could do anything. Surely he'd help him find the mermaid again.

Celtigar stood for a long time on the reef, the sound of the waves hitting the shore bringing him both pain and comfort. The sunlight wasn't bright, so his eyes felt fine. Downcast, he thought of his mermaid. It still didn't have a name. When he realized that, it was already too late. But he could come up with a name for it when he got it back. Maybe he could give it a human name. It had all the cleverness and traits of a human—or perhaps it was humans who were like mermaids.

The waves hit the shore. Something small washed up and bumped into a nearby reef. Celtigar couldn't see what it was, but he heard the muffled thump it made. He guessed it was a large piece of trash.

THIS STORY originally appeared in *Future Science Fiction Digest*.

DAI DA IS a science fiction writer who now lives in Guangzhou, China. She loves to read, cook, sleep late and walk aimlessly. She seeks to build a more interesting world in her stories.

S. QIOUYI LU WRITES, translates, and edits between two coasts of the Pacific. Ær debut biocyberpunk novella *In the Watchful City* is out now from Tor.com Publishing, and ær other work has appeared in several award-winning venues. You can find out more about S. at ær website s.qiouyi.lu or on Twitter @sqiouyilu.

MATER TENEBRARUM

Pilar Pedraza, translated from the Spanish by James D. Jenkins

THE GRAVEDIGGER BASTIÁN emerged from the nightmare that had tormented him during the few hours of sleep he managed to get after his drinking binge the night before and opened his eyes to the light of an unpleasant day. His mouth was thick. A burning sourness rose from his belly to his throat. The efforts he made to belch brought on a fit of coughing. Remembering the work he had left not even half done, he muttered some blasphemies that didn't give him the slightest relief. He was on the verge of yielding to the temptation to roll over and go back to sleep, but one of the voices in his head told him that he had to finish digging the grave if he didn't want the people from the day's first burial to arrive and find no hole for their deceased. The local council was so poor that he couldn't afford an assistant to help with the hardest work, although sometimes the coal merchant's son, the red-headed Candido, who had devils in him, would lend him a hand in exchange for some tobacco.

Lupo came out to meet him, wagging his tail. His drooling tongue hung out between his fangs and he was panting, choking with servile passion. He slept in the tool shed on a pile of empty sacks. All the mud in the cemetery seemed to have stuck to his hairy coat. On his back he had some reddish scabs that never managed to heal. And far from lessening his ugliness, the tenderness of his expression accentuated it. But he was a good dog. He happily joined the gravedigger in the rain: they would not leave each other's side all day long. Since old age had made them retire from the world, all they had was each other. Their mutual company was enough for them, along with the proximity of the dead people, who were no bother, absorbed as they were in musing on their nothingness. At most they gnawed discreetly at their shrouds if Bastián had drunk a lot, or they drummed with their bony fingers on the wood of their coffins, not to cause a fuss and have someone open them, but only for fun. Bastián felt an immense tolerance towards them.

When they were near the half-dug tomb, Lupo lowered his ears and began to tremble, scratching at the muddy earth with his paws and recoiling. But Bastián knew the animal was no coward. He was never frightened by the will o' the wisps of decomposition, nor the strolls of the lost souls in the blackness of moonless nights, nor the boys who threw rocks at him when he prowled outside the walls of the cemetery seeking relief for his masculine urges in the bellies of the female dogs. This, however…

"Bloody hell! What is this?"

In the grave he had begun to open last night, before getting so drunk he couldn't even see where he was putting his shovel, there lay a dark and suspicious lump.

"What the dickens is this corpse doing here?" Although he hadn't checked whether it *was* a cadaver, for him any body in that position had to be. Bastián's world was made up of those who were dead and those who weren't yet. And he went on planting them, a devout gardener, in order to fertilize the world.

With the handle of his shovel he moved the lump, which stretched and let out a groan. From the pile of old rags a thin little face and small hands, bony, bluish like diluted milk, filthy with red mud, emerged into the ashy light of the rainy morning. This wasn't a corpse, it was hard but not stiff, and beneath the blue and mauve whiteness of cold there were purple transparencies that announced the bloody warmth of life.

"Well, well! Good morning, girl!" the straw-hearted man exclaimed with thick irony.

She sat up. She sat there at the bottom of the hole, looking at him balefully with her green little eyes. She was a girl as old as the world, scrawny and pale, bleary. A mop of unkempt red hair stuck out from between the creases of the thick garment covering her, which appeared to be a military cloak.

"Come on, get out of there! I have to finish the grave."

He offered his callused hand to the girl, who spurned it and climbed out like a spider, gripping the soft walls of the hole, at whose edge she sat down without saying anything.

"Better hope you haven't caught cold or damp or anything, if you slept in this hole."

She didn't open her mouth. After a while, Lupo, who at first had growled, scrunching up his muzzle and showing his fangs, approached her. In his pupils strange fires burned. The spirit of the old dog in him was working for the first time in a long time, and it did so painfully since up until then happiness for him had consisted in the cultivation of apathy. Something simultaneously sweet and bitter was taking hold of him, flowing towards the deepest fibers of his canine insides like a love potion, or a death one, at the same time as he felt something tighten around his neck, pulling him towards the girl who had risen up from the earth.

Bastián began his work, making sure to pay no heed to the girl, who didn't stop looking at him with her bleary little eyes, whose dark circles underneath, like the marks of a beating, seemed on the verge of spreading across her face. She had a large mouth, lipless like a snake's, and she was graceful as a kitten, but there was something about her that was disturbing, insect-like.

The man got out of the hole and sat down to rest beside her.

"I don't know you, girl. You're not from around here, huh? What's your name?" he asked as he chewed a piece of tobacco, looking out into infinity.

"My name is Ángela, and I'm not from anywhere. I have to go now."

She rose and, bundled up in the rain-soaked cloak, she started to walk without turning back. She slipped between the tombs and the cypresses like a shadow. Lupo followed her for a moment with his eyes. When he was about to lose sight of her, he got up and ran barking after her with the happy energy of one who has finally found his reason to live.

BUT THE JOB was not a comfortable one. There was a lot of walking and not much eating. All day they traversed vacant lots, following paths that didn't seem to lead anywhere, skirting walls furtively. Lupo missed the slop and scraps Bastián gave him, the warmth of the fireplace, and even the sounds the dead people made when they stretched their bones.

Ángela and Lupo advanced along silent streets. In the city everyone was asleep except the cats in heat and a mare who was miscarrying in the southern suburbs. Her moans were carried on the breeze. The night would have been lovely, had there been eyes to see it. When the moon peeked out between the clouds, the world turned gray and black, every detail sharp as in an engraving. And when it appeared in the middle of a clearing, it was terrifying. Beams of white light filtered through the treetops and traced a changing lacework on the ground, turning the rough brick arches and wall parapets into marble and the tears seeping from the stones into diamonds. A mercuric cloak had fallen over the world. It was not possible to imagine hearts beating beneath that frozen platinum veil, nor love, nor warm limbs entwining on feather mattresses. Perhaps, yes, snowy bodies trembling with impotent love between crisp starched sheets.

Ángela used the stars to calculate whether it was a propitious moment for what she was planning. The Star of Bitterness was in the exact center of the night. In the darkness evil swelled, ripe, about to fall in one's hands like a fruit. It was time.

The old door of the charnelhouse opened at a push from her little hands. The spectacle offered to her view in the moonlight didn't make

the slightest impression on her. She was used to it. They were familiar
to her, the stiff corpses of the condemned that hung from the beams in
the courtyard like hams, those who lay piled up on the ground, those
stacked up rotting under the porticos.

Lupo, believing he'd figured out his new mistress's intentions,
walked ahead, ripped off a corpse's left hand with bites and tugs and
dropped it at her feet like an offering.

"This mutt must be an idiot!" the girl exclaimed in a low voice.
"That's not what we're here for, you silly fool. Why are you in such a
hurry?"

Lupo, whose greatest misfortune was understanding human
language, which made him an object of scorn to dogs and cats, felt
something like the desperation of an aging lover for his girlfriend,
although neither he nor Ángela knew that, both being creatures little
inclined towards love. But anyway his rheumy eyes filled with tears
that ran down his muzzle, and his heart shrank.

Unconcerned about the movements of the beast's soul, she headed
with decisive steps towards the corpse of one of the hanged. Stiff and
lifeless, it swung in the night's quiet air because a bird that had nested
in its belly had come flying out at the sound of footsteps. The cadaver's face was handsome in the moonlight; in it there was a definitive
quietude.

"How lucky you are, you dead bastards, not having to run around
trying to earn a living."

But remembering that her father, shut up in a deep dungeon,
wouldn't be long in joining them in the same club of those who
danced at the end of a rope, she fell silent out of respect and went to
work.

He had a good set of teeth, a shame about the incisors that had
been broken by a blow, perhaps from a rock, which had also cut the
upper lip. Ángela rose up on tiptoes but couldn't reach. She looked
around and found only a block of stone long detached from the wall
and black with moss. Faced with the effort that awaited her, she gave a
kick of impatience.

"Damn you, you son of a bitch!" she rebuked the hanged man. "They could have hung you lower!"

The stone was porous and light like a rotten tooth, but for the girl's bird-like strength it meant pain if she lifted anything weighing more than the folds of her cloak. She managed to drag it, however, and climbing up on it she reached the scarecrow's mouth, from which she pulled out several molars with skilled and vigorous little tugs, paying no heed to the stench coming from the black hole and the blue tongue.

In the western part of the ramparts there stood an abandoned turret, in whose damp ruins old Crisanta, a third-rate witch and sorceress, lived all by herself. She had seen better days, but too much tippling had made her lose many of the gifts she had received from her female bloodline, which had passed down from mothers to daughters the pact with Satan, ratified with a drop of blood. If she appeared to be a beggar, it wasn't from poverty but from the worst of miseries: avarice, which left her uncomfortable, dying of hunger and dressed in rags, although she was sitting on treasures that she hid in her magpie's nest.

She received Ángela with a grunt and invited her to sit beside her on a bench in front of the fireplace, where a charred log was burning out and about to disintegrate into ashes. The girl remained standing, took a packet from a pocket of her cloak and set it noisily on the table, saying with the dry voice of a little despot:

"I brought you this, Crisanta. Let's see what it's worth."

Without looking at her again, Crisanta stirred the fire with an iron fire shovel, her eyes fixed on the embers which shone for a moment like rubies.

"What is it?" she asked, feigning indifference.

"Molars freshly pulled from a hanged man."

"Molars from a hanged man! Right!" mocked the sorceress. "And how do *I* know they're from a hanged man and not waste from the barber's?"

Ángela didn't respond. Crisanta turned towards her and fixed her dust-irritated eyes on the girl's, which reflected the purest and most innocent evil in their greenish waters. In all the days of her life, she had never seen eyes like those. It was whispered at the sabbath that they were the devil's eyes, but she had never been permitted to see those. How come this little brat just happened to have them? What had she done to deserve them? When the women's glances met, it poisoned the air to the point that Lupo raised his head, anxious as though he scented danger.

"If I say they're from a hanged man," the youngster muttered between her teeth, her face pale with rage and her throat swollen, "then they're from a hanged man."

Her eyes had hardened like stones. Some dark spots on her irises painted figures of black toads on the green water.

"I'm not interested," replied the old woman, turning her glance away towards the fire, which had gone out again. "Right now I'm mixed up in something big."

"Big? What do you mean, big? Spoiling some woman's love affair or making her miscarry. Beyond that, I don't know what you're capable of."

"A hand of glory. You don't happen to have a hand?"

"There's a loose one in the charnelhouse. If you want, I'll bring it to you. My dog tore it off, but I didn't know it was good for anything."

"It's no good, girl, it's no good. I need a fresh hand, with blood in its veins, not the dried-up rotten things you're in the habit of carrying about."

"Fresh!" Ángela remarked in a falsetto voice. "Is it to eat or what?"

The old woman explained to her what a hand of glory was and how to make it. To begin with, she needed the hand of a hanged person, not like those rotting in the charnelhouse, but rather a fresh one.

"From a man or a woman?"

The girl's question caught the sorceress by surprise. She didn't know.

"Doesn't your guide show you?"

She was referring to an enormous book Crisanta had, which was called *Great and Universal Elucidarium*, an inheritance from those who had preceded her in the art and the source of most of her knowledge. It was so large that to finish reading a line, she had to take a couple of steps in front of the lectern. It was written in black ink that was so corrosive it had eaten through the paper in many places, and in spiky handwriting like the devil's own.

"It just says a hanged man's hand," the old woman responded with a sigh of impatience.

"Well then, it has to be a man's," the girl judged. "It's a shame because in the city a few days from now they're going to hang the coal cellar murderess. The one who killed her three children and hid them in the coal in the kitchen."

"We can try. We have nothing to lose. With what they'll give us for a hand of glory we won't be poor anymore."

"Why are you talking in plural like the bishops?"

"Because I'm referring to you, too. If you help me, we'll share it. I'm no longer up to jaunts through cemeteries and you have a knack for getting into tricky places. Go on, girl, bring me a fresh piece and you won't regret it. Don't waste time with this crap," she said, sending the hanged man's molars into the fire with a sweep of her hand. A thick but ephemeral smoke rose up, as if from the other world or in a theater.

Ángela had remained thoughtful, with Lupo nestled up at her feet. She seemed to be attentive to the sound of the wind which, crashing against the tower, howled furiously in search of other paths between the holes in the rocks and the thorny shrubbery.

AT DAWN, lost among the crowd, she attended the execution of the infanticide in the market square. When the fury of the storm provoked by the departure of the condemned woman's soul dispersed the people and there remained only two guards watching over the corpse, which would hang from the gibbet a couple of days as a warning and lesson to bad mothers, Ángela took shelter from the rain with Lupo in the vestibule of the Church of St. Justa. From there she could observe all that happened at the gallows and its surroundings.

Not even she herself knew for certain what she was going to do. She counted vaguely on the guards' getting drunk that night and sleeping like logs. She trusted in the dark force that seemed to have been hovering over the city for some time. Caught up in her plans, she remained motionless all day, curled up like a cat. She was cold and hungry, and she knew there was no use in staying there while it was daylight, but she was bound by a leaden laziness that had been overpowering her to the point where she was unable to move.

Her presence made the woman who usually begged in the doorway cower in her spot as if she wanted to disappear. She was a young blond woman with no arms, but with the beautiful legs of a tightrope walker, an idiot angel fallen from the archivolt. Passing in front of her, a lay sister who was coming out of the temple stopped and tossed some coins in her lap. The girl raised her ingenuous iris-blue eyes and smiled kindly and gratefully. Ángela, who was watching the scene a few steps away, let out a mocking chuckle. The old woman fled in terror. For a moment the two girls had seemed to be one, and that one, the devil.

The hours passed like those in a feverish dream, sometimes slowly and at others so fast that she would have said the tower clock had gone mad. Its clapper sounded not like bronze but iron. The dampness of the stones had gotten into the girl's soul and, arriving at her frozen heart, had turned to frost. Lupo shivered along with her.

The dead woman's long hair fluttered against the inclement sky like a black flag. Wrapped up in their cloaks, the guards paced around in circles without neglecting their watch, but when that time of night arrived when there is a wrinkle in the fabric of the world and senses and natural laws cease to reign, they fell asleep, and Ángela prepared to take advantage of their slumber.

But a troop of silent shadows overtook her, emerging from the corners of the square and flowing together like a river. Surrounding the gallows, they lowered the hanged woman without delay. They were her relatives, fed up with so much scandal. They weren't inclined to have shame brought on them for a single minute more. They had come to an agreement and they were carrying her off. This was unknown to Ángela, who in her capacity as an innocent though diabolical child saw only the skin and guts of the world, but not the schemes of men. She followed them like one more shadow through the maze of the upper-class neighborhood, with which she was unfamiliar, and passed in front of the Casa de las Rocas where they kept the elephant given by the sultan of Egypt, which trumpeted at the sound of people. Lupo stifled a panicked bark, cut short by a kick from his mistress that instantly made him keep quiet. Then they crossed the river and headed to Los Cigarrales, entered the estate and deposited the dead woman in the crypt after they had put her in a coffin and the curate had said a funeral prayer at top speed.

When everyone had left, Ángela opened the coffin, grabbed one of the dead woman's arms and pulled on it until the hand was outside, with the wrist on the edge of the wall of the box. There was something in the air just then, barely an icy breeze circulating through the black and gloomy dampness of the crypt. But the girl was used to the groans of the souls who resist leaving their bodies for good and the murmur of those that remain stuck to the flesh. She knew she didn't have to pay any attention to those phantasms, smoke from a bonfire that has gone out and a siren's songs carried on the wind from the region of shadows. She took a firm grip with both hands on the hatchet Crisanta had lent her, raised it as high as she could, and, collecting her scant strength, unleashed it again and again on the dead woman's stiff left wrist until the hand came loose. She then groped with her own hands until she found it and put it in a pocket of her cloak.

Then a hair-raising creak made Lupo's fur stand on end. The door flew open. In its opening, silhouetted in the paleness of the sky, which was beginning to be tinged with pink, there appeared a tall, white figure. Something dark oozed from its mouth and its clawlike hands opened and closed like those of an automaton.

Ángela squeezed the murderess's hand in her pocket and gulped. Her fright was giving way to awe. Because she was beginning to realize who the woman was who, for her part, was looking at her with relief.

"Señora…"

"None of that señora stuff. I'm calling it a night. Can't I be left alone in my own house?"

She sniffed.

"There were people here."

"Yes, señora. The hanged woman's relatives stole her from the gallows and brought her here to bury her. They left her in this coffin."

"And what are you doing here?"

"I came for a hand to cast a spell."

"Well then, if you've finished, get lost."

When the vampire returns to her lair, she won't be happy at finding you there, Ángela remembered from a song from her childhood.

"Good, girl, good. We can make use of this. It's not too spoiled yet," Crisanta said, palpating the pale severed limb and squeezing the horrid wound with expert fingers. Her beady eyes gleamed with satisfaction and wilfulness. "Someone," she remarked, "should have given this broad a reading before it was too late. It's obvious from these lines that she was going to come to a bad end," and she traced them with her index finger on the dead flesh. "They look like flies' legs. Now we have to make the brine of glory."

"How?" asked Ángela.

"The brine of glory," the old woman said slowly and solemnly, as if she were reading, "is made with salt, saltpeter and pepper, and a pinch of gunpowder if you have some, all mixed together. You put the hand in it in a clay jar and leave it there fifteen nights. It says so in the book."

The witch carried out her schemes in the presence of the girl, who didn't miss a detail. She absorbed the knowledge with the cold avidity of the disciple who knows she will betray her teacher and neither feels any scruples nor anticipates any remorse.

"Look how lovely, my dear," said Crisanta with giddy enthusiasm when the salting time had passed. "Dry and clean, it doesn't even seem to be from a cadaver. Like the hand of a virgin at the altar."

Ángela assented earnestly, although the thing reminded her more of a hen's foot.

"The nails are broken," she pointed out.

"So what?" replied the other, annoyed. "It doesn't matter. Now I just have to grease it and it'll be ready to burn for hours."

"What do you make the grease out of?"

"With fat from a hanged man or a cat, it's all the same. We'll use some from a cat. There are women who have qualms about killing cats because they think they're guardians of the home, but I have no such scruples, nor do I believe in superstitions. Cats are cats, they can't do anything to us."

"Which one should we kill? A black one? Or the neutered tabby, which will have more fat than any of them, with that belly of his hanging down to the ground?"

"It can't be a neutered one," the old woman said. "Fat from a castrated cat is easy to get, since they let you cut their throats without fighting back, but it has less power than fat from an intact male. Go and see if you can find the striped one with the yellow eyes. He's probably sleeping on the steps in the sun."

Lupo went out with her into the splendor of the blue morning. Soon they found the cat, curled up into a ball between two rocks. He awoke at hearing them, cast a sleepy golden glance and yawned, showing the beautiful teeth of a miniature wild animal.

"Come on, mutt, time to earn your keep."

The dog obeyed to the letter. After a brief skirmish full of sound and fury, from which he emerged bleeding, he deposited the soft palpitating prey at his mistress's feet.

WITH NO SMALL DIFFICULTY, Ángela was reading her way through the *Elucidarium* during the old woman's absences, sneaking a peek whenever she was alone in the tower, feigning fatigue or menstrual pains, which had come to her for the first time on the day when Lupo killed the cat so they could extract its fat. She learned from the book that the hand of glory was a tool used by robbers in their exploits, since it had the virtue of making all the inhabitants of a house, masters and servants, fall into a profound sleep, and opening all the doors and locks for as long as the fingers of the hand were lit like candles. She fantasized about what she could get for herself with the help of the hand Crisanta was preparing, and she dreamed of getting hold of the book. It contained many other invaluable secrets and it would help her make her way in life and go from being a scavenger to someone with real power. But before she had the chance to carry out the plans she was concocting in her imagination to make off with those treasures, the people who had ordered the talisman showed up.

They came enveloped in a cloud of dust, two men and a woman. The men entered the house, but the lady remained in her saddle, her head covered in a wide-brimmed black hat that permitted only the gleam of two eyes like embers and the tip of a haughty nose to be seen. She wore a dirty but elegant black and green dress that brought out her good looks. She must have been very young and arrogant.

Crisanta took the dead woman's stiff hand from a fine crystal cheese dish where she kept it and, setting it atop a cloth on the table, showed it to her clients, exaggerating its virtues and the efforts it had cost her to acquire it.

But with a sweep of his hand, the younger and more quarrelsome of the two men threw both cheese dish and carrion to the ground, where they smashed with the sound of broken glass.

"It cost you a great deal to get hold of this rubbish, old woman? And you had us come here for that?"

"What's the idea? You know more than I do about how these things have to be made!"

"I won't say anything about making it, but you're not going to deny that this is a female hand. You're a lazy good-for-nothing."

And to show that no one made fools of them, and also as a warning to incompetent witches, they cut off Crisanta's left pinky and took it with them, saying it was a good talisman against senile old women who tried to con them. The girl and the dog trembled when they heard the young lady in the black hat laughing.

"I told you so," mumbled Ángela again and again while the old woman, howling in pain, applied a poultice to the wound.

After chewing some henbane leaves, she fell into a doze. She appeared greatly relieved. Before losing consciousness, she said to the girl:

"Get out of here. Since you started hanging around this house I've had nothing but hassles. I want to be alone."

Ángela set out walking and, followed by Lupo, headed towards the nearest cemetery, Santa Rufina, in search of a night's lodging in the mausoleum of the Mira Valdesúa family, which could be opened easily, but then she thought better of it and hurried her pace towards Los Cigarrales. She felt an irrepressible desire to see the inhabitant of the crypt again. What's more, since the vampire wouldn't return until dawn, she had time to sleep for a while.

There, hidden between two old caskets, she overheard an entertaining and instructive conversation between the two women, who had become friends. The vampire was dripping with blood, the other was a melancholy, one-handed ghost. When the monsters had set off on their nocturnal errands, she threw herself into the infanticide's coffin, which being new was the most comfortable, and she slept divinely until dawn.

That night Ángela conceived the idea of getting hold of a hanged man's hand and using it to escape from poverty.

THE STORM RAGED, surrounding the turret in lightning and thunder. The smoke from the fireplace seemed possessed: it came in instead of going out. Shadows not justified by the candles' light danced on the walls. Ángela had stopped what she was doing and watched them with furrowed brow as though she found some flaw in their movements. The skull she was polishing with a piece of agate rested forgotten in her lap. Now and then Lupo sniffed at it apathetically.

Suddenly Crisanta leaned against the kitchen sink, raising her hands to her chest. She was turning blue. When she fell to the floor emitting terrible spluttering sounds, Ángela was on the verge of running away. She had to get out of there because if that old hag died, the devil would surely come for her soul and she didn't want to be around when that happened.

"Help me," panted the old woman. "Help me or I'll curse you with my dying breath!"

Lupo had taken shelter trembling in a corner. A hissing wind crept through the chimney, which besides smoke also scattered ashes from the hearth across the room. The pale lightning flashes lit and then extinguished the light of the world. Each time it thundered it seemed the turret would come tumbling down. Ángela dragged the old woman's body to the bedroom, pulling her by the feet. It cost her a painful effort to lift her up and put her in the bed. When she had managed it, she remained seated on the floor for a moment without moving, recovering her breath, while the old woman wheezed in a pure death rattle.

"The pact! The pact must be undone!" she exclaimed all of a sudden with a voice that didn't seem to be hers, stretching one hand towards the girl. Ángela got to her feet and approached her. Both were terrified. "In the dresser drawer ... the parchment ... take it out and burn it, and help me to make the act of contrition."

In that wobbly and dilapidated piece of furniture, enormous as a mausoleum, there were all kinds of rubbish, mixed with the very finest linen, silverware, and objects of value. Ángela rummaged frantically until coming upon a roll tied with a black ribbon. Her excitement was such that she didn't realize she had poked herself with the tine of a fork. A drop of blood stained the parchment.

The heaviest thing, she told herself, was going to be the *Elucidarium*, because as for the rest of it, she only planned to grab the highest-priced objects, which were small. At first she intended to put it all in a sack, but then she considered that if she used a very fine damask pillowcase she had seen in the depths of the dresser to pack the things in, she would kill two birds with one stone, so she took it out of the drawer and laid it out on the floor.

"What are you doing, my child?" asked the old woman, sitting up again, with a firm and clear voice little in keeping with her deathbed condition.

The girl did not answer. She put half her body under the bed and dragged forth a little coffer, which she placed in the center of the pillowcase.

"No way, not that," shouted Crisanta angrily. "It's taken me a life-time to acquire it!"

"Shut up, grandma, you're going to make yourself worse. What does it matter to you anymore? It won't do you any good now... It's better if I take it, since after all I've been the one who's taken care of you..."

"You'll bury me at least? Look, if you leave me here, I'll rot, and my soul will be furious, and I'll bring harm to you and..."

"Yes, woman. Calm down."

But when the old woman breathed her last breath, resembling a belch, and remained quiet for good, Ángela no longer thought of anything but getting out of there as quickly as possible. She finished making a bundle with the pillowcase, put the book in it, and left the turret dragging it like the ant drags its booty against wind and tide.

ALTHOUGH SHE NO LONGER NEEDED TO yank molars out of corpses to earn small change, wealth didn't go to Ángela's head nor cause her to abandon her habits or her work. She studied the *Elucidarium* with eagerness day and night, until her head was bursting and her eyes were filled with grit. There were things she didn't understand, but she made great progress. And when they condemned Pedro Madruga, who was said to be her own father, she saw the perfect opportunity to get hold of a good hand with which to make a powerful talisman. This time she wasn't going to sell it cheap to some young gentlemen like Cristina did with her work. She would use it herself to her own benefit. Thus she used all her astuteness, patience, and ability to slip through the cracks like lizards do, until she managed to get hold of that magnificent member, strong from having come from a son of the village and at the same time with skin soft like silk from not having worked in the rough and vile jobs that destroy body and soul. And she started marinating it in the brine of glory.

At the same time, she learned from the *Elucidarium* that leaving a sorceress's corpse uninterred brings bad luck. Remembering that Crisanta was rotting unburied in the turret, she felt a great cold rise up from her belly to her throat while sweat pearled on her forehead.

"That's just stuff and nonsense, right, mutt?" But this time the dog didn't agree with her. The book didn't lie.

"Fine, even if that's how it is," she said, reading his thoughts, which she could do because she was the one who made them up, "I burned the pact the old woman had with Old Nick, and thus she was off the list of sorceresses. So it's all the same whether she's buried or not."

But, unable to deceive herself with that argument, she finally decided to return to the fortress and take care of the corpse. And one night she went out from the river mill with Lupo, took the rough road along the walls and circumvented the ditch on the western side, climbing the embankment covered in nettles, which cruelly punished her audacity by breaking the crystalline capsules of their poison on her skin like Bolognese tears breaking at Carnival. The old mutt was no longer up for adventures. He gasped for breath on the way up, but followed his mistress indefatigably. The cancer of love had grown until it completely took over his heart, turning him into a gooey emblem of fidelity.

Ángela was scared. She had learned from the book that a dead person's hatred was a poison worse than a viper's venom. She had supplied herself with a crucifix and some branches from a white hawthorn, a good remedy against bloodthirsty spirits. Around her neck she wore a silver choker with a sapphire stolen from Crisanta, and a jet amulet a pilgrim had given her in exchange for letting him touch the budding firmness of her breasts. But the terror of the serene night was so great that it flooded her spirit, opening ulcers in it for which there was no cure.

The turret rose in the middle of an ocean of silence, enveloped in the scent of the wild fig that grew in the ditch, fed by the putrefaction of the corpse of a large animal that had fallen to its death. Ángela was surprised there was no smoke coming from the heights of the fortress like before, when the old woman had kept the hearth fire lit. The door was neither closed nor open: it was now no more than a dried-out piece of wood, the wind's plaything. She fumbled for the table in search of the candle, but her hand found only dust and some small dry objects. Finally she came upon a stub of a candle. She lit it and stuck it to the dirty table with wax drippings. In the doorway leading to the old woman's bedroom she thought she saw eyes like coals watching her malevolently.

"It doesn't smell of death here," she said aloud, and Lupo appreciated the information, since he no longer had a sense of smell.

In the bedroom there was nothing. No bed, no corpse, no dresser, no trunk. Only the bare walls, which were beginning to crumble from dampness and neglect.

The heat of the night was beginning to give way to the coolness of dawn. The girl shivered as she leaned against the door jamb, staring like a madwoman at the empty bedroom, inhabited only by uneasy echoes.

ONE DAY the hand of glory was ready. Large, well cured, shiny with grease, its fingers seemed candles capable of burning for a long time. She made a little base for it so she could stand it on its wrist like a five-armed candelabra. She felt that the hand loved her, could imagine it caressing her hair or giving her pats on the shoulder. It kept her company. She remembered that she had met Madruga once at a crossroads and the bandit had given her a handful of nuts and spoken to her kindly, calling her daughter. But she didn't know if that had happened in her dreams or in reality.

She chose as her victim a usurer named Catuja who was as rich as a queen. She was said to have great treasures, guarded with the help of three very ferocious mastiffs. No one went near her house without being invited. When a peddler had tried to, they'd eaten him up on the front steps.

The day recommended by the stars arrived. The girl had gotten a sack for the plunder and carried the hand of glory in a pocket of her cloak. She had thought about leaving Lupo locked up so he wouldn't bother her, but the mutt was obstinate. He stuck by her, assumed the bearing of a greyhound to hide the fact that his lungs were destroyed, that he could hardly see, that he stayed alive only through force of will. She brought him with her, not out of pity but out of habit.

There wasn't the slightest breath of wind. She could light the talisman outdoors in front of the garden gate. It was like Madruga's hand was impatient to go into action. The fingernails caught fire with a cheerful crackling, five perfect, serene little flames arising from them, whose light, at first bluish-gold and then orange, filled her soul with confidence. Scarcely had the light started to shine when Catuja's garden gate opened without a sound, as if it had recently been oiled. The garden was a tangled mess of confused plants, whose life seemed to be in their center, like animals, and not spread out through cells and fibers. Rose bushes and nettles embraced. In a bed of lilies a poisonous oleander bush grew. In the back the house rose up, silent and unlit, like a mausoleum.

Hearing the sound of steps on the gravel path, the mastiffs came. They were enormous and so similar to each another that one would have said it was just a single dog that had inexplicably multiplied, like a Cerberus duplicated beyond just the heads. Their eyes shone in the darkness, their butchering fangs, their drool. But when Ángela held out towards them the lit hand that she held in hers, they dropped drowsily to the ground. Lupo, who had been terrified at seeing them approach, stood still with his ears perked up, looking at them incredulously. Then he approached them with great caution, with movements more of a cat than a dog, and seeing them so docile, he dared to confront them, showing his teeth and growling.

Black like the night thanks to her cloak and light as a breeze, Ángela headed for the door of the house. The dogs followed her, wagging their tails. And this time too the dark door opened soundlessly, slow and solemn, leaving an open passage towards the shadows of the hall. Everything was perfectly calm and in darkness. Lighting her way with only the light of her bandit father's hand, she ascended the stairs to the bedrooms of the upper floor, where Catuja's chamber was.

It is bad to let a sorceress rot away alone, sounded an echo in the girl's head. She couldn't allow herself to be scared, but fear comes whenever it wants. It had entered the house like a breeze and it was in her heart and in her legs. Lupo felt it too. He trembled and was wary of the other dogs, although they remained docile and behaved with Ángela like loving pets.

The old usurer's door opened, at first so slowly that Ángela feared the talisman was failing. But it ended up opening all the way, revealing the immense room, whose size made it seem an attic or a barn. There were dozens of candles burning in it, whose light cast a glimmer on the objects placed on the furniture. On one rough and peeling wall hung many floor-to-ceiling mirrors that cried out for a return to reflecting scenes from palace ballrooms, and paintings and tapestries dulled by dust, in which the gold threads gleamed and the silver ones were turning black. On a sideboard there was a little coffer with the appearance of containing jewels.

Catuja was sleeping in a bed that was somewhere between a straw mattress and a nest. One would have said she was dead if it weren't for her breathing, which though not quite a snore, was at least a happy snorting. She must have been dreaming of something pleasant, for in her face was reflected a happiness that came from within.

Ángela had placed the hand of glory on a nightstand and took the coffer in her hands. It was small but very heavy. When she opened it, she was dazzled. Diamonds like raindrops wounded by the sun and a bleeding ruby necklace sparkled in the light of Madruga's fingers. *Let's go, don't get bewitched now,* said a man's voice, and another: *There's no need to rush, kid, you did enough of that when you left the sorceress unburied.* The girl looked around. She didn't know what to grab. Everything was within reach and everything was tempting. The fingers of the talisman had burned down halfway. *There is time.* But when she was putting a handful of beautiful, worthless necklaces that she had found in a drawer into the bag, she heard a loud noise behind her. Lupo had stumbled against the nightstand that was serving as a pedestal for the hand, which had fallen to the ground. *Bad, very bad.* Three fingers had gone out, and on the others the little flames were in their death throes. They didn't take long to go out.

All of a sudden, the mastiffs recovered their ferocity. As if they were coming out of a dream, they shook themselves, stretched, and turned fierce again. Their barks awakened the whole house. Catuja shot up in bed as if propelled by a spring, yelling:

"Burglars, burglars, burglars!"

The hunt began.

Lupo and the girl flew down the corridors, descended the stairs in the blink of an eye, crossed the hall, went out into the garden like in a dream. They carried the mastiffs with them, fastened to their bodies. They felt their fangs tearing their flesh, cracking their bones. In the night, sweet with blood and noisy like a celebration, shouts were heard and lights were lit. The thorns of the rose bushes caught in the folds of the cloak, feet tripped over paws, hands groped desperately at the garden gate until managing to open it.

No one had ever been able to catch Ángela, who knew how to scurry through cracks like a little viper and knew all the city's labyrinths. Though she was injured now, they weren't going to catch her this time either. She hid in a doorway. She descended stairs to forgotten basements, sneaked like a rat, coughing bloody froth, through damp passages, then along tunnels, through sewers, until she emerged at the surface, very far away.

Finding herself once more under the stars in the serene night, without shouts or commotion, or any other danger now that death was nesting in her wounds, she sighed with relief. Lupo had followed her. He was missing an ear, he was limping so much that he was really just dragging himself along on his stomach. He was black with blood in the moonlight. *How much blood it costs to reach the end.*

"Stupid fucking mutt..." she murmured with something vibrating in her voice, perhaps a little tenderness.

What shone in front of her like a white ribbon wasn't the river but the wall of the cemetery.

"Look! We were always meant to wind up here!"

THE NEXT MORNING when Bastián neared the pit he had left half dug the previous night, he knew that something was going on. It wasn't merely a feeling: a trail of blood, coming out of a bush, came to a stop at the hole.

"Damn it! Now the dead are coming on their own two feet and putting themselves in the hole all alone," he said aloud to relieve himself from the sudden terror that had gotten the better of him.

He leaned over and cast a fearful glance: for the moment, he didn't want to notice too many details of whatever was there, he only wanted a general idea. The first thing he saw was a wrinkled cloak that seemed familiar to him. He forgot the blood and felt better.

"Eh, girl! Having a free sleep in my inn again?"

She didn't move. Nor did the shapeless and dirty lump that lay curled up in her lap.

"Oh, Lupo, you senile old bastard! I knew things weren't going to go well for you out there! Why did you need to suffer hardships at your age?"

And although prudence didn't advise it, he filled the pit with dirt, planted a white rose bush on top, and kept that little secret in his old heart.

THIS STORY originally appeared in *The Valancourt Book of World Horror Stories*, edited by James D. Jenkins and Ryan Cagle.

PILAR PEDRAZA (b. 1951) is a film professor at the University of Valencia, who over the past thirty-five years has also produced an impressive oeuvre of fiction, including both novels and short stories. Curiously, although Pedraza is well known to horror readers in her own country, where she frequently features in anthologies, and though there exists a book-length study in English of her work, Kay Pritchett's *Dark Assemblages: Pilar Pedraza and the Gothic Story of Development* (2015), none of the author's work has previously appeared in an English translation. "Mater Tenebrarum" (the title is Latin for "Mother of Darkness") is probably Pedraza's best-known story; like much of her work it is a very Gothic tale, peopled with horror fiction mainstays like witches and vampires, and featuring her trademark blend of horror and macabre humor.

JAMES D. JENKINS is the co-founder of Valancourt Books, an independent publishing house specializing in horror and LGBT-interest fiction. He is the co-editor of *The Valancourt Book of World Horror Stories*, which was a finalist for the Shirley Jackson and World Fantasy Awards, and the four volumes of the acclaimed *The Valancourt Book of Horror Stories* series. He holds a B.A. in French and an M.A. in Romance Languages and Literatures, and has published translations of short stories from a dozen different languages. He is currently at work on an anthology of horror stories written in endangered languages.

VIK FROM PLANET EARTH

Yevgeny Lukin, translated from the Russian by Mike Olivson

FINE RESORT. Great planet. Not too many visitors, though. The reason is simple: the locals are rather particular about the ecological state of their home. They dutifully protect species that many would argue should not be allowed to exist to begin with. At times, it seems that their respect for the horrifying things that inhabit the planet takes on a religious fervor.

The plant life around the resort looks picturesque, but it is there that one can run into rakes and eight-tooths. Though unmistakably different in appearance, they belong to the same species, as the eight-tooths are pre-pubescent rakes. Not that it makes them any less dangerous.

The natives consider being eaten by the wildlife a privilege. They refer to it as "becoming one with nature." They don't understand the concept of a cemetery or even a crypt. When they reach a certain age, they say goodbye to their loved ones and walk out (walking may not be the right term, as they actually crawl on their forty-two pseudolegs) into the wilderness, where they are immediately devoured. The more painful the death, I'm told, the more bliss they will enjoy in the after-life (or perhaps the after-digestion life).

The tourists are just here on vacation, however, and don't find the prospect of being eaten appealing. Sure, nature is well protected from us, but we aren't in any way protected from nature. If a sentient being kills any local beastie—be it by accident or on purpose—they risk a hefty fine. That is why every tourist is allowed to bring a pet to ensure their own safety.

You see, local laws allow a non-sentient being to kill other non-sentient beings without limit or consequence, even if it is done at the explicit command of the sentient owner. They are odd customs, to be sure. The sort of pet you bring is entirely up to you, although lately a few exceptions have been introduced.

For example, the pet you bring with you must be a multi-cellular organism. That requirement came about after an unfortunate incident when a tourist brought a vial containing a pet virus. The virus proceeded to wipe out the entire species that happened to be at the top of the local food chain. The natives still haven't recovered from their grief.

I tried to talk about that incident with my next-door neighbor. He is a small, sabre-toothed humanoid, accompanied everywhere he goes by an enormous, hideous monster with deadly-looking pincers. My attempt at conversation revealed that the pincer-monster is the guest and the two-legged toothy dwarf is the pet, a ferocious, difficult-to-train beast named Uhrl. That was a very short and uncomfortable conversation.

I must admit: humanoids are a weakness of mine. What marvelous creatures! When I meet one, I freeze, forgetting all rules of etiquette. I stare agape at their impossible acrobatic act of balancing on just the two legs that nature has given them. I feel a strange mixture of pity and awe. How does one even survive having only a pair each of eyes, ears, and nostrils? Why even have two for that matter, since each one is so close to their counterpart? Yet, judging by their disposition, they don't even realize how disadvantaged they are.

There is only one sentient humanoid at the resort at this moment. His name is Vik, and he is from a planet called Earth. More about him, later.

As for myself, I require no pet or guardian. In a strange coincidence, I resemble the predator species that was wiped out by the virus. Upon seeing me, all other predators play dead, since they remember that resistance is futile.

I knew, though, that coming here without a pet would present all sorts of bureaucratic hang-ups, and so I brought a harmless cilium, named U. Because of me, U now has the reputation of the fiercest bodyguard on the planet, with the exception of Vik's critter.

As far as I know, only one tourist was allowed to come and stay without a pet. He came from a faraway world with a methane atmosphere, so he is encased in a crab-like suit with impenetrable armor. It wouldn't allow oxygen through, let alone a rake. I'm not sure what enjoyment he derives from being here. Perhaps when he returns to his home planet, breathes in some fresh methane and gets his hands on a nice cup of chilled hydrocarbon, he'll enjoy telling his friends tall tales about the dangers he encountered on his trip.

There's one other tourist who arrived without a pet, but since he's a plant-based life form, all he has to worry about are the herbivores. So they forced him to rent a local bodyguard. A trained rake was too expensive, so he settled for an eight-tooth. He immediately attached himself to it with his tendrils and began using it as a surprisingly convenient mode of transportation. Now he can venture into the wilderness, where only I, the methane-breather and, of course, Vik from Earth, dare to tread.

Not that he doesn't have to deal with any problems; first, while on resort territory, even a trained eight-tooth has to have his teeth capped. All eight of them. The second issue is my presence. Just like all the other fauna on the planet, his eight-tooth faints at the sight of me and it takes him a while to recover. I never even got to learn the eight-tooth's name.

What a bother these pets are. Most pets, fierce predators and loyal guardians on their worlds, prove completely ineffective here. Their owners are forced to spend the entire vacation confined to the resort compound. At times, the upkeep of the pets exceeds the cost of the vacation.

My cilium is cheap on the upkeep. It never complains, and eats table scraps. But Vik from Earth—that's another story. He is forced to drag around a whole box filled with little tins of food for his pet. Fortunately for him, it seems to hibernate most of the time (perhaps the climate disagrees with it). In case of danger, Vik has to violently shake it awake; I've seen this personally. Strange creature, this pet. It seems an inconvenience for Vik to constantly carry it in his arms, but humanoids appear to enjoy discomfort.

Recently, I asked Victor if his pet had a name. It was a tongue-twister, which took me three attempts to pronounce:

Modernized Kalashnikov Rifle.

***

THIS STORY originally appeared in *Future Science Fiction Digest*.

EVGENY LUKIN IS the author of seventy-five books, some of which have been published in Germany, Poland, and Bulgaria. He's the winner of multiple Russian literary awards. In 2015 he was awarded the title of European Grandmaster by the SEST (European Science Fiction Society). He resides in Volgograd, Russia.

MIKE OLIVSON LIVES in Brooklyn while dreaming of living somewhere else. When he is not watching, discussing, or writing about hockey, he indulges his legendary love of quality sci-fi and fantasy, and complains about the lack of civics education in America today.

BIOGRAPHY OF ALGAE

Martha Riva Palacio Obón, translated from the Spanish by Will Morningstar

(Shortlisted for 2021 Rosetta Awards)

For the astrobiologist Antígona Segura,
who knows about plants in other worlds

BANGIA FUSCOPURPUREA

ALTHOUGH DARK MATTER exerts a gravitational effect on ordinary matter, we can't observe it directly. That's why we call it dark, but it might be more precisely described as matter that is invisible across the electromagnetic spectrum. Dark matter makes up eighty percent of the universe. Like agar culture medium, this is what holds things like galaxy clusters—and galaxies themselves—together.

We make our home within the Virgo Cluster.

In biology, the term *dark matter* is used for all the microorganisms we have not yet been able to isolate and identify. Holobionts—every body is an ecosystem, inside of which live, perhaps, more life-forms than there are stars in the universe.

Agar, or agar-agar, is derived from a type of red algae.

The wavelength of cyan is 476–497 nm. The word *cyan* derives from the Greek *kyanos*, which is sometimes translated as "dark blue." You once read an article that said the ancient Greeks couldn't see the color blue. The author cited as evidence some passages from *The Odyssey* in which the sea is referred to as "wine-dark." Purple, not blue.

But then again, we have *kyanos*.

When they first announced the ATKIN-5 project, you were in the sea, which didn't look blue to you either. This was the day you almost drowned. You were eleven, and you had swum out far from the shore. You remember the rise and fall, the salt on your face, and the piece of seaweed, of macroalgae, that you were playing with. You never saw the wave coming at you from behind. You didn't see the next one either, nor the one after that.

"The samples taken by ATKIN-5 will allow us to determine whether there is life on Europa," the project leader explained to the press, at the same exact moment your mother was trying to revive you on the beach. One of your obsessions from that day forward would be trying to make sense out of coincidences like this.

CORYNEPHORA MARINA

Approximately four billion years ago, in a hydrothermal vent rich in iron and sulphur, inert matter came to life for the first time on this planet. That first microorganism is known as the last universal common ancestor, or LUCA. In theory, LUCA is where we would land if we went far back enough in our genetic family tree. But it's also possible that there exists a LUCA-2, a second common ancestor from which descended all the organisms we are so far incapable of detecting.

Life developing in parallel lines.

In the mid-nineteenth century, Anna Atkins used cyanotype to document the different forms of algae in Great Britain. Potassium ferricyanide—the Prussian blue trace of an organism that has long since turned to dust. For many years after her death, Anna Atkins fell into obscurity. Her work was almost entirely disregarded. Once, a Victorian academic even suggested that the AA that appeared in the volumes of *British Algae* stood for "Anonymous Aficionado."

Every time you write about yourself, you use the second person. It's the only way that makes sense to you. To talk about what happened to you, you need a *you* to encompass the *I*, which most of the time feels like someone else.

We search for life in other worlds on the basis of what we know of our own, but scientific paradigms aren't infallible; we could be overlooking a key part of the story. For example, no one would have thought organisms could survive in a lake of sulphuric acid, but they can, and do.

When you were young, you couldn't reconcile the idea that the woman whose depressive episodes would last for weeks was the very same woman who was strong enough to pull you out of the sea and bring you back to life. It's such a monumental contradiction that you once forgot she was the one who saved you. You only began to understand one morning when you, now an adult, couldn't get out of bed either.

Ghost population—the possible remnant of a long-extinct human group in our own DNA.

As the ATKIN-5 team tests its space probe in Antarctica, you are under the covers again, now a shadow of the melancholy that every woman on your mother's side of the family must try to outrun. The tests at the South Pole fail, and it dawns on you, seventy-five hundred miles away and two days after your last shower, that you've forgotten the name of one of your great-grandmothers.

ECTOCARPUS LITORALE

Terrestrial plants are believed to have descended from a group of green algae called Charophyta. Two orders of charophytes, Charales and

Coleochaetales, are closely related to what were likely the first plants to spread over the earth's surface: bryophytes.

Moss is a bryophyte.

Cyanophyta, or blue-green algae, are not in fact algae; they are bacteria. Cyanobacteria were the first photosynethic oxygen-producing organisms and, as such, had an important role in determining the course of life on earth. The oxygen content of the atmosphere is maintained at a constant 20.95 percent.

The sun is as necessary for photosynthesis as for the creation of cyanotypes and, although it may seem unrelated, you always enjoyed looking at moss up close and imagining you were zooming in on a forest from outer space.

No matter how hard you try, you can't remember the exact moment you lost consciousness underwater, just seconds from returning to a state of inert matter, but even though you can't access the information, it's still in there, interfering with your other memories and causing you, on occasion, to lose your sense of space-time.

Sargasso is one of your favorite words, and you don't know why.

Sometimes you're able to function in what we call the present, but sometimes you get lost within yourself. The ATKIN-5 launch countdown begins and you, on a bench in the botanical garden, are struck with an unfiltered awareness of the sea of green surrounding you. In every chloroplast, a miniature thunderstorm.

IRIDAEA EDULIS

Overproliferation of algae can significantly reduce oxygen levels in water, leading to the death of entire populations of the other organisms that call it home. Climate change has led to more and more of these blooms, and more and more oceanic dead zones have appeared in recent years. The Capitalocene and its ironies: we can destroy new life-forms before we even discover them.

The pesticide Zyklon B is composed of cyanide impregnated into secondary materials such as diatomaceous earth, a sedimentary rock formed from the cell walls, or frustules, of millions of microscopic marine algae. The Nazis used Zyklon B in their extermination camps.

Sometimes it leaves a trace of Prussian blue.

The ocean is your obsession. You can't stop talking about it, but even so, you remain at the edge. You'd like to learn to dive in, but you're too scared. Every time you get close, you push yourself deeper into your prison of rituals and fixations, your supposed defense against this terrifying piece of you that threatens to burn down everything you love.

This paralyzing fear is the force that pulls you toward the bottom, making you see the things you'd rather ignore. Like the garfish thrashing around on the floorboards of the pier. On the ferryboat with your family, you thought about the sea needle's last water-seeking gasps as it drowned in the air. A man had stepped on its mouth to keep it from flopping back into the water. The horror, the violence that is such a part of our world, the salt in your eyes, a fish that won't die. The next day, you would be the one thrashing, under the waves.

The ATKIN-5 probe circumnavigates Mars to gain momentum toward Jupiter as you, millions of miles away, wake up again screaming.

NACCARIA WIGGHII

Life springs from order and chaos, the product of a series of accidents and coincidences without which nothing would be as we know it. Two planets colliding, an atypical moon, tides that affect the rotation of the earth. The very same entropy that will one day consume the universe is what has allowed us to be here in the first place.

Cancer—a proliferation of cells reproducing uncontrollably, a survival impulse in overdrive.

Anna Atkins died in 1871. Various causes of death are noted, including paralysis, rheumatism, and exhaustion. She left her algae and fern collection to the British Museum.

Biological witness—a sample of algae, a moment in the earth's history, told in cyan.

Sometimes you feel like you're drowning again.

During your mother's fifth chemotherapy session, poison drips into the line and through the cannula and you are outside yourself. You are overcome with the knowledge that one day you will lose your last link to this shared piece of your life stories. Your mind falls into a black hole at the exact moment ATKIN-5 begins its descent onto the surface of Europa. All you can think of as you run from the hospital is Moshio salt.

Salt made from algae, and the unavoidable fact that all things must end.

POLYSIPHONIA SUBULIFERA

When the first photosynthetic organisms appeared on our planet, the ozone layer had yet to form. Life on earth began in the oceans in part because water, in addition to being a solvent, served to shield the first life-forms from the sun's ultraviolet rays. These days, in our atmosphere, yellow photons with a wavelength of 560 to 590 nm are the most prevalent.

Our sun's light determines the color of plants on earth. There could be other planets that revolve around a dim star with vegetation that live off of infrared light. In such a world, kelp forests would be black.

Black—a melancholy color, like blue. An inundating aqueous humor that leaves you, sometimes, unable to breathe. You have turned your mother into a specter that haunts you, that tries to drown you, so you won't have to face the fact that the only one holding your head underwater is you.

An experiment carried out on the International Space Station showed that algae, unlike us, can survive in space.

After many years, you and your mother return to the beach where you almost drowned.

She lies back in the shade, and you go down to the water. The story, with some differences, repeats: you swim up to the point where the waves crashed into you when you were young, and you are surprised to find your feet touch the bottom. It makes sense, but you still weren't expecting it. Like you weren't expecting how quickly you would reach the age your mother was when she rescued you. She couldn't help you now, not anymore, even if she tried. She's sleeping in the shade, a silk handkerchief tied over her bald head.

The uncertainty of death means it doesn't even come when you're expecting it.

Thousands of nanorobots emerge from ATKIN-5 to traverse the frozen surface of Europa. Below the ice lies an ocean whose tides are pulled by Jupiter.

SARGASSUM VULGARE

Most of the oxygen we breathe is produced by microscopic algae called diatoms. Their silicon skeletons are formed from minerals deposited by rivers and glaciers into the oceans. The dust of our ancestors' bones, our crumbling mountains, all flows back into the sea. When diatoms die, their skeletons are laid to rest on the sea bed.

Much of the salt we consume comes from a prehistoric ocean.

Broadly—and imaginatively—speaking, we might say our ancestors are what sustain us. The rocking of the waves, the salt in your hair, the algae-covered rock you're sitting on. You become aware of the fact that you are a small piece of an indifferent universe in which nothing goes to waste, and you smile.

Dark matter—everything that exists on the edges of the story you tell yourself to keep the illusion of continuity alive. The blind spots, the ambiguities, the ghost-memories; a biography made up of nothing more than a collection of disjointed notes on the back of an algae catalogue.

(Any relationship between headings and the rest of the text is purely accidental.)

A nanorobot pokes through a crack in the ice, takes a sample of orange material, and analyzes it. And twelve hours later, at long last, the ATKIN-5 team receives the message they have been waiting for.

THIS STORY originally appeared in *Strange Horizons*.

MARTHA RIVA PALACIO OBÓN is a Mexican sound artist and author. She studied a BS in Psychology and an MFA in Visual Arts, and is part of the art and science collective Cúmulo de Tesla. In 2020, she was granted the Otherwise Fellowship with her interdisciplinary project *Following Crickets Around the House* and has received awards like the 2013 Gran Angular Prize for YA Literature. Her sound works have been presented in spaces such as the Tsonami Festival, Radiophrenia, Sur Aural, the Centre for Complexity Studies (UNAM) and the WFAE world conferences. Among her published works are the novellas *Orfeo* and *Frecuencia Júpiter*. Her story *Biography of Algae* appeared in *Strange Horizons* magazine, and she's the human behind Sono-bot, a bot that creates an infinite inventory of probable and improbable sounds on Twitter.

WILL Morningstar is a freelance editor and translator from Boston whose translation work has appeared and is forthcoming in *Two Lines*, *Latin American Literature Today*, *Strange Horizons*, and the *Massachusetts Review*. He works with both prose and poetry for children and adults, having collaborated with authors from Mexico, Argentina, and Spain.

THE POST-CONSCIOUS AGE

Su Min, translated from the Chinese by Nathan Faries

ONE

I MASSAGED MY TEMPLES, and looked sideways out the window at the mass of gray buildings. From here on the 28th floor, the ground was invisible. The only green was a few plants dangling out of a window across the way. I barely had a chance to catch my breath between appointments before my sixth patient knocked at the door. He was a slightly balding, middle-aged man. His body was stiff, and his movements—closing the door, walking to the chair—were deliberate. I knew he was an anxiety patient before he spoke a word. He sat up straight, like a puppet, two eyes staring forward vacantly.

"Make yourself comfortable," I said to him. "You can lean back, adjust the chair as you like."

He allowed himself to recline against the chair cushion, just slightly, yet he remained rigid. I offered him an approving smile, encouraging his effort.

I opened with my standard greeting, "What brings you here today?"

"I think I'm being controlled by something." He once again sat straight and still in the chair, if leaning slightly in my direction. "A lot of the time I feel that it's not me talking, like there's something controlling what I say."

He spoke almost in a whisper, as if he were telling me a secret; patients with delusions of being controlled are often like this. I simply wrote down the words *delusions of control* in my notebook and asked him, "Can you tell me something about the last time you felt you were being manipulated?"

"The last time was in our company conference room. I was meeting with a certain client of mine to discuss a proposal. I was well prepared for the meeting, and my thinking was sharp, clear. I was explaining my plans to the client, using my hands to clarify certain points." He did not—perhaps could not—move his hands now.

"Then I saw, just outside the window, the holiday cactus that was planted there—the flower pot had been there as long as I can remember —suddenly tip and fall. The conference room is well-insulated; you can't hear anything that happens outside. There was no sound, though I knew that since the pot fell from the ninth floor, it must have been destroyed. It was as if the plant had fallen into a bottomless pit.

"I did not stop speaking; I continued with my presentation, concentrating with all my might. But after a while the client stopped me and asked, 'Why are you crying? Are you okay?' Only then did I realize I had been weeping. Something else must have been controlling me. It must have been..."

Then he kept repeating versions of the same phrase: "I am sure this thing that won't stop talking is not me."

I wrote, *Uncontrolled emotional outbursts, crying without clear cause* and interrupted him by asking, "Did you like that particular cactus?"

"No, I wouldn't say that. It's just that every time I gave a presentation in that conference room, I could always see it out of the corner of my eye. It was something that drew my attention."

"Can you tell me something about the cactus flowers? What were they like?"

"Its leaves were always coated with a layer of gray. It didn't look like it could possibly live very long, yet last week I saw it bloom."

"What were the flowers like?"

"Small, like fingernails. Red like a rose."

"You clearly observed it carefully. Although you say you didn't particularly like it, your subconscious actually saw it in detail."

He choked up a bit, and his body slid down slightly along the back of the chair. That was good. He was starting to relax.

I pressed my advantage and asked, "Is that client very important to you?"

"Yes, very important. And in two weeks I have my promotion review. Every account is important now."

So this was a case in which the motivation to succeed was so powerful that it became counterproductive. As I took a moment to think about what to say next, I glanced out the window, and felt suddenly that I was just like him, concentrating on the plant in his periphery while talking with clients about their projects.

"Then you must have put a lot of effort into this account." I had to offer him approval before I could expect him to listen to what I was about to say.

"Yes... I have to work hard. I can only keep working hard."

"Do you ever feel that sometimes the goal toward which you strive is too distant, that it is out of reach, and that therefore..."

A large shadow flashed past the window, falling, like a heavy black trash bag dropped into a dumpster. It moved so fast, there was only time for me to catch a glimpse of the shadow's edge before it disappeared. A man's black leather shoes. It was a person.

"...therefore you are not fully absorbed in your work?" I completed my speech fluently, without a pause, as if someone else were speaking through me. My visitor was covering his face and wiping tears from the corners of his eyes. He had apparently not noticed the scene outside the window.

Strange, unnatural feelings swept through my heart, but I did not have time to consider them. Practiced words of comfort flowed out of my mouth: "After all, people are not machines, and even machines cannot always maintain a perfectly functional state."

My timer buzzed gently, and looking at the visitor I pursed my lips slightly toward the sound, politely signaling that his session was over.

"I recommend that when you go back to work, do your best to adjust your goals. Don't put too much pressure on yourself. For example, take the sense of accomplishment you feel with each account, any one account, and regulate that feeling to the level that you now feel after closing three successful accounts."

He nodded, got to his feet, and left wearily. I set down my smile as if laying down a heavy load. I was finally done.

TWO

Stepping out of the office building, I saw a group of people forming a circle in front of it. I knew it must be where the man had landed. The body had already been carried away, but there were dark-red blood stains on the ground, and a single black leather shoe. It was the one I had seen through the window in my office.

Someone in the crowd whispered, "Who was it? I can't think of who that…"

"I know him. It was that sales rep from the insurance company on thirty-four. His name was Shen Xin. He always did have a bit of an odd look."

Once I heard the name Shen Xin, I remembered that I had met him once myself. I had run into him in the elevator, a young man in a proper suit, his tie straight. As a salesperson, he seemed to have boundless enthusiasm for his work: he enthusiastically asked me what floor I was going to, enthusiastically pressed the button for me, enthusiastically introduced himself, and then enthusiastically tried to sell me an insurance policy.

Yet he still had a sense of the meticulous about him. He held his shoulders straight and rigid, and every high-pitched greeting seemed to be pre-recorded and played back. It seemed that observing fixed forms was in his bones. Why would this utterly conventional young man jump off a building?

Then there was the mystery of my reaction. This had to have been the first time I had witnessed someone jumping to their death, yet I had neither stopped what I was doing in amazement, nor had I cried out in panic: "Someone just jumped off the building!" Instead, I had smoothly continued telling my patient precisely what I thought I should tell him. A sense of unreality again spread through me, like an eerie touch from a ghostly hand.

I shuddered and quickly shook these thoughts away. I did not have time for foolish ideas; at home, I had to face a daughter who never stopped crying and a husband who didn't do anything at all. There was no room in my brain for foolish notions.

When I pushed my apartment door open, there was my daughter, two-and-a-half years old, sitting on the floor, barefoot, playing clumsily with a doll, and giggling idiotically. The picture book I had bought for her had been tossed carelessly aside.

My husband Rick, the man whose singing used to move me, sat to one side of this scene cradling his guitar and playing a cheerful tune without a hint of anxiety or care. Seeing me come in, he raised his head and looked at me with his simple, artless eyes, like a child expecting praise.

I stepped forward and pressed his guitar strings with my palm, silencing the instrument. He was stunned, his puzzlement showing plainly on his face.

"We agreed you would read that picture book to our daughter from seven to eight in the evening. What are you doing?"

"I did. I read to her. She didn't like it. You can see how happily she's playing now."

"She's almost three years old. Our daughter can only say a few words; she can't put together a complete sentence. Aren't you even a little concerned about that?"

"Look, she's laughing. She laughs as soon as I pick up the guitar. Her musical sense is highly developed. Maybe she has a gift for music, like me!"

This man who had aspired to be a musician, but ended up a music teacher—wasn't he embarrassed to talk about musical gifts? I couldn't stop myself from raising my voice. "This has nothing to do with gifts!

I have told you many times. Ages two to three are critical years for developing a child's reading skills and logical capabilities. After this crucial period is over, it doesn't matter how hard you work, there is no way to catch up on those skills!" I heard myself overstating for effect, reciting the most rigid of the older theories.

"Wen…" He said my name as if he wanted to placate me, but I was in a rage, and there was no stopping me.

"After age two, she immediately enters the stage of making calculations and connections. If our daughter's language and logic skills are not well-developed, she'll have more trouble with the next stage of concept formation. She'll fall behind her peers. Can't you be a little more responsible, a little more like a father?"

"Wen." He called my name again, apparently louder this time, but I only saw his mouth open and shut. Whatever he was saying, I could not hear it clearly. I kept talking, like a loose slot machine spitting out coins.

"I know you're psychologically immature. I know this. You've always been like a big child in this marriage. This was pre-determined for you by your original family circumstances, because when you were young your father abandoned your mother, so your mother spoiled you. I don't blame you for this. But we have a daughter now, so can you just pretend to be an adult, just a little?"

"Wen!" He had raised his voice again. "She's crying!"

"I know that!" I yelled, though in truth I had only just noticed. My daughter's sobs had turned into an open-mouth wail. The sound of the crying upset me, made me anxious. "But I have to make you understand that our marriage constitutes our daughter's original family and will determine her future. Do you understand that you are influencing her just like your family influenced you?"

"Fine. You've said your piece. Good. Are you done?" Now he was furious as well. "Don't spout your psychological theories at me."

"She will grow into a child who does not have a sense of trust in men. She will not be able to understand or rely on half of the members of society!"

"Wen!" he burst out suddenly. "Would it actually be so difficult for you to talk to me like a human being?"

The blue veins in his neck protruded, and his voice was heavy as a drum. It echoed through the room and resounded in my ears. I finally was quiet.

The scene from earlier in the day floated up before my eyes.

The heavy, black garbage bag fell.

"Do you ever feel that sometimes the goal toward which you strive is too distant, that it is out of reach, and that therefore…"

Men's black leather shoes flashed past the window.

"…and that therefore you are not fully absorbed in your work?"

Was that really what I had said? Was it really me saying it? As a man jumped to his death right before my eyes?

Ghostly hands spread across the dark room, reaching toward me, grasping at the back of my head. My body slowly stiffened, and I lost all control over my limbs.

THREE

"I think I'm being controlled by something."

At these words Professor Xu, sitting across from me, displayed a broad smile, and the fine lines in the corners of his eyes wrinkled softly, very different from my own dry and shriveled smiles.

Professor Xu was a veteran consultant with twenty years of experience. He had been my practicum advisor in school and became my own therapist—a therapist for therapists. More than that, he was a friend I trusted implicitly. Only here with him could I let down my guard and speak my true mind. With him I could enjoy a self-indulgent tone, almost like a spoiled child, and say such foolish things as "I think I'm being controlled by something."

He did not criticize me for my lack of professionalism, but simply asked kindly, "Communication with Rick is still rough?"

The problems between me and Rick had been going on for a long time. I was a very deliberative person, and Rick was used to doing whatever he felt like in the moment. The strange thing was that I did not realize this until we were already married.

When we were younger, we talked about everything. We would meet on the university quad, chatting from the bright afternoon to the slight chill of the moonlit night. I thought we were sufficiently familiar with each other. I thought that continuing our relationship was a rational decision founded on adequate communication, but clearly he had approached the situation differently. Perhaps for him our relationship was nothing more than a romanticized manifestation of long-repressed hormones.

I sighed. "We had another argument last night, and it made my daughter cry."

"The evolution of intimate relationships requires time and patience, and during this process it's best if you can avoid quarreling in front of your daughter. Even if she is only two-and-a-half years old, such scenes can have adverse effects."

"I know that. Of course I know. The problem is that even when I clearly saw her crying, I was still fully engaged in explaining my reasoning. Somehow I couldn't stop myself and comfort my daughter first. It's not that I don't know the importance of promptly consoling my child. How could I have set my sobbing daughter aside for the sake of an argument?" I pounded my forehead with a fist in self-recrimination.

"First of all, Wen, don't rush to blame yourself." Professor Xu's voice was full of comfort. "You have always been a highly rational person with a great deal of self-control. Have you recently encountered any additional stressful situations?"

Dark ghosts again enveloped me, and I told him about the man who had jumped from the building.

Professor Xu calmly wrote something in his notes and then said to me, "Is it possible, because you saw this man falling from the building and you yourself did not take any action, that you feel some guilt because of your passivity?"

"But I didn't know him at all. I had only seen him once. I barely knew his name."

"Can you tell me something about the circumstances of the day you met him?"

I thought back to that day.

"Just as I had done every day, I folded myself into the flow of commuters pouring into the office building. I stood quietly at the elevator door and waited. At the ding of the elevator bell, people entered, hurriedly but still keeping a polite distance from one another.

"There was a brief period in which voices called out floor numbers and polite thanks to those who pressed the buttons, followed by a stillness like dead water. In that silence, only Shen Xin was able to speak, to look into the cold and indifferent face of someone near him and introduce himself.

"I did not respond to his self-introduction or to the ovarian cancer insurance policy he presented to me. When I walked out of the elevator, he was still talking, giving his pitch every last ounce of his effort, and I didn't even turn my head to look back at him.

"Later, he fell to his death right before my eyes, and again I was indifferent, did nothing, did not even give him a second of my time."

When I finished describing the scene to Professor Xu, his response was familiar: "See, you remember it all very well. You are not as uncaring as you think."

I was pierced by an icy arrow that flew out from the darkness around me. I held tightly to the armrest of the chair, swallowed by the shame that seeped from my wound.

⸻

AS ALWAYS, I rode the elevator up to my office, but on the way I could not recover any sort of calm. The elevator rose and stopped, rose and stopped, and the red number indicating the floor continued to rise.

The twenty-eighth floor arrived, my floor, and I did not get out. Professor Xu's words still echoed in my ears: "The feelings of guilt come from a kind of fantasy that if only you had done something, taken some action, you could have prevented the undesirable outcome. If you were to go and try to understand this man's life and the cause of his death, you would naturally find many factors over which you could have had no control whatsoever."

Perhaps to atone for my indifference that day, I pushed the button for thirty-four. I would try to understand the man's life and why he had died.

HIS FLOOR WAS EXACTLY the same as the floor where I worked. The ceiling was low, and the space was carved up into several office areas separated from the hallway by frosted glass. The door to each area was affixed with a company name. I saw a door labeled PEOPLE'S INSURANCE COMPANY and knew that must have been where Shen Xin had worked.

I told the receptionist at the front desk that I was looking for Shen Xin. She wrinkled her nose, as if she smelled something odd, and told me coldly that he was dead. I confessed awkwardly, "I know. I just wanted to ask, why did he commit suicide?"

"Who knows? He was always a little strange. There was a period when he worked like mad, like sales was his whole life. He would sell to anyone. As long as he was talking to a person, he could make a sale. He was top salesman for several months. But recently, in the last sales period, he hadn't closed a single deal for a few weeks in a row. Then he just jumped."

It sounded like his suicide was related to work frustration and this professional setback. "Did anything specific happen just before he committed suicide? For example, did the company plan to let him go?"

"What would I know about that? I only know what I hear from my coworkers. His mother's here today. Why don't you ask her?" Her plump finger pointed toward the interior of the office. An elderly woman, dressed like she had arrived directly from the countryside, was packing up one of the work stations. She was hunched over and appeared frail, a figure stricken with grief.

I moved toward her and saw Shen Xin's name still printed on the cubicle nameplate. The old woman was a little embarrassed, not knowing what to do about my presence. I hesitated for a moment, then said that I was a friend of Shen Xin's.

"Oh, oh…" the old woman responded. She apologized repeatedly for not knowing me, saying that her "Little Xin" had not talked to her very much about his life. Even the things he had told her, she simply didn't understand.

I helped the old woman pack up the few items Shen Xin had left behind. We put his tea cups, pens, books, and folders one by one into a cardboard box. On Shen Xin's table, there were several large volumes on scientific subjects. This I had not expected to see.

The old woman chattered on long-windedly about the past. She talked about how Shen Xin had grown up polite and with a good understanding of things, and how he'd always studied diligently. Although she and his father were both illiterate farmers, Shen Xin's dream had been to be a scientist.

He originally wanted to continue his studies as a graduate student in biology, but then his father found out that he had stomach cancer, and the treatment was very expensive. Hearing that salespeople could make fast money, Shen Xin went to the city to sell insurance.

So, it turned out Shen Xin had been forced by the exigencies of life to give up his dream, I thought to myself.

"My little Xin, he was a good boy. Why did he take everything so hard? Why would he…?" The old woman choked with sobs and wept soundlessly.

"Perhaps he simply felt that life was too exhausting." I tried to comfort her with these words, although I did not really know anything at all.

I wanted her to answer her own question. Why did she think Shen Xin had committed suicide? But this was not the time for such pointed questions, and in any event, the elderly woman would not necessarily have any clear insight into her son's motivations.

The receptionist came over from the front desk and politely asked us to be a little quicker in finishing our task. The old woman stopped crying; I lowered my head and silently continued packing things into the box.

A notebook about the size of my palm fell out of a book titled *The Robot's Rebellion*, and I immediately squatted down to pick it up. I stayed there behind the desk for a few seconds, flipping quickly through the notebook. The first line on the first page brought me up short: "If I die someday soon, know that I did not kill myself."

The densely packed text was thick as grain in the field, and the thin sheets of paper etched deeply by the heavy handwriting gave off a strong air of the personal; these notes were clearly not related to his work. I stealthily tucked the notebook into my coat pocket. The answer to the riddle was surely within. It burned me through my clothes like a glowing piece of coal, but I could not throw it away. I could not wait to open it as soon as I had returned to my office.

FOUR

"They have been controlling me for a while already. I have encountered the following situation many times: I meet a new person in a public place. We exchange the conventional pleasantries, talk about the weather and so forth. After this initial greeting, I immediately and involuntarily start in on my sales pitch for an insurance policy.

"At first, I didn't think this was a problem. I thought it would improve my sales numbers. Maybe, I thought, it was actually me subconsciously trying to improve my numbers. After all, I had practiced so many hours in front of the mirror, how to greet a stranger and how to talk spontaneously about the products I was trying to sell.

"Eventually, however, there were times when I clearly saw the disgust in the face of the person I was talking to. In those moments, I should have known how to be tactful and stop talking or change the subject, but I found myself unable to stop. It was as if I were an actor, and the lines I had memorized must all be recited before I could leave the stage.

"(Conclusion: They are not able to discern human emotions.)"

This read like the typical ravings of a patient suffering from delusions of control, but the detailed descriptions that followed drew me in and kept me scanning the pages.

"LATER, the situation developed to the point that every person I saw became a potential customer, no matter who it was. I would try my pitch on literally anyone I met; it didn't matter whether they were realistically a potential client or not. Whenever I saw a person, I automatically began the process of greetings, small talk, and then sales, as if a switch had been flipped.

"For a while, I sold ovarian cancer insurance, but I even tried to sell it to men! When one of them swore at me and walked away, something terrible happened. I still couldn't stop talking, and the torrent of words poured out into the air, directed at nobody, until I had finished describing every last detail of the product.

"(Conclusion: They probably have no sense of sight.)"

A KNOCK ON THE DOOR; my next patient had arrived. I hurriedly shut the notebook, adjusted my posture, and said, "Please come in!"

It was the anxiety patient from two days previous. He sat down opposite me, still stiff.

"How have you been feeling?" I asked him with a smile.

"Doctor, I don't think I'll ever get better." His dejection and hopelessness were beyond my expectations. "I think the situation is worse. I can't stop talking about my account proposals with people, even people who are not clients. I'm less and less able to control myself."

"What did you say?" I couldn't believe what I was hearing.

"I can't control myself."

"No, before that, please."

"I can't stop talking about my accounts, going over my presentations and proposals, even with people who are not my clients."

These words, so perfectly consistent with the description in Shen Xin's notes. Could it be mere coincidence?

FIVE

"I work in a building with thirty-eight floors. There are approximately twenty thousand people working in this building. I have tried to sell insurance to practically every one of those twenty thousand people. There have been some successful attempts, but many more failures. I have seen everyone's indifference, if not their hostility. Before I fall asleep at night, those faces play back one after another in my mind, each one carved with contempt, contempt for me. I don't know how to go on living like this."

When I finished reading this passage in the midst of turbulent rush-hour traffic, remorse once again oppressed me. Mine was one of the contemptuous faces that had haunted Shen Xin in the night.

When I got home that evening, Rick was watching TV in the living room. He chuckled at something on the screen, and his silly expression was exactly like that of our daughter when she played with that doll. I was suddenly and violently irritated at the thought that my daughter had inherited half of her genes from him.

This world might possibly be undergoing a complex and radical transformation, and he was completely unaware. He was still watching his favorite variety show and laughing sardonically. His ignorant and happy eyes turned to me, and he uttered a completely insubstantial, "You're back."

"The new clothes I bought for her online should have arrived today. Are they okay? Is there any problem with them?"

"Clothes? Ah, when I got back today, I forgot to go pick up the package. I'll go tomorrow."

Again, thoughtless. I thought of Professor Xu's advice, "Don't carry stress with you into the home." With great effort I resisted the urge to spit a complaint at my husband. Instead, I went directly to the bedroom and opened the notebook.

"I became reticent, afraid of talking with anyone. And that worked.

After I stopped talking, they could not control me anymore, but the price of this freedom was that my monthly sales numbers dropped to zero.

"The manager called me into his office and berated me harshly. He gave me a new insurance product and said I had to sell at least five policies within the month or I would be let go. There was no way out.

"I went home and began to familiarize myself with the new policy documents. As I recited the materials softly to myself, they took control of me again. They forced me to talk to myself in front of a wall for two hours. They made me describe every single insurance product I have ever tried to sell, one after another!

"Like a dog that has been stuck in a room for too long, it runs even faster and more wildly than usual as soon as door opens. And this dog had been stuck in the room for a very long time. It went crazy.

"But these things are different from dogs. They are of a collective. They are used to doing things as a group. All it takes is for one of them to be mentioned, and then the other ones that are linked with it will pour out of one's mouth.

"I have done experiments to test this hypothesis. They do not respond to random everyday words unrelated to any system. Only words that belong to a certain systematic framework will bring about the endless talk. They are essentially like genes, each of which is composed of a specialized vocabulary. The particular set of words that belong to it are like the specific nucleotide sequence that comprises a particular gene.

"Their reproductive instincts are also the same as genes; their goal is to make as many copies of themselves as possible and thereby expand their population! And human consciousness is their medium; linguistic communication between humans (both oral and written) is their vector of transmission!"

"THAT FEELING that we talked about last time, the feeling that you were being controlled—has that situation improved?" Professor Xu's mild voice embraced me.

"Ah? What?" I snapped out of a reverie. Shen Xin's dense handwriting still floated in the air around me, as it had for more than a week.

"Have you experienced any compulsive behavior recently? For example, any movement of your body that you feel did not originate with you?" Professor Xu continued, "If so, it may be an anxiety disorder."

"It's not anxiety." I spoke in a low voice. "It's them. They have taken control of me. They are controlling humans." My body trembled unnaturally, and I knew I probably sounded incoherent.

"Wen? Are you all right?" Professor Xu asked. "Are you feeling controlled right now? Wen, just stay calm. Do you hear a voice in your head? Are you seeing something unusual?"

He went on in one long breath to talk about all the symptoms and principles of delusion, but I didn't hear a word of what he said. Why was he talking at such length about all these things? These are principles with which I was quite familiar. Was Professor Xu also being controlled? He sounded like Shen Xin, unable to stop talking until he had finished his entire sales pitch.

As I walked down the road that led toward home, it seemed that the voices of the people on the street became drawn out and attenuated. A man holding a mobile phone talked without pause about a certain plan of his, all the way down the street. A salesperson at the door of a store introduced her product in full detail without taking a breath, a tedious and redundant recitation. The huge electronic screen in the city's central plaza was broadcasting a program about the law, and the lawyers in their impeccable suits rattled on and on about the legal clauses and subclauses of some legislation. Every voice was so strange.

Were they all being controlled? Or was this how the world had always been? Was it merely that Shen Xin's notebook made me pay attention to these details?

My head was buzzing. No. I had to find more reliable evidence.

SIX

"I found a forum about them on the internet. There's a group of people like me who suffer under their control. I try to tell people around me that they are here, trying to control humans.

"At first, I was able to talk without interference about the forum and the name those victims gave to 'them'. What I mean is that, even though people often looked at me strangely, nevertheless, I was able to speak about 'them' unhindered. But very quickly it all changed, and I could not mention details about the forum, and I could not say 'their' name to anyone. I only have to try to mention that term, and I am instantly mute, as if I have a sensitive word filter in my brain.

"I suppose this is proof that that name is the true name of the collective. They can cause me to rattle on endlessly, or they can hide away in my consciousness and refuse to come out. If this is true, very likely they control human thought simply by deciding what to output and what to block. Here I enter the most frightening territory, and this is why I am writing down these words.

"I have an ominous presentiment. If some misfortune should happen to me, please look at chapter seven of *The Robot's Rebellion*. The name is there."

***

THE ROBOT'S *Rebellion* was the book on Shen Xin's desk from which this notebook had fallen. His mother had taken it away with her. I searched for the book online, and it was there. The seventh chapter was titled "From Genes to Memes."

The chapter opened, "Meme: an element of a culture or system of behavior that may be considered to be passed from one individual to another by non-genetic means, especially imitation. Just as genes are transferred from one individual to another through sperm and egg, memes are propagated from one brain to another to carry out cultural reproduction."

After a little time with a search engine, I soon found the forum that Shen Xin had written about. I read page after page of posts, read until my palms were sweaty and my head burned. The experience of being controlled that the members described was virtually the same as Shen Xin's. Although, because of their different occupations, each individual had been colonized by different types of memes.

For example, mathematicians were colonized by memes from within the mathematical system, and architects were colonized by memes related to construction and design. Advertising agents were colonized by their own marketing campaigns.

I could even analyze the similarities in their descriptions to abstract the symptomatic stages of meme control. First, there was the inability to stop speaking to people when it was clearly appropriate to stop. Then there was the rigidity of the body, anxiety and tension. Then the steady flow of speech with total disregard for one's audience, if there even was an audience.

God, I was a psychiatrist, a scientist. Was I actually going to blindly accept the statements of a delusional patient? The only way to disprove or confirm these statements was going to be through experimentation.

I FACED THE MIRROR, took a deep breath, and arranged for myself a simple experimental method. I spoke the first word: "Hello."

My throat and palate vibrated softly, causing the air in my ears to ripple as if with small concentric waves of water. After the brief quavering of sound dissipated, the air recovered its calm, and I did not continue to speak or excite any other special response.

I continued on to my second experimental phrase: "My name is Wen."

No response.

Once again I drew in a deep breath and carefully enunciated the third statement of my experiment: "Subconscious."

That one word was all I had planned to speak, but then I saw, or thought I saw, a dark-yellow, creeping vapor surge from my mouth like a dense swarm of bees.

"This refers to those things that cannot become conscious under normal circumstances, such as desires that are repressed deep in one's innermost being and cannot be considered by the conscious mind…"

They were here. They occupied my brain and used my throat as a channel. I desperately tried to cover my mouth, but they flowed out through the tiny gaps between my fingers. I smashed the mirror and pushed down a towering pile of books, but the loud noise failed to shake the momentum of their inexorable march forward.

Rick rushed over from the living room and shouted my name through the locked door. Paralyzed, I slumped to the ground. I was unable to open the door or respond. He forced the door and entered, shocked to see the disorder in the room. He held me and asked anxiously what was going on. But I could not reply. My linguistic capabilities were entirely under their control.

"…Freud believed that the unconscious functions actively, that it spontaneously exerts pressure and influence on human character and behavior…"

"What's wrong with you? Why are you talking this way?" Rick asked.

"…Things that may seem insignificant, such as dreams, words misspoken or miswritten, and clerical errors, are all initiated by latent triggers in the brain. They reveal the hidden, unconscious self, though their appearance in these forms constitutes another kind of disguise…"

"Oh, now I understand what you mean. I get it." Rick laughed bitterly. "You're saying that because I forgot to pick up the package for our daughter and didn't read the book to her that that's all intentional, that it means something! You've decided in your heart that I'm a child with no sense of responsibility, and now you think I'm making these unconscious mistakes because I want to escape responsibility. Is that it?"

I couldn't explain to him what was going on; I kept spitting out words like language-repeating software. Rick flung the door open and was gone.

Theories of the subconscious are vast and labyrinthine. I had opened the floodgate, and it could not be closed again. After Freud's dynamic unconscious, I talked about Jung's collective subconscious in minute detail, followed by Adler's inferiority complex and Fromm's social unconscious. As the misty dawn brightened the sky, I finally stopped talking. Heedless of my extreme thirst and burning tongue, I rushed to the office as quickly as I could and pulled all of our practice's client files from the past three months for statistical analysis.

* * *

ONCE I EXCLUDED all patients who began their therapy earlier, I discovered that the number of new anxiety patients had tripled in the past three months. The symptoms they described all included stiffness, sometimes paralysis, delusions of being controlled, and workplace situations during which the patient was unable to stop speaking once they started. These all demonstrated a high level of consistency with each other as well as with the descriptions by those who posted to the online forum.

Trembling, I printed out the reports and went to find Professor Xu.

The corners of his eyes again creased with gentle wrinkles, and he asked me kindly what was the matter.

"This is extremely urgent, Professor Xu," I said. "Many of our patients are being controlled by cultural memes and are in grave danger. We must do something now."

"What are you talking about? What memes?" Professor Xu looked at me, puzzled.

"I know this sounds absurd, but it's true. I have experimental evidence and data to back it up!"

I handed the reports over to him. He looked them over solemnly for a time, and then, his face gentle as before, said, "Wen, your findings are correct. In recent months, cases of anxiety and delusions of control have increased, not only in our practices—they have increased all around the world. However, your conclusions are wrong. The situation is not what you imagine; in truth, there is no meme controlling humanity."

"Then what is the truth?"

His smile was both mysterious and oddly gratified. "The truth is, humans have evolved."

SEVEN

The psychological community had never held a news conference on such a grand scale. There was not an empty seat in the auditorium, and even the aisles were packed tight.

I took a closer look at the podium and the table at which sat the distinguished panel of presenters. In addition to psychologists, top scientists from every field crowded the front row of seats, alongside reporters from all of the major media platforms around the world. Their cameras flashed without pause at the stage and the words projected on the screen behind it: *The Evolution of Human Consciousness: A National Academic Report*.

Professor Xu stood up on the broad rostrum, and on the screen was now projected a massive and detailed schematic of the human brain. This image was different from the typical diagram in that here the surface of the cerebral cortex was blanketed by a network of fine lines, like a spiderweb, and this net was highlighted in glowing green.

"The past six months have seen a marked increase in patients all over the world complaining of intense anxiety. Many of our peers in the psychological community have noted this phenomenon. Psychologists have performed many independent and in-depth investigations into the reasons for this, and have finally discovered these nodes that form a net around the brains of these anxiety sufferers.

"The links between these nodes are marked on this image with thin green lines. At first, the researchers thought that these were brain lesions indicating pathological mutation, but it was soon discovered that these tissues and the structures they form could also be found in the brains of many control-group individuals, subjects with no complaint of acute anxiety.

"These other individuals were found to be primarily professionals in fields requiring a relatively high degree of dense cultural knowledge —such as scientific research, law, and finance—and without exception, these subjects were all outstanding members within their field, with a prodigious capacity for knowledge acquisition and clear logical thinking.

"After completing complex comparative research, psychologists have concluded that these net-nodes are not pathological, but rather evidence of the evolution of human consciousness! The anxiety disorder that has appeared in the past six months is merely a symptom of an individual's unsuccessful adaptation to this new stage of human evolution."

Cameras flashed and reporters' hands shot up. The theory had been published, of course, and a few articles written already in the previous month, but no interviews had been granted. Everyone wanted to be the first to ask a question. Professor Xu, however, carried on with his prepared speech. I sat quietly, thrilled to be in the room. I'd never imagined that I would witness such an important scientific discovery in my lifetime.

Pictures of the brain's net-nodes were frequently cited in academic papers and were even quickly added to scientific textbooks. And Professor Xu's speech at the conference, like a manifesto for a new age, flooded people's eyes and ears wherever they went.

Professor Xu was on TV, dignified in his suit: "We all know that human beings emerged out of fifty million years of ceaseless evolution. Only after those eons were they able to transform themselves from their origins among ancient ape-like species into what they are today. Human psychology and consciousness have also experienced a prolonged period of development, even longer than the evolutionary history of the human form."

Professor Xu's statements appeared on the front page of the newspaper: "From the first appearance on earth of a single-celled organism worthy of the name 'life,' each stage of the species' development has left significant traces in human consciousness, just as ancient creatures, long-extinct, left their fossils in the rock layers of different ages. Fear, escape, attack, predation—these are instincts developed in the cold-blooded reptilian stage. The emergence of mammals necessitated the development of more delicate perceptions and emotional responses and led to the construction of what we now call the subconscious as the basis for human psychology."

Professor Xu's speech was even on the big screen in the city's central plaza: "It was not until humans developed language and used that language to communicate that humans truly possessed consciousness, reason, and intelligence. Only then were humans able to create such a rich and magnificent civilization. And now, after instinct, the subconscious, and consciousness, the human brain has evolved a higher level of psychological mode: the post-conscious. The birth of post-consciousness benefited from the advanced development of human language and reason. It closely follows the organizational structures of rational logic and knowledge. Post-consciousness will transform humanity into a higher-order civilization!"

Every time I heard that last sentence, I got goosebumps, as if the initially neutral word "post-consciousness" were suddenly and roughly brushed over with red paint. The shock this discovery brought to the psychological community was tremendous. One conference followed right on the heels of the previous one. Scholars did battle with words, their mouths like weapons; I could see them, or thought I could, spout forth all different colors of writhing vapor. Some people's light-colored smoke was swallowed by the darker, denser smoke of others, leaving only the most powerful vapors to blend together and evolve into blurry and indistinct new colors.

Those with anxiety disorders and who thought they were being controlled were considered to have a post-conscious maladaptive disorder. The psychological community quickly developed a drug for the treatment of these patients: Levizodone. Its principle was more or less the same as that of antidepressants that eliminate depression by regulating hormone levels. Levizodone reduced the activity of the brain's limbic system, which is mainly responsible for producing the subconscious mind, thereby expanding the space available for conscious and post-conscious activities.

THE MIDDLE-AGED MAN with the anxiety disorder came to consult me again. He told me about the day he had found the smashed pot of the holiday cactus in the dumpster behind the company building.

"Its bulbs were completely exposed, and several limbs had been broken. It was too horrible to look at. I couldn't stop myself from crying when I saw it." He went on, "You were right. I actually did really care about that plant, subconsciously."

"It's okay. These things don't matter anymore," I said.

I made a note in his file recommending the prescription, two courses of Levizodone. "Go down to Psychiatric to pick up the prescription. After you take this, you won't have any more trouble."

He took the referral slip and left, half-believing and half-doubting. But he faithfully took the medicine according to the treatment course, and when I saw him again a week later, his condition was much improved. He showed no signs of stiffness, and his speech had become easy and fluent again, although he didn't talk about anything other than his advertising accounts, which was tedious for me.

THERE WAS a bottle of Levizodone in my pocket also, which Professor Xu had prescribed for me. I hadn't taken it yet; I hadn't even torn open the packaging. The idea of needing the medicine made me feel powerless, like admitting that I really was seriously ill and unable to rely on my own resources to make myself well again.

The vapor I saw spewing from my own mouth when I spoke was gradually changing into the same color as that of my colleagues in the office. The sense that I was being controlled still afflicted me, and the stiffness in my back prevented me from falling asleep at night. I was becoming an insomniac on top of everything else. Already I could no longer say the word "meme" to others, just like Shen Xin before he died.

The online forum was inexplicably shut down. All online articles on meme theory, already very few in number, also disappeared, as if they had never existed.

At the same time, the concept of post-consciousness spread quickly. It spread in-person, too. Its color was an ashy-blue. It had tough roots as well as strong legs and feet. On many occasions I had seen it dashing from one person to another in the exchange of smoke from their mouths, so very fast it was. And it quickly rooted deep in the minds of everyone I knew… except for Rick.

Rick was the only exception I knew personally. He didn't seem to have any of these things in his mind, and there was no filthy smoke in his mouth. He remained pure as the afternoon we first met in college when we sat on the quad, separated only by a few blades of green grass, silent.

He had fiddled with the strings of his guitar and raised his eyes from time to time to meet my gaze. I'd held a book, but had forgotten I was supposed to be reading it. Two people growing first warm toward each other and then passionate.

But all of that was far behind us, and it could not be recovered. And yet I could not wholeheartedly accept this new world. Which was more absurd, really—to believe that one was being controlled, or to believe that humanity had evolved into post-consciousness?

I walked to the window and opened it, my head pounding from lack of sleep. I climbed half over the railing, straddling it. Vertigo made me dizzy, and my legs went soft. Before I lost consciousness, I saw Rick rushing toward me, his face pale, his lips trembling, and I saw deep within his enormous pupils nothing but the most pure fear and the most genuine concern. This is what I saw: the final innocence of humanity.

EIGHT

When I regained consciousness, I found myself lying in a hospital bed. The bottle of Levizodone, which had been in my pocket, now sat on the bedside table. The packaging was torn, and the bottle's seal was broken. The hallucinations that had long troubled me had disappeared, and the feeling that I was being controlled was gone. My entire body felt relaxed as never before, and I was alert and clear-headed. I felt as if I had become smarter.

"You're finally awake." Rick's face appeared before me. He seemed to be crying tears of joy, just as foolish as ever.

Professor Xu stood beside my bed as well, with a rare expression of severity on his face. "Being a doctor yourself, how could you not take your medicine? Your anxiety worsened, and you almost jumped out of a window. Fortunately, Rick was there to save you."

I laughed. "Huh. If I had known it would be like this, I would have taken the medicine. I feel much more comfortable now."

WHEN I GOT HOME, I found Shen Xin's notebook was still on my desk. I opened it again, but inside the pages were blank, not a word written on them. Half of the pages were deformed by what seemed to be water damage; the paper was covered with ripples and bumps and discolored patches. It really had been a delusion, after all, memes controlling humanity. I laughed derisively at my own foolishness and tossed the notebook into the trash bin.

More and more people adapted successfully to post-consciousness. The number of academic papers on every subject in every field grew exponentially. New theories and technologies emerged constantly, and with no end in sight.

Aerospace research, which had been stagnating for quite some time, now made rapid progress again, and even migration to alien planets soon came within our reach. The media were full of programs focused on various professions, while shows produced merely to make people laugh and other simple-minded entertainment all but disappeared.

I watched the people on TV with keen interest. They spoke faster and faster every day, and every day I consumed ravenously all the new knowledge and novel concepts I could find.

For my part, I did my best each day to produce and verbalize valuable new ideas. Human culture was a train moving at full speed along its track, and there was no stopping it. People's daily communication omitted a great deal of complicated etiquette and small talk; everything was more efficient.

But Rick never changed, and that was odd. He neither developed a complete post-consciousness nor did he show signs of a post-conscious maladjustment. He was like a static, unevolved man. I talked to him less and less. He never could keep up with my train of thought, and I felt that his words were invariably vacuous. Listening to him was a waste of time.

I read the latest research that claimed some human beings were incapable of developing post-consciousness and that this was a normal phenomenon in times of evolutionary shift. Such people would gradually be eliminated in the course of natural selection.

Professor Xu explained that Rick and those like him would eventually be completely unable to understand the language of post-conscious humans. This, he said, was akin to how two AIs, after long communication with each other, will generate a unique AI language system that humans cannot understand. When that time comes, people like Rick would hear the conversations of post-conscious humans without the slightest comprehension. Rick and I would eventually be people of two worlds.

But my daughter was still young, and her tender and malleable brain was still in the developmental stage. If she continued to have contact with Rick as she grew, she would be affected negatively. This would not be conducive to the successful development of post-consciousness.

To make it easier for Rick to understand this matter, I described the rationale behind our divorce in a letter and gave it to him along with the divorce agreement. It was gratifying that he signed the agreement quickly, and I obtained full custody of my daughter.

When that was settled, I sent my daughter to a post-consciousness training institute that had been set up especially for children. My daughter quickly reached the linguistic level expected of post-conscious humans, so I no longer worried about her development.

One day, when I brought my daughter home from the institute, I ran into Rick at the door. It cost him great effort to make me understand that he wanted to have a cup of coffee with me and spend some time with his daughter as well. He missed her very much. Out of pity, I decided to satisfy his simplistic emotional needs, and my daughter and I walked with him to a nearby cafe.

Rick called out to the girl using her old nickname, trying to start a conversation with her, but she held tight to the institute-issued electronic screen the entire time, her plump fingers dashing back and forth over the touchscreen.

"Say hello to your father." I pointed to Rick as I spoke to my daughter.

She looked up for a moment and then provided a perfectly coherent and correct definition: "Father: a form of address for a man with children."

The electronic screen recognized the girl's words and gave her a congratulatory cheer: "Correct!"

The girl continued speaking: "In the biological sense, a father is a male who has contributed half of the chromosomes to his children."

The electronic screen gave her a more enthusiastic commendation: "Correct! The second-level cognitive association has been achieved!"

Rick's expression darkened.

I smiled. "Her post-conscious language learning progresses quickly."

"It's okay," he sighed. "I'm actually just here to see whether or not I made the right decision that day."

I could not stop to listen to him as I excitedly began to elaborate on post-conscious language learning.

"Their post-consciousness training is based on micro-current stimulation of the cerebral cortex, combined with medications that reduce the activity of the limbic system, coupled with cognitive association training to promote the formation of net-nodes on the cerebral cortex..."

"These past few years you and I quarreled constantly. You were always saying things that I didn't understand. Then you said that memes were controlling you. I know that no one else believes in memes now, but I believe, because I saw that your fear was real and urgent, even as your mouth was saying something unrelated or irrelevant.

"That night you tried to jump out the window, I saw your eyes. They were asking me for help. *You* were asking me for help. I knew that it wasn't you who wanted to jump. That thing controlling you wanted you to die. You were resisting it; you had been fighting it all along.

"When you arrived at the hospital, Professor Xu said that you had tried to kill yourself because you hadn't taken the medicine. He said that you had become another kind of human being, and if you wanted to live, you must take the medicine.

"He asked me to make the decision. I couldn't watch you die, but I didn't know whether or not after taking the medicine you would be completely controlled by that thing, whether or not you would still be yourself. I decided to gamble. I let them give you the medicine to keep you alive.

"I was betting on you, betting that even if you took the medicine, you would still be able to fight that thing until the very end."

"...After only a month of training, her cerebral cortex had already formed two net-nodes in the post-consciousness network..."

"So, I came to ask you, somewhere inside this thing that speaks through you, are you still yourself? Are you still the girl who sat with me on the grass pretending to read as the wind rose and the evening fell?"

"...As long as she persists in her training for half a year, her post-consciousness network will be able to mature fully, and she will be among the first cohort of human children to use post-conscious thinking from such a young age…"

"I know you can't stop saying what you're saying. It's OK. But if you are still that girl, if she's still in there, just blink your eyes, just one time."

I blinked, one time, and forced a single warm teardrop to fall from the corner of my eye.

THIS STORY originally appeared in *Future Science Fiction Digest*.

SU MIN IS a Chinese Sci-Fi screenwriter and writer. Her novel *Niche Psychological Cases* was signed to China Literature Limited. Her short stories, mainly published on such online magazines or platforms in China as Non-Exist, Douban, and JingRenYuan, include "Inverted Reflection of Earth," "Substitute Vessels," and "The Post-Conscious Age," which was voted as Best Short Story of 2020 at the Galaxy Awards, a Hugo-esque award in China.

NATHAN FARIES TEACHES Chinese language and literature at Bates College in Lewiston, Maine. He has translated several stories for *Future Science Fiction Digest*.

JUST LIKE MIGRATORY BIRDS

Taiyo Fujii, translated from the Japanese by Emily Balistrieri

IN THE CENTER of the zero-gravity lab, in which I was alone, a wind with the salty smell of the air eighty meters above the East China Sea was blowing at 50 kph.

Floating with my body parallel to the floor while I was controlling the wind, I placed a hand on the titanium cage surrounding the round, two-meter observation stage in the middle of the room, and pulled myself toward the blue glow inside. It was interesting how my fingers on the inside of the cage felt a slight gravitational pull.

On the stage where the 50 kph wind was blowing, the gravity was also matched to the 0.973 m/s^2 of the sky above that specific region of the ocean.

In the center, a swallow I'd named Akane was flapping his wings.

I'd messed up when it came to the gender. It was after I gave him the Japanese female name Akane that I realized the swallow that had been sent from the Philippines was male.

Behind Akane was a breathtakingly sparkling blue sky, and the deeper blue of the sea—projections. I knew the same sky and sea were being projected on my fingers and face.

As I watched Akane beating his wings with all his might, the wind suddenly whipped at my face as it changed direction.

Turbulence.

Akane was blown toward my side of the stage.

When I murmured, "Begin log," the brain activity captured by the fMRI sensor fixed to the cage was overlayed on top of Akane. Of course, the video was an augmented reality only I could see.

I climbed up onto the stage, and, resisting gravity for the first time in a while, peered into Akane's face. With the East China Sea projection-mapped on my own face, he couldn't see me.

I saw a yellow spark shoot in C12, the region that governs a swallow's migration.

Neurons firing.

The yellow spark born in the C12 region traveled as a signal to the bases of the wings and tail.

A twitch of his flight feathers shifted Akane's posture, and he headed back toward the center of the stage. Watched from the ground, the action appears smooth, but if one observes the nerve movements from this close, you can tell it's a set of digital motions.

With the signal of just a few hundred synapses firing, Akane can set his course and fly. The event is practically a reflex, bearing little resemblance to thought as we humans think of it.

Why do animals migrate?

After extinct Japanese eels were hatched in an ocean trench off the Philippines, they swam for Japan's rivers, and wildebeests endure hunger and thirst to traverse half their great continent. Sea turtles return to the beach of their birth after two or three years of ocean living.

Of course, we know the reasons they do it. They travel for food, or a breeding ground, or in response to seasonal climate changes.

But—just as I thought that, there was a movement on the horizon line crossing my face.

Pulling away to look at the screen, I saw a stratovolcano with a beautiful base showing up small. This was the Fuji of Satsuma, Kaimondake, which towers at the tip of the Kagoshima Peninsula.

Little on the horizon, Kaimondake was a hazy purple through the steam rising from the Japanese Current; I gasped at the sense that I was really there.

I was sure that if it felt this real, even Akane would be tricked.

I slipped out of the gravity-equipped stage, and pushed off the cage with my feet to fly through the lab's zero-G space over to the apparatuses fixed to the wall.

Trapping a migratory bird in virtual reality and observing its trip was my research. I'm second-level professor of Zhejiang University's Institute of Natural Engineering, Tsukasa Hibino.

By placing a stage with gravity controls capable of reproducing slight geoidal variances at the center of an omnidirectional projection-mapping screen and blowing a wind comprised of minute, custom-printed atmospheric particles, I was reproducing the swallow's migration from the Philippines back to Kyoto in its entirety.

Gazing between my floating feet, at the stage filled with the shining ocean, I refocused on the life-sized augmented-reality video of Earth, a meter in diameter, floating beyond it.

I was on a space island.

Once called space "colonies" or "stations," an island is a human facility for living in orbit. If not for the zero gravity, it would be impossible to reproduce a specific geoid. In labs on Earth's surface, you can't fabricate gravity lower than your location, but here on Taiji Tianlou, with its graviton spiral accelerator (GSA) emitting two trillion gravitons per second, it's possible to create as much gravitational interference as you like, anywhere on the eighty-five-kilometer facility.

I made use of that to reproduce a perfect East China Sea inside the lab.

The experiment was proceeding favorably.

If the setup worked this well, maybe next I could do a huge aquarium to investigate tuna or krill migrations. If I continued expanding the area of my research, maybe I'd be able to study the near-life phenomena we were finding on planets outside our system.

Then we'd get a better understanding of what they are.

I noticed a few streaks of light fly away from the Earth on the wall.

The thirty million Chinese people who had returned to Earth would be arriving home to Taiji Tianlou the next day.

And then the Earth would recede.

Its plane of revolution and Taiji Tianlou's orbit around the sun at a tilt of thirty degrees mean we only approach the planet once a year. The date we come nearest is controlled by the huge number of gravitons being emitted by the heart of Taiji Tianlou, the GSA. This year, 2120, it was January 30.

Looking at the label on the streaks of light headed this way, I laughed in spite of myself.

"Chunyun Special."

Even in the 22nd century, the Chinese living on space islands make the annual journey home for Lunar New Year. It goes without saying that those living in stationary orbit, such as on space elevator stations, go home, but those on Mars do, too. Supposedly there are something like seven hundred million or a billion of them, and, thanks to the space travel infrastructure improved to service their annual travels, it has gotten much easier to travel to and from Mars.

Though I belong to Zhejiang University, the reason someone like me, from the minor nation of Japan, can live on Taiji Tianlou, to simplify it quite a bit, is the rocket network built for the Lunar New Year trips.

"A million thanks to the *kakyō*," I found myself murmuring.

The Chinese living in space have been called kakyō since the middle of the previous century. The second kanji in the compound is from an archaic version of the word that meant "Chinese merchants abroad"—the previous character had come back into style since the crowning radical is the same as the one in both characters that make up the word for "space."

I searched for the Chunyun Special Flight that had departed from Fujian Spaceport and dropped a pin.

My friend from college, now living with me on the island, lab engineer Hefei Ye, was on that rocket.

As I touched the augmented reality with a finger, the "He'll never agree..." slipped out.

I hadn't even asked the question, but I knew he wouldn't react well. I reread the message I had received the previous day.

"Hey, Hefei Ye. I think of Taiji Tianlou as my second home. If I were to return somewhere, this place would be fine. And when I move to the next place, that'll be my home."

Imagining Hefei Ye sitting in the cramped rocket seat, and his face, I voiced the question I wasn't sure if I could ask:

"Why does it have to be Fujian for you?"

"I'M BACK."

With a whoosh of compressed air as the plug door opened, a familiar voice echoed in the room.

"Good to see—whoa!"

When I turned around, my field of vision filled with him as he leapt from the door. He wasn't used to the gravity, which was set to only half of Earth's.

"Sorry!" Hefei Ye shouted as he tackled me.

I took his fingers from my shoulder and gently bent them backward.

When his arm extended reflexively, his back, rounded from his two weeks at home, naturally straightened as well. That stabilized his posture after he had lost his balance.

"Sorry, I'm not acclimated." He scratched his head sheepishly.

"That can't be helped. You were on Earth for two weeks. Welcome back."

"Thanks."

We hugged now that he was standing up straight. Whenever he was freshly back from Earth, his hugs were always a little forceful. Feeling my breathing get constricted, I yelped in spite of myself.

"Sorry, did I hurt you?"

"Not as bad as all that, but you could watch your strength."

"Right."

Releasing his arms, he was about to turn toward the container he'd left near the door, but I sandwiched his cheeks in my palms to stop him.

"You can unpack later. I'm going to make tea—which do you want?"

"I've had too much Wuyi and Maofeng, so I'll have Japanese tea."

I told him okay and readied tea cups and a small pot while trying to think of the best way to broach my topic.

After three minutes, the room was filled with the aroma of green tea. Hefei Ye and I sat across from each other at the dining table and chatted about what had happened over the past two weeks.

Once I had made our third cup (I can never get Chinese people to understand, but when making Japanese tea you need new leaves each time you add hot water), I was finally able to bring up what I needed to talk to him about.

"Do you remember Uluru?"

"It's a settled planet in Cetus, right? Or was it Ophiuchus?" He sounded nervous as he asked.

I nodded and pretended not to notice. "Yeah. The fourth planet in the Tau Ceti system, Uluru." I pronounced the name, which was neither English nor Chinese, respectfully, with the correct intonation. Uluru is named after a place sacred to a group of Aboriginal Australians.

The Australian planet development company, based in the New Sydney district of the space island La Grange 2, chose five thousand Aboriginal Australians to be the first immigrants and later the administrators.

I don't know why they specifically chose people with aboriginal roots as immigrants. Maybe the president of the development company, with roots in Victorian England, felt guilty for the massacre his ancestors had committed against the indigenous peoples, or maybe it had something to do with the anti-orbit globalism movement troubling space islands here and there. But since the company that had sent the ship off went bankrupt, there is no longer any way to investigate its management decisions.

The ship departed twenty-seven years ago, when it was still the 21st century.

Regardless of the how or why, the Aboriginal Australian immigrants headed for the fourth planet of the Tau Ceti system, 11.9 light years away, using a graviton disruption lens to navigate a black hole fall. Having achieved 99 percent of the speed of light in three years, the immigration ship reached its destination fifteen years after departing. Time moved more slowly on the ship itself, traveling at near-light speed, so only seven years passed inside.

Taking the same three-year period as they had accelerating, they decelerated to Tau system orbital speed and put the ship in stationary orbit as set out in the Exoplanet Development Agency's terraforming procedures.

Looking down on the fourth planet with their naked eyes for the first time, the immigrants were captivated by the earth, orangey with a thin layer of mercury sulfide and sparkling through the primarily methane atmosphere. I heard the color and the giant landmass, visible even from orbit, reminded them of the huge sacred stone Westerners had once called Ayer's Rock.

Along with notice of their arrival, the immigrants reported to the Earthsphere that the new land, which had hitherto only been known as "the fourth planet" would be called Uluru, and that their capital, of the moment, at least, would be named after another sacred place, Kata Tjuta.

This had happened twenty years ago.

The news that took eleven years and eleven months to cross space and reach Earth had arrived two weeks previously.

I had stopped Hefei Ye as he was packing for his Chunyun Special Flight and told him about the new planet humanity had reached.

He said that even in his home town, the kakyō who had returned from orbit had gathered and discussed it excitedly.

How would resources be brought into orbit from Uluru, which had four times the mass of Earth? How many space elevators could be built? Was terraforming possible? And if so, how would the earth, coated in orange mercury sulfide, and the primarily methane atmosphere be replaced? And would it be possible to shorten the fifteen-year voyage from Earth? That the conversations didn't stop at the fantasizing of technical experts is the formidable thing about the kakyō.

During the two-week Chunyun period, the number of planet development corporations registered in China topped five thousand. When Hefei Ye VR'd me from home, he had winced as he said, "Ninety percent of them will dissolve, though," and then he'd ftold me he had even joined two ventures related to space flight systems as technical officer.

The two of us laughed at how quick to heat up and just as quick to cool down these off-planet Chinese entrepreneurs are, but then again, if five hundred companies remain, all I can say is that I'd expect nothing less from kakyō.

The space island where we live is supported by kakyō technology. The recycling plant that closes our resource cycles, the gravitational field navigation that makes it easy to change the orbit of our eighty-five-kilometer space island, the graviton disruption lenses with plasma trapped inside that make tiny nuclear fusion reactors possible—all invented by kakyō. They've filled the area this side of Mars's orbit with space islands.

It's even said that the lingua franca in the field of technologies related to living in space is Chinese.

But the further you get from Mars, the less you feel the kakyō presence.

Japanese space immigrants—*nikyō*—are working hard in that treasury of resources, the asteroid belt; the ones pumping up the helium 3 that fuels nuclear reactors from Jupiter and Saturn are American energy conglomerates, and the same Arabian corporations that had dealt in oil in the Middle East.

The ones who sought a way out of the solar system were the European Union, the island nations of the South Pacific, and the Australian company that bet its fate on developing Uluru.

Kakyō have the largest share of the market for fusion reactors,

GSAs, the most comfortable residential plants, and so on, but you rarely see any of them in person outside the orbit of Mars.

The reason—those of us living in the space age laugh as we explain —is that they won't go anywhere they can't get back from for Lunar New Year.

Of course, that's a joke, but as Hefei Ye enjoyed his first Japanese tea in a while, I couldn't manage to bring up the important thing I had to discuss with him. That said, there was no way he would overlook my hesitation.

He set his tea cup on the table and looked at me. "So, what about Uluru?"

The tea in his cup seemed to sway endlessly due to the gravity of only .6 of a G.

When I didn't say anything, he smiled and offered a topic. "Now that you mention it, the second report from Kata Tjuta hasn't arrived yet, huh? The gravity wave transmissions with the Tau system can send a megabyte per second, was it? They haven't finished down-loading the initial survey results yet, or something?"

You're so nice.

I had looked it up a thousand times, but still couldn't say it smoothly, yet here was Hefei Ye with the name of Uluru's capital and the transmission speed off the top of his head. He must have looked it up just now in order to stay on the topic of Uluru. He must have noticed I was lost for words.

At any rate, I replied. "Yeah, seems like they haven't managed to download it all yet."

Hefei Ye seemed relieved and continued down that line of discussion. "We knew from the advance survey that there was no civilization using gravity, electromagnetic, or space-time waves, right? Any remains?"

"Apparently they found some structures larger than a meter, as deep as twenty meters underground."

"Any trees or anything? The drone photography showed something that looked like cedars, remember?"

"Those ended up being mercury sulfide crystals. Hexagonal pyramid-shaped fractal structures. Did you see the enlarged photo?"

"Would be neat if they could be sold as Uluru Crystals or something. So there was nothing organic?"

"Not more than what's created in lightning strikes. We know there are bubbles of fat floating in the inland waters, but no self-replicators, like RNA, have been found. There are different colors around high-energy craters."

"So the stage where something might become life, then. Have the seas been surveyed yet? There's an ocean of water, right?"

"Yeah... they're doing a survey of the ocean."

Perhaps noticing the awkward pause in my reply, Hefei Ye leaned back in his chair. "They found life or something like it? Is it still confidential?"

After I nodded, I swiftly shook my head. "Sorry, it's not actually classified. I think the release will be out this week."

"Is there life?"

This time I nodded slowly. "It's not confirmed yet, but they say they observed something moving against the sea current from Kata Tjuta."

"From Kata Tjuta... you mean from stationary orbit? Something big enough to be seen from 40,000 km above was moving down there?"

"Yeah. The movement would be comparable to krill on Earth, mass-wise."

"Tsukasa, I thought you worked on swallows; do you do marine animals, too?"

"My specialty is animal migration. Uluru's axis wobble is fast, so in a revolution—a year—there are three or four summers. Apparently that matter migrates between the north pole and the equator between summer and winter."

"Just like migratory birds?"

"Yeah. Which is why the government of Uluru reached out... Will you come with?"

He dropped his gaze to the floor.

I knew he wasn't hanging his head because he couldn't answer.

Hefei Ye wasn't that much of a wimp. He looked toward the floor to look through it—to confirm the location of home, which was ten seconds away by lightspeed.

From Earth's orbit, it took eleven years and eleven months to get to Uluru.

At the fastest speed in the universe—light speed—by electromagnetic waves, or even gravity waves, the fourth planet in the Tau Ceti system, Uluru, was eleven years and eleven months away. If you took one twin from a pair of entangled particles and put it there, the states of both particles would be determined simultaneously, but no information would be transmitted.

Raising his head, Hefei Ye tightened the corners of his mouth and asked, "Did they decide how settlers would be adapted to the environment?"

I brought the message to settlers up on my workspace and read off the gene therapy they would receive upon arrival to Uluru. "Resistance to harsh environmental exposure is required. VEMG."

"Vacuum, electricity, magneticity, and gravity? The first immigrants to an exoplanet will live on a station, so I guess that makes sense. Even in the Earthsphere, lots of the builders get those. What else?"

"ATP chain reactions will be altered for methane respiration."

"You have to?"

"While they're doing remote surveys from Kata Tjuta, it's not required, but once they switch to surface surveys, it'll be necessary."

"Wow," he murmured, his breathing slightly erratic.

The gene therapy would replace all the mitochondria in my body to switch my carbon dioxide metabolism to a methane-based system. If you want to breathe in Uluru's atmosphere without a pressure suit, it has to be done.

The cost would be covered by the autonomous government of Uluru, of course. It put pressure on their budget, but it was more realistic than terraforming the whole planet. More importantly, the massacre of all indigenous life would be unforgivable. But switching your metabolism at the genetic level causes another problem.

Stabilizing his breathing, Hefei Ye looked me in the eye. "So you're quitting being human, Tsukasa?"

I couldn't say anything.

You change species.

Of course, it's not as if Uluru would be the first example of this.

As of the year 2119, on the fifteen exoplanets humans have settled so far, we've witnessed the birth of humans who breathe fluorine, humans who use ammonia instead of water and tolerate extremely low temperatures, humans who traded carbon for silicon to support electric metabolisms, and more. The methane respiration therapy I would undergo was already in use on two planets in the Teegarden starzone of Aries. There were already 100,000 of those people, and two generations; their subspecies had been named *Homo sapiens methanum spiritus.*

They're incapable of having children with the current humans, *Homo sapiens sapiens.*

"Wait, I haven't decided for sure that I'll do it."

"But you will, won't you? You'll be studying life forms. Everyone else'll be breathing methane and you're gonna lug an oxygen tank? You'd need an oxygen chamber to sleep in, too."

I couldn't argue. Though I'd been invited, I was only a single researcher. Surely at some point I would have to stand on Uluru's surface and breathe methane.

I made up my mind and said, "I guess—" but Hefei Ye spoke first.

"Why do you have to go as far as gene editing?"

"Because there's no coming back," I retorted.

Hefei Ye looked puzzled. "What?"

"Because once you go, there's no coming back."

I'd been thinking about this ever since I heard from the Uluru government, so the words came out smoothly.

"Trips to new exoplanets are one-way only. Uluru just got a station put in orbit twelve years ago, and it'll be another fifteen before they have space elevators to pull resources into orbit. They can't be bothered about building ships to get back to Earth. Even if they start, it won't be for another half century or so."

"If you could come back, you'd stay human, you mean?"

"Yeah, if I thought I could come back to the Earthsphere…" I tried imagining it. If people who went to an exoplanet could return to live in the Earthsphere, if I could come back to live in this room on Taiji Tianlou again… "I'd probably lug the tank. I'd put a pressurized base on the surface."

I looked at Hefei Ye. Now it was his turn to fall silent. He didn't have any other words to persuade me.

"Let's go."

"Mmm…" he trailed off.

"Let's go. I want to go together. If I can live with you, then I can stay on Kata Tjuta forever."

Hefei Ye didn't answer.

———

FIVE YEARS LATER, on the day of my departure, Hefei Ye was not beside me.

I boarded the second immigrant ship, dubbed the *Birrarung Marr*, alone and headed for Uluru along with five thousand others.

The voyage aimed to be "as diverse as possible," so it included five hundred kakyō who had given up their customary Lunar New Year trips.

We were traveling for six years, so I fell in love during the flight. By the time we reached Uluru, I had just ended the relationship with my second partner.

The first was an agricultural engineer from Germany. We dated for quite a while and had fun, but around the middle of the trip, he got busy, and our relationship cooled off and faded away. The second was a kakyō by the name of Qingming Huang, chief engineer on the improved GSA. Since he wasn't hung up on the Lunar New Year or other parts of Chinese culture, he was easy to date, but he reminded me too much of Hefei Ye, so I distanced myself, unable to deepen the relationship.

When we landed, my subjective age was thirty-seven. By the

Western calendar, which didn't mean much at that point, I was forty-eight. Either way, I would never return to the Earthsphere.

I started spending more time at the lab in pursuit of the piecemeal Uluru updates.

The objects moving with the seasonal changes had been found to be bubbles of fat that couldn't quite be called life just yet. Still, we knew the bubbles moved seasonally in groups of like chemical makeup, to places where it was easier to maintain surface tension. Though it was unclear if they had metabolisms, much less intelligence, I was excited to see them traveling together, but the survey had ended there.

The survey on the ground to ascertain what was inside the bubbles was entrusted to a team of five that I would lead.

Having agreed to gene therapy for methane respiration, I and my team members, who were also immigrating to study the life forms, analyzed what little data there was. We could hardly wait to land on Uluru. By the time Tau came into view, sparkling pink, in January of 2133, we had resolved to set foot on the planet.

That was when it happened—unexpected news arrived.

"Chunyun Special Flight?"

I repeated what the team member who brought the report said.

"Where is it planning on returning to?" another confused team member asked.

"China, apparently."

"Even if they hurried using the latest black hole fall drive, it would take thirteen years. Even light takes eleven years and eleven months."

"Yeah, I know. But they told anyone who wants to go to gather at the GSA tower—the central lobby. All the kakyō are there."

"...Seriously?"

When I took my staff and went to have a look, there was an apparatus we'd never seen before in the back of the lobby.

The easiest way to explain it would be a dome that ten people could fit under. It was attached to a graviton track branched off from the accelerator.

There were kakyō working around the dome. Surprisingly, their leader had been my partner up until recently, Qingming Huang.

Once the ring of people watching them work had grown two and then three thick, Qingming Huang stopped working, projected himself via augmented reality, and began to speak.

"Everyone, I'm sorry to have kept this quiet until now. We Chinese immigrants brought gravitons entangled with the Earthsphere on this trip."

Confusion spread throughout the immigrants who were listening to his explanation.

Everyone knew that the states of twin-like particles would be the same at the same time across space—that's quantum teleportation—but we didn't understand what it had to do with the Chunyun Special Flight.

Faced with the murmuring crowd, Qingming Huang scratched his head self-consciously. "We were entrusted with these particles thirteen years ago, but even we don't know what will happen as a result of this experiment. After all, our knowledge on the matter stops thirteen years ago."

A voice rose from the gallery. "Experiment? You're using the GSA?"

"Yes, we were told to put fifty trillion entangled gravitons into the accelerator and observe them in this dome. We have no idea how much progress our friends in the Earthsphere have made in the past thirteen years. It might be that the gravitons simply evaporate, but..."

I spoke up. "It doesn't matter what happens if it *doesn't* work. What are you trying to accomplish?"

Qingming Huang looked at me.

"Hefei Ye is on the other side."

When my eyes widened, Qingming Huang told me the experiment was already starting and turned to face the dome.

The kakyō stopped what they were doing and stood up.

Light began to gather at the center of the dome.

"It's a wormhole," Huang Quingming said. "Using the interference of the gravitons positioned in the same location in the Earthsphere, we've created a wormhole. We opened a hole in space."

When the light faded, a different space was visible inside the dome.

Hefei Ye was there.

I was about to leap for him, but Qingming Huang spread his arms and barred my way.

"Sorry, we go first."

"Let me through!"

"We've been waiting for thirteen years to celebrate Lunar New Year. Okay, everyone, let's go home."

The kakyō passed through the hole in space.

After they had all gone in, Hefei Ye walked out from the other side and wrapped his arms around me.

He seemed slightly older than he should have been from memory, but my body remembered his strong hugs. My tears overflowed.

"I made it," he whispered.

"Huh?"

"I caught you before you could stop being human. I could keep us from becoming another species. Now we can go anywhere in space and still return."

"Oh, oh yeah."

Before the emotions rising in me rendered my speech mere sounds, he whispered, softly, something so kind: "Just like migratory birds."

———

THIS STORY originally appeared in *Future Science Fiction Digest*.

TAIYO FUJII WAS BORN in Amami Oshima Island—that is, between Kyushu and Okinawa. He has worked for stage design, desktop publishing, exhibition graphic design, and software development.

In 2012, Fujii self-published *Gene Mapper* serially in a digital format of his own design, and became Amazon.co.jp's number one Kindle bestseller of that year. The novel was revised and republished by Hayakawa Publishing in 2013 and was nominated for the Nihon SF Taisho Award and the Seiun Award. In *Gene Mapper* he explored in detail the AR/VR communication, GMO plants and terror for infrastructure.

The second novel, *Orbital Cloud*, won the 2014 Nihon SF Taisho Award and Japanese Nebula Award.

In 2019, his novelette collection *Hello, World!* won a mainstream literature award: the Yoshikawa Eiji Literature Awards for Young Writers.

Fujii attended as 18th president of Science Fiction and Fantasy Writers Japan and developed a strong connection with science fiction communities all over the world.

Emily Balistrieri was born in 1985 in Wisconsin and is now based in Tokyo. Published translations include Eiko Kadono's *Kiki's Delivery Service*, Tomihiko Morimi's *The Night is Short, Walk on Girl* and Takuji Ichikawa's *The Refugees' Daughter*. He has also translated fiction by Shaw Kuzki, Ao Omae, Mikoto Mashita, Kugane Maruyama, Carlo Zen, and many others.

He did the English subtitles for Takahide Hori's film *Junk Head* and translated Cocosola's mobile game *The Witch's Isle*.

Follow him on Twitter: @tiger.

THE WITCH DANCES

Thiago Ambrósio Lage, translated from the Portuguese by Iana Araújo

(Shortlisted for 2021 Rosetta Awards)

Five, six, seven, eight.
One leg right,
One leg left.
Raise arms, half a pirouette.
Kick the air with the left.

IN THE DISTANCE, I see the end of the empty street. I feel their eyes on me. Through the cracks and slits of the houses, they watch me. Fear, curiosity, fascination. A witch dances. The Witch dances. In a village like this one, we need no names. The Witch, the Priest. I don't see him, but I know he's there, on the bell tower, watching me. We thought about using the bell to set my pace but decided against it. It could disturb the rhythm of the fae. The pace of the Priest was the repose. Leave the scene and let the others dance.

Slap the right thigh.
One more step, one more pirouette.
Turn. Sigh.
Bang the staff thrice on the ground.

I conquer the distance of a few more houses. In between moves I can hear the whispers behind closed doors, the small cries. I feel their bewilderment. "Where is the Priest? How can he let her do that?" I am but a witch, but to them, I am the Witch that crossed a line today. I have always had my duties, and the Priest had his. He had the answers for the maladies of the soul; I had the cures for the maladies of the body. Everyone went to my hut outside the village. They paid upfront. It was best to already have left a chicken, some eggs, a few yards of fabric or even some coins than have to return to the Witch's house. In exchange, they were cleansed, and took home herbs, teas, concoctions, charms.

Repeat from the top, thrice.
Change the pace. Arm, arm.
Aim with the staff, recite the rite.
A wide step forward, a short step back.

I could have chosen a simpler dance, but it wouldn't be as effective. We had to defeat the Violet Vesicle. My medicines weren't enough, and I could tell by the fresh graves on the tiny cemetery behind the church that many villagers had already been taken. It was impossible to dispel the disease with the incantations and dances of a Witch, so I was left with the duty of frightening the villagers into their homes, where they'd watch me from a distance. That was the only way to make sure that the fae, at their own pace, would visit them all.

Wiggle, turn, repeat, repeat.

More houses conquered. Now only halfway to go.

Left leg.
Right leg.
Cross and uncross the arms. Squat.

Each fae carried two things: a vial and an imp. It was the little devils' duty of stabbing the villagers with a needle. Singe the needle, dip on the vial and stab. Singe, dip, stab. The villagers would only feel a sting, and upon not being able to see the imp—made invisible by the craft of the fae—they would assume it was just a mosquito. It had been hard to convince the Priest of the need of the imps, but even if the fae could touch the iron needle, they lacked the fire to perform the delicate procedure. Hence, the tiny creatures were left with the mission of disguising the imps and carrying the vial with the golden liquid. Those were their steps in our choreography.

Burst with a scream.
Slap the left thigh.
One more step, a backwards pirouette.
Turn. Sigh.

The Scientist was the newest resident of the village: he had come from the City, from the University, claiming the air here would do him good. He had a small garden but didn't work the land like the Gardener. He was skilled with glass, metals, and wood but not like masters Glassmaker, Smith and Carpenter. He was wise but unlike the Priest, he didn't have all the answers. To tell the truth, he had more questions than answers. Many of those questions were directed at me, and he was the only villager who wasn't afraid. He came to my hut frequently, only to drink tea and talk. In one of those visits, when the disease was already taking men, women, children, and elders without distinction, he brought me the golden vial. My herbs and ointments appeased the fever and the pain, but I had already lost all hope of saving the sick from the fate waiting for them behind the church. That golden medicine filled me with hope, but we had two problems: it had to be applied *before* the person fell ill, and it had to be done through the pinch of a needle. "It'll be impossible to convince people of this madness," I had said. He laughed and pointed at my hut and my glasses of dried herbs, saying that "impossible" was the very thing I did every day.

That night, we made our plan.

Turn the staff thrice. Repeat.
Repeat everything three more times.

I spoke with a fae princess who thought that the whole thing was delightful. Besides, with all the deaths, the few offerings her people received were now bathed in tears, and everybody knows that fairies prefer sweet over salty. The Scientist spoke with the Priest, whose prayers and miracles, he was reluctant to admit, were powerless against the disease. One day and one night without church bells and without a mass: it was all we need to open the village for the forest people, the people of the deeps, and me. The Scientist and I had to work together to get help from the people of the deeps. It took at least four hands in a ritual to summon a prince of Hell to make a request. The Scientist, that fool, happily paid the price, giving away something he thought he didn't have. Deals done, I only need to finish my dance and trust my partners. Each one of us who cared was in their place, performing their duties. Even the villagers, just by staying at home. Soon we would be rid of the disease.

What about the Alcaide? Well, he is a moron that insists on smearing urine and manure in the wounds, and other things that only got in the way.

Everyone had a pace and helped. Not him.

THIS STORY originally appeared in *Eita!* magazine.

. . .

THIAGO AMBRÓSIO LAGE IS A PROFESSOR, scientist, and writer who lives in North Brazil. He has a diverse range of interests: from biotechnology, his area of expertise, to fairy tales, through linguistics, and astronomy. In fantasy and science fiction, he found the freedom to explore this diversity of themes. His hobbies include calligraphy, lettering, and watercolor painting. He has published a few SFF and horror short stories, in Portuguese unless noted otherwise: "A Bruxa Dança" (The Witch Dances) independent, "Carnaval Encarnado" (Incarnated Carnival) in *A Taverna*, *A Cidade do Átomo* (Atom City) in *Futuro Infinito/SESC*, "Malus restituta" in *Maçã do Amor*, "The Witch Dances" (in English and shortlisted for the 2021 SSF Rosetta Awards) in *Eita!* Magazine, "Teste Anti-Turing" (Anti-Turing's Test) in the science fiction collection of LGBTQIA+ authors titled *Violetas, Unicórnios e Rinocerontes*, by Patuá publisher, "Patrícia" in the *Casa Fantástica* Collection by Presságio Publisher, and "Plano de Ensino: Introdução ao Voo" (Flight 101 – Course Plan) and "Portabilidade" (Portability) both in *Faísca Mafagafo*. He also co-hosts a podcast called Incêndio na Escrivaninha (Fire in the Desk) about literature with the Brazilian writers Ana Rüsche and Vanessa Guedes. He writes biweekly in his newsletter *Mercúrio em Peixes* (Mercury in Pisces/Fish).

IANA ARAÚJO WAS BORN in 1989 in sunny Recife, Brazil. She is a teacher, writer, editor, and a critical reader and translator (EN-PT) for indie authors, literary agencies and publishing houses in Brazil. She is editor-in-chief at *Eita!* Magazine, publishing Brazilian SFF in English, and co-editor at *Pretérita Revista*, a Brazilian zine of historical fiction. She can be found surrounded by her four cats and an unfortunate pile of to-be-read books.

FORMERLY SLOW

Wei Ma, translated from the Chinese by Andy Dudak

1

Wednesday. 00:02.

Xia Mang's biological clock woke him from a deep sleep.

His daughter Weiwei was one month old today, and today would be her dormancy test. Starting tomorrow, she would be a Wednesday citizen of Shenli City, like Xia Mang and his wife Xiao An.

Weiwei was still asleep.

Xiao An got up and stretched, then went to the kitchen to fire up the coffee maker. Xia Mang sat on the sofa, yawning as he poked around on his mobile. TV images appeared on the opposite wall.

The COG TV logo flashed in the upper right corner of the screen, and morning news headlines revolved eye-grabbingly in the lower left.

The familiar face of the Wednesday announcer appeared:

"Yesterday, the Statistics Bureau released last year's Shenli Economic Development Findings Report. The numbers show last year's per capita GDP at 137,654 U.S. dollars, for a growth rate of 113 percent, surpassing Shanghai for the third year in a row, and holding onto first place in the world for a city's per capita GDP. At the same time, the report's questionnaire investigations, considered highly reliable, indicated a satisfaction rate exceeding 85 percent with regard to a composite index of our city's economic development, environmental quality, public security, crime rate, and so on. Shenli, the first city in the world to implement a Cyclic Freedom-of-Movement System, and an experimental pilot city using dormancy technology, shows favorable momentum by all indicators, drawing attention and approval from various governments around the world…"

Xia Mang changed the channel.

"…the Shenli City Immigration Bureau cracked down on 323 cases of illegal entry this month. Illegal immigration numbers have risen little by little in recent months. The Population Management Bureau reminds city residents to maintain heightened safety awareness. On your Freedom-of-Movement days, keep your eyes open for suspicious strangers."

A montage of fierce law enforcement illustrated the announcer's words.

Xiao An sat down beside Xia Mang and gave him a coffee.

"Scary!" she said, brow furrowed. "These people will do anything to get in."

"And for what?" Xia Mang said. "Without dormancy qualification, it's not like life on the outside of the city. Six days a week you'd be shut indoors, unable to venture out on the streets. So why even come to Shenli?"

Xiao An stared at him in amazement. "Are you thick? Of course there are good reasons! How about Shenli's clean air? How about taking a subway without getting packed in like sardines, or seeing a doctor without queuing up, or not having to worry about turning around to find a pickpocket fumbling for your wallet? How about high wages, a good environment, a higher quality of people? Even without dormancy qualification, life here is just better!"

"Alright alright, my mistake," Xia Mang said, growing contrite.

"Of course it's your mistake!" Xiao An stared at him, coldly contemplative. "But to be fair, in Shenli, the dormancy qualification really makes all the difference. I mean, all that hard work back then was worth it." Xiao An took a deep breath, then smiled in perfect contentment. "You don't even know... in our company, people without dormancy qualification are forever consigned to odd jobs, errand running, unskilled labor with no tech element. Promotion will never be a prospect for them. You wouldn't understand, Mr. Relaxation..."

Xia Mang was an influential and bestselling science fiction author. When Shenli City was first established, the then-subversive Cyclic Freedom-of-Movement System, along with dormancy tech, had triggered global controversy. To win support, Shenli had offered a batch of free dormancy qualifications to attract interest from various spheres. In particular, the elite of forward-looking domains had moved to Shenli and given their endorsements. Xia Mang had been among them.

"You got dormancy in order to get promoted?" Xia Mang jokingly asked.

"Of course not!" Xiao An glared at him. "Do you remember Yaya? She entered the company at the same time I did. She still hasn't qualified for dormancy. We were born in the same year, but now she looks just over forty." Xiao An touched her cheek. Her tone relaxed and cheerful, charm dialed to ten, she said, "And me, I still look twenty-eight."

"Pff." Xia Mang couldn't help laughing.

"What's so funny?" Xiao An punched his shoulder.

Seeming to cater to their conversation, another news item came up on the screen:

"Last month, Shenli received 7,680 new dormancy applications. Fifty-three qualifications were signed and issued. This issuance rate is a new low, indicative of tightening standards for investigating dormancy applications in our city..."

Ding-dong!

The doorbell rang, interrupting the news.

Xia Mang opened the door.

"Good morning... very early morning, that is, Mr. and Mrs. Xia. I'm the service worker sent to conduct your daughter's dormancy test run." The man at the door was dressed in the SIP company red-and-white uniform. He held a compact, pink dormancy module at his side.

Xiao An gave Weiwei a thorough bath, breast fed her until she was full, and, reluctant to part with her, played with her a bit.

Xia Mang was a bit uneasy as he placed Weiwei in the dormancy module. "Can you guarantee that dormancy tech is safe for an infant her age?"

The worker smiled. "Rest assured, dormancy tech has been used on newborns for more than a decade. There's never been a problem. Our company guarantees the absolute safety of this technology."

Xia Mang nodded.

"But, if you have misgivings about dormancy tech, you may consider postponing this—"

The worker had not even finished his sentence when Xiao An and Xia Mang interrupted him:

"No need!"

Weiwei, sated on milk, gave a satisfied burp, then directed a confused expression at her diffident, guilty-looking parents.

Due to health and safety concerns, newborns under one month couldn't be dormancy-induced. Xia Mang and Xiao An had been obliged to forgo dormancy themselves for the past month, to care for this annoying little tyke all day, every day. They had never been so tired in their lives. They'd just about reached their limit.

"Okay then," the worker said, smiling. "I will now begin to induce."

"Weiwei... see you next week." Xia Mang kissed her little face.

"See you after a good sleep," Xiao An said, following suit.

She said that deliberately, forcing the sense of separation from her words and her tone. Xia Mang could hear it.

Weiwei was sent into a deep sleep, her plump little hands beside her tiny round face, the corners of her mouth sometimes drawing back in a sweet smile, no different than any normal, peaceful time.

The worker closed the dormancy module and showed the parents the display data.

"Everything's normal. She'll have a good sleep."

Xiao An and Xia Mang felt relieved, and they felt guilty for feeling relieved. She would sleep six days a week now. They were her parents and they'd barely have to care for her anymore.

The two of them accompanied the worker to the door, and they were just about to close it.

"Waaaa!"

The familiar cry echoed through their home. The three adults stood dumbfounded at the door. Xia Mang was the first to react, rushing back inside.

Weiwei was red-faced, crying angrily and kicking at the module. Xia Mang hastily retrieved her and got her gently rocking in his arms. "Okay okay, good little Weiwei. Daddy's here."

"This... how is it possible?" The worker stared wide-eyed. "The data showed all was normal just now." He examined the module. "Strange..." Confronting Xia Mang and Xiao An's vigilant, uneasy gazes, he said in haste, "I... I'll just give the company a call. I'll get a tech specialist to come have a look. Sorry!"

THE FOLLOWING WEEK, five groups of people came from SIP, not just dormancy tech specialists, but also neuroscience medical professionals. They examined Weiwei carefully, conducting no less than a dozen tests. All results came back normal, suggesting Weiwei should be able to enter dormancy fast and without complication, but every time they tried, she would wake naturally within five minutes.

FINALLY, SIP put out its report, verifying that the current dormancy system was unable to induce sustainable dormancy in Weiwei. As for the cause, the medical experts' preliminary opinion was that Weiwei's brain, in some regions, experienced physiological stress in response to the dormancy command. They'd never seen anything like it, and for now at least, had no solution.

"No solution? Really?" Xiao An couldn't restrain her anger. Just after receiving the report, she had called SIP. "My daughter has her qualification and yet she can't enjoy dormancy, and you're telling me there's no solution!?"

Xia Mang hunted down a phone number left by a doctor who had come to examine Weiwei a few days before.

"In other words, this physiological stress response to the dormancy command… it had no other ill effects on her growth or health, right?"

With the doctor's affirmative reply, Xia Mang allowed himself to relax a little. He hung up.

Xiao An was still roaring into her phone: "It's not just her with the problem! My husband and I can't go dormant either! Do you get that? In Shenli this is a serious matter! Are you understanding me? How can your company treat clients so irresponsibly?"

Xia Mang entered the bedroom. Weiwei's sleep had been disturbed by her mother's tirade. She was rolling over in the middle of her crib. Xia Mang patted her lightly and crooned a song.

Because of this issue with Weiwei's dormancy, Xiao An had been fretful for the past few days, like the sky was about to fall. But Xia Mang didn't share this feeling.

Because one thing science fiction writers are expert in is being used to a world different from what they imagined.

2

Weiwei's issue soon became news.

"Dormancy tech has perhaps run into a stumbling block, and the Shenli City myth has encountered a challenge."

This was not just Shenli news sensationalism; it was causing a huge controversy outside the city.

For a brief time, Xia Mang's family became a beleaguered media focal point. Journalists hung around outside their apartment block and kept watch, hungry to land an interview.

XIA MANG, unable to go dormant, sometimes got bored. He would stand beside the window and watch the journalists downstairs. The interesting thing was, no matter how dedicated to their work, in Shenli City, Tuesday journalists always had to hurry home before midnight, before Wednesday, while their Wednesday colleagues couldn't turn up early for their shifts. Around 11:40 PM, Xia Mang would start to see journalists beating a hasty retreat, and starting at ten past midnight, the new batch would begin to turn up.

As if separated by time, like two different worlds, Xia Mang thought to himself.

REGARDLESS OF HOW Xiao An would have preferred it, Weiwei's dormancy issue couldn't be resolved, in the end. Thus, SIP proposed a compensation plan, while vowing to continue regular examinations and dormancy tests of Weiwei. Shenli City even made exceptions for the family, granting an extraordinary privilege: total freedom of movement.

This meant they were no longer bound by days of the week. They could walk out of their front door any day they liked, and venture about the city. This was just about the highest status one could achieve in Shenli.

Xia Mang and Xiao An agreed that while Weiwei's issue remained unresolved, they would temporarily renounce dormancy. The two of them would care for Weiwei together.

"IF WEIWEI CAN NEVER GO DORMANT," Xiao An said, late one night in the darkness, "what'll we do?"

"We move forward with her, awake. What else?" Xia Mang held Xiao An. "We make it work, just like all the unqualified of Shenli."

"But we worked so hard to be different from them." Xiao An turned over, escaping Xia Mang's arm.

The two of them were silent, and already worlds apart.

***

THE FOLLOWING year was actually not so bad for Xia Mang.

Xiao An wasn't comfortable going out on any day but Wednesday. She said it made her feel unsafe. Xia Mang knew that she would, one day, return to her former way of life. She did not want to connect with the world beyond her Wednesday domain.

***

ACTUALLY, Xia Mang did have some trouble adapting at first.

The first time he brought Weiwei out on a non-Wednesday, it was a Saturday.

The media's short-lived enthusiasm had finally receded. There were no reporters lurking downstairs. It had been too long since Weiwei had been outside, and Xia Mang had decided to take her to the park to get some sun.

Before going out the door, Xia Mang subconsciously glanced at his mobile. In gaming terms, although the government had removed obscuring fog and cleared the entire map for them, the enchantment that had harnessed Xia Mang's psyche to Wednesdays was not so easily dispelled.

***

THEY'D GONE OUT for some sun, but the world seemed dark to Xia Mang. Everyone he should have known well was unfamiliar: the convenience store clerk, the apartment building security guard, the cleaning lady, the café barista.

The worlds of Wednesday and Saturday were completely different.

Xia Mang felt like a stranger in this city for the first time. It was as if he'd always been gazing at one face of a Rubik's Cube, completely ignorant of what was happening on the other faces.

"Oh, what a little cutie!" Two women pushing a baby stroller through the park had spotted Xia Mang holding Weiwei, and were heading over.

"We like to come here on Saturdays for a little fun," said the thinner, older one, a woman with a warm tone but doubtful eyes. "How have we never seen you two before?"

Xia Mang recalled the illegal immigration warnings on the news. This woman was on high alert.

"We're..." Xia Mang found himself tongue-tied, not knowing how to explain himself.

The other woman, the young mother, wasn't paying attention to the exchange. She lifted her son from the stroller so he could play with Weiwei. The two children grabbed each other with glistening, saliva-smeared hands.

The thin woman gave the young mother a stealthy poke.

The younger woman glanced uncertainly from Xia Mang down to Weiwei. "Huh... why does she look a bit familiar?" Having recalled something, she cried out, "Ah ha!" then fiercely seized her son's hand, swung him away from Weiwei, and retreated several steps.

"No, not in your mouth!" She pulled the little hand that had just touched Weiwei away from the boy's lips, and went to vigorous work on it with a wet wipe.

The woman was taken aback by the young mother's reaction and moved the pram into a flight-ready position. The younger woman seemed to become aware of her rudeness and forced an embarrassed smile. "It's her, right?" she said, seeming to speak to the woman but also as if asking Xia Mang. "The one on TV who can't go dormant, right?"

"Well, yes." Xia Mang shifted Weiwei and held her close to his chest.

"Oh!" the thin woman shouted, wide-eyed, like a squawking chicken. She lowered her voice and said, "Such a pity..." She shook her head, yet managed not to look very sympathetic.

"It's not so pitiful," Xia Mang said, suppressing his temper. "All children grow up. Some grow up fast, some a bit slow, that's all. It's no big deal."

"Well that's nice," the woman said. "Trying to look on the bright side and take things philosophically is best. Hey, by the way..." She seemed to recall something. "This disease of hers, is it contagious?"

The young mother pricked up her ears.

"She doesn't have a disease," Xia Mang began, but saw the women weren't really interested, and let it pass. "I don't know, the doctors didn't say."

Xia Mang smiled with grim anticipation.

"Well, we have to go," the woman said. "I do hope we have the chance for another play date..." The two women, faces utterly changed, hurried away with their pram.

"We need to get back and sterilize his hands." The old woman's words floated back to him from a distance. "Some people... well, they're just doomed that way, and there's nothing for it!"

Okay then, Saturday was not so inviting, Xia Mang thought to himself.

3

Although Saturday had not left a good impression, Xia Mang and Weiwei ran into some interesting people on other days.

Their Monday citizen neighbor was an idol celebrity. He explained that being an idol in Shenli didn't leave much opportunity for advancement. There was never a way to make a Tuesday citizen love a Monday idol. The gap wasn't just a day's time, but more like a dimension.

"No matter how I go about it, I just can't raise those fan numbers. There's no heat, it's boring, really. But there are benefits too." He ran a hand casually through his bangs, shaking them out, and smiled handsomely. "One time at a news conference, I had chosen a striped outfit. I was about to go on stage when my manager said that the previous Wednesday, a famous fashion critic had decreed stripes the most out-of-date thing of the season. This manager wanted me to go change. Guess what I said." He reached out and tickled Weiwei's chin.

She gurgled cheerfully. "No way! Monday people live in Monday, so who cares what Wednesday people say!"

"No wonder you're popular," Xia Mang said merrily. "That's character, the It factor!"

"Yeah, well whatever, who cares!" The idol threw up his hands. "I don't want to stay here anyway. This is supposed to be temporary. I want to be successful back outside the city, make movies, get awards."

"You can't make movies here?"

"How? Think about it… with cast and crew working one day a week, a movie would take, what? Decades? You start out shooting a young, fresh film, and by the time it's done it's a nostalgia piece."

The two of them laughed together.

"Well then, if you're pursuing that sort of career," Xia Mang said, "why on Earth did you come here?"

"Well…" The idol seemed a bit embarrassed, but went on: "Careers have their ups and downs, you know. My last down was an actress who spread the rumor that I am a cheating two-timer. The media and anti-fans were out for my blood! I was pretty stressed, so I came here to hide. The idea is to wait several years and go back out, not having aged. The fans meanwhile have moved on to new scandals while mine vanishes and disperses like smoke. As far as Out There is concerned, I'll be like a new person. I've got my acting skills. Going out and getting popular again is no problem."

"Very slick!" Xia Mang said after some thought.

4

Auntie Li, responsible for Thursday cleanings of the apartment building, came to trouble Xia Mang again to take soup to her daughter.

Her daughter, Miss Chen, had Friday Freedom-of-Movement. When they wanted to meet, they had to apply in advance for temporary Freedom-of-Movement allowances. Auntie Li didn't like to waste money, preferring to hoard it for her daughter's dormancy application. It had been several years since the two of them had met face to face.

The habitually quiet Miss Chen took the insulated thermos from

Xia Mang, but suddenly said, "Mr. Xia," just as he was about to leave. "My dormancy application was accepted."

"Well that's good news! You haven't told Auntie Li? She'll be over the moon!" Xia Mang couldn't help being happy on behalf of mother and daughter.

"You really think so?" Miss Chen lowered her head.

"Well, you don't seem so happy." Xia Mang grew puzzled.

"I'll only be able to have mom's homemade soup once a week." She twisted open the thermos lid, and fragrant chicken soup vapor floated out. "A few dozen soups, and mom will be a year older. Mr. Xia, if I go dormant, mom will age much faster than me. Can you imagine that?"

Xia Mang understood well.

If his own parents had not already passed away, Xia Mang would certainly not have agreed to come live in Shenli. Aging at a different rate than close kin: although it was only a nominal distance, it could be as unbearable as the permanent separation of death.

"I can go over to her and..."

"No, Mr. Xia. Don't tell her anything." Miss Chen lifted her head and smiled briefly. "She has saved all her life for me, just for the chance to live here. I can't let her down."

Xia Mang nodded.

"Papa," Weiwei said, lying on his shoulder and looking back as he departed. "She cry." Not understanding, she pointed at Ms. Chen, who was slowly squatting down in the doorway.

"Yeah, her chicken soup is too hot."

Having learned her daughter had obtained dormancy rights, Auntie Li was, sure enough, wild with joy. She even became short of breath in her excitement, had to support herself against a wall and breathe heavily for a while, mouth agape. Eventually, something seemed to occur to her. Her smile eased a bit, and she muttered, "I won't be making as much soup from now on."

Xia Mang chose not to interrupt her train of thought. He politely took his leave.

Time and space self-righteously completed each other. Love

between human beings was all too easily obstructed by unrelated things, rendered non-transmissible. And in Shenli City, the conveyance of emotion was all the more intricate and obscure.

Weiwei whispered in his ear, "Grandma cry."

5

Of everyone Xia Mang and Weiwei encountered, Big Li was Weiwei's favorite.

In the old days of Wednesday Freedom-of-Movement, Xia Mang loved working in the café downstairs from his apartment. Big Li was the shop assistant there.

He was also Xia Mang's only friend in Shenli City.

The first time they'd met, Xia Mang was hiding in the café's back door alley, sneaking a cigarette. Shenli City had comprehensively banned smoking, but to Xia Mang's mind this taboo could never reduce the number of smokers. As long as you had money, getting a few packs of cigarettes from outside of the city was no great matter.

"Hey!"

Xia Mang was interrupted mid-smoke by a hand on his shoulder. He turned to meet Big Li's penetrating gaze. The man looked not fully awake, perhaps, yet capable of violence at any moment. Dumb-founded, Xia Mang gave an embarrassed smirk and tossed the cigarette on the ground, then crushed it underfoot.

"Oh, come on!" Big Li rolled his eyes, squatted, and grabbed the butt. "Fire hazard."

From that day on, the two of them often squatted together in the alley behind the café, smoking and chatting.

After gradually becoming familiar with each other, Xia Mang knew Big Li had been a popular rock singer outside Shenli. He claimed his mere glance could undo women's undergarment clasps.

On hearing this, Xia Mang's first instinct was to rebuke Big Li for boasting, but then he recalled their first encounter, that look, those eyes, and he swallowed his words.

"Shouldn't a rock singer be roaring, 'I want freedom, and fuck tomorrow!' to a drunk and hypnotized audience? Why the hell would you leave that life of wild crowds and come here to Shenli to be a waiter?"

"To wait for death," Big Li said.

"Oh, nonsense," Xia Mang, finally unable to keep from scolding him. "You have dormancy rights. It's going to take a long time, if you're really waiting for death. You must be going crazy with boredom."

Big Li started laughing. That was first time Xia Mang saw him laugh, though he wasn't sure what was funny.

AFTER BIG LI MET WEIWEI, he started smiling and laughing more.

He didn't talk much, but he could toss Weiwei into weightlessness mid-air, and catch her again with assurance, making her giggle uncontrollably. He could also get on his guitar and sing for her. Weiwei didn't like his quiet songs, so Big Li resorted to his louder material and frenzied strumming, and Weiwei would recklessly thrash her limbs, until laughter made their centers of gravity unstable and had them rolling on the floor.

Every time she had to say goodbye to Big Li, Weiwei would cry herself hoarse, or hug his neck and not let go, face covered in tears. It could even make Xia Mang feel a bit jealous.

"Come!" she would often shout at Xia Mang, as she watched Big Li vanish into the distance.

"Alright, he'll be back, he'll be back. Next Wednesday, Papa will take you to play with Big Uncle Li."

"No!" Weiwei protested. "Morrow morrow!"

"But tomorrow Big Uncle Li will be asleep. And the next day, and the day after that, and the day after that, Big Uncle Li will be asleep..."

"Waaaaa!"

Shenli City had what amounted to a cement boundary between itself and the outside world. As far as the city was concerned, Xia Mang's family was a chink in this armor, a flaw in the magical boundary.

People here lived as in air bubbles in the ocean of time. They followed one of seven non-intersecting trajectories, jumping from one air bubble to another. The lives and times of the other six trajectories were completely cut off from them, had nothing to do with them.

Xia Mang and Weiwei were like fish in this ocean, darting back and forth. Time flowed along their bodies continuously, dense, adhering them to all that surrounded them. Every change in this world left its mark on their bodies.

Xia Mang had not felt this in a long time. So long, in fact, that he'd forgotten he liked it.

Xiao An, however, did not like it.

6

"We need to talk."

One night, after Weiwei had gone to sleep, Xia Mang discovered Xiao An sitting in the living room waiting for him. She did not seem happy.

"What's wrong?"

"Xia Mang… today my company decided to give my post to Yaya."

"Why?" Xia Mang was shocked.

"She landed her dormancy rights."

"But you have them too."

"Do I? Do I really?" Xiao An raised her head, looking fierce and agitated.

Xia Mang knew what she wanted to say. "I don't know what your company's employment standards are exactly," he said, his tone harsh, "but are mere dormancy rights so important?"

"Of course they are!" Xiao An stood up. "The brain is faster with analyses and data after dormancy, several times faster than normal. Don't tell me you don't know this! Do you have any idea how my work efficiency has suffered? To be honest, if I were in charge over there I would have made the same decision!"

"I mean, it's ridiculous!" Xia Mang said. "No matter how fast a computer computes, it can't just phase shift into an AI. The difference between people doesn't lie in their thinking speed, but in their thinking quality."

"I'm talking about reality here, not your great abstract truths!" Growing frustrated, suddenly crying, she said: "I can't go on like this! You know how hard I worked to get where I am. Of course I want to be there properly for Weiwei, but if I continue like this, I'll go crazy! I don't want Weiwei to see her mother like this..." The more she spoke, the more upset she became, suffering and squatting on the floor.

"Okay, I know." Xia Mang hugged her. "I can take care of Weiwei."

"But that wouldn't be fair to you." Xiao An wept spasmodically in Xia Mang's embrace.

"I love Weiwei, and I love you. Fair doesn't mean anything to me. I just need the two of you to be happy."

Xiao An lifted her head, swollen eyes locked briefly on Xia Mang, and she held him tightly.

"Oh, that's right!" She'd suddenly remembered something. "The doctor called today. He says he's prescribed a new medicine for Weiwei, though he couldn't say for sure it would regulate her brain's stress reaction to dormancy. Go get the med from him tomorrow and come back and let Weiwei try it, okay? If she can finally go dormant without issue, then our family's troubles are over."

"Okay," Xia Mang softly agreed.

FOR THE NEXT TWO YEARS, Xiao An returned to a state of normal dormancy. She only woke on Wednesdays, interacting briefly with Xia Mang and Weiwei. She went from being a permanent character in their lives to an honored guest doing cameos.

"Mama's always sleeping," Weiwei learned to complain.

Xia Mang had picked up the doctor's prescription, but he hadn't given it to Weiwei.

He knew Shenli life was making him feel off, but he couldn't say exactly how.

Until he got that call from Big Li.

IT WAS ON A THURSDAY AFTERNOON.

Xia Mang stared at Big Li's name on the mobile screen, and repeatedly glanced at the date, which was clearly a Thursday. The name and day in combination made him feel a practical joke was being played.

"Hey. I'm dying. Was hoping you'd bring Weiwei to see me."

BIG LI LAY in the hospital bed, body invaded by tubes and connected to machines. He gestured weakly with his finger at Weiwei, inviting her closer. Giggling, Weiwei threw herself at his bedside.

"Big Uncle Li!"

"Good kid." Big Li touched Weiwei's head, his expression tender like never before.

"When did you get sick?" Xia Mang asked hoarsely.

"A while back. On the Outside, I was already late-stage." Pale, wan, Big Li still managed a smile. "Didn't I tell you? I came here to wait for death. But coming here to hide like I did, I didn't expect to just fucking muddle along through my last few years."

Xia Mang moved his lips, but no words came out.

"It really wasn't worth it. My years here have been like a prison term." Big Li's former expression was back: disdain for a situation beneath contempt.

"Prison?" Xia Mang said with resentment, knowing Big Li preferred him talking this way. "But no one forced you to stay here."

"Time kept me bound here. And the prison cell that held me was called Wednesday."

"Look at the state of you!" Xia Mang said. "It's disgusting, really. Still writing lyrics at this point!"

The two of them erupted with laughter.

Xia Mang felt a tickle in his nose. He turned around, not wanting to be seen crying.

Weiwei had at some point crawled onto Big Li's bed and was wildly strumming on his guitar.

"Weiwei, very good. Just as I thought."

"What do you mean?" Xia Mang said, confused.

"When I knew I wasn't going to live through today, it really scared me. I mean I've never been so terrified in my life. The thought of dying on a Thursday... where nobody knows me, a stranger in a strange land, that's Thursday. I felt this coldness penetrating me to my core. I mean, you live your life, but don't get to see anyone you know before you die... that's scary, isn't it?"

Xia Mang was stunned by his words.

"After coming to this lousy place, the more I lived, the more... muddled I became. Sometimes I'd wake up and couldn't remember why I came, couldn't remember my plan. To me it was just a series of Wednesdays in a row, but placed in the context of this world, it's a pile of fragments, smashed and scattered. Like a musical note leaping into existence in a song, and I'm forever unclear on its tone. Such days are really fucking tedious!"

"There you go," Xia Mang said, interrupting his dispirited rant, "still handing down judgment on what's meaningful and what isn't, even now."

"Fortunately, there's still Weiwei." Big Li gazed at the ceiling and let out a long exhalation. "Thinking of Weiwei and her free, easy life in this world... it's like catching hold of a ball of light amid pitch black night. There's warmth and relief, allowing you to fall asleep. Xia Mang, thank you." Big Li's voice grew softer. "Weiwei. Wei—"

The sound of that final "Wei" became a breath. The light in Big Li's eyes went out, and they became two orbs of cloudy gray.

The equipment near the bed emitted a sharp braying. Xia Mang rushed over and picked up a startled Weiwei. He hugged her tightly, as if she were ungraspable light.

7

A month after Big Li had died, on a Wednesday, Xia Mang was in his kitchen cooking a nice spread, waiting for Xiao An to get off work.

"Why did you prepare so much meat?" she said when she arrived. "Weiwei's teeth haven't all grown in. She'll have a tough time chewing."

"Sheesh, my teeth have grown in!" Weiwei opened wide to illustrate.

Xiao An stared, dumbfounded. She didn't talk much during the meal.

AFTERWARD, Xia Mang set Weiwei up in her room with an animated film. Then he and Xiao An cleaned up together.

"Weiwei's teeth have grown in..." Xiao An said to the window as she put plates in the sink. It was like she was talking to Xia Mang and thinking aloud at the same time. "When did that happen? Last time I noticed her teeth, I feel like she only had eight. She grinned, showing four little upper teeth, so white, so tiny, like rabbit teeth. How can they have grown in after only a few visits?"

Xiao An's voice began to choke with sobs.

Xia Mang embraced her shoulders. "Xiao An, I've decided I want to take Weiwei and leave Shenli City."

Xiao An turned around, fierce, wide-eyed with disbelief. "Excuse me? Are you crazy?! This is Shenli City! Outsiders do anything to get in! Residents don't want to leave!"

"It's not that they don't want to leave, it's that they don't dare to. They're afraid. They wonder what's to be done if this is the best possible future."

"And it isn't?"

"For you it is. For me it isn't. For Weiwei it definitely isn't."

"I don't understand," Xiao An said, shaking her head.

Xia Mang met her gaze.

"When I was a kid out there in the world, there was a peach tree in front of our house. As soon as it was planted, I ran out every day to see it, from germination, growing branches, blooming, pink petals falling, the sprouting of green, slender leaves. The first year, the fruits it bore were small and tart. I took a bite and it was so sour I cried. But by the third year, it was bearing tasty peaches."

Xiao An didn't interrupt. She seemed to guess his meaning.

"I liked eating sweet peaches, but more than that I liked the waiting process. I know each and every step of a bud becoming a rosy, perfect peach. I know how it happens, why it's able to happen. The answers of the world, for me anyway, aren't hiding in that final sweet peach, but in that waiting process. Xiao An, Weiwei should get to wait for her own sweet peaches."

Xiao An shook her head. "I don't understand. Weiwei wouldn't miss anything living here."

"Really? Didn't she just miss a..." Xia Mang paused, then said: "A mother who knows when each of her teeth grew in?"

Xiao An stared blankly for a long time, then smiled bitterly. "So you're saying I'm no longer qualified to love Weiwei?"

"No. Of course you love her. But Xiao An, Weiwei is my sweet peach. And your sweet peach, that has never been Weiwei."

Xiao An's lip shivered, tears again flowing.

"I..."

Xia Mang hugged Xiao An.

"I want to say you're wrong," the woman wailed into his shoulder, "I really do! But I can't."

Xia Mang's heart grew heavy.

He recalled that Tuesday night long ago, the heavy rain, Xiao An in a gray sweater standing inside the door, he on the outside.

"Shouldn't you be getting back?" Xiao An had yelled over the rain's clamor. "It's almost midnight!"

"The sun's old color changes slowly,
Car, horse, and mail all sluggish.
A lifetime is just enough
To love one person."

Xia Mang hadn't answered Xiao An's question, but recalled this old poem they both adored.

Xiao An had watched, startled, understanding what was about to happen.

Bells rang at the arrival of midnight.

Xia Mang had extended a hand toward her. "Xiao An, the future is very slow in coming. Would you like to go there together?"

Clocks still striking midnight, Xiao An had rushed into the rain, and Xia Mang's embrace.

———

Now, Xiao An would continue toward that creeping, slow future, and he and Weiwei could no longer accompany her.

8

"Xia Mang, have you thought it through?" Xiao An said in the airport lounge. "I mean, the reason you find the world so beautiful, worth Weiwei perceiving every second of it uninterrupted? Maybe it's because your starting point, yours and hers together I mean, is Shenli City. Here we sacrifice your so-called sense of life's continuity in exchange for the comfort of less crowded, relaxed streets, for clean air and a safe environment. Maybe a world made of fragments is not sufficiently complete, but at least it's secure."

Xia Mang found himself at a loss. It was like Xiao An was once more that rational young woman who had first captivated him.

"I don't know if this is the best future here. But here at least is one possibility. And I will wait for you and Weiwei here. I will wait for the day you two choose this future."

THE FLIGHT LEAVING Shenli City was Weiwei's first time in an airplane. She was very excited.

"Papa, why isn't mama coming with us? Where is she?"

"Mama's waiting for us in the future."

"But Papa, where are we going?"

Xia Mang thought about this for quite a while, then replied: "Into the past."

THIS STORY originally appeared in *Future Science Fiction Digest*.

WEI MA IS an anime playwright and SF writer who began her professional writing career in 2008. She spends most working hours on serialized comic playwriting, and writes stories for children, screenplays, and SF stories, as well.

She is a lifelong SF fan, having been one since she subscribed to *SF World* magazine in elementary school, and hopes to have more time to write SF in the future, meanwhile earning enough to cover the living expenses for her children. (^_^)

She now lives in Shanghai, China, raising two kids.

ANDY DUDAK'S fiction is featured in *Jonathan Strahan's Year's Best Science Fiction*, *Neil Clarke's Best Science Fiction of the Year*, and two volumes of *Rich Horton's Year's Best Science Fiction and Fantasy*. His stories have appeared in *Analog, Apex, Clarkesworld, Interzone, The Magazine of Fantasy and Science Fiction*, and in *Science Fiction World* (科幻世界), which boasts the largest sci-fi readership on the planet. His story "Love in the Time of Immuno-Sharing" was a finalist for the Eugie Foster Award. He also translates Chinese sci-fi. He likes frogs, and believes in the healing power of *Dungeons & Dragons*.

MENOPAUSE

Flore Hazoumé, translated from the French by James D. Jenkins

I'VE ONLY JUST RETURNED from a two-month vacation to Cape Lake when I rush to the phone and dial Clémence's number. I need her so much. Only she will be able to comfort me. When a young girl's voice responds that Clémence no longer lives at that address, I'm gripped by a senseless fear.

"It's not possible! No, it's not possible."

The voice on the other end hesitates.

"Wait a moment, I'll get my husband."

I hang up. I slip on a jacket and get in my car. I shiver. Could Clémence already have...? No, it's not possible; she's only six months older than I am.

Nervously, I bring my hand to my throat. I feel the soft skin flee from my fingers. I park my car in front of Clémence's house. I ring. The sound of steps on the gravel. Flipper, the dog, barks. The door opens halfway, a young woman smiles at me. She looks like a twenty-year-younger version of me. She looks like my two daughters, too.

"You're the one who called just now? My husband was sure you would come. He's waiting for you in the living room."

She signals me to follow her. I observe her. Women in our world have always been lively, young, and beautiful. I've never seen a woman grow old, but next to this young girl, I feel withered, rough, like a piece of burlap. I follow her anxiously down the corridor, Flipper at my heels. Clémence's favorite paintings are still hanging on the wall. The notes of our theme song, the hard-to-find original version of "Afrikan Krystal" sung by Daya Smith, are coming from the living room. Clémence had promised to give it to me for my birthday in a few days. I look around. I understand everything now, I feel like laughing. Clémence is playing a joke on me. Nothing has happened to her. She hasn't changed. She's still the same. She's waiting for me, smiling, in the living room in front of a cup of tea. I walk with a more assured step.

The young woman opens the door for me. Clémence is sitting with her back to me in an armchair facing the window. I see only her dark hair where, to my great surprise, some white strands have blended in. My anxiety vanishes. I can confide in her without fear, explain without shame what's happening inside me.

"Clémence! I was so worried; you really scared me, it's really bad of you to…"

She turns around slowly, I can see half of her face. The end of my sentence hangs in the air. A cry of horror escapes me. There, in Clémence's armchair, a middle-aged man looks at me with a calm expression.

"What's wrong? Do you feel ill? Why don't you sit down."

"I… I'm looking for my friend Clémence, she lives here, she lived here, I… I don't know anymore."

I collapse into a chair. My head is all muddled. The man puts his hand gently on mine.

"Your friend no longer lives here. She is gone."

"Gone? No, it's impossible, a person can't just go without taking anything with them, leave everything behind. The photo of her husband, the one of her wedding, of her daughters, a person can't just leave like that! No one can change to that extent," I say under my breath, scrutinizing for a moment the stranger's impassive face.

I cast a disoriented glance around the whole room. Flipper has come up to the old man and is licking his hands, how strange! They act as though they've known each other forever. A mad thought crosses my mind; but I don't want to believe it. Could Clémence...? I reject that idea. And yet, that way of running his hands through his hair, of stroking his chin with a dreamy look. So many details remind me of Clémence. I stand up, in the grip of a great agitation. At the doorstep, the man places his hand affectionately on my shoulder and murmurs in a comforting voice:

"There are many ways of leaving."

As he says these words, he plunges his clear gaze into mine. For a fleeting moment I have the strange sensation of having always known him, of finding a friend I thought I'd lost.

That evening, Claude and Pascale, my two daughters, Frédéric and Joël, their husbands, as well as my two granddaughters come to my house for dinner. This familial interlude is good for me and forces me to take my mind off things. I have just enough time to fix dinner and get dressed. I choose a skirt that covers my calves, a long-sleeved blouse. I prefer outfits that are lighter and less covering, but for the past few weeks... Let's not think about it anymore!

At 8 p.m. the doorbell rings. I assume a calm expression. My two daughters kiss me, my granddaughters Emmanuelle and Paule hop around me. I stroke their curly hair as they pass by. My two sons-in-law, so alike with their timeworn faces, shake my hand. I seem to sense an unusual warmth, a complicity, in the smiles they give me. Claude, my eldest daughter, joins me in the kitchen where I'm arranging some glasses on a tray.

She looks at me insistently. Is it that noticeable?

"You look tired, Mom!"

My lips pursed, I don't say anything. She takes a couple steps. I anticipate her gesture. I start to take a step back, too late! She has already run her hands through my hair.

"You're losing your hair, Mom! Look!"

Do I need to look? I know that trivial spectacle only too well. Every morning on my pillow I gather up handfuls of hair. With every passing day my hair grows more and more sparse.

I manage to stammer a response.

"I… I went to the doctor. Apparently it's menopause; I'm following a treatment. Everything will go back to normal. Come on, it's late, let's sit down at the table."

During the meal only my daughters and I speak. My sons-in-law say almost nothing. Men, in our world, speak little. They look out on existence with an expression that reflects all of mankind's wisdom.

Is it their function that surrounds them with this indefinable aura? Here, men make up a separate clan, an inaccessible caste. Beneath their idle appearance, they hold power, wisdom, knowledge. The very balance of our society is in their hands. The women, simultaneously the ants and the grasshoppers, are the lifeblood of our world. They are the future and they beget the future. For those aging sphinxes, stuck in the wanderings of their thoughts, women are a kind of short-lived turbulence that barely disrupts the order and functioning of the society they have skilfully built.

For the first time in my life, I find myself admiring them. I feel close to them. I feel like talking to them, learning their opinions, their thoughts, and thus having a foretaste of what perhaps awaits me… I turn towards them. Our glances meet. One of them slides his hand towards mine and squeezes it with emotion. I read the profoundest respect in their eyes.

When dinner is finished, we make ourselves comfortable in the little sitting room. My sons-in-law smoke their cigars with a vacant look. My daughters have a discussion, carefree. My granddaughters sit on footstools, playing at my feet. I relax and softly hum "Afrikan Krystal," my favorite song. I think of Clémence. Without noticing, I've crossed my legs. My skirt has slid up, revealing my ankles. Paule, my younger granddaughter, caresses my legs. Unsuspecting, I indulge myself in that soft contact.

"Oh, Granny, your legs, they're like a cat's back!" she yells, pulling on the long, hard hairs.

"No, more like a black rabbit," retorts Emmanuelle.

With a brusque movement, I fold my skirt back over my legs.

Instinctively, I turn towards my sons-in-law, as if only they could come to my aid. There's an awkward silence.

"It's getting late," they say finally in a single voice. "It's time to leave."

My daughters, uncomfortable, remain silent. Have they guessed? They won't say anything, I won't say anything. It's the law, this stage of life is lived alone, far from the gaze of others, with courage, with modesty. I had almost forgotten.

Once I'm alone, I go up to my room. Tonight I have the courage to face my own image, this strange body which yet is mine.

I stand before the large mirror, completely naked. I close my eyes, unable to bear this horrible vision, this grotesque reflection of myself. Yet I must! I open my eyes. I can't help flinching in repulsion. With horror, I notice the extent of the illness that's devouring me. My breasts are completely covered in short, bushy hairs. Is this arm mine, this hairy chest? These arms, these legs, made up in a long, hideous down? Is this really me, this hermaphrodite, this unnatural thing?

My eyes wander for a moment over the bedside table where the photo of my husband is. At least he would have helped me to get through this stage of my life. Only today do I realize how I miss his silent presence and what a void his death has left. Exhausted, I swallow two sleeping pills.

For several days I don't notice anything abnormal. My transformation seems to have stopped, the growth of my body hair seems to have balanced out. Only the forerunner symptoms of menopause persist and reassure me: dizziness, hot flashes, bloating.

On the other hand, my skin worries me. Some already-existing wrinkles have become accentuated; others have appeared on my forehead. Bags have formed under my eyes. Now I look like a middle-aged woman. After all, maybe that's what getting old is, maybe that's the menopause the medical books talk too briefly about. I suddenly realize I'm the first woman to see herself grow old. In our world, women never reach old age, what becomes of them? I know the answer. I refuse to believe it. But can one struggle against the order of things?

In the street, no one notices me. The couples are all alike: young women in the arms of their middle-aged husbands, families built on the same model: young girls holding the hands of their mother and their worthy father, in the prime of his life. They all pass close by me without noticing anything. Maybe people take me for what I'm not. The other day, coming out of a store, a young woman bumped into me and said: "Oh! Sorry, sir!" It's true that I was wearing pants.

So I've decided to shave my legs and arms and wear dresses again. What a pleasure to see those vile hairs drowned in the bathtub! I'm finally going to put on an elegant dress. Who cares if my face is marked with age, my legs are still respectable. I take a dress from the wardrobe and slip it on. I have the impression that it used to fit a little tighter at the hips. The anxiety of the past few weeks must have made me lose weight. So much the better! There, all done.

I turn towards the large mirror. I look at myself, I burst out laughing. I laugh until it hurts, no, it's not me, this miserable clown. I laugh harder and harder, no, it's not me, this grotesque creature, this transvestite, this weirdly attired caricature in a dress that hangs everywhere, this woman with no breasts, no hips, no curves. And I laugh over and over without realizing that my laughter ends in tears.

I GOT UP EARLY this morning. A sort of intuition forced me to get out of bed. I feel that something irreversible happened last night. I avoid the large mirror. I run my hand over my face. Under my fingers my skin is as rough as that of a man who hasn't shaved in several days. The mirror behind me mocks me. I won't look at myself. I already know what I'll see.

I take off my nightgown unhurriedly. All the hairs have grown back, my breasts have totally disappeared. I hold my breath. My heart beats harder and harder, faster and faster. Gently, slowly, I lower my eyes towards the only feminine symbol I have left. I can hardly breathe, my vision goes blurry, I put my hand between my thighs, I'm reeling, I'm losing my mind. Under my fingers, an unambiguous growth. In a final cry of horror I lose consciousness.

It's dark, I must have slept a long time. My memories are confused. I have the impression of living a second life, in a new skin. I'm sitting in the living room, in an armchair. An appetizing smell is coming from the kitchen. I get up, I light my pipe. I am very elegant tonight in my three-piece suit. Dominique told me that we'll be receiving guests. An old friend, it seems. Here she is. She smiles at me, young and radiant.

"Did you sleep well, darling? Clément and his wife won't be long."

A ring at the door. They're here. Standing on the doorstep are the young woman and the man who are living in Clémence's house. He looks at me in silence and hands me a record: "Afrikan Krystal."

"Happy birthday," he says to me, with an attitude of complicity.

THIS STORY originally appeared in *The Valancourt Book of World Horror Stories*, edited by James D. Jenkins and Ryan Cagle.

FLORE HAZOUMÉ WAS BORN in Brazzaville, Congo, the daughter of a Beninese father and a Congolese mother. She grew up in France and is now a citizen of Ivory Coast, where she has lived for more than thirty years. Enriched by these different cultures, she considers herself above all a citizen of the world. She is the author of ten books, including novels, story collections, and works for young adults. Her writing deals with themes connected to African societies, contemporary history, and family. She is at present the head of the nongovernmental organization Audace-C, which works in the fields of art, culture and education, and she is the founder of *Scrib Magazine*.

JAMES D. JENKINS is the co-founder of Valancourt Books, an independent publishing house specializing in horror and LGBT-interest fiction. He is the co-editor of *The Valancourt Book of World Horror Stories*, which was a finalist for the Shirley Jackson and World Fantasy Awards, and the four volumes of the acclaimed *The Valancourt Book of Horror Stories* series. He holds a B.A. in French and an M.A. in Romance Languages and Literatures and has published translations of short stories from a dozen different languages. He is currently at work on an anthology of horror stories written in endangered languages.

THE MOLE KING

Marie Hermanson, translated from the Swedish by Charlie Haldén

ONCE UPON A TIME, there was a King who couldn't bear life aboveground. There were demands on him to make wise decisions, to allow and to forbid, to lead and command, condemn, punish and reward. He neither wanted to nor knew how to do any of this. He tried to avoid it as much as he could. Told his councilors to wait, asked for more time to think, locked himself in his chambers and cried. He often lay sleepless through the night, worrying about all the problems he had to solve in the morning. When he finally fell asleep, sleep itself was a difficult chore, and he awoke tired, though he had accomplished nothing. He knew the whole castle talked about his incompetence. All he wished for was to not have to be King. But this was an unattainable wish, for he was his father's only son, and his life was woven into the heavy crown.

One day he was walking the grounds, deeply despondent, when he came upon a large tree that had been uprooted by the storm. He looked upon the hollow by the upturned roots, and he remembered crawling into a hole just like that once, as a child, and staying there for a good long while although everyone was looking for him. It was a pleasant memory. The King glanced around, and then crawled into the hole. He lay there, looking up into the gray clouds covering the sky. There was a slight breeze, and the dead tree branches rustled. He felt something resembling calm. And he fell asleep.

When he awoke, it was night and dark. For the first time in many years, he felt rested. He walked back to the castle. In the dark, his life seemed more bearable. But the next morning, it was just as difficult again. As soon as he could get away, he headed for the woods. He walked far, and when he found a cleft of rock, he crawled inside to lie down. The peaceful sensations from the hole by the uprooted tree came over him again. He fell asleep and did not wake up until night had fallen. With great effort, he got up from the cleft and fumbled his way home through the dark woods.

From then on, the King escaped into the woods as often as he could find the time. He could not resist the vast attraction pulling him to various kinds of cavities. As soon as he found a suitable space, he curled up in it, and all his heavy thoughts left him while sleep crept in. When he awoke, he felt like he had regained health and strength after a long illness. He trained his eyes to spot hollows and crevices. On his wanderings, he inspected the mountains in the hope of uncovering hidden caves or clefts. He always walked around any old oak tree to see if its trunk might be hollow. In the dense brush, he sought for openings that would fit his body. When in council with his closest advisors, he couldn't help peering down into the dark crannies under the table, or wondering whether he could flatten his body and press it against the floor so it would fit underneath the big cabinet that held the laws of the kingdom. While he wondered, one of his councillors reported on the very precarious plight the country was currently in.

Then one day, they received word that the enemy had attacked the country's borders. The King was expected to lead his troops into war. The King was not afraid of dying himself, but he didn't want to lead other young men to their deaths. He didn't want to make their wives into widows and their children fatherless. He didn't want to ride into war knowing beforehand that he would lose. This time, he felt, what they expected of him was something he could not possibly achieve.

And at the same time, being the King, it was not possible for him to refuse to defend his country. He felt cornered on all sides. As usual, he asked for some time to think. The councillors looked at him with dismay and disdain.

"Surely Your Majesty realizes the urgency of this matter?" one of them exclaimed.

The King blushed and nervously fidgeted with his mantle clasp. His head did not even hold heavy thoughts any longer. It was empty.

Suddenly, he turned his back on his men and bolted through the big stone hall, out of the castle, across the courtyard, past fields and pastures, and into the woods. The councilors ran after him, and some soldiers joined in the pursuit. They chased him over hill and dale, and the King's eyes filled with tears of shame and despair as he ran on. His crown fell off and his clothes tore and ripped on branches. All the while he searched for a hole, just like a rabbit running from a pack of dogs, and to his great relief, he found one. It was the entrance to an abandoned badger's den, and he crawled down as far as he could go. "They won't find me here," he thought. It was completely dark in there, and a faint, strange scent of badger tickled his nostrils.

He lay in the den all day. He heard shouts and steps, but nobody found him. After a while he fell asleep, as usual. But he did not crawl out when he woke up. He stayed in the den all through the night and the whole day after. They searched after him with dogs. Petrified, he heard paws scraping and noses snuffling at the entrance to the den. But the badger smell threw the dogs off the scent and they disappeared.

The King didn't dare stay in the den. But he didn't dare get out either. No, he could never ever get out of there. When on the third day he heard the dogs again, he thrust his hands into the wall of earth and started digging inwards. And on that day, his underground life began.

HE STAYED between half a meter and two meters below the surface. He did not know which direction he was digging in, and soon he lost his grasp of time. There were periods of ferocious hard work, when he slashed his way forward like a plow, relishing the strength of his arms. In other periods, he lay still and curled up in one place.

He listened to the soft, muffled sounds of the underworld. The rustling shoveling of earth from a persistent mole. The curious pattering of a vole gliding through its tunnel just below the surface. The purring sound the badgers made when burrowing in the earth for bugs. He learned to recognize the faint sound of earthworms munching on soil, and the tingling of their wanderings up and down their tunnels. Sometimes he plunged his hand through the earth, clutched the wriggling body, and devoured it.

He discovered how many had chosen to live in the sheltering darkness like himself. The earth was a well-spun web of tunnels for different creatures.

Meeting a mole always filled him with a gentle joy. He could feel the warm breath from the animal's searching snout. They inhaled each other's presence and went on to dig their own tunnels. Silent, blind encounters with no questions. Why could people not meet like this aboveground?

He fed on earthworms, bugs, and roots. When he was thirsty he dug downward, until water flowed into his tunnel and reached his mouth. Occasionally, he found the underground wells of the moles. His fingers brushed a dozen of the marvelously soft animals who had gathered down here to drink. If they did not know him, they swiftly scattered into their safety tunnels. But often, they were old friends, and then they went on drinking while he listened to the sounds of the water trickling down their earthy throats.

Once in a while, he left his underground life for a short spell and crawled up out of the ground. He only ever did so at night, and only for a few short minutes at a time. The potent air tore and clawed at his lungs.

Sometimes, he dug himself new tunnels, sometimes he crawled along in his old ones. He crawled without aim. Once he crawled backward for a change. He did not have to explain his path to anyone. On one occasion, he happened upon a tangle of roots. He got stuck, and while he fought to get free, he felt great relief that nobody could witness his embarrassing plight. Now and then he encountered a rock face and had to turn around, but he did not mind at all, since nobody observed his retreat.

He wondered why he felt such joy. "It is because I'm free," he thought. "You can't be free until nobody sees you."

As time went on, both his body and his senses adapted to underground life. His arm muscles developed. His hands grew large and broad like shovels. Because he used his head to shove aside the earth he had shoveled away, his neck muscles grew stronger. His eyesight deteriorated, his eyelids grew swollen, and his eyes turned into narrow slits.

At times, a great tiredness overwhelmed him. He stopped crawling then, and lay still for a long time. He didn't know how long. A week, a month, a year. He felt his pulse slow down and his body grow colder. He lay there slumbering, enjoying his feebleness. A mole or two passed by, gave him a friendly and understanding sniff, and burrowed pleasantly along. He could hear everything that was happening around him. Even the sounds of the very small creatures. All these lives sharing his aimless crawling around in a sightless existence. Beetles, wood lice, and centipedes weaving a cocoon of vigorous, determined sounds around him. A whispering, rustling murmur filled his entire being, and he fell into a deep sleep. A long while later, he woke, with a voracious hunger and an uncontainable urge to move, to crawl. And so he continued on his underground journey.

After some time, he noticed that the worms were behaving strangely. They seemed distressed, and they wriggled back and forth in their tunnels as if they didn't know which way they needed to go. Later, he too felt that there was something unusual happening. A faraway rumble rolled over them, and the earth shook slightly. He dug upward to find out what this was. The top layer of soil was damp. He emerged somewhere in the woods at night. It had just stopped raining, and drops were falling from the trees. He sat down beside the mound of soil he had flung out and waited for his eyes to adjust to the moonlight that came and went between wandering clouds. Then he heard the rumbling again. It was significantly stronger overground, and the sky above the treetops lit up with a red blaze. "This must be war," he thought. The stars gazed at him through thousands of eyes and pierced him with guilt. Hastily, he crawled back down the hole.

He dug himself far away from the rumble and the tremors. But they caught up. He dug even farther, but the rumbling grew stronger, the ground trembled as if there was an earthquake. The war was right above him. It was the same wherever he crawled. The war seemed to be everywhere. Gradually, he got used to the noise and felt thankful for the protection of the earth. He was just a few meters away from bloody battles, but still untouchable.

As time went by, things turned calmer above him. The worms went back to their normal behavior, venturing up to the surface whenever rainfall moistened the soil. Often, he thought about how the lives of the worms ran parallel to his own. They were meant to live underground, everything they needed was provided here, but they seemed to always long for the surface. Even though their visits there often ended in death, they couldn't resist the urge to crawl up there after the rain. In dry weather too they often lay in the topmost parts of their tunnels, right by the surface, feeling the clear air of the overworld on their heads. Oftentimes, a robin would spot them. He felt the vibrations of their terrified, thrashing bodies, and then the short, satisfied chirp of the bird.

He was made to live aboveground. He had been given legs to walk with and eyes that could tolerate the sharp daylight. And yet, all his life he had carried a longing for the underworld.

PRINCESS ESMERALDA SAT in her tower. A beautiful lynx in a golden harness lay on the floor before her. Esmeralda rested her bare feet on his back, using him as a footstool. She loved running her toes through his pelt, and the lynx purred and kneaded the floor with his front paws.

Esmeralda was beautiful and intelligent, but she caused her father a great deal of worry. For several years, suitors had come riding from faraway lands to win her hand in marriage. There had been magnificent tournaments and all manner of contests and trials to let the suitors prove their courage and strength. But the princess just shrugged her shoulders. She didn't want any of the young, handsome men who went clanging about in their armor. She found them silly, and the jangling of spurs was as painfully irritating to her as nails on a chalk wall.

Her father, who realized that the pool of suitable candidates for marriage was not bottomless, wrung his hands and pleaded with her to choose someone. But Princess Esmeralda said that she was fine with things the way they were and had no interest in getting married.

It was late at night and everyone was sleeping, apart from the guards who walked back and forth along the walls. Esmeralda went out into the castle park to walk the lynx. During the day, he was content to lie around being lazy, but at night he wanted to go out. She let him loose to hunt birds and mice while she slowly strolled around the nocturnal park. She stepped in among the dense bushes where the darkness was so thick she didn't know where she was. She liked it when the darkness stroked her from head to toe, making her smooth and flat and calm.

Suddenly, she heard the lynx growling and yapping. She found him among the fruit trees. Between the lynx and the wall were several dug-up mounds of soil that looked like oversized molehills. The lynx seemed to have caught some prey. Something large, something that fought back. She edged in closer and clasped her hands over her mouth in horror. She saw a hand and an arm flailing, another arm, a bloody head… Half a human! But when she looked closer, she saw that the human was not halved but half-buried in the ground, only visible from the chest upward.

"Stop it! You're killing him!" she shouted at the lynx, yanking its harness to make it let go of its prey. She had to use a broken branch to push the animal away, and then tied it to a tree trunk.

Princess Esmeralda studied the strange creature. Was this really a human? The protruding head leaned its forehead on the ground, arms resting in front of it. The body parts were filthy with blood and dirt. Esmeralda thought the creature looked like a macabre, withering plant. It did not utter a sound. She crouched by the head and carefully lifted the stiff clumps of hair. There was a large gaping wound at the back of the neck. She turned the head to one side and saw a face that seemed overgrown, almost obliterated. The creature was unconscious from its injuries or from fright.

Esmeralda considered summoning the guards, but decided not to. Instead, she gripped the creature tightly under its armpits and pulled him out of the ground. This was easier than she had thought. The robust shoulders and arms were not proportionally matched by his lower body, which slipped out of the hole like some sort of flaccid appendage. With a firm grip around his chest, she dragged the under-ground creature through the park. She left the lynx by the tree. Right beside the tower, she waited under cover of darkness, letting the sentry pass by before she made her way up the stairs unseen with her peculiar cargo.

Only when she had washed him clean did she start to feel certain that what she had pulled out of the ground was a human. Underneath the dirt, his skin was white as snow. She laid him on some blankets on the floor, bandaged his wounds, and then inspected him closely by the light from a candle.

"What a pitiful creature," said Princess Esmeralda, fascinated.

At that moment he suddenly awoke and whimpered, seemingly terrified. He started scrambling and scrabbling and scratching wildly at the floor. When Esmeralda touched him, he anxiously curled up and tucked his legs under him, like a hedgehog in hibernation.

When morning came she carefully locked the door, went down to the park, untied the lynx, and asked a servant woman to take care of it. She was afraid it might hurt the stranger more if she let it up into her tower.

All day the man lay curled up in a corner. The blankets that the princess had laid out were no longer on the floor; he had instead heaped them up over his body. She sat down on a chair beside him. She tried using him as a footstool like she usually did with the lynx. After a while, he seemed to get used to it.

Esmeralda told nobody what she was keeping in her tower room. She had learned that it was best to keep quiet about things that meant something to you. She told the man stories, she sang to him, she caressed his back with her toes.

After a month or so, he started speaking. He complained about the light. The princess tore strips of fabric from her dress and tied them over his eye slits like a blindfold. He thanked her, and a few days later, he told her his story. Princess Esmeralda listened, and then said in surprise:

"The war you speak of ended fifty years ago. But there's not even one wrinkle on your face."

She continued:

"Everyone has always warned me against sunlight. It ruins the complexion. If you want to stay young, you should avoid the sun. How youthful it must make one to spend all one's time in darkness, like you!"

Princess Esmeralda told him more about the war:

"The war annihilated almost all of your people, and the enemy too. It went on for many years. Those who did not fall in battle soon starved to death, since fields and barns were burned down. Many died from plague as well. The land lay dead for long. But all the fires had made the soil fertile. Therefore, my people moved here to plant seeds in the ashes."

The princess tended to the man's wounds and sewed him new clothes. She called him the Mole King and fed him bread soaked in water and earthworms. She brought several large horse blankets from the stables for him to crawl around under. But when he asked her to take him back to the park, she refused.

"You can have anything you want up here in my rooms. But I'm never letting you go."

The Mole King yearned for the underworld. Air was such an empty element. He felt vulnerable and fragile. Again and again, he dreamed of scrabbling at the stone floor. A flagstone was loose—he pried it free, darkness came flooding up—he widened the hole and crawled in. But when he woke, the floor was smooth and impenetrable, and he was still a prisoner in the overground.

He always kept his blindfold on. But one day, while giving him his feeding bowl, the princess stroked his cheek and happened to nudge the blindfold, and his eye was exposed. The shock made him open it. Her white-hot blondeness blazed toward him. Her eyes flashed blue in every direction. He closed his eyes and adjusted the blindfold. His eye had almost been burned through, as if someone had poured a drop of poison into it. After she had left, he knew what she resembled. She was like the royal crown he had lost in the woods. Shining, with sapphires sparkling blue.

One night, he cautiously lifted a corner of the blindfold. The princess lay sleeping in her bed. There was moonlight in the room. He felt she was made of liquid silver. When dawn came, he looked at her again. Now she was lead. Gray, heavy, muted. In the sunrise, she was copper. At dinnertime, when she brought him food, she was gold. And when she combed her hair at sunset, she was made of copper once again.

When the Mole King was by himself, he tried standing up. After some time, he could hobble around, holding on to pieces of furniture. He started taking off the blindfold altogether at night, and when he looked around the room, he felt a strange sensation. These eight walls embraced him and brought memories of a calm, light world. At the same time, everything was new and unfamiliar. The walls were covered with tapestries showing animals and people from faraway lands.

The balcony door was open, and he forced his soft legs to walk there. Out in the night air, he recognized his surroundings. He was back in his own castle, in the tower room where he had lived with his nursemaid as a little boy. The tower room had windows to the north, south, east and west. The light up here had always been so airy and blue. He remembered his nursemaid and her generous lap, where he had ridden in comfortable walks and wilder canters. Gingerly, his thoughts touched this part of his past, and to his surprise he found no pain.

When he looked down he saw that several of the smaller buildings around the castle were gone. Gaping foundations showed where they had been. Some had been replaced by new structures.

The Mole King returned to his mound of blankets. He tied the blindfold so he wouldn't be caught unawares by the bright morning light. Princess Esmeralda slept above in her bed. Her breathing was rhythmic and unyielding, like the footsteps of the sentry outside.

ONE DAY, Esmeralda's father called her to him. He took her for a walk.

"You are my only child," he said. "If you don't get married, our line will die out. I am old now and growing less strong. Grant me the joy of seeing you married before I die."

"I would love to give you joy, Father," said Esmeralda.

"But none of the suitors please you! Is there then not a single man in my large kingdom that you would want?" the King exclaimed, spreading his arms toward fields and forests and mountains in the distance.

"No," answered Esmeralda. "Not out there. But up in my tower I have a man I want."

"Really? A man you want? A man who is good enough for you?" the King asked incredulously.

"He'll do," Esmeralda said.

"How did he get here?"

"I dug him up."

"Well, that's just like you. But it doesn't matter. Now, I want to see him, and then we're going to throw a wedding."

They climbed up to the tower room. The Mole King was sitting on his mound of horse blankets.

"Could you not have given your suitor a nicer spot to sit?" Esmeralda's father asked.

"He's not a suitor," Esmeralda answered.

"What now? Hasn't he asked for your hand?"

"No."

"But how do you know he wants to marry you then?"

"If I've dug him up, he's mine," said Esmeralda. "And he likes the horse blankets."

The King approached the man, crouched down, and inspected him. Then he returned to his daughter's side.

"Why is he wearing a blindfold? Can't he see?"

"Yes. But he doesn't want to."

"He seems sickly. He's very pale," the King pointed out.

"Father, can't you see his lovely complexion? If my skin were that white and smooth, I would be very pleased."

"Yes, his complexion is extraordinarily fine, it's true," the King muttered. "He must come from a good family."

"He has royal blood," said Esmeralda.

"I can see that. I can see that. But his hands are rough."

"He has used them to work hard."

"Manual labor and royal birth. A good combination," the King nodded. "You have my blessing, Esmeralda."

And with this, the King left the throne room. At last, his heart was at ease.

EVEN THOUGH IT brought him pain, the Mole King often lifted the blindfold a little to look at the princess.

"Good," said the princess one day when she noticed him watching her.

"When we get married, you can't wear the blindfold at all. If you take me as your wife without looking at me, you'll make me a laughingstock. And you have to learn to walk properly. Come, let's take a walk in the park so you can exercise your eyes and legs."

They went outside. The Mole King supported himself with one hand on a cane and the other on Princess Esmeralda's arm. Two guards walked in front of them and two behind them. They were surprised by a shower of rain. The princess pulled her fiancé in under a willow tree. The guards stayed outside.

"Have you been married before?" Esmeralda asked.

"No," said the Mole King. "My relatives introduced me to several young women, but…" He fell silent and cast his eyes down.

"None of them interested you?" the princess prompted. "I understand perfectly. We will be well suited."

The rain whipped through the park, but the dense foliage of the willow protected them like the walls and roof of a house.

"I hope there's thunder as well. I love a storm," said Esmeralda.

"If we marry—does that mean I will be King?" wondered the Mole King.

"Yes. When my father dies. And don't think you can slip down some hole again. I will keep you under surveillance."

Small drops of sweat crept forth on the Mole King's forehead. Esmeralda tried to kiss his cheek, but he hid his face in his large collar.

"I'll support you. Don't start brooding over that yet. Oh look, there's a wrinkle on your forehead! You shouldn't worry so much. It'll damage your beautiful complexion."

The rain stopped and they made their way back to the castle, accompanied by the drenched guards. The fragrance of the flowers had been freed by the rain, and a rainbow spanned the turrets of the castle. The princess talked rapidly about her plans for the seven-day wedding. The Mole King was silent. His eyes were stinging and he felt utterly exhausted.

On the walkway, the earthworms had crawled up to the surface. There they lay, blue like veins and utterly vulnerable. The Mole King halted and pushed his big toe into the ground, trying to send the vibrating warning signal. But he had forgotten how it went. The worms stayed still. As princess Esmeralda talked about her bridal gown, all the courses of the wedding dinner, the gifts she might receive, the slim lavender-gray bodies were crushed under her heels.

When the wedding day came, the Mole King had put aside the blindfold, but he couldn't manage without his cane. Esmeralda's father had ordered there to be rumors of how his daughter's betrothed had been wounded in glorious battle.

The wedding celebration took place in the largest castle hall, which was illuminated by a multitude of torches. Their light was not as bright as the sun's, but it was more unpredictable, and it was intensified by all the shiny objects in the room. It ambushed the Mole King from every direction, and he didn't know where his eyes could rest. If he looked straight ahead, a thousand needles of light pricked him from the necklace of a lady-in-waiting. Over her shoulder, he saw rows of torches, multiplied by their gleaming brass holders. Turning his gaze upward, he was met by massive chandeliers swaying like ships ablaze at sea. And if he lowered his eyes, the sparks from a well-polished spoon struck him. He closed his eyes, opening them only now and then to look at Esmeralda, who seemed to him lovelier than ever in her bridal finery.

A never-ending stream of serving plates filled to the brim were brought out. There was eating, dancing, games, walks in the park, and yet more eating. On the seventh day, Esmeralda's father stood up to give his speech to the newlyweds. But before he could say a word, his face turned scarlet, he clutched at his side, then his chest, and fell face-first onto the table with a grimace of pain. Groaning, he rolled from side to side, and his face, having landed right in his plate, was smeared with pheasant sauce. The King gripped the edge of the table to try to stand up, but crumpled to the floor instead, lying where he fell, with eyes staring vacantly. The Royal Physician, who had been sent for, could only conclude that his highness was dead.

When the dead King had been carried out and the shock had dissipated, someone called for a toast to the new monarch, and everyone turned toward the Mole King's chair. But it was empty. He had instantly realized the implications of the event and, giving in to an overpowering urge, had crawled under the table. There was quite a bit of searching before they found him. The new King of the realm lay curled up in his mantle like a tortoise in its shell. They dragged him out, hoisted him in the air, carried him to the throne amid shouts of celebration, and pushed the crown down on his head. The Mole King looked out over the sea of people, food, candles, torches. All eyes were upon him.

"All this light," he mumbled, and everyone fell silent, thinking this was the start of a speech.

Whispering, he continued:

"Darkness. I want to eat darkness like the worms eat soil."

And with a sob, he leaned his head in his hands, and stayed like that until all the guests had left.

———

Now that he was King, the Mole King had to leave his mound of blankets in the throne room and move into the Royal Chambers together with his Queen Esmeralda. Not once during the wedding night did he touch her. And not any of the following nights either. She asked:

"Why won't you touch me? You're my husband now."

"I can't touch a woman made of brass or copper. Not even a woman made of silver," he answered.

Esmeralda found heavy dark blankets for the bed and had someone sew her a little moleskin cloak. When night fell, she crawled under the blankets to the King who lay hidden there and gently sniffed him. And in the darkness they made love like two little moles in the underworld.

———

The Mole King was now reliving his old life. Every morning, he met with his councilors in the very hall where he had sat in council many, many years ago. He felt the same insecurities. The same anguish over decisions that affected other people. But at the same time, he realized that the expectations upon him were less than before. He was pale and sickly, half-blind and lame. His unbelievably smooth skin that Esmeralda had marveled over was turning rough and coarse. The Mole King couldn't help noticing the servants' scorn behind his back, the mumbling in the Council Hall before he entered, the cunning looks exchanged by some of the councilors. He lamented this to Esmeralda.

"You're being much too suspicious," she said. "Don't worry so much. I do believe there's another wrinkle here! Worry and sunlight are the very worst things for the complexion."

Regarding the latter, Esmeralda need not have worried. The Mole King hardly ever ventured out in the daytime. But when evening came, he set out on long walks. With no crown on, his mantle like a cowl over his head, leaning on a cane, he looked like a beggar. A short distance behind, the guards followed him like shadows.

From the throne room, he had seen a hill with a single tree. One evening he made his way there. He found that the hill was a church-yard and the tree a large oak. He sat down under the oak. The guards rested by the gate and round the outside of the wall. All was calm. The Mole King sat listening to the whispering of the leaves that swept through his thoughts, dispersing and dissolving them. When the moon rose, he set out homeward, feeling something of the quickening that had once filled him when sleeping in a hole by an uprooted tree.

But every day, more wrinkles appeared on his face. He started to look old. One morning, a chambermaid overheard the Queen calling her husband the Mole King. She found this so apt and amusing that she told some of the other servants, and before long, he was referred to as the Mole King throughout the castle. With his squinting slits for eyes, a mole was just what he looked like.

In the beginning, the nickname was uttered carefully, in whispers. But as time went on, the voices grew louder. Once the court and the servants realized that the King did not punish those who mocked him, they grew ever bolder. He was openly ridiculed, and his poor eyesight taken advantage of for mean jokes. But when the Queen was around, the jesters kept a low profile. Esmeralda doled out harsh punishments to anyone who did not show her husband appropriate levels of respect.

When the two of them were alone, the King would repeat his plea to Esmeralda that she set him free.

"Everyone wants to get me off the throne. And I myself wish for nothing more than to leave it."

"Nonsense," said Esmeralda.

But the Mole King was not mistaken. There was a rumor around the castle that the old King had been poisoned by some of the councilors. And it was precisely those councilors who exchanged cunning glances during meetings and came together to plot in the concealed nooks and crannies of the castle.

One morning, when the King was on his way to the Council Hall, masked men ambushed him and dragged him down into the castle dungeons. He was left there while the leader of the plotters declared himself King. He had garnered support among the soldiers, and anyone who protested this turn of events was sent to the dungeons. Queen Esmeralda hid with the servant woman who took care of her lynx. The woman was responsible for tending the vegetable gardens, and she lived in a small cottage at the far end of the park. Esmeralda spent the whole day there, and with the help of the servant woman she and the lynx were able to escape when night fell. She sought refuge in the great woods, but did not want to go too far away from the castle before she could find out what had happened to her husband.

The King's enemies had no idea that they had put him in just the sort of place he had so long been yearning for: a dark, secluded space with an earthen floor. To them, the name Mole King held no other meaning than a certain similarity of appearance. Therefore, there was great surprise when a guard opened the door after a day and a night, and found only a large mound of earth and a hole.

Soldiers and hounds were sent out to search the area. "He can't have gotten far, being lame and half-blind," they reckoned.

But when Esmeralda was reached by a message from the servant woman and learned how the King had disappeared, she smiled and said:

"They'll never find him."

And Esmeralda ran through the trees, and her lynx followed. She wandered the deep woods, filled with joy. The lynx caught hares and pheasants for her which she cooked over an open fire. She swam through water lilies in dark, silent lakes. Now and again, she climbed a tall tree to see if there was a town nearby. But all she saw was woods and lakes and mountains, and she was content.

One evening, she was standing by a brook, combing a small branch through the long hair she had just washed. She sat down on a rock to let her hair dry, running her toes through the lynx's pelt, and she thought: "I'm sitting naked in the woods and nobody can see me." Over and over again, she thought this. She said it aloud, and for every time she did, she felt happier and happier. And she realized that you can't be free until nobody sees you.

The Mole King dug his way forth with great effort. He hadn't been digging in a long time, and his arms were not as strong as they used to be. His whole body had grown weaker. He felt that the time above-ground had turned him into an old man. But his digging was not aimless. He had carefully taken his bearings beforehand. He was heading toward the hill and the oak where he had found such peace. Even before he reached the wall, he was welcomed by the roots of the tree. He followed them to their center and curled up in their embrace. Once again, he felt the drowsiness. His blood flowed slower, his pulse relaxed, his thoughts started to dissolve, lose their shape, move beyond his grasp. He knew he would not wake from hibernation this time.

The Mole King dreamed. He heard the dead whisper warm, friendly words. One of the voices sounded like his old nursemaid who had rocked him in the tower room. The sap pulsated through the roots of the tree. He thought he felt the silent mouth of a mole kissing him —or was it Esmeralda in her moleskin cloak?

To the people in the castle and in the land, the King remained missing. All the soldiers could find was a row of unusually large molehills. The new King ruled the country with an iron fist. He soon executed the councilors who had supported him through the coup. After some time, a war broke out that lasted for many years, laying all the land to waste.

THIS STORY originally appeared in *The Big Book of Modern Fantasy*, edited by Jeff and Ann VanderMeer.

MARIE HERMANSON (1956–) is a Swedish writer who studied literature and journalism at Gothenburg University and later worked as a journalist at daily newspapers. It was then that she began writing stories infused with elements of fairy tale and fantasy.

Her novel *Himmelsdalen* (2011) became her first book to appear in English when it was released as *The Devil's Sanctuary* (2013) in a translation by Neil Smith, and adapted into a TV series, *Sanctuary*, in 2019, starring Matthew Modine. Her mystery novels are huge bestsellers in Sweden. "The Mole King" was originally published in her 1986 collection *There's a Hole in Reality*.

CHARLIE HALDÉN IS A TRANSLATOR, writer, proofreader and audiobook narrator who lives in Stockholm, Sweden. They have a degree in Translation Studies from the University of Stockholm, where they specialised in fiction translation and wrote their thesis on translating fantasy and treating the genre as the serious literature it is.

Since graduating, they have been working as a freelance translator, with projects ranging from short stories and song lyrics to museum audio guides and sexual health information for LGBTQ groups. They have also taught at the Translation Studies university program.

Charlie works from Swedish to English and English to Swedish, due to being bilingual from the age of four. They have lived in Botswana, the UK and Ireland as well as in Sweden. Language is one of their passions, and they have studied French, Spanish, Russian, Italian, and Dutch, and wish to someday decipher the intricacies of Irish.

Stories are another passion, which is reflected in their spending a lot of time LARPing – specifically in the Nordic tradition that focuses on narrative and collaborative storytelling – and their home consists of roughly 50 percent bookshelves. Charlie also writes poetry and songs.

THE ANCESTRAL TEMPLE IN A BOX

Chen Qiufan, translated from the Chinese by Emily Jin

(Shortlisted for 2021 Rosetta Awards)

"Mr. Huang has a few words to say…"

Everyone in the room stood up at once. The intelligent care robot, however, slowly turned its face in my direction. Emojis flashed on the blue screen. I wasn't sure whether I understood what those emojis meant.

"…to *you*, in private," the robot continued.

I took a deep breath. All the pairs of eyes landed on me at once. It was as if my body were soft mud and the gazes of my family members were loaches, about to rip apart my skin, penetrate my flesh, and bury into my body. I knew what they were thinking; but now, I have lost all the strength to fight back.

The man who used to carry himself with such pride and charisma lay before my eyes, shriveling, crumbling, and wasting away, leaving behind an empty shell made out of thin paper. I was scared that even a heavy sigh would blow him away. A rotting scent permeated the air. Every fifteen seconds, the automatic mist spray system would purr lightly, as if a cat had sneezed. The flow of time in this room, thick and sticky, indefinitely slow, felt like resin gradually hardening into amber.

Fear rose up in my stomach and gushed up my throat. Yet I quietly waited for Father's last words. For all my life, every conversation I have had with my father usually ended with his scolding and my utter silence. I was afraid that this time it was finally Father's turn to be the silent one.

"Sonny, you're here…" Father's trembling voice tore through the silence. His accent, laden with the scent of soil from Southern lands, sounded distant and strange. Our family had left our Teochew homeland long ago. More so, ever since I chose to become a wanderer in the virtual world, busy occupying myself with technology, I have long been estranged from my kin. "My time is up. There's one last thing I want to ask from you. Only you can do it for me…"

"Don't say that, Dad! No matter what you want to do, once you recover—I'm sure you will—we can do it together…"

"There's no need to comfort me. Isn't it strange? The older you get, the more things from your childhood you are able to recall. Remember that story I told you? When I was seven, my father—your grandpa—took me to our ancestral temple…"

I had no idea what he was about to tell me. A few years ago, when machines had revolutionized the traditional craft industry, the impact also extended to our family business: handmade gold-lacquered wood carving. I, an advocate for using new technology to aid traditional arts, had been completely at odds with Father who'd insisted upon doing things the old way. Back then, our conversations were nothing but explosive arguments, often ending in cold wars that lasted for days. At some point, he'd even considered kicking me out of the succession line. *What's the point of telling me this story again?*

"The wobbly car ride went on for hours. I couldn't even feel my own butt anymore. Finally, we arrived at the Huang clan's ancestral temple. What an enormous space! The pond in front of the gate was symbolic for 'collecting a pool of wealth.' A pair of proud stone lions, male on the left and female on the right, guarded the gate. The top of the roof was decorated with figures from mythology: birds and animals, *long* and *feng*, rows and rows of deities…"

The image of a Disney carnival parade flashed through my mind as Father carried on, describing every detail of that mysterious building. I shook my head to get rid of the ridiculous thought.

"The memorial tablets of all our ancestors lined the large altar in the main hall. Dad ordered me to kneel and kowtow, to pay respect to our ancestors. I refused. *But I don't even know them, why should I kneel to them?* I argued. So Dad scolded me for being disrespectful and spanked me. I cried and cried…"

Father's voice grew weaker. He was like a balloon, hanging limply in midair, about to let out its last breath. I could almost see him sinking deeper and deeper. I leaned forward and pressed an ear close to his lips. The rotten smell was so heavy that I almost couldn't breathe.

"That happened eighty years ago. Back then I didn't understand why honoring our ancestors was important, but now I do. Every falling leaf must return to its root. After I am gone, sonny… Visit me at our ancestral temple often. *Please.* By then, you'll be leading the Huang clan…"

Clearly, Father's consciousness was slipping away. His words did not make much sense. Halfheartedly agreeing to his request, I fumbled for the emergency button next to the hospital bed. The last time Father even went home to visit had been a few decades ago. I was pretty sure that his memorial tablet did not make it into the ancestral temple. Even if it did, how on earth would I be able to visit the place *often*, given that it was thousands of miles away? As for leading the Huang clan… That sounded more like a joke to me than anything else. The families in our clan were at each other's necks fighting over inheritance. Yet gazing at Father's dying face, I couldn't bring myself to ask him about his will.

"Promise me you'll go there…"

"Yes, Dad. I promise you."

As if some mysterious force squeezed the last air out from the humanoid balloon on the sickbed, the rotten odor disappeared at once. The automatic mist spray system sneezed again. Doctors and nurses rushed into the room with more machines. Stiffly, I stood by the bedside in silence and waited for a death sentence that had, in fact, already arrived.

THE THIRD DAY after Father's funeral, I discovered a red envelope he'd left me. In the envelope was a small card printed with an IPv6 address and a strange logo.

It took me a while to locate an adequate access device for the address. Tech geeks call the adapter "the white box," a kind of advanced virtual reality system that could scan your neural patterns and mix them in with an algorithm to produce a quantifiable, controllable neural signal input. The white box was much more effective than all the other virtual reality devices, and yet more feared: no doubt, it would change your fundamental cognition in some way that you could not predict.

I had no idea how Father came across such hip, quirky technology. My impression of him was still frozen in the moment when he bellowed at me for my ignorance and disrespect toward my ancestors and forgetting my roots, because I had dared suggest that we replace traditional craftsmen with machines. Heavily panting, eyes wide and cheeks beet red, he'd resembled a dragon about to spit fire.

That dragon now lay six feet beneath the ground, in a small wooden box, accompanied by nothing but darkness and dirt.

Without further hesitation, I connected myself to the white box, entered the IPv6 address that Father had left for me and pulled the soft eye mask over my eyes. Not only that I wanted to honor my promise to Father, I was also curious about what he was up to. The system logged me in immediately after scanning my iris. Seemed like someone had already registered an account for me.

At first, I was surrounded by thick, pale fog. My eyes couldn't discern anything. A few moments later, I heard a feminine voice echoing faintly in my ear, "Mr. Huang, we have detected that the default travel speed does not match your neurological composition. Would you like to switch over to fast mode? Please confirm."

The walking figure of Father, limp and slow, flashed through my mind. I understood what she meant. Father had been the first to access this IPv6 address, after all.

"Confirm," I responded.

All of a sudden, the center of gravity shifted. Terrified, I crouched to the ground and pressed my palms hard on the floor to keep steady. The fog gradually dissipated. I looked down and found myself hovering ten thousand meters above the earth. A village surrounded by mountains and rivers, spread out like the pattern on a turtle's back, lay beneath my feet. The next second, the landscape gushed toward me like a ferocious tide, rapidly enlarging in my sight. I could even see the gray ridgeline of the village house roofs. *I was falling.* I shut my eyes tightly and swallowed a scream.

After what seemed like forever, the fall came to an end. I slowly opened my eyes and found myself standing on a vast plaza. The brightness of various objects shot up as my eyes landed on them, highlighting them from the background, as if my gaze was some kind of a spotlight. The voice in my ears explained each object to me as I peered around—now I understood it was a beginner's tutorial.

No doubt, this was the place of Father's last dream. The placid pond, glistening in the light; the horse-hitching post, erect by the gate; the magnificent screen wall, inlaid with colored porcelain that depicted the shapes of sika deer, qilin, and wing-spreading cranes; the roofed porch and the gate frame, made of gray-white marble; the black-lacquered wooden plaque, engraved with four characters in calligraphy that shimmered with gold, "Huang Clan Ancestral Temple"; porcelain statues of mythical creatures and deities on the roof ridgelines and eave corners... I stood, stunned, my mouth hanging open in awe.

Father had not been exaggerating. The ancestral temple he'd described to me really existed.

The glorious sight did not reduce my confusion, though. Someone out there, for some unknown reason, had gone to all the trouble to reproduce the Huang clan's ancestral temple in a virtual space. It was a most unlikely combination. Wasn't it the ancestral temple, a standing embodiment of ossified traditions, that had restrained Father from embracing the bold technological inventions of the new world? Now, it appeared to me that the older generation was preserving such tradition by betraying it. Why had Father led me here? To become a replica of him, abiding by our ancestor's values, following every single rule that was ever written, and watching with hopeless eyes as our entire clan declined?

Trotting along the path, I entered the gate and walked through the front courtyard. The sun shone from behind the hollow-carved grill door, casting strands of light onto the floor of the middle hall that reminded me of the shape of a barcode. I glided through the back courtyard. Everything before my eyes unfolded with symmetry, structure, and routine, characteristic of the era that Father had lived in. *An era long gone.*

My revolutionary vision was to introduce embodied robots to the traditional craft of gold-lacquered wood carving. A robot like that could connect to and synchronize with every muscle and nerve signal of a human gold-lacquered wood-carving craftsman. In a way that magically resembled traditional one-on-one master-student learning, the robot would observe and learn every intricate detail of the craftsman's hand movement, then reproduce the choreography on digitalized raw materials in a virtual space. The simulated mechanics of materials are as precise as four decimal places. Coupled with generative adversarial networks, relying only on a small set of data, we could train highly efficient robot craftsmen. What's more, a robot craftsman would never experience fatigue and illness or need any breaks at all; its spatial perception and accuracy of motion are literally two orders of magnitude higher than that of humans. Honestly, I couldn't think of any valid reason to reject this proposal.

It had been Father who'd buried his head in the sand, refusing to confront the machine-dominated reality.

I finally arrived at the heart of the ancestral temple: the main hall. Otherwise known as the slumber chamber, it was the place where spirits of the dead rested in peace in their eternal sleep. Colossal red-painted wooden structures extended upward like Aztec pyramids, as if about to disappear into the vast sky beyond, yet once I fixed my eyes on them, they appeared to be confined by the enormous hall. An impossible optical illusion. Memorial tablets of my ancestors, carved from camphor wood, lined the wooden structures like books on the shelves of a library. They were organized by the order of relatedness to me: from the most distant relatives to the closest blood kin. I searched for Father's name in the forest of memorial tablets. Whichever tablet my gaze landed on, the name carved into the tablet would glow with a golden light. Amongst all of the Huang-surnamed ancestors were all kinds of people, government officials and wealthy merchants, peasants and commoners, yet at this moment, they were all equals to me. Every single one of them was a cog or gear on the giant machine of the Huang clan's collective memory.

Father's memorial tablet was there, too. I gazed fixedly at Father's name as I murmured to myself, "Dad, I'm here to visit you."

The guide spoke. "Mr. Huang, would you like to activate the system?"

"Activate?"

"Please kneel on the mat, put your palms together, and kowtow three times."

***

"WHAT THE HELL?" My eyes widened as I saw Father, looking about ten years younger, emerge from his memorial tablet. *Just like witnessing the genie squeeze out from Aladdin's lamp,* I thought to myself. Father, shifting around and stretching his arms and legs, seemed to be having some mild difficulties with his new body. He was only an AI-generated virtual avatar, after all.

"Sonny, you're here," he greeted me. Even his accent and the slow, sluggish way he spoke were perfectly reproduced. *How much money had been spent on this thing?*

"Uh… yeah. It's me. I'm here." I didn't know what to say. It felt way too awkward to call this avatar "Dad."

"I knew you'd come. You're different from the rest of them. You're smart and curious, a real fast learner…"

How ironic. Those were the exact words that Father used to scold me with. I assumed that he had sent the same invitation to my older brothers, too—my competitors. Although our ages were not so far apart, their views on technology and art very much aligned with that of Father's. *Abandoning our traditional handicraft is the same as betraying the art, betraying our ancestors, and the generations of wisdom they passed down.* The same old words. I secretly speculated that if given the chance, they would probably tattoo the word "traitor" on my forehead and kick me out of the family.

"I'm sure right now you are wondering what this is all about," continued Father. Seemed like he was programmed to finish this conversation no matter whether I responded or not. "Thirty years ago, Mr. Ma launched his new project on the digitalization of Teochew ancestral temples all around the world. That's right—*the* Mr. Ma who single-handedly founded the biggest technology company in Asia. What a sight, that ancestral temple of the Ma clan! Mr. Ma believed that ancestral temples serve the same purpose as instant message software: it brings together people of the same clan, regardless of their generation or geographic location. Many young people, however, have long forgotten about ancestral temples. Mr. Ma's vision is to revitalize ancestral temples with the help of technology."

I cut him off. "Aren't you against the idea of using technology to change traditional culture?"

"Sonny, you must understand that there are certain things I cannot say out loud. I need to be careful with my words in front of the clan, but you're different. You belong to the new generation, and you don't have to watch your mouth when you speak…"

"Isn't it too late, though? Look, if the line of succession for our business is determined by age and seniority, then I am neither the oldest nor the most experienced. As for you, you're already…" My voice cracked and trailed off.

I must admit that this AI avatar of Father was extremely well made, in particular its speech communication, to the point that I couldn't help but feel like I was speaking to Father in person once again. The word *dead* choked in my throat.

"I am already dead, you're right," the younger version of Father before my eyes grinned at me, a painful resemblance of his living self. "But the rest of you are alive. You are the future. Tell me, why do you want to replace humans with machines?"

"Everyone is using machines. They are faster, more stable, and cost-efficient. If we don't jump on the trend, the entire market will be taken over by machine-created wood carving. By then, there will be nothing left for us to profit from."

"Well, nowadays, humans are colonizing space; 3D printing is everywhere. Why do people still care for gold-lacquered wood carving? Because they are cheap? Easy to carry? Sturdy? Or beautiful?"

I was stunned by this question. I was born into a family that had practiced gold-lacquered wood carving for generations and took fierce pride in their skill; yet with my head buried in digital art and cutting-edge technology all the time, I had never put any thought into it. I knew nothing, I realized, about the symbolic or realistic implications, the aesthetics or the history behind this specific form of craft. *How had it survived thousands of years?*

"Perhaps people were just nostalgic," I answered, hesitating, my voice timid.

"Heh! You're too smart for your own good. You think with your brain all the time, yet you never *feel* with your body. Look…"

He pointed at the marble columns shaped like elongated winter melons. Above the columns was the major summer beam, hovering over the secondary beam that signified fruitfulness and prosperity. The column caps, beams, dougongs, girders, and lintels glistened with a gold spark. I recognized immediately that they were gold-lacquered wood carvings.

Legend had it that this craft had originated in the Tang dynasty. Equipped already with unparalleled wood carving skills, those Tang craftsmen drew inspiration from the cavalier perspective seen in

Chinese ink wash paintings and had attempted to recreate the same effect on wood: merging scenes from different time-spaces together into one grand visual narrative. The scenes were depicted by intricate openwork carving on wood, layered one next to another, so that they could be represented in the same space altogether. Finally, the craftsmen had painted the wood carving in rich, thick gold. The finished artwork thus became a limbo where the real and the imaginary, the prologue and the denouement, the cause and the effect collided and melted into each other.

What did Father want me to see? I swallowed my question when, all of a sudden, all the wood carving came alive.

The crabs crawled along the wires of their cage like fruits on a vine. Magpies, startled by the crabs' snapping claws, spread their wings and scattered across the sky. The eight immortals crossing the sea made a zigzag instead and ran smack into the outlaws about to take refuge in the Liangshan Marsh. The heroes of the Three Kingdoms swore their oath to become brothers in the Peach Garden, and their witnesses were Mencius' mother, who raised the sage alone, and the ancient giant Kuafu who chased the sun. This small, confined carved sculpture became a hodgepodge of endless time and boundless space.

I stared at the scene before my eyes, utterly spellbound. The legends that Father had told me back in my childhood all came to life at once. "You mean the gold-lacquered wood carving is also a kind of historical synchronic narrative?"

"Well, I think wood carving is the best way to talk and learn about history. When you were a baby, you used to spend ages lying on our bed, caressing the wood carving while muttering syllables to yourself. Remember?"

Of course I remembered. The hard and cold texture of the wood and the hills and pits of the complex carvings had been my first introduction to the world beyond my own body. My fingertip, brushing past the arcs, curves, and undulations, was like a time traveler who embraced lives and stories from a thousand different worlds. Fictional or real, those stories, shimmering with gold, were ingrained in my memory through touch.

I was beginning to understand why Father had wanted me to come here.

"Speaking of the robot you've been meaning to use, the art it creates is completely soulless if there isn't a real craftsman to guide its hands. People nowadays are so obsessed with the virtual world that they keep on forgetting that physical bodies are a thing!"

Coming from you, a virtual avatar! I muttered to myself. "So you're not against technology, after all?"

"Using technology right is like adding wings to a tiger, you can only make things more powerful. Using technology the wrong way, though, will only bring harm and ruin our ancestors' efforts. You know why I never agreed upon your plan in the past? I was worried that you were dreaming a little too big..." Father paused for a second, "Or, *not big enough.*"

"Not big enough?"

"Sure, technology will enhance production efficiency, but what more? Your proposed innovation is superficial; it changes the flesh, but not the soul. I think technology has a lot more to offer us. Technology can lead to the rebirth of the gold-lacquered wood carving by reconceiving it, instilling in it new aesthetics, and adjusting it to fit into our future."

Father was right, I realized. Originally, I'd thought about having robots learn the craft of wood carving and gradually replace human craftsmen in the next three years, so we could mass-produce gold-lacquered wood carving like never before. Yet, if we took the memory and the sentiment away—the *human* essence of handicraft—would anyone truly care for those assembly-line produced, soulless things? Mass production at its best would only help us win a low-price competition, nothing more. This future I envisioned for the Huang clan was a dead end. In Father's words, we needed to take the best of both worlds and produce something new: gold-lacquered wood carving that combined the advantages of both machines and humans, fit for our contemporary time. No matter how much its form and shape shifted, it would always preserve the essence of artisanship.

"I think I know what you mean now. But my brothers..."

"Look back at the way you came," responded Father.

"What?" I turned around. My gaze passed through the back courtyard, middle hall, front courtyard, and landed on the glistening pond outside the memorial archway. My brain reminded me that something was not right.

"So what did you see?" asked Father.

"Well, if the entire ancestral temple was built on the same horizontal plane, it would be impossible for me to see all of its structures at once. Which means..."

"The ancestral hall is designed in a three-part structure. The front courtyard to the middle hall is the first part, the back courtyard to the main hall is the second part. Every part is about three feet higher than the previous part. Thus, walking into the ancestral temple is like climbing up the ladder of success: with every step you take, you get a little higher."

"You mean..."

"I mean that you need to see past the land beneath your feet. Only when you are standing up taller can you expand your horizons and see what's out there in the wider world. Your brothers have already agreed that you're the best person to take the Huang clan's wood carving art to a new level—to make it into something that truly fits the needs of this era. Don't worry. No matter what you choose to do, you will have our support."

I swallowed hard, trying to get rid of the lump in my throat. I gazed into Father's eyes, utterly wordless. He had planned everything out long ago; and yet for almost his whole life, I had accused him of bigotry and conservativeness.

"Why didn't you tell me this earlier?" I stuttered, my voice trembling.

"You didn't really give me a chance, did you? You haven't contacted me in so long, let alone visited home. Was I really going to go looking for you in the virtual world?" Father's words sounded like a familiar scolding, yet his voice was gentle, even melancholic. A slight smile emerged on his face, "I didn't expect that my time would be up so soon, though. Sonny, I wish I could have talked to you more..."

"Dad…"

Tears rushed out of my eyes. Instinctively, I turned my head toward the pond to avoid Father's gaze—yet I forgot: registering my real tears was evidently not programmed into the now-virtual Father's algorithm.

I took a deep breath and turned back again. Father had already vanished into the forest of memorial tablets.

His mission was complete, but my mission has just begun.

In the virtual main hall of the Huang clan's ancestral temple, my brothers and I knelt together and kowtowed three times. Then we waited.

Everything was the same as the first time. The rather ridiculous-looking old man, clumsy and plump, wiggled out from his memorial tablet. "Sonny, you're here," he exclaimed.

My brothers were clearly not expecting to see this. Stunned, they stared blankly at Father. Gods know how much effort it had taken me to convince them to celebrate Chinese New Year with me in this absurd way.

Trying to alleviate the awkwardness, I waved my hand at Father. "Dad, it's New Year! We're here to visit you. We brought a present, too!"

My gesture summoned a wooden box. The box hovered above the pond at the gate of the ancestral temple, glowing as the sunlight reflected off of its reddish-black surface. Its reflection on the water surface vibrated, just like how my body was trembling from the nervous energy.

To create the desired visual effect, I changed the object ratio of the box to 1:1000. Gazing out from the main hall, I could see that the box was virtually the size of half a soccer field. Dazzling gold light seeped through the few arc-shaped cracks on the box, as if hinting at the magnificence confined inside.

"I knew you'd come. You're different from the rest of them…"

"Dad, don't you want to look at our gift first?" I cut him off. The intelligence level and social awareness of this simulacrum were the same as the weather in June—you could never predict its highs and lows.

"Yes, yes…"

The three of us stood together and piled our right palms on top of one another, our faces completely solemn. A gold light rose from our hands and ripped through the air, aiming for the wooden box. As the light passed by the back courtyard, the middle hall, and the front courtyard, all the porcelain statues also came to life: the cranes flapped their wings, the qilin dashed off into the distance, deities and demons alike played instruments and danced, forming an orchestra of harmony… I made a mental note to myself to praise the advertisement team that I'd hired to do the job. Today was the big day. Better put on the best performance we could manage—for the dead, for the living, and for the three hundred thousand viewers out there watching our livecast.

The gold light struck the box. Ripples of light dissipated in every direction. "Also Sprach Zarathustra" by Richard Strauss, and Howie Lee's remix of Teochew Yingge folk dance music, vibrated through the sky and rang in everyone's ears. The sublimity of mysticism, underlain by the rowdy rhythm of mundane everyday life, was disassembled in a way not unlike drawn thread work, and then rewoven into a vast Dolby holographic sound field. In turn, the sound was delivered to the bone conduction headphones of each viewer watching this virtual livecast via the white box. The auditory sense was integral to this ceremony; hearing would help the viewers empathize better.

Slowly, the wooden box opened.

The scene before everyone's eyes was the exemplar of a new era of enlightenment: a piece of art co-created by machines and humans, a hybrid of a Rube Goldberg machine and the Lu Ban Burr puzzle. Magnificent, delicate blocks of gold-lacquered wood carving were assembled together in a mortise and tenon style. The space frame, transcending even the wildest imagination, was something completely impossible for mortals to create. If you restore the order and perspective angle of those arbitrarily positioned blocks, though, they would at once transform into a stage play about time-space and human history. Thanks to the mechanics, all of this was able to take place without any external power source. This tiny wooden box was the nutshell that encapsulated infinite space, the oyster that held a thousand worlds.

What's better, I had been able to incorporate Father's idea into my design. Every box told a story: from eons ago to the modern age, from the oldest myths to the latest technology, from abstract ideas to concrete artworks... machines couldn't draw inferences between seemingly unrelated elements, conceptually or visually, but the human brain could. The box in front of us right now told the long story that began with goddess Chang'e abandoning her mortal life, through drinking an elixir that gave her the ability to fly to the moon, and ended with the establishment of the Moon Base. It was a narrative complete on its own, concise, powerful, vivid, and rich with symbols.

The live viewer count grew steadily.

By solving the puzzle of a wooden box, you could understand a history, apprehend a concept, immerse in a story, or even experience an entirely unfamiliar culture. In this process, however, you are required to interact with this heavy box with your physical body: caressing it with your fingers, smelling it with your nose, interpreting —deciphering—*feeling* its intricacy and glory from every possible perspective. It will become a part of your body memory, just as once Father had told me. This unique experience, grounded in physicality, is exclusive to humankind, irreplaceable by robots or algorithms.

You could even customize a box that contained the story of your family. By handing the box to the people you love and care about, the memory gets passed on—to Teochew, to California, to Mars, to the end of the universe. These boxes are ancestral temples that you can hold in your hands.

And today, through livecasting a carnival in a boxed-up ancestral temple, I was able to demonstrate the concept of our ultimate product to eight hundred thousand—no, one million—people in this world. I knew that those people would in turn spread the word and idea around like nuclear fission.

Father glided toward my brothers and I and patted us on the shoulders, though I couldn't feel his touch at all. He nodded in his ordinary matter-of-fact way, "Not bad. Looks like you didn't disgrace the Huang clan after all. Have you thought of a name for it yet?"

I glanced at my brothers. "We're still talking about it. I insisted that the character *chao* must be a part of the name."

Father was silent, as if lost in thought. I didn't know whether there was a glitch in the algorithm or if he was simply pausing for effect.

"*Chao* as in *Chaoshan*, the Mandarin name for us Teochews, means tide. Wherever there is gravity, there is tide; wherever there is tide, there is life. It's the ebb and flow that makes up a long and prosperous life. *Chao* is good, *chao* is good..."

Father's words were interrupted by firecrackers that crackled and spluttered noisily. The box finished unfolding itself. The entire history of humankind conquering space now lay before our eyes, shimmering with glorious gold. Magically, I realized this was how I remembered New Year to be as a child: a fresh start to nearly four hundred new days of hope and positivity. Now so many years have passed, and the only way I could re-experience the New Year of my childhood was in a virtual ancestral temple.

All of a sudden, I yearned to return to a different reality, to give my family a hug—even though they may not be the most amiable or understanding people you can find. At least I still have a physical body that could embrace, experience, and feel all the imperfections of this world.

Maybe it was time to leave the box behind.

TRANSLATOR'S NOTE on Teochew culture:

The Teochew (Chaozhou) people are native to Guangdong province, China, and are spread across various Southern regions and Southeast Asian countries. The Teochew prefecture in Guangdong, known as Chaoshan in Mandarin, traditionally included Shantou, Chaozhou, Jieyang, and Shanwei. Teochew people speak their own dialect, the Teochew dialect, which is a derivative of the Minnan dialect of Southern China. The gold-lacquered wood carving (jinqi mudiao) mentioned in this story is a traditional art of the Teochew people.

THIS STORY originally appeared in *Clarkesworld*.

CHEN QIUFAN (AKA Stanley Chan) is an award-winning Chinese speculative fiction author, translator, creative producer, and curator. He is honorary president of the Chinese Science Fiction Writers Association, and has a seat on the Xprize Foundation Science Fiction Advisory Council. His works include the novel *Waste Tide* and, co-authored with Kai-Fu Lee, the book *AI 2041: Ten Visions for Our Future*. He currently lives in Shanghai and is the founder of the Thema Mundi Studio.

EMILY XUENI JIN is a science fiction and fantasy translator, translating both from Chinese to English and the other way around. She graduated from Wellesley College in 2017, and she is currently pursuing a PhD in East Asian Languages and Literature at Yale University. As one of the core members of the Clarkesworld-Storycom collaborative project on publishing English translations of Chinese science fiction, she has worked with various prominent Chinese SFF writers. Her most recent Chinese to English translations can be found in *AI2041: Ten Visions For Our Future*, a collection of science fiction and essays co-written by Dr. Kaifu Lee and Chen Qiufan, and *The Way Spring Arrives*, co-published by Tor and Storycom, the first translated female and non-binary Chinese speculative fiction anthology (scheduled to publish April 2022). Her essays can be found in publications such as *Vector* and the *Field Guide to Contemporary Chinese Literature*.

NO ONE EVER LEAVES PORT HENRI

K.A. Teryna, translated from the Russian by Alex Shvartsman

I ENTER the bar and all conversation ceases, like in a trashy paperback novel. Patrons turn and stare at me. Francois must've already spread the news. Not that I was going to hide it—you can't hide something like this, tomorrow it'll be in the papers. But for now, I was unsettled.

What dragged me to Azure anyhow? I knew Francois couldn't keep a secret; his nickname—Loose Lips—was well-earned, after all. The thing is, when your mind is preoccupied with difficult problems, your feet carry you along the familiar path. Doc César calls this a "behavioral pattern."

Doc's here too—where else would he be? Hidden away in a dark corner so you can only see his eyes. Those eyes are filled with a devil's compassion. Others look at me with equal parts jealousy and genuine happiness for my fortune.

Their stares only serve to anger me. Especially César's. If not for his stories, I'd be the happiest man in Port Henri. But now?

Now I feel like a man at the edge of the abyss.

Not that I can explain this to any of them.

They aren't thinking of me, or of my son. They think of their own children who lost the most important lottery of their lives today. What future awaits them? They'll become fishermen and prospectors. Some, who are very lucky, might join the Cayman Guard. The not-so-lucky ones will become miners.

I've seen child miners. Grim, exhausted faces. Eyes that have absorbed the darkness of the mine shafts. It's as though they've seen things beneath the mountains that have changed them forever.

Any resident of Port Henri will tell you: the mountains are populated by demons who loathe parting with their treasure. They demand human souls in exchange. That's why children make the best miners: their souls are purer, tastier for the demons. A child carries such a demon back from the mine inside them, like an incurable disease, and the demon slowly devours the young soul, leaving nothing but a walking skeleton.

At first glance the people of Port Henri are like everyone else. Not better, not worse. At first glance you can't tell they carry the sorts of stories inside that make even my stomach turn.

"What are you standing over there for, Joe?" shouts Francois. "Buy a round for the good people, my friend. Surely you won't forget your old pals now that you're practically an Olympian?"

"That's Mr. Joseph Fellow to you, Loose Lips."

Francois grins a pocked smile at me.

They love nicknames in Port Henri. Seven years ago someone started calling me Convict. I had to break several noses to put an end to that.

I nod to the bartender. I've seen what's to come time and time again. Whenever fortune smiles upon some poor prospector he becomes an instant celebrity for a day. His meager handful of emeralds will barely cover a round for the barflies. And he'll spend it all, instead of buying a new dress for his wife, to bask in the smiles and approval of his buddies. That's how things are done in Port Henri.

I have no choice but to undergo this ordeal. Congratulations, friendly slaps on the shoulder. Everyone tries to shake my hand. The bartender asks for an autographed photo to put up on the wall. And why not—the Azure will become a celebrity hangout now. They might even rename Caipirinha into Joe Fellow in my honor.

The thought makes me sick. I down a shot of cachaça and ask for another.

***

THE TROPICAL NIGHTS sneak up on you, quiet and stealthy, like dexterous thieves. Perhaps the night *is* a thief, but what does it pilfer? And if it doesn't, then why does it sneak up on me so suddenly? Life taught me that every living thing has its agenda. But can the night be considered a living thing? When you think of it, even inanimate objects have a will of their own.

Take my grandfather's favorite fishing rod, which he used on the Little Tennessee River. When it didn't feel like working, the fish wouldn't bite for anything. I don't know what it whispered to the bass, but nearby fishermen reeled them in one after the other while Grandpa caught nothing but some peace and quiet.

I realize that last shot of cachaça had been too much. My thoughts are tangled like the narrow Port Henri streets I'm traversing.

This won't do, Joe, I tell myself. You can't fall back on your usual solution of getting drunk instead of dealing with the problem. Not today. Sober up, convict. Sober up now.

Last time I got this drunk was five years ago. I was in my right, then. All fathers get drunk when their sons are born. The wives think of us as terrible egoists and weaklings for doing so.

The woman carries the child for nine months inside her. This miracle is a part of her, gradually becomes a part of her world. The same miracle catches the man by complete surprise. The new dimension opens in front of him, like a hole that leads into a parallel universe. Like a sunrise after a night that lasted a lifetime. As though he were falling into the abyss and had realized, just above the ground, that he knew how to fly.

That's why a *real* man must get drunk as many times as he has children. But no more than that. Not even if his son's life is on the line. Especially not then.

I look around. The nights in Port Henri are murky and thick. It's not easy to orient myself in the dark. But the sense of smell never fails me. I sniff at the air. Among the aromas of spices and the sea I smell the waft of typographer's ink.

The sounds confirm it. I hear the rattle of the printing press from the basement of the nearby building. The lights are on within the second floor. No doubt, these are the offices of the *Free Guanahani*. The newspapermen work best at night. I imagine the editor, his hair unkempt, a cigarette dangling from the corner of his mouth. He stares grimly at his typewriter, dissolving his writer's block with strong rum.

I don't have to look over his shoulder to learn tomorrow's headline. I already know it.

"King Henri IX Chooses Heir" will be printed in huge letters across the top. A few lines about the poor young Henri IX will follow. They'll praise his bravery, the strength and grace with which the young king faces certain death. Underneath, it will say:

"His Majesty has finally reached the decision all of us have been waiting for with baited breath. He chose the five-year-old Nicholas Fellow as his heir. As per tradition, Nicholas will adopt the name Henri, and under that name will become the tenth king of Guanahani."

Next to that paragraph will be the photo of my son.

Then, in small print underneath, they might add:

"Keep in mind that all ports will be closed until Sunday night in celebration of the coronation."

I hear a shuffling of steps behind me. I recognize them without turning. Doc César.

The stubborn old man gets right to the point. "What are you going to do?"

"Go to hell, Doc."

"You won't solve your problems by drinking cachaça, Joe."

"Leave me alone. I don't want to talk to you right now."

"Don't be a fool, Joe. You have to do something. You can't—"

I shove him. Not too hard by my standards, but he falls onto the ground anyway. This damned town has changed me. I fight old men now.

"Sorry, Doc." I offer him my hand.

He gets up, dusts off his clothes, adjusts his glasses. He goes on as if nothing has happened. "You have to decide today, Joe. Tomorrow will be too late."

As if I didn't know this.

"When will they close the port?" I ask.

"They already closed it. They put up the celebratory flags."

"So there's no way to get the motor boat."

"No, no way."

I could take Francois's boat, but there's no point. It's a slow tub. Won't get far.

"No amount of money will rent you a motorboat," says Doc. As though I had the money. The lack of funds is the one constant in my life. "But it's possible to steal one."

Doc raises an eyebrow at me, as if to say: *You're a thief, Joe. You could easily do this.*

People in Port Henri are stubborn. Once they got it into their heads that Joe Fellow is a first-rate thief, it was impossible to dissuade them. They'll nod as they listen to how I ended up in prison as an innocent man. How the jurors were idiots, the judge was a scoundrel, and my attorney was a hack. And how I was the fool who was doing research for a book about the Parisian underclass and decided to collect some material in person. How I had nothing to do with the robbery and especially the murder of that old man—I only waited by the car and smoked a bunch of cigarettes. They'll nod and smile, and won't believe a single word. Joe Fellow is a first-rate thief, but he loves to spin a yarn, they'll say.

I tell Doc to get some sleep. Then I head to Madame Simone's. Her establishment is open all night.

Simone greets me personally, seats me in an armchair and brings me strong coffee. The old woman knows more about men than any other woman. More than we know about ourselves.

"Is Monty upstairs?" I ask.

She shrugs, as in: where else would he be?

I'll wait for him here. The important thing is not to fall asleep.

I stare at the faded figurine of the Virgin Mary in the corner for so long that Simone begins to make excuses: it's well overdue to be painted, but there's never enough time.

I don't hear her, just like I don't see the faded Virgin Mary.

I escaped Hell's Island, the most heavily guarded prison in French Guiana, where escape was said to be impossible. Surely I can find a way to leave the peaceful, quiet Guanahani.

———

I HAD ALMOST CHOKED on my rum when César came to me a week ago and told me that Nicki would be made king. The sun had been setting in the blue sea. It had been devilishly beautiful.

I never really came to like Port Henri. It's a shameful feeling, akin to hating one's own father. Or rather, a stepfather. Port Henri accepted me as one of its own. It forgave my sins. Gave me a wife, a son, friends. Fed me and kept me warm. But in seven years I never acclimated. Two things made the town tolerable: its sunsets, and my son.

When the sun had set and Doc began telling me about the *Sek*, I had to go get the second bottle of rum.

We'd known each other for seven years. You might say I owe him my life. That was the only reason I hadn't thrown him out and had politely listened to his nonsense instead.

I had listened and said, "Doc, this is nonsense."

"Have you never wondered why, seven years ago, none of your compatriots survived?"

Of course I had wondered that. Although I tended to frame the question differently: why had I survived?

We had been practically corpses when we reached Port Henri. We'd spent two weeks on the open water in a dilapidated river boat which had nearly sunk in the first storm. Sun and salt had wounded our skins. Dehydration had made me hallucinate. I had thought I was back in my cell on Hell's Island, and that all other prisoners had been released due to amnesty but I had been forgotten in the dank, moldy basement. I had desperately knocked on the bottom of the boat, sending unrequited messages to an imaginary neighbor in the next cell. I had talked to dead people. They had shown up in the boat one by one, glaring at me silently from the next bench. I saw my grandfather, who died before the Great War. Saw my father and mother. Saw the German soldier whom I had shot in the leg. The girl from Amiens whom I had once promised to marry. I was guilty of some slight toward all of them, and this guilt ate at my soul like salt that ate at my skin. I confessed and I prayed, but my only reply was silence.

When I had heard the cries of seagulls, I was certain it was another mirage.

Even the healthiest man might not recover from such a journey. I hadn't been healthy to begin with. I was a pale scarecrow who had crawled into the sunlight after five months spent in the dungeons of Hell's Island, where water flooded my cell up to my waist at high tide.

The three of us had escaped together. Me, Antoine, and a kid whose name I never learned. None of us knew the ways of the mariner. It was a miracle our fragile vessel reached the shores of Guanahani.

Port Henri is a mecca for the convicts of French Guiana. It was the dream that gave me strength on Hell's Island. The oasis in the middle of the watery desert. There were many stories about it, but I only cared about one: unlike Trinidad, Curaçao, and Grenada, it didn't extradite runaway criminals.

When I regained consciousness in the Port Henri hospital, I learned that my compatriots were dead. I was the only one granted the miracle of survival.

Sometimes I wonder if perhaps I'm still there, on the boat, this life a fever-dream of a man dying of dehydration.

"I'll listen to your theories, Doc. But I can't promise to buy into them. You're not yourself today."

"These aren't theories, Joe. When you were brought to the hospital, the first thing they did was check your blood type. Of the three of you, you were the only match. When His Majesty learned of this, he dispatched his personal doctor."

"And who was this doctor?"

"Me, Joe. Me."

Such news after seven years of acquaintanceship, almost friendship. I never suspected Doc to be so complicated a man. Outwardly he seemed a typical old man from Port Henri—dark skinned and short. A regular at Azure. Someone who enjoyed a good drink, telling a good story, and listening to one. Unbelievable.

"Are you saying the others were left to die?"

"No, they were treated. But they weren't treated by me, so their chances weren't good."

"What's so special about my blood?"

It was a surprise that old king Henri VIII, grandfather of the current king, Henri IX, had taken personal interest in my fate. It was almost something to be proud of.

I've always been impressed with the fair structure of the Guanahani monarchy. When the king lacked direct descendants, he chose an heir among the children of regular citizens. In one hundred plus years Guanahani had seen ten different monarchs. Five of them were from the families of miners and fishermen.

It wasn't a big surprise. After all, the first King Henri had been a slave, bore the surname of his owner, and spent half his life roasting under the sun in the sugarcane fields, until the revolution of 1813. They say the rebels killed all the Europeans on the island. They had apologized later, but I suspect those apologies weren't especially sincere.

"You can't imagine, Joe, how important a thing blood is. Augusto Medina, my predecessor in the post of the royal doctor, once said that Henri planned on marrying one of the granddaughters of Queen Victoria. Believe me, had he made that decision, neither the Queen, nor the British parliament, nor the granddaughter herself would have been able to deny him. But Henri changed his mind when he learned that Victoria's descendants suffer from hemophilia."

"Which Henri was this? Fifth or sixth?"

"Joe, you haven't been listening. There had been no fifth or sixth. Just like there had been no second, third, etc. There has ever only been one Henri. One and only."

Heavy steps on the staircase. That must be Monty—Mr. Smith, the American consul.

The consul and I share a complicated relationship. Monty knows that it was I who taught everyone to call him by his first name. It annoys him, but there isn't much he can do. He'd be thrilled to extradite me back home, but he doesn't have the juice.

One thing I like about this portly gentleman: he knows how to keep a poker face. When he sees me, he only raises a single eyebrow.

Simone escorts us to a tiny room that serves as her office. Better than heading upstairs, to one of the bedrooms, I suppose.

I tell Monty Smith about the Sek, about the king, and about my son.

"Fellow, you aren't making any sense. How much have you had to drink?" he asks.

"Not that much. Practically nothing. Listen, Monty, you don't have to believe me. I'm offering you a once-in-a-lifetime deal."

"Why would I piss off King Henri?"

"Because you get *me*. You'll be a hero and finally get off this stupid island. Guanahani is a dead-end assignment for a diplomat. I can't even imagine how you must've screwed up to get this post. But I bet you'll be glad for the opportunity to fix things. To return to the civilized world where you'll be Mr. Smith again. Admit it, you hate when everyone in Port Henri calls you Monty."

"You suffer from delusions of grandeur, Fellow. Back on the mainland you're nothing, zero, an empty space. A deserter, a thief, and an escaped convict who once managed to write a mediocre novel. No one remembers your name."

"My name, dear Monty, is always on the mind of a certain senator who, I hear, stands an excellent chance of becoming the next president."

I seem to have nailed the target. I don't have a lot of skills, but I can read faces with the best of them.

"Why do you think your son will become king? I heard no such thing."

Monty is especially funny when he puffs his cheeks like this.

The American consulate in Port Henri is mostly fiction. Words on a sheet of paper. Smith has a grand total of three marines and two clerks on his staff. Most of his activity is focused here, in Madame Simone's establishment.

"Loose Lips—that is, Francois—and I finished early today. A wasted day, the fish weren't biting. The Cayman Guard were waiting for us on the pier, handed me the official notice. Do you think Caymans joke about such matters?"

Monty frowns. "Okay, Joe. I'll hear you out. But I warn you: I won't do anything that might be interpreted as interfering in the internal affairs of Port Henri."

That's something already. He's ready to discuss a plan, which is all I need. I have a good scheme, so long as Smith agrees to help.

"If you're right and everything I told you is nonsense, then nothing will happen. It would mean that it makes no difference to the king whom to select as his heir. Some other boy will be selected to become Henri X."

"Of course I'm right. Joe, you're a writer, an educated man, even if you're a criminal. How in the world did you come to believe this malarkey?"

I don't believe because of words, or because of Doc César. I won't say it out loud, but it's because of the nightmares.

I never remembered my dreams before. Not even on Hell's Island, in a cell, burning with fever. Not even then.

But now the nightmares come every night. The Port Henri of my nightmares is covered in gray spider silk. Its residents look like scarecrows with empty eyes and stitched mouths. All of their movements are controlled by the spider web—as though they're marionettes in the paws of a spider. The spider is always nearby. Hiding behind the corner. Looking at me through the irises of a passerby. Waving at me with the dead hand of a doll held by a scarecrow child. And then there's the screech. Barely audible but alarming, like whispers coming from the next room, when you're certain no one but you is in the house.

When I leave Simone's it's still dark. But I'm well-familiar with the cunning of Caribbean nights. I have to hurry. I go to visit Jose. Somewhere ahead, the network of his little ragamuffins passes along the news of my impending arrival.

SEVEN YEARS AGO, when I first arrived on the island, Jose courted me in hopes of recruiting a first-rate thief into his operation. To be honest, I was somewhat disappointed that I wasn't the man everyone took me for. I was curious to learn what sort of a heist required a professional thief on an island where no one locks their doors.

My refusal struck a blow to Jose's ego, and then I managed to do so again by stealing his girl. At least that's what Jose thinks. Truth is, Valerie chose me. This woman always gets what she wants.

I enter without knocking and head to the patio, where Jose is waiting for me. The bottle of cachaça and a plate of sliced limes are on the table. Knowing ahead of time about my visit and setting out my favorite drink is a special treat for Jose, a confirmation of his ephemeral power. The island has no organized crime in the usual sense of the word, but Jose is in charge of all the smugglers, unlicensed prospectors, and port beggars.

Jose's skin is dark like charcoal. He looks down on the natives like a crown prince upon his bastard half-brother. Jose's father walked on Africa's soil, breathed its air, and was never a slave. Over a glass of rum, Jose likes to brag that he carries a small part of Africa within him.

"I hear congratulations are in order, Fellow. You're no simple convict anymore. Now you're convict, father of a king."

One doesn't have to beat around the bush with Jose. Without preamble I tell him everything. I watch his obsidian face, hoping to understand his reaction. I'm sure of one thing: Jose isn't surprised.

This scares me more than my nightmares. What if they all know?

Have always known, closed their eyes, hiding behind bright-colored walls, picturesque flags, cocooned in their benevolence so that the darkness of this knowledge doesn't disturb them?

But Jose says: "I've never heard a more foolish tale, Fellow. You stole my woman and now you want to steal a king? It's no wonder you ended up in prison."

He says more, but I can see past his sharp words: Jose will help me. This man truly is made of stone, and his feelings are etched into that stone. Several years are but a moment for stone. He still loves Valerie.

BY THE TIME I return home, it's almost morning. I enter the bedroom. It always smells of cinnamon and lavender. Valerie is asleep.

Nicki is sleeping next to her.

I'm a bad person. Unlike most people, I recognize this fact about myself. Some will say it's just pride talking, but to me, one sin more or one sin less doesn't make much of a difference.

I was seventeen when I killed a man for the first time. It was an honest fight. My opponent, should fortune have been on his side, would have done the same without hesitation. The argument was over a woman. I don't recall her face, her smell, or her voice. Only her name. Agnes. She couldn't seem to choose between the two of us, so she gave herself to both of us.

This other man was the son of a senator. Even then I didn't put my faith in a trial by jury, so I didn't wait to be arrested. I hired on to the first ship heading for Europe. Decided to become a writer. But first, I had to experience more of life. In France I volunteered for the war. I was no ideologue. I didn't care about the Germans, the French, the English and all their politics. I wanted to get to know war. One battle taught me everything I wanted to know about the subject. I deserted. Headed to Paris, wrote a stupid novel, which to my then surprise and current regret, was published in a small print run. I was so proud of myself. After the book came out I thought people would begin recognizing me in the streets. They didn't. I bought my novel, reread it, and my disappointment was limitless. I decided to write another.

Instead, I got myself thrown in prison.

When Doc César nursed me back to life, I was certain that my time had come. Finally, I knew life and all the things I wanted to write about. I had experienced adventure enough for ten men, first hand. And, of course, I was very much inspired by Port Henri in those early days.

Port Henri is the sort of quiet place every writer dreams of. The writer tells themselves: one day I'll go to a nice tropical island, sit under the palms and listen to the cries of seagulls as I shape all the thoughts that have accumulated in my mind into beautiful sentences.

Lies.

No one has ever written anything of note in a place like Port Henri.

I'm a murderer, a deserter, a worthless writer, and an escaped convict. But I hadn't managed to commit my worst crime.

Seven years is a long time. Ever since I left Illinois at fifteen, I never spent more than three years in any one place. I'd intended to leave Guanahani several times. I had no qualms about leaving Valerie. When she'd told me she was pregnant, I'd decided I'd wait for her to give birth. I'd wanted to meet my son and leave with the memory of him.

But having held newborn Nicki in my hands I knew I would never leave him.

Valerie opens her eyes.

"Valerie, do you recall what Padre Anjel said when we got married?"

"Lots of things. Once Padre begins to talk, it's not easy to stop him."

Wrong opening. Padre Anjel isn't an authority for Valerie. The old man likes to drink but isn't any good at it. There's no better way to disappoint a woman.

"There was something from St. Peter," I say. If St. Peter isn't an authority for her, then my plans are ruined.

She stares at the ceiling, remembering.

"Husbands ought to love their wives as their own bodies. Do you love me, Joe Fellow?"

"I love you, Valerie." A familiar lie. Love is a word, and words, as is well known, were invented by women. "What else? There was something about an obedient wife."

"As the Church submits to Christ, so also wives should submit to their husbands in everything." Valerie frowns.

"Exactly. I've never demanded such obedience from you, and I won't now. But I'm going to beg. I beg you to be a good wife and ask no questions. Promise me."

She nods. Good.

"Get dressed. Pack Nicki's things."

"Something happened," she says. It's not a question.

"When you're ready, we'll go visit Mr. Monty Smith."

"He's disgusting."

"It's not for long. You and Nicki are going to take a boat to Florida."

"Without you?"

Clever girl.

"I have to stay behind for a day or two. I'll catch up." This lie comes almost effortlessly.

Valerie's eyes grow wide. I know what she's going to say. Two years ago I tried to leave Guanahani—along with Valerie and my son—and take an English ship to Wales, where they say there's no better reference than being convicted by the French. Valerie refused. She said no seafaring adventures until Nicki turned at least ten years old. Valerie knew what they do with children aboard ships.

Every ship has a special person whose job is to find homeless boys in port and recruit them by promising work, food, and a hammock. Hungry demons who live in the ocean demand tributes from every ship that dares a cross-continental journey. Small dark-skinned children are mercilessly thrown into the ocean while rich Europeans dance on the upper decks to the Caribbean music. The bodies of those children forever wander the ocean floor, searching for the way home. Worse yet, some of them find it.

I don't want to hear her agonize about that again. Such tales make me nauseous. So I rush to say, "Jose is going to escort you."

I pause, but there's no reaction. She's stone-faced. It seems she has realized that things are serious.

PORT HENRI IS WAKING up early. In the morning it looks like a shiny toy or a bright picture in a children's book. One-story houses are painted in every bright color imaginable.

We walk past the barber where I get my hair cut each week. Raul waves his greetings. Old men sit on wooden stools outside the barbershop and discuss baseball as they wait their turn. In front of their houses, owners put out tables filled with merchandise. Everyone in Port Henri sells everything. Dried herbs, rocks of every shape, fruit, spices, painted clay figures of animals, jars and pots, bottles with lizards preserved in formaldehyde, stuffed birds, amulets for all occasions, home-rolled cigars, and home-distilled cachaça. During siesta the sellers rest on their patios, leaving the merchandise in the street.

Valerie stops in front of a friendly dark-skinned old woman, picks out a blue necklace and begins to haggle with her in earnest. I whisper in her ear that we're in a hurry.

Valerie tells me, *"Husbands ought to love their wives as their own bodies,"* and I pay for the necklace.

Nicki is enthralled by the wooden knives set out right on the ground by another seller. I buy him one. I figure he'll have something to remember me by.

We pass by an old mustached greengrocer. He pushes his cart slowly, deliberately, as though each step is measured in advance to help him last the entire day. A young man on a bicycle races past us. When he sees Valerie he begins to show off; he lets go off the handles and stretches, interlocking his hands behind his head. He nearly rides into a tree.

I ask for today's newspaper at the cigarette stand.

"They haven't come in yet," says the merchant. "Rumor is, the king has selected an heir. Something like this has to be written about using special words, so they're taking their time."

I look around. Could it be that no one is spying on us? They must be, otherwise this entire performance is for naught. I notice a dark-skinned sailor in a blue uniform who takes a suspiciously long time studying his reflection in a store window. He doesn't look away even when a gaggle of girls in airy, bright clothes showing a lot of skin pass him by. No sailor would resist staring at a sexy woman.

So they are spying on us, then. Good.

We turn toward the consulate, toward the old Spanish quarter which was built back in the days of Cortez, when the town was still called Santa Anna. The colors are less bright here, the lines more severe. Dark walls stare in opprobrium at neighboring streets.

VALERIE and my son are on the patio, flipping through a world atlas. Every once in a while Valerie sighs theatrically. Smith and I are sitting in the study.

Smith tugs nervously at his mustache. He is sweating profusely.

"When will your man be here?"

"Soon."

When I asked him to send a marine to the underground tunnel that led to the southern piers from the basement of the consulate, Monty gasped in surprise.

"How do you know about the tunnel?"

"Please, Monty. The entire town knows about it."

Jose had left in the morning to get the boat. I'm beginning to worry too, but I'm not letting it show.

An hour ago Doc César had joined us. Knowing that he was going to worry, I'd called him from the consulate. Doc brought a basket of food for Valerie and Nick. Idiot that I am, I hadn't even thought about packing food.

Finally, I hear steps in the kitchen. A marine who had been sent to the pier comes in. Jose follows him.

Jose's shirt is soaked in blood.

"The guy didn't want to give up the boat," Jose explains. He sees the grimace on Smith's face. "Be calm, Yankee. Everything is all right. He's going to live."

While César tends to Jose's wound, I pull Smith aside.

"Send at least one marine along," I ask of him. "You can see Jose isn't doing great."

Smith doesn't budge.

"No marines, Fellow. It's one thing to host an American citizen in the consulate. It's another to assist in the kidnapping of the future king of Guanahani. Do you understand the difference?"

Damn politician. Of course, he won't let me go, either. The plan I proposed is too appealing to him.

Doc César says, "I'll go with them."

He's a saint of a man. Useless in a fight, but it still makes me feel better.

I say goodbye to them in the basement. I kiss Valerie and tell her everything will be all right. I hug Nick.

I tell Smith to lock the door and to order the marines not to let anyone in. Under any circumstances.

***

By nightfall Monty feels more confident.

"Drink?" he offers. "I'll have one. It seems all deadlines are past. No one is searching for you, except maybe a psychiatrist. What a story you made up, Fellow! I'm not upset. I have you, and an excellent anecdote to tell."

"Shut up," I tell him.

He shuts up. I think I can hear the sound of footsteps over broken glass.

Imagine you're having tea on the veranda with your favorite aunt when you realize there's a pack of velociraptors hiding in the back yard. There's no evidence of this other than a strange whistling noise, but that could be anything—perhaps a neighbor kid who snuck onto your property to pick apples. But no, you're absolutely sure: it's veloci-raptors. You look at your aunt and realize she feels the same thing. The world around you hasn't changed, the tea tastes the same, the air smells of autumn and fallen apples, but the velociraptors are about to charge from around the corner.

That's how I feel now. Nothing appears to have changed—the lights haven't gone out or even blinked. Birds are chirping in the palm trees. But I realize: it's beginning.

Smith plays the role of the aunt to perfection. His head shrinks into his shoulders and he shudders like a bird. He regains control of himself and moves toward the door.

"Don't you dare open it, Monty," I whisper.

"Nonsense," he says.

He opens the door wide and catches a bullet in his stomach.

The Cayman guards enter the study. Through the door frame behind them I see a marine on the ground, with a surprised expres-sion and a cut throat.

THE ROAD LEADS UPHILL, which means I'm being taken to the citadel.

The citadel is the highest point of Guanahani. The fortress built by the first King Henri after the revolution. They say more slaves lie dead in the foundation of the citadel than perished in the war with the French. Even so, the residents of Port Henri are proud of their fortress.

In my dreams the citadel is the huge ink blot inside of which hides the spider.

In my seven years in Port Henri I've never quite seen the citadel. It's difficult to see it from the town below. Even on the brightest of days, the sky seems to find a few clouds to obscure it. On a rare day when there are no clouds, the citadel looks like one itself. Its walls are painted blinding white.

The truck shakes as it traverses the boulders on the road, but I don't care. I think about little Nick, and about Valerie. In a few hours they'll be in Key West.

The truck stops. Cayman guards roughly toss me outside, and I scrape my knees and palms on the rocks. It's nothing compared to what awaits me. Probably execution by firing squad. I'm surprised to realize that I'm not afraid at all.

I look around. Close up the fortress doesn't look all white. Its stones are covered with red moss. The walls are three times as tall as an average person. This wouldn't be an easy place to escape from. Good thing I don't plan on running.

A WOODEN COT is set against stone walls of my cell. The moss turns to dust and falls with the barest touch. A narrow window is situated just below the ceiling. If I stand on my toes I can just make out the shoes of the Cayman guards by the lights of their torches.

This isn't the worst dungeon I've ever been in. At least it's dry and devoid of woodlice.

The door creaks open behind my back. I don't turn around, preserving what's left of my dignity.

"Leave us. I wish to talk to him alone."

A woman's voice. That intrigues me. I turn around.

She's wearing a severe dark dress, closed to the neck. Something that's gone out of fashion two generations ago. A wooden cross dangles on a strap of leather over the dress. Her hands are gloved. She places a kerosene lamp on the cot. She looks like Valerie, but older by about fifteen years. Her light-brown skin, blue almond eyes, ink-black hair. The Port Henri women are very beautiful. Sun mixed with spices, sea salt, and clear sky. This island has collected the best of many different peoples and gifted it to its daughters.

There's only one woman for whom all doors of this fortress are opened. Camilla. Cami, as the locals call her. The daughter of old king Henri, who died six years ago. The mother of the current King Henri.

I sit down on the cot, breaking etiquette. It's a tiny, indulgent form of rebellion.

She's silent. I don't rush her. Perhaps she wants to see the man who voluntarily refused the throne for his son? Who knows what's in the woman's head?

"Do you know what the Sek is?"

The question catches me by surprise, but I don't let it show. I shrug. "César told me."

She frowns at the mention of his name. Is it anger? Contempt?

"You know the word, but the meaning escapes you."

"I don't believe in the afterlife."

"The Sek isn't an afterlife, Mr. Fellow. The Sek is like a sealed room where you relive the worst moments of your life, time after time."

What was the worst moment of my life? The cell filled with woodlice? The boat shared with dying men? The battle of the Somme? The moment my blade entered the heart of a senator's son?

"If there's a hell, we'll all get there. I've never met a man who managed to remain innocent by the time he reached adulthood."

"My son was seven when old Henri decided it was time to begin a new life. How much do you think he had managed to sin?"

I don't know what to tell her. Now that Jose had taken Valerie and Nick away from here, all of this seems like an illusion. Even the memory of Consul Smith's death is uncertain. Perhaps I have gone mad.

"You're a fool to think your family is safe. No one ever leaves this town without Henri's knowledge. Everything happens according to his plan. Every time. If he has decided to steal your son's body, then he will. You won't be able to stop him. Your boy's soul will go to the Sek, following the souls of all the others. They'll wander there forever. Think about that, convict. Eternity is worse than death."

Damn, I think. Word for word, she's repeating what César had told me. What if they're in cahoots? Feeding a bunch of lies to a trusting gringo. Is all of this about the throne? Perhaps she wants to become queen after her son dies? She could have convinced the Doc to spin some tales and set all this in motion.

I nearly slap my forehead. What a simple answer. Goddamned Occam's Razor. All of this adds up, even the delay in the morning papers. I drive away thoughts of nightmares and Monty Smith's death.

If this turns out to be a run-of-the-mill palace intrigue, I'll be quite relieved.

"Why have you come?" I ask, stressing frustration in my voice.

Cami looks at the door fearfully, as though she hears some distant sound. There's nothing there, woman. No one needs us. She comes closer and whispers: "I never loved my father. He's not easy to love. It's like loving this fortress, with its darkness and rot. But I was an obedient daughter. I had borne him an heir. If I knew then what he had planned I would have killed my son with my own hands. Do you believe me?"

She asks the question, but doesn't seem to expect an answer. She smells like Valerie, of vanilla and cinnamon.

"He told me everything after the coronation. Pride, Mr. Fellow. He sought a witness. Someone to appreciate his greatness. He's frustrated that everyone around him sees only a child. He needs fear. He came to me and told me in detail of everyone he had sent to the Sek. He told me that entering another's body is akin to rape. He said this in a voice of a seven-year-old child, looking up at me with the clear eyes of my son. Can you imagine?"

Fine, I'll play her game. "Why didn't you kill him? It's easy, especially now. His illness has done half the work for you."

"He forbade it," she says, a bitter smile on her lips. "His power is limitless. You'll murder your own mother, if he orders it."

"You could've told someone. Like you're telling me now."

"He forbade me to talk about it outside the walls of the citadel. Left himself an opportunity to be amused. Because of me, three people have died. He forced a young Cayman, a god-fearing Catholic, to open his own veins. He forbade the second man to drink. He locked me in the room with him for several days, along with many jugs of water."

"What happened to the third man?"

Why do I ask this? I don't want to know. None of it can be true. Just ravings of an insane woman.

"He killed the third one by my hand."

Cami says this evenly, with no emotion in her voice.

She gingerly removes her cross.

"Don't move," she says. "Be still. He didn't forbid me from coming here. Didn't forbid me from giving you a gift. Lower your head."

I obey. I've learned not to argue with the insane. Cami puts the string with the cross on my neck. The silk of her gloves tickles my ears.

She holds me by my wrists. Leans in. Whispers: "Don't touch this cross unless you want to die."

"Magic again?"

"No, foolish Yankee. It's poison. If it gets into the bloodstream, it'll kill in seconds. An adult or a child. Think about that, Mr. Fellow. Think hard. You can't kill Henri. But if you kill your son, Henri will be stuck in his current body. And then he'll die. If that happens, all of them will be free. Do you understand? All his victims, free. He'll go to the Sek in their place."

"Don't mess with me, woman. I'll never kill my son."

She stares into my eyes, as if trying to see the contents of my mind through them. I know this look. It's how I look at people.

Read me, woman. I have nothing to hide.

She lets go off my wrist. She says, regretfully: "No. You will not."

And then the door creaks and she's gone. The women of Port Henri are like the tropical nights. They arrive when you least expect them, and leave before you can come to understand them.

I shake my head. Was she ever here? I reach for the cross but stop myself from touching it.

I CAN TELL time pretty well when I'm sober. I learned this on Hell's Island. Time can be measured in breaths, heartbeats, steps of the guards.

The door opens again an hour and a half after Cami leaves. The grim Cayman tells me to follow him.

We go through a maze of corridors, descending and ascending again via staircases. This fortress had been built by a madman. Somehow I'm certain I'm about to meet the king. The newspapermen describe him as a kind child, very polite and considerate. I'm sure he'll gently inquire as to why I'd caused all this drama, kidnapping my own son. I have no idea what I'll tell him. I feel like an idiot, to be honest. Much worse than when the French policemen had accused me of murdering that old man and I responded by mumbling something about seeking inspiration for writing a novel.

We arrive. The room doesn't look like a child's bedroom, and even less like a royal hall. A low-hanging lamp with a dozen candles barely illuminates the center of the room. The walls and ceiling drown in darkness. The room is empty. Our steps echo.

The Cayman pushes me so I enter the circle of light. He remains by the door.

A small silhouette moves toward me from the darkness. A boy in a wheelchair. King Henri IX.

The residents of Port Henri are in awe of their king. He was only seven when the old Henri died. His illness has turned him into a skeleton. His dark skin has acquired a greenish tint. His eyes are sunk deep. For a moment he looks more like an old man than a child.

"Thank you, Jorge. You may go."

His voice is low and weak. Very boyish. But in it I hear pure, unadulterated power.

After Jorge leaves and closes the door behind him, Henri says: "The Caymans are loyal to me, but they're like children. Never tell children the entire truth, Joe. Their souls are too fragile."

The axles of his wheelchair emit a barely audible screech. I recognize this sound. I've heard it in my nightmares.

He's right next to me. I realize that I'm lost.

I believe. I believe every word of what César had told me. Of what Cami had told me.

I could kill him right now. But Henri says, "Stay in place," and my legs refuse to move. They feel like lead.

Henri smiles winningly, like a child. His eyes are blue. Just like Valerie's. Just like my son's.

I don't want to look into these eyes, but I can't turn away. It's as though an enormous hand is holding me by the back of my head, forcing me to look. As if I'm falling into the abyss. No twelve-year-old boy can have eyes like these. Not even a hundred-year-old man could. I'm staring into the succession of centuries.

"You shouldn't have staged this circus with the consulate. Smith's death is on your conscience. Come to the window, Joe. Look outside."

I watch a pickup truck drive up to the gates. Valerie, César, and two Caymans climb out. One of them is holding my sleeping son.

"No one leaves Port Henri without me knowing, Joe."

All of this had been for nothing.

"My plan worked, as it always does. You see, Joe, I don't need your son. I'm too tired of being a child. To be five again? No, thanks. Let him grow up a bit first. For now, I'm going to be you. The father of the king. That was the plan, Joe. All I needed from you was to believe. And Doctor César, a man of immense value in every sense of the word, has provided that for me."

The Caymans come in, followed by César. Valerie follows, holding the now awake Nick by his hand. She runs up to me, ignoring the king. She wants to hug me but I catch her by the shoulders and kiss her forehead.

"They killed Jose," she whispers. "He shot one of them in the leg, but there were too many of them. They cut his throat and threw him into the water, to the sharks. It was a bad death."

A bad man died a bad death for the woman who didn't love him. If there really is an afterlife, I hope this will outweigh many of the other things he had done.

"I think," says Henri sweetly, "that your wife and son should rest after their journey. What do you say, Joe? You'll see each other again soon. All will be well."

"Go with the Caymans, Valerie." I take her hand into mine. "I love you. And I love Nick. I love you both."

Perhaps for the first time, I'm telling the truth.

"Belief is a funny thing," says Henri after they leave. "If you didn't believe in my powers, I wouldn't have been able to stop you from killing me. Have you heard about President Harding's death? It was quite painful. He made two mistakes. First, he wouldn't leave Guanahani alone. You Yankees love to appropriate others' belongings. You know this better than most, thief. Do you want to know what his second mistake was? He *believed*. He believed that his death was within my power, and it became true. Now I have no problems with America. Harding's successors remember what happens to disobedient presidents."

I don't give a damn about Harding. I stare at César, who is rummaging through his medicine bag. I'm trying to understand how he's so calm. Is he under Henri's power or is he helping him of his own volition?

"Listen carefully, Joe. This is an order," says Henri. "Come closer, and look at me."

My feet make several steps against my will. My head turns. I try to close my eyes, but I can't.

"Do you know why I showed you your wife and son, Joe? I wanted to be certain that you won't pull some sort of trick at the last moment. I want to make sure that you let me in, voluntarily. I can't order this. You have to let me in yourself. I hate it when they try to resist. Fools. I can't be stopped. I'll break past any door if I have to. Have you ever had to break a door, Joe? It's somewhat painful, but worse, there's this feeling like you're not respected. Like they didn't prepare for your arrival. Didn't tidy up. They twitch and scream. Then I have to clean up myself. Wash off the blood. Repair the door. That isn't nice, Joe. You can't treat guests that way. That's why I like children. They're so nice, so trusting. It's easy to fool them. But I'll be honest with you, Joe. Our dear doctor is going to finish the necessary procedures and you're going to be a good boy. You'll open the door, let me in, and head into the Sek. The doctor told you about the Sek, yes? I won't lie, you won't like it there. Just think about your wife and son. It could be much worse for them here. Do you understand me, Joe? Nod if you understand."

I nod.

César picks up a curved knife and approaches the king. Henri tilts his head forward. The doctor makes a cut along the nape, just under the hairline. Then he retrieves a syringe and quickly draws blood from Henri's vein.

He walks toward me, blood dripping from the syringe across the floor. I let César make a shallow cut on my neck.

I wonder, what will happen with the body of the child in the wheelchair when the spirit of Henri leaves it to occupy mine?

It's as though Henri can read my mind.

"Don't worry," he says. "He'll last until the coronation. Just like Consul Smith, by the way. Have you heard of chickens who seem alive even after you cut off their heads? They run. They worry. You wouldn't guess that they're dead. People aren't much different from chickens. So long as you know a few tricks. César, leave us."

César backs up toward the door.

"That's it," says Henri. "Wait for me, Joe. I'll be there soon."

His eyes gloss over. His head falls onto his chest, and then the boy's entire body falls forward until he's lying on the floor, unconscious.

Then nothing happens.

Except for the spider which climbs from the cut in Henri's nape. This is impossible. Spiders don't live in human heads. Yet here it is, in front of me. It descends to the stone floor and runs toward me along the path of blood left for him by the doctor. If I could only take a few steps, the spider would never find me. But Henri forbade me from walking away.

That's okay. I have another plan.

The spider jumps onto the hem of my trousers and climbs up my back. I feel its cold legs on my nape.

It's time.

Once I feel the spider inside me, binding, I grab hold of the cross gifted to me by Queen Cami.

I hope, my dear, that your poison is truly strong.

Of all the deaths, I chose the most ridiculous.

I could've died from the knife wound to the heart.

I could've caught a German bullet in the battle of the Somme.

Could've perished in the cell of Hell's Island.

Could've drowned in the vast expanse of the Atlantic Ocean.

My last thought is: who knows? Perhaps that's what happened. Perhaps I died a long, long time ago.

THIS STORY originally appeared in *Galaxy's Edge*.

K.A. TERYNA IS an award-winning author and illustrator from Russia. English translations of her stories have appeared in *F&SF*, *Asimov's*, *Apex*, *Strange Horizons*, *Samovar*, *Podcastle*, *Galaxy's Edge*, and elsewhere. She lives in Moscow. Her website is www.k-a-teryna.blogspot.com.

ALEX SHVARTSMAN'S translations from Russian have appeared in *Tor.com*, *F&SF*, *Clarkesworld*, *Asimov's*, and many other venues.

COUSIN ENTROPY

Michèle Laframboise, translated from the French by N. R. M. Roshak

(Shortlisted for 2021 Rosetta Awards)

SOMETIMES I THINK that all God did to create our universe was to burp it out, then let it inflate like a balloon.

In that first fraction of a second, the compressed matter of His Burp sprayed out its offspring in waves. First came a crowd of misbehaving neutrinos, followed by a flood of photons.

The universal balloon became transparent. As it swelled, the thick quark soup cooled enough to settle into atoms and stars.

But along with His Divine Burp, God ejected laws, which He stuck like price tags onto our slowly expanding cloud... laws which included a meddlesome pair of cousins, Enthalpy and Entropy.

The cousins' fingerprints are on everything: on the atoms being forged in the hearts of stars, on black holes, on galaxies, on dust clouds, even on planets—including the planet that birthed, and bid farewell to, our species.

Cousin Enthalpy's always on her best behavior, but bursting with energy. She gives what she gets. A joule for a joule. I imagine her as vast and golden, her face perfectly symmetrical.

Cousin Entropy is another story, though. She is a wastrel who skims a little off of every energy exchange, a bit like the percentage that banks once levied on every transaction. And what does she give in return? Nothing but chaos.

Cousin Entropy's effect on the universe is like the effect of a little kid on a nice, tidy room: you come back to find all your stuff dumped on the floor.

But when I picture Cousin Entropy, I don't see a little kid. I see a great, greedy mouth with blood-red lips—not that I've *had* lips, as such, for the past twenty billion years—sucking the energy out of the universe with a straw. Just a mouth: no teeth, no tongue, and especially no eyes.

Because, if she had eyes, Cousin Entropy would see the dead end that she's dragging us all toward.

Oh, how I hate her.

Of course, Cousin Entropy isn't inherently bad. She's just a perfectionist. She wants everything to be perfectly equal, uniform, and desolate.

Desolate and cold.

I BLAME Cousin Entropy for the mess I'm in.

And she's also to blame for the mess the over-inflated Universe is in.

Thanks to Cousin Enthalpy, the Universe's been cooling as it expands. But, no thanks to Cousin Entropy, it's also been falling into degeneracy, blurring the lines between types of particles. Greedy Cousin Entropy siphons heat from the nuclei of heavy atoms that don't have enough energy left to get cracking (in any sense of the term).

She's the one pushing the Universe's temperature down, down, down toward the point of no return, where all that's left will be nuclei drifting in disorganized isolation, sluggish electrons clinging to them like an icy mantle in the absolute-zero vacuum.

It'll be a neat and tidy vacuum, utterly free of radiation. Not a single stray ray.

It'll be lifeless.

There are no bright stars within sight, now. Oh, there are plenty of red dwarfs, those ubiquitous nobodies crowding our fading galaxy, but their glow's as dim as a failing flashlight.

And even those dim lights are going out. The nearest ones are spinning into a final, fatal dance that will land them in the vast black hole beneath my feet.

Not that I have *feet* to speak of. But that doesn't stop me from joining the dance.

Okay, so I'm staying a prudent distance from the supermassive black hole (don't mess with power, as the historian said). Just shy of the event horizon.

Here's the thing about dancing this close to the event horizon, though: like it or not, the rest of the universe speeds up around me. The closer I get, the faster the dying stars dance.

ONE OF MY buddies decided to take matters into his own hands, to end himself before Cousin Entropy ends us all for good.

He slipped over the event horizon and let himself fall into the black heart of the galaxy, gaze turned outward.

He had time to tell us how beautiful it was to see the remaining stars darting like moths, flitting and spinning faster and faster...

I don't know if he'll still be watching when the last stars go out.

But if I adjust my scopes and aim a precision laser just right, its light falls on his round body, which, for me, is endlessly falling.

And he isn't alone.

There are so many celestial and post-human bodies piled up at the event horizon that they form a shining vortex of memories.

I said "he." I could've said "she," or "ze." Gender doesn't mean much to the UnAttached.

I'VE BEEN around for about twenty billion *years*—an obsolete unit, given that the ancient Sun long ago met its dramatic end, taking several inner planets with it. Even what remained, an insignificant little dwarf, has long since cooled into a dark, mute ball.

Eternity has lost its meaning, now that the center of our once-vibrant Galaxy is nothing more than an ocean of dead dust, slowly swirling into an invisible singularity.

For now, the remaining friction between bits of dust still gives off a little light, a trickle of heat, which I soak in with all my pores.

My body's well-constructed.

Too well.

As the eons passed, we UnAttached added everything to our bodies that we could possibly need, in order to survive anything.

Even the nothingness.

Few of us still remember the distant era when our species lived on the surface of a single rocky planet... except through HearSay.

AFTER THE FIRST humans tamed fire, they sheltered in boxes made of wood and dirt.

When they tamed Cousin Enthalpy, they harnessed her and channeled some of her energy into lifting off into space, Detaching themselves from planet-bound life.

They sealed themselves in metal boxes at first, out of habit. Pressurized, shielded tin cans, to protect their bodies from the steady rain of live, energy-rich particles that danced through the universe at the time.

Gradually, medicine and micro-robotics came together to change those soft, weak Attached bodies into bodies that could live outside the boxes.

That first generation of UnAttached was glorious!

They still had arms, legs, even *genitals,* all proving their attachment to the primal human form.

They gave themselves radiation-shielded torsos and skulls. They spun their hair of magnetic wire that waved and curled in the vacuum, tracing out its own sign language.

They gave themselves eyes that could see the whole electromagnetic spectrum, which spawned a rash of exciting discoveries.

And they gave themselves wings, vast nets that unfolded from their backs to catch the same flux of energetic particles that had so threatened their soft, Attached bodies. Cosmic rays turned from threat—to dinner!

That first generation still needed boxes for *in vitro* gestation and birth, but they were nearly there.

Their first UnAttached newborns were turfed out of their boxes straight into orbit, like baby birds being pushed out of the nest. They stretched their rumpled little wings and flew straight into the waiting arms of their parents.

And their freshly-minted UnAttached minds came with added storage: memory banks filled with HearSay. Even back then, HearSay's store of accumulated human knowledge was a deep well that we UnAttached could sip from at will.

These fresh UnAttached had also been grafted with new organs that let them communicate without vocal cords. And their advanced polymeric skin tingled with new sensations.

Meanwhile, the Attached stayed firmly planted on the ground, marveling at the dance of these cosmic butterflies that glowed bright as the aurora in the solar wind.

IN ALL THE EXCITEMENT, everyone forgot about Cousin Entropy.

Humanity had discovered her, measured her, calculated her slow drain on the Universe's energy. And we had decided her effect was negligible. We dismissed her thieving ways as a minor counterpoint to the glorious harmony of the Universe.

But Cousin Entropy never forgot about us.

HUMANS HAD BEEN SO accustomed to life with a horizon, that that horizontal bar had soaked into all our art—into our very souls. Many people just couldn't handle life in three dimensions, with stars as the only scenery.

None of the colonists who'd settled off-Earth planets wanted to become UnAttached. They'd struggled too hard to keep their fleshly bodies alive to sacrifice them in exchange for life in the vacuum.

Thus began the First Division. We harassed each other, for a while: UnAttached versus Attached.

Off-color jokes made the rounds. Did you hear the one about the UnAttached who fell for an Attached? He convinced her to climb to the top of the tallest tower for a single kiss...

But then the Second Division began. And it was even less amusing than the jokes.

TO UNATTACH, we had to learn to change our bodies and our brains to survive in the vacuum. And we decided: why stop there? We had developed the power to become anything we could imagine.

Our clever UnAttached scientists lengthened our telomeres. They peppered our chromosomes with novel proteins. They multiplied our neurons, with compound interest. And finally, they tweaked the speed with which messages fly down our axons from neuron to neuron, until they could control the very passage of time—subjectively, at least.

That last came in handy for flitting between solar systems without suffering the twin depredations of old age and boredom.

To hell with the deterioration and decay Cousin Entropy had planned for us!

And the light-speed cosmic speed limit is no more than an inconvenience, when thousands of years pass in one long blink.

But our extended lifespan was the seed for the second great Division of humanity.

***

THE SECOND GENERATION of UnAttached made themselves useful: they ferried box after box of hibernating Attached to their future colonies, like seeds waiting to root and cover the planetary surface with roiling masses.

The UnAttached sprouted reactors for the journey, and shields to let them shrug off cosmic rays and debris.

And after dropping off their cargo of Attached, they simply traveled on, drinking starlight and stowing away knowledge.

There was rarely any discord among the UnAttached, given our reduced needs and our diaspora's dispersion across parsecs.

Several of us chose glorious solitude, drowsing alone in distant nebulas.

Little by little, we lost track of the Attached.

Their brief lives—longer than baseline, but only by two or three centuries—flickered by too quickly for us. We couldn't really get attached to any individual Attached. It would've been like befriending an ant.

That's not to say we *forgot* them. The deep pools of HearSay still held the memories of these grains of human dust.

The UnAttached shed crystal tears when the supernova formerly known as the Sun incinerated humanity's cradle.

Alone, or with another UnAttached, I watched stars evolve before my eyes. Each nova was its star's apotheosis, which we would've applauded if we'd had the appropriate appendages.

I also attended the birth and death of civilizations. Tens of thousands of human anthills rose up and crumbled. Sparring empires bloodied every arm of the galaxy.

A new wave of Attached, disgusted by the unending wars, rose up to join us in the peace of the void, their bodies barely recognizable as human.

WE'VE FIXED ourselves up pretty well since the butterfly generation.

Those long-ago cosmic butterflies wouldn't have been able to hover, as I can, over the vast whirlpool at the center of the galaxy, slurping up the X-rays shooting from the poles of the supermassive black hole's accretion disk, while contemplating the Hawking radiation that's slowly evaporating that black hole into nothing.

A baseline Attached, if there were any of those left, would be like a speck of dust on my skin. And a first-generation UnAttached would be like a fly squashed on the windshield of my eyes.

These anachronistic comparisons bubble up to me from the vast depths of HearSay that are pooled within me.

An Attached's puny three pounds of brainmeat wouldn't be up to the task of constructing an inner life spanning eons. And its mere ninety billion neurons would be pathetically inadequate for storing all the memories of our extensive past.

Paradoxically, it was these recently-UnAttached, the ones fleeing the galactic wars, who'd really given us the drive to *remember* our species' history.

I contemplate the cosmos—or what's left of it—with the multiplicity of eyes dotting the oblate spheroid of my body.

About my eyes: forget the lashes, irises, and pupils of old-timey bodies. In their place I have dark wells, endlessly searching. And why would I make do with a mere two eyes? I have over eight million with which to sweep the depths of space, in every EM frequency, with complete efficiency.

Same goes for the angelically long hair of the first UnAttached.

Forget hair. It's gone. And my bald skin is wrinkled, to help me capture the kinetic energy of every speck of stardust that hits me.

An old UnAttached like myself is eons past aesthetics. I look more like a planet than anything else.

I cast nets of carbon atoms to tap into the immense source of radiation at the center of the galaxy.

And I use as little energy as possible. Ever conscious of the red ink on the universal balance sheet, I forbid myself from feeding too much to Cousin Entropy.

***

EVERY SOCIETY IS ENRICHED by the arrival of new members. Despite the fears of a few of the first and second generation of UnAttached, most of us welcomed and helped the refugees of the galactic wars.

It was no small task. We had to re-accelerate our subjective time to be able to communicate with this third generation, until they adapted.

But it was worth it.

It was these refugees that, rich with the fruits of thousands of years of scientific progress, brought us new techniques for probing the innards of the universe.

These new techniques harnessed not Cousin Enthalpy, but a weighty aunt: Gravity herself.

But that's not all. In negotiating the unending conflicts of their Attached era, the refugees had learned the wisdom of *listening*. Now they stretched their ears out again, taking advantage of their newly slowed subjective time to listen in a new way.

And they found that the galaxy was alive with conversation.

The play of dark spots and jets, of ion flux and gravity waves, the heart-song of supernovae: these made up the chatter of hundreds of billions of entities.

If our species' limited brains had been able to self-assemble from chemical stews of carbon and hydrogen, with impulsively sparking neurons... then imagine the scope of a consciousness that assembled itself from an immense stew of molten metal!

The stars were talking to each other.

THE GALAXY WAS A GREAT CITY, in which spun hot blue divas, yellow main-sequence conformists, diamond-bright little neutron stars, drab red dwarfs, and silent black holes.

There were lively stars, packed into the noisy downtown. And there were lonely stars, moping in the suburbs of the far-flung tips of the galactic arms. The latter got the occasional visit from itinerant comets, though these made feckless messengers, prone to letting themselves be captured by weightier celestial bodies.

Some stars were too generous. The massive Wolf-Rayet stars were burning their helium at both ends, creating a vast stellar wind that carried their outer layers away at 2000 km/s. Their neighbors waited patiently for them to come to a violent end.

At the other end of the social spectrum, a huge mass of brown and black dwarfs were chilling in obscurity.

Between these two extremes, the yellow stars wondered about the meaning of life, traded black-hole jokes, and bragged about the size of their planetary systems.

When we UnAttached managed, by dint of carefully-tuned emissions, to communicate with the stars, they were astonished to discover that one of their planets, although now vanished, had first borne this progeny. The news took a hundred million years to spread to every galactic neighborhood.

But the most emotional moments, for us, were when we overheard the stars measuring the widening distance to the galactic cities where their sisters spun, and mourning the ever-increasing delay in their responses.

Cousin Entropy was working in the shadows.

THE UNIVERSE COULDN'T CARE LESS about Attached and UnAttached, blue giants, or red dwarfs. It just kept on plugging on its own deliberate project of expansion.

And the temperature of the vast, infinite void kept on dropping.

Cousin Entropy wants us all to be the same, everywhere.

Frozen.

Completely frozen.

THE BEAUTIFUL BLUE giants were the first to disappear.

One by one, their swan songs shone out across space. In death, these superstars spread the rosy veils of new stellar nurseries across parsecs.

The newborns that sprung from these nurseries were too lightweight to become anything more than yellow dwarfs.

The stars' conversations took on a more anguished tone. Their sisters in other, receding cities were now too distant to respond to their final messages.

The black hole jokes died out.

The new yellow dwarfs were a pessimistic generation. Few of these young stars could bring themselves to put together a solar system worthy of the name.

Venomous disputes broke out between binaries. White dwarfs bled their companions dry to gain themselves a bit more time.

Worried stars passed around tips to prolong their lives, without pausing to think that a tip that worked well for a yellow dwarf could be a catastrophe for a Wolf-Rayet star. And the quasars didn't listen to anyone. They were too busy channeling their existential anguish into the long, poignant poems they screamed out into the void.

The stars were no more resigned to their deaths than humans.

You've really got to hear the heartbeat of a red giant that's trying to restart its hydrogen-to-helium fusion, but is running out of hydrogen.

Its heart keeps contracting.

At a hundred million degrees, the star suffers a heart attack:

helium starts fusing into carbon and oxygen, triggering a meltdown. The whole core fuses at once in a helium flash. The star swells, then expels its outer layers in a great, final cry.

The marvelous consciousness built over billions of years is crushed, transformed into inert iron. The white dwarf that remains has no memory of its previous existence.

Four or five billion years later, the pessimistic generation of young yellow dwarfs had themselves gone out, leaving behind still-smaller dwarfs. Their robes of interstellar dust were too thin to form planetary entourages.

Meanwhile, the red dwarfs, the oldest of which had been born not long after the beginning of the expansion, carried on shining as dully as dark lanterns.

These dim, isolated stars didn't have much to say.

Even with the patience of an UnAttached, one quickly tires of listening to "How's it going?" and "What's up with you?"

COUSIN ENTROPY RE-INTRODUCED herself to the last of the Attached.

As the red dwarves and the stars of the galactic suburbs went out, the cold forced the remaining Attached civilizations to migrate toward the galactic downtown's island of warmth.

Ferocious wars burst out between the factions of Attached for control of the best neighborhoods. The wars lasted for hundreds of thousands of years—by UnAttached standards, the blink of an eye.

The Attached latched on to downtown's flickering stars with the energy of despair (a concept Cousin Entropy could never understand).

We UnAttached also wanted to escape the death's-waiting-room that the galactic arms had become.

Moving through a field of dead stars was risky. With no stars, we couldn't pick out black holes by the way they curved starlight. Keeping ourselves out of these invisible, rogue death pits required energy-intensive gravitational sensing.

I had no choice but to say goodbye to all my suburban friends. *Everybody's leaving the neighborhood,* they sighed as they cooled.

Wrapped in their stardust, I set myself up downtown, a mere eight-million-year commute from my former home.

So now, I dance above the heart of downtown: a supermassive black hole, surrounded by the spiral of luminous gases it's drawn in. I sip energy from the powerful X-rays that periodically burst from its poles.

At this last act of our little corner of the universe, each of us has our own table manners.

A hundred parsecs from me hovers a giant silver coin, one face turned toward the black hole, the better to capture its energies.

The coin's diameter is greater than the ancient Earth's orbit.

This UnAttached is so thin as to be translucent. As the galactic center's light passes through it, variations in the thickness of its material outline a profile crowned by leaves. From my well of HearSay, I dredge the name of an ancient Roman emperor.

Could the original, Attached Augustus of antiquity have conceived of the stellar scope of this tribute?

I recognize it as a manifestation of our duty to remember, a duty dear to the third-generation UnAttached—the ones who built themselves from the ruins of worlds destroyed by war.

The downtown isn't bustling anymore. Our proximity to the immense gravity well slows our senses.

The outward-facing residents discussed the flight of the other galaxies, their lacy loops of stars shining darker and darker red.

Finally, the last purple loops of lace disappeared from view. Even the giant coin's ocular network, the best any of us had, couldn't track them. A measly few photons still reach us, at the furthest end of the infrared: their wavelength is longer than the diameter of the ancient Milky Way.

My HearSay processors breathlessly evaluate the current size of our universe.

It's over a trillion lightyears in circumference.

The sky is empty.

OUR GALAXY of dying stars is forevermore alone. The last red dwarfs are quietly going out.

The forecast is for a meager 0.05 degrees Kelvin.

When there was nothing left but a cluster of icy bodies, Attached and UnAttached found ourselves in the same boat (so to speak).

The spaceship holding the last twenty billion Attached is hard to distinguish from the giant coin.

Our psychological timescales are still far apart, but over the eons, the Attached had kept working at self-improvement. Their specialty was pocket environments.

To get an idea of what they look like now, imagine a large, transparent, flattened orb, filled with billions of little bubbles jostling each other in a thick amniotic fluid.

Each bubble is an Attached. Or rather, an ex-Attached, their translucent body swollen around their conscious biosphere, their eyes and senses turned toward the others.

AFTER 887 BILLION YEARS, new subjects of conversation are hard to come by.

"Hey, Augustus! You still kicking?"

"You old bastard, haven't you frozen up yet?"

WE KEEP ourselves occupied by studying history, by comparing our pools of HearSay. Every now and then, the Attached send out a lightning-brief burst of information, but their lifespans are too microbially fleeting to permit any real conversation.

The cold creeps into us, as our internal energy dwindles.

We warm ourselves back up as much as we can, by capturing the X-ray jets streaming from the black hole's poles. But you can't hold yourself too close to the axis: more than one UnAttached has gotten an overdose of X-rays right in the smacker.

We rub our toughened outer skins against each other to gain a tiny bit of energy. Obviously, we pay for these momentary lapses in lost matter.

This bodes poorly for the future.

When Cousin Entropy finishes evaporating the galactic black hole, the curtain will fall on the final act.

Actually, the curtain will freeze solid at absolute zero.

JUST WHEN I was starting to be tempted to let downtown's central supermassive black hole compress me into a tiny speck, the colony of Attached made an unexpected discovery. Our distant cousins had managed to decode the black hole's emissions. Their brief lives were the key to this achievement, given that we UnAttached could barely make out the black hole's rapid blabber.

It turns out that the singularity is a first-class chatterbox, as if to make up for the silence of all the stars it had swallowed.

A keen intelligence bubbles under its secret horizon. Heat and light swirl there without too much distortion, as the black hole's immense size mitigates the tidal effect.

That's when we understood that Cousin Entropy had been keeping a card up her sleeve, all these eons.

An ace of spades.

An ace as black as the dark energy that so mystified ancient scientists!

Along with Cousin Enthalpy and Aunt Gravity, she'd been cooking us up a superb Napoleon pastry for dessert all this time.

Far from being selfish, Cousin Entropy had been filching excess disorder in order to pierce an inconspicuous little hole between two no-longer-theoretical membranes.

Where one universe ends, another begins.

None of the galactic spheres gave a damn about ever-widening distances or about light years. Their singular hearts were busy weaving webs of interdimensional string.

When we're ready to take the plunge, all we have to do is politely let our galactic center know.

And restrain ourselves from telling any more black hole jokes.

ALL OF US, UnAttached and Attached alike are preparing for the big move. Augustus has wrapped the Attached orb in his immense body. All we UnAttached gather tightly around them, as though the cluster of Attached were a small, fragile bird.

Humanity, reunited, will let itself fall into the star near the pole, just outside the emissions cone. And then we'll take advantage of a lull in the X-rays to slip across the secret horizon.

The black hole advises us not to wait too long, given that the manoeuver to relocate us into a baby universe requires as much mass as possible.

I don't know what the other side will look like. I imagine those Cousins, Entropy and Enthalpy, swimming in an immense white fountain.

Our march toward the event horizon will take up a brief millennium or two.

As humanity sets off on its journey, I have one little twinge of regret:

Leaving downtown is never easy.

THIS STORY originally appeared in *Future Science Fiction Digest*.

MICHÈLE LAFRAMBOISE FEEDS coffee grounds to her garden plants, runs long distances and writes full-time in Mississauga, Ontario.

Fascinated by the sciences and nature since she could walk, she studied geography and engineering, but two recessions and her own social awkwardness kept the plush desk jobs away. Instead, she did a string of odd jobs to sustain her budding family: some quite dangerous, others quite tedious, all of them sources of inspiration.

With words or drawings, Michèle creates worlds filled with humor, invention and wonder. She's gotten a lot of novels and graphic novels out, but publishing houses tended to flop behind her like those rope bridges in adventure movies... So she ran faster forward.

Michèle now has about twenty novels out and over sixty short stories in French and English, earning various distinctions in Canada and Europe. Her most recent SF book, *Le Secret de Paloma* (David, 2021) deals with teen angst and grief on a remote, hostile world. It is currently in translation and waiting to start its quest for a good home.

You can stop by at her website (michele-laframboise.com) to say hello, or visit her indie publishing house (echofictions.com) to get a taste of her fiction!

N. R. M. Roshak is an award-winning Canadian author and translator. Their stories have appeared in various anthologies and magazines, including *Galaxies SF*, *Daily Science Fiction*, and *Future Science Fiction Digest*, and have been translated into several languages. They live in Ontario, Canada, with a small family and a loud cat. You can find more of their work at nrmroshak.com.

THE CURTAIN FALLS, THE SHOW MUST END

Julie Nováková, translated from the Czech by the author

"She knew about theater and life. He wanted to ask her whether it was not possible to create an artificial life for oneself, so similar to the real one that it could be mistaken for it, and which one could master. Was it not possible to build tragedies into the days, operettas with deep and lingering punch lines? What was the stage then? After all, people cried and cheered for a play, crimes were committed and fear flapped its wings against paper walls. Making a destiny out of the whims and idiosyncrasies of the heart, for oneself and for others, just as one makes landscapes and cities in the theater out of wood and cardboard - was that so difficult?"
— *Severin's Journey into The Dark* (Paul Leppin, 1914)

A HIGH-PITCHED SCREAM, and an "I've got you at last!" echoed in the auditorium drowned in dark.

Muffled laughter filled the vast empty space. Then light appeared: someone had lit a match. The flame revealed the faces of a wide-smiling man and a young woman with reddened cheeks.

"You're such a stupid fool, Stefan," the girl said, not altogether disapprovingly.

Stefan grinned. "Couldn't resist, Hanna! It's spooky here in the middle of the night, isn't it?"

Her face grew serious. "No, it's not. There's nothing to fear here. Come on, we've got a job to do."

"You still don't believe I can do it."

"Let's see," she said diplomatically.

Stefan drew a deep breath. "Fine. Would you do as I say?"

"Unless I think you've got some ulterior motives."

He ignored her remark, ignited another match, and lit a small candle. Then another one. He continued until a circle of candles surrounded them on the stage. Hanna scrunched her nose. The candles exuded a strange smell, but not an unpleasant one. It resembled freshly mown grass. The color was unusual too, a deep olive-green.

Meanwhile, Stefan began drawing on the boards. The chalk scratched on wood with high cadence, fast and resolute. Hanna watched the circle infused with myriad symbols close in around them.

"Done," Stefan exhaled. "Sit down opposite me."

Hanna complied, trying to set her doubts aside. *It would simply be a foolish adventure. God knows we need some these days!*

Grandmother had always told her fantastical tales of ghosts and poltergeists haunting theaters, especially opera houses. She'd told them as if she had personally witnessed them. Hanna had always assumed there was a lot of imagination involved, even as a child. She loved them. But that didn't mean she believed them.

Yes, there were a lot of stories of theater hauntings, and perhaps some were true, but she always found it suspicious that ghosts and news of such had largely stopped appearing over two decades ago.

So when Stefan proposed to *summon* one, she couldn't help being somewhat skeptical.

"You don't have to say anything," Stefan continued. "I will say the invocation. Just… try to lure it here with your thoughts."

Like wishing upon a star? Hanna didn't say it aloud. Stefan always took pride in claiming that his uncle had once been an exorcist in this theater. If the stories were true, he'd lost several years' memory and almost his mind too in an exorcism gone awry. But there was hardly anyone who could corroborate that, and she knew well enough that

Stefan could make up anything. She sighed inwardly. *Why do I always fall for these types? Head in the clouds, empty pockets, boasting and swaggering, and always a handy tale to tell if a girl asks an inconvenient question…*

But as he started chanting in what may have been old Greek (sounded impressive, she had to concede), she tried to focus on wishing for a ghost to come.

Stefan's chanting continued, and Hanna grew uncomfortable. The stage felt increasingly hard and cold underneath her folded legs. She shifted in her position. And the damn draft…

Suddenly, with a chill, she looked at the candles' flames and realized the draft was coming from the center of the pattern to all directions. Her breath caught.

Stefan uttered the last word, and heavy silence fell upon the stage. It was like the moment after a particularly powerful aria ends and everyone is too mesmerized for a fraction, before they snap out of it and start clapping. Now, for an audience of two, a special performance commenced.

A human-like shape shimmered in the center of the chalk circle.

They both remained silent. Perhaps neither had believed the ritual would work. But the apparition was now so close that they could easily touch it.

Stefan raised his hand slowly and did just that. He flinched as soon as the tips of his fingers reached the outline of the misty shape.

"It's so cold," he breathed out.

Hanna watched the specter with eyes wide open. "Who are you?" she whispered. Her voice resonated with emotion, barely containing it. The acoustics of the theater carried it to the farthest reaches of the auditorium.

The specter inclined her head—for a moment, Hanna was sure she could make out a woman's features in the fuzzy shape—and then emitted a long high-pitched wail.

Hanna and Stefan both gave a start.

"Don't be afraid!" Hanna cried out and instantly realized the absurdity of her words. *She* was telling a *ghost* not to be afraid. "Do you… understand us?"

But she couldn't recognize the ghost's face well enough to read any emotion off it. It might be friendly and start to talk… or turn against them at any moment. A chill ran down her spine. How good were the protective wards Stefan had drawn around them?

The apparition just floated there. In a way, it was scarier than if it shrieked again or moved.

"We'd better release it," Stefan mumbled. His face was pale as death itself even in the warm candlelight.

"How?" Hanna breathed.

"There's another ritual, a reverse one of a sort." Stefan straightened his back, exhaled, and started incanting again. Hanna sensed a change in the air: for a fraction, it felt warm and smelled of freshly mowed meadow, like a summer day, but this was abruptly replaced by a bone-chilling whiff carrying a stale stench of death.

All the candles went out at the same moment. The apparition was gone.

A new light appeared as Stefan struck a match. Hanna would never forget his face: so awed, full of part-fear, part-excitement. It looked like a statue or a mask in the long shadows cast by the single match. Was she harboring a similar expression?

"It's real," she breathed and immediately felt stupid for stating the obvious. "Who… who do you think it was?"

"I have no idea," Stefan shook his head. "Let's get out of here. This place…"

"It feels haunted now," Hanna finished for him and gave him a little uncertain smile.

Out in the street it felt much safer, despite the late hour. Stefan offered to walk Hanna to her flat, and she was too sensible to decline. Neither spoke for most of the way; only she finally broke the silence when they reached her street. "If the stories told by my grandma were true, ghosts usually harm living people, even if they don't intend to. But… do you think you could use one as a protector spirit, a sort of a guardian angel?"

"There are some myths of that in various cultures, but I've never heard anything specific, or modern." Stefan shook his head.

"If it were possible, we could try to do it. To protect us, the theater, all good people…" Hanna fell silent for a moment. "I fear we might need it."

Stefan embraced her. It was an utterly non-romantic, comforting, warm embrace of two lost people shivering in the darkening night.

MORNING GREETED them with a cacophony of raised voices. Everyone was talking about the same thing: at dawn, German troops had entered Austria. There were talks of a coup, or even of annexing Austria to Germany, but no one knew anything certain at this point.

There was perhaps nobody in the theater who hadn't had at least a passing thought: *Would we be next?* Only the response it elicited differed. Most feared this happening; few had no opinion; some, however, would welcome it.

As they started preparing to try the set for the upcoming premiere of *Karl V.*, the tension grew almost palpable. However, the scenographer Feistel held a firm grip on the works and commanded the stagehands and lighting technicians, even though he'd made it no secret that he loathed this piece.

Hanna was in her tiny room working on the costume the wardrobe master had assigned her, when Stefan burst in. "Come. Director Eger wants to speak to everyone in the auditorium."

Again? She bit down the remark. The director was probably trying his best to maintain professionalism within the theater staff and motivate them. But the speeches grew more frequent—and so did the tensions.

Eger stood on the stage, the ominous emperor's deathbed behind him. Was he unusually pale and tense, or was it just the sloppy work of the lighting techs, too tired of Feistel's commands?

"We have probably all heard the news by now: the German army has crossed the Austrian border, and it may be a start of an annexation. We, for now, are safe. You may think what you want of the action, but I strongly urge you not to let it get in the way of professionalism. What is happening just outside our borders is disturbing, and we will do as much as we can to help any refugees from Austria if it comes to that."

Hanna set her jaw. The theater was already at the legal edge of its capacity of employing foreigners, who could comprise up to thirty percent soloists and couldn't be employed in the chorus or orchestra, and getting a Czechoslovakian citizenship in order to gain better job prospects was near-impossible. She was still a German citizen herself. Eger may have *wanted* to help, but how exactly was he planning to do it?

"We can't make decisions for politicians and don't have the power to stop the military," Eger continued, "but that doesn't mean we have no power. On the contrary—we possess the power to change people's minds through our work. We should use it wisely..."

"What is *really* going to happen?" a voice suddenly called out from the back. It was Felix Jentzsch, actor. "We've had the Schiller Theater Berlin guest-starring here just a week ago! Do we have to accept more of this German influence in order to survive? Are we going to stand up, or stand back?"

"Welcoming the Schiller Theater Berlin on our stage was a diplomatic act suggested by our government," Eger reminded him firmly. "We are *not* showing any kind of support of the German political regime. Also, need I remind you that we had a Czech-German cultural event just the day before, or that we performed Čapek's *Mother* the previous week?" He raised his voice slightly to address everyone. "We come from many different backgrounds, even speak different mother tongues, but in these times, we need to stay strong together. Our work is still needed, perhaps more than any other time. Our theater is *national*, and proudly so, but it is not *nationalist* and never will be. Now, we have work to do!"

With that, everyone started dispersing slowly to resume their jobs.

Hanna exchanged a short glance with Stefan.

It's going to be all right, he seemed to be saying, reassurance in his hazel eyes.

I wish, she thought. *But I don't believe it will be.*

THE PHOTOGRAPHIC PORTRAIT of a smiling mustached man on the wall seemed to exude almost inhuman confidence and energy to Paul Eger, who himself felt exhausted and beaten.

"Six years of running the theater, trying to live up to your example," he said to Angelo Neumann's picture, "and what of it? It's crumbling down beneath my very hands."

Eger had to overcome an almost visceral feeling of aversion before he grasped a pen and pushed himself to work. The theater needed him, he kept reminding himself. He may not have been a second Neumann, but he was doing his best in keeping the business together. The show must go on.

"I wonder what you'd think of the theater nowadays," Eger sighed aloud while going through the contracts. "Fifty years' time... We've even had the *Meistersingers* at the semicentennial. I wish you could have seen it. I dare to hope it would have made you proud."

I'm insane, he thought for himself, *talking to a photograph.* But the truth was, he had no one else to talk to like this, except perhaps his wife, but he didn't want to place all of his burdens on her.

The *Meistersingers* had gone brilliantly, but no one from the outside could see the painful process that had preceded it. It was a popular comedy and the theater's opening play fifty years ago, so there was plentiful reason for doing it; but it was also Wagner, a choice that could hardly stand as apolitical these days. Moreover, the figure of Beckmesser elicited feelings ranging from reluctance to pure revulsion, especially among the Jewish members of the ensemble. Eger was more than happy to tone down the anti-Semitic original portrayal of the character, but that for a change upset several Wagner purists.

"I bet you'd had your own problems with the opera. This one just doesn't go lightly," Eger murmured. "It was worth it, I just wish I could consult with you, learn from your experience..."

In theory, he had reasons to be happy. The president had visited the semi-centennial and had promised more funding for the theater. But the political tensions threatened to tear it apart from the inside.

Thespians were never inclined to blindly follow suit and go quiet, and usually it was a good thing, but not if it made any working together increasingly more difficult. After all, political tensions were ripping apart the Brünnish scene at this very time.

Well, they should start pre-dress rehearsals of a new piece, Ernst Křenek's *Karl V.*, in a week; perhaps the exciting work would bring them together. It would be a world premiere of outstanding importance. Yet Eger feared it would not be an easy collaboration, especially since Křenek first intended the piece for the Vienna State Opera five years ago, but the opera house had been pressured from Germany to abandon the play, and Křenek was essentially blacklisted in Germany, and now perhaps in Austria too. This would undoubtedly call the wrath of the neighboring states down on the Neue Deutsche Theater. The cast wasn't satisfied either; the piece's twelve-tonality was difficult to work with.

Eger set aside his pen and looked up at Neumann's picture. "What would you do? I can't just cave in and only select easy, uncontroversial pieces. We would become a trifling provincial theater like that; it would be just a way into obscurity, against everything you and all the other directors before me had worked for. I suppose we just have to persist against all the odds, don't we?"

The picture remained silent, smiling its enigmatic smile frozen in time.

STEFAN FOCUSED on the stage with all the attention he was capable of. This was just the first ensemble rehearsal with a piano corepetition, but he wanted to do his best anyway. This performance would be hard not just on the singers and orchestra, who had to work in a different tonality, but on the lighting crew too. The director had decided to make the emperor Karl V.'s deathbed the sole piece of scenery, while lighting would create all the spatial effects.

Stefan looked forward to it immensely—and dreaded it at the same time.

"Indessen wurde ich Kaiser des Reichs, ich kam zum Reichstag nach Worms, und Widerspruch und Zwang fielen mich gewaltig an. Als ob es eben jetzt geschähe, höre ich das misstönende Lärmen der Fürsten im hohen Saal. In unbegreiflichem Streit fahren sie aufeinander los. Wie ein Kessel voll kalten Nebels ist dieses germanische Land," the dying emperor sang of lament and quarrel, with padre Juan de Regla leaning over his deathbed.

Stefan felt a wave of admiration and a slight pang of envy as he listened to Pavel Ludikar's portrayal of the king. As a boy, he'd sometimes dreamt of being on the stage himself, but he'd never gotten even into the chorus. Being a carpenter and training for a lighting assistant was the closest he could get to the stage.

Most of the technical personnel looked unimpressed and just went about with their jobs. Stefan, however, felt he could appreciate the strange intensity of the piece.

"Wir wußten es nicht. Nur daß in ihm ein Dunkles sein mußte, das ein Dunkles wachrief im Wesen dieser Deutschen, daß sie in ungeheure, zügellose Bewegung, maßlose Unbotmäßigkeit gerieten." The excellent Pavel Ludikar as Charles V. lamented the tragedies of life, all the dark and the madness.

A strange chill went down Stefan's spine.

Stefan clasped the nearby railing more tightly. Was the song so powerful? But the feeling was so peculiar...

With a start, he realized when he'd felt exactly like this: the summoning. Just before the ghost had appeared.

No, it can't be...

The corepetitor's outcry made the singers stop. Stefan looked at the piano and his eyes widened.

It still played, but the tune changed, and no one's hands were touching the keys.

No material hands, at least.

For a split-second, Stefan was frozen in half-surprise, half-fear. Then he desperately fished in his memory for anything that might stop this.

The actor playing Juan de Regla, perhaps carried away by portraying a priest, was the only one to act: he took a few steps toward the haunted piano and said, shaken at first but in an increasingly loud and firm voice: "*Sancte Michael Archangele, defende nos in proelio, contra nequitiam et insidias diaboli esto præsidium...*"

Mid-note, the playing stopped. Deafening silence ensued.

The actor took another step forward, reached very slowly to the piano, and touched a key.

The fallboard slammed down on his hand, and he shrieked.

A grayish shape shot out of the piano and above the stage. The rigging started swaying.

Stefan gulped. Fear almost paralyzed him for a moment, but he collected himself and recalled what he was searching for. He whispered a protection spell under his breath.

Everything was still.

De Regla clutched his injured hand and moaned, and two of his colleagues were tending to him. The rest were suspiciously looking around, as if expecting to see a monster leap at them from anywhere.

Stefan began shaking so badly he was afraid to leave the catwalk.

A sole horrible thought permeated his mind: *Was it my fault?*

NEUMANN'S PICTURE was looking down on Eger serenely, but Eger still had the feeling of the famous director's eyes burning through him and reaching the furthest depths of his soul.

"An exorcist," the stout man opposite him repeated hollowly after Eger, which snapped the director back into the real world.

"Yes. I can't imagine how we'll manage without one if the... *ghost* returns."

His friend Max Brod shook his head. "You're asking for a world that doesn't exist anymore."

"I suppose it's useless to send word to Vienna."

Brod shook his head. "Not under the current situation."

"But Paul, perhaps..."

"Paul is here, yes, but you'd need to go talk to him. I won't be an intermediary. I'm sorry."

Eger tried to read more from Brod's face, but the older man's expression was indecipherable.

"Anyone else?" he asked, allowing himself a spark of hope.

Brod's eyes unfocused, and a very sad smile played on his lips. "Not many from our circle left, are there? Some left for Vienna, I imagine they're fleeing elsewhere now... some died... some are living in France, Mexico, America... Paul might know someone from the purely occult circles, perhaps."

"Perhaps," Eger echoed. So this was the word that the fate of the Neue Deutsche Theater hung to. The outcome of Angelo Neumann's legacy.

A perhaps.

STEFAN WAITED for Hanna until she was able to leave work. "Do you think we've done that?" he asked almost breathlessly, as soon as they were a safe distance from the theater.

"How could we have? You banished the ghost back!" Hanna tugged at her coat nervously. "It must be an accident."

"You don't believe that, do you? A ghost hasn't appeared in the theater in over two decades, we summon one, and a week later another one *accidentally* manifests!"

Hanna stopped despite the light rain and looked him in the eyes. "You're right. But what if we are to blame? We don't know how to drive the ghost out, so we can't help. What do you think would happen if we just strolled into the director's office and told him what happened? He'd fire us! What are the chances of finding another job now?" She shook her head. "I don't like this any more than you do, but we must be silent. The director will sort it out."

"But knowing the truth might be useful for getting the ghost out!"

Stefan's lower lip trembled. It almost pained Hanna to see him like this—and to have to crush his ideals. "He'll manage that anyway," she said with all the confidence she could muster. "Do you want to lose your job? No? We—must—not— talk!"

He inhaled sharply. "Fine," he said, attempting a firm tone and failing abominably. Then he just turned on his heel and walked swiftly away. She almost called after him, but decided not to. *He'll be thinking about it and wallowing in his feeling of guilt all evening. Best if he's left alone to make peace with it. Tomorrow, everything will be better.*

For a moment, she closed her eyes, focusing on that thought. Light rain droplets settled on her eyelids and slowly formed small streaks like tears. She heard trams from the distance, a dog barking, someone laughing, and smelled wet soil and cobblestones. It didn't feel like the world was ending.

But still, she couldn't make herself believe her own thoughts.

THE SMALL GROUND-FLOOR flat in Slezská street was cluttered and somewhat shabby. Eger had never been here before; when they had Leppin's two plays in the theater, they always met there or in some café.

Leppin's wife Henriette answered the doorbell. "Herr Eger?" she recalled his name. "I'm afraid Paul is a little indisposed, but if you come tomorrow morning..."

"Who is it?" a call came from inside.

"It's Paul Eger, director of the theater!"

"Let him in."

So Eger entered the cramped antechamber and continued to the equally cramped living room. There sat Paul Leppin in a chair that seemed to loom above him.

Eger hadn't seen the writer for nearly two years and was surprised at how much Leppin had deteriorated in that time. Perhaps the death of his only son a year previously had affected him so badly. He rarely ventured out after that tragedy.

"Herr Eger! What a surprise to see you." Leppin smiled. His youngish smile was the one thing that had not changed about him. "Sit down, please. Would you like some tea?"

Eger sat down uncertainly and accepted a cup. The spare chair creaked uncomfortably under him, probably used to holding books and newspapers more than human beings anymore. "How have you been?"

"Well..." Leppin's gaze fell upon a small stack of papers. "I've been writing. New stories and poetry. The first part of my *Prager Rhapsodie* was just published..."

After a few minutes' talk, Eger coughed and changed the topic: "I'm afraid I'm here for more pressing reasons. It's the theater. We... have a ghost."

Leppin's eyes lit up. "Tell me more."

Eger recounted the incident. The old writer listened attentively in silence.

"Interesting," he breathed when Eger finished. "So you've come to me..."

"To ask for help in exorcising the ghost, yes. You have some knowledge in this matter, don't you?"

Leppin chuckled slightly. "A little. But no personal experience, if you don't count the seancés at Meyrink's over three decades ago..."

"You're not serious," Henriette breathed; hard to say which of them she was addressing.

"Nevertheless, if you were willing to be of assistance—" Eger continued.

"It would kill him!" Henriette retorted sharply. She looked from Eger to her husband with a mixture of anger, love, and worry.

Leppin raised a hand, smiling gently. "Calm down, Henriette. You are right, of course... but what if it does? I'm sick and old."

"Don't talk like that."

His light smile widened slightly. "It's true, my dear. No need to call things false names." He turned to Eger. "I accept. If you're content with your exorcist being an old man who most certainly cannot climb rigging or run fast."

Eger reciprocated his smile. "I am."

THE THEATER just before dawn always seemed somehow out of time to Eger. The ornamental building was shrouded in a gray veil of mist. Statues were emerging from it, truly ghost-like.

A strange expression flickered through Leppin's face as he saw the Neue Deutsche Theater.

"The last time I was here on a job, you were giving *Der Enkel des Golem*. It was just before Christmas and freezing to the bone," he said for himself. "Seems like a lifetime ago…"

A lifetime ago, Paul Eger had accepted the position of the theater's director. The year had been 1932 and, despite the crisis, he'd had no idea what the position had in store for him.

"Come," he said now, averted his gaze from the gray stone faces of Mozart, Schiller, and Goethe, and led Leppin inside. But before they stepped on the stairs, Eger glanced back up, above the artists, at the tympanon depicting a poet on a Pegasus, ascending to the heavens with Orpheus's lyre in his clutch. The scene was magnificent, and yet it now seemed ominous to Eger.

No one ever said if the victorious poet was the one speaking for peace and truth.

They arrived at the empty auditorium. "Do you know that I've known two exorcists in their time?" said Leppin dreamily. "Gustav Meyrink, of course—or Meyer, as they called him here—and Jiří Karásek, whom I met through the *Modern Revue*. Karásek was an exorcist for the National Theater, before he committed to his literary career. But he soon ran out of money and had to accept a position at the post office, where he'd briefly worked before joining the theater. Much like my life—only I stuck with the post and never became an exorcist."

Leppin turned to Eger. "I would have recommended you to ask Jiří instead of me, but he's traveling at this moment and I don't know how to reach him. But I'm reminiscing too much and exorcising too little, right?" he laughed. "Forgive the old man. This world brings back many fond memories."

He hissed as he walked the small stairs on the stage, clutching his side. Eger couldn't fail to notice that, and worried whether inviting Leppin had really been such a good idea. But who else?

Leppin bent down with a visible strain and scratched on the boards curiously. "Look. A warding mark. An old one."

"Yes, I believe these were carved here by Meyrink, or someone else of his time." Eger nodded. "Um, do you think they're... still powerful?"

"I wish I knew," Leppin admitted. He walked center stage, frowned and bent down again. Eger noticed the tiny vial on a chain that slipped out of Leppin's waistcoat when he leaned down. There was something iridescent-blue in it, some little crystals perhaps? But the writer tucked it back in hurriedly. Eger decided not to ask for the moment.

Leppin scratched at a small gap between boards. "When did you last use chalk here?"

"We were preparing the scenery, so we used chalk lines... Why?"

"It's probably nothing." The writer stood up. "It feels strange here, but it may well be just my aching bones. Let me try something."

Eger watched half-curious, half-horrified as the old man turned his head up and started uttering words in ancient Greek. Well, old—just three years older than him. But unlike Eger, he *looked* old.

Leppin finished. It took a while, however, before his gaze focused and he looked back at Eger. He seemed tired, but smiled faintly. "I looked this up yesterday evening, after you visited. Jiří has given me this text long ago—one of the simpler rituals. What you've had here really was a ghost. And... I *may* be wrong, but I think the ghost was... summoned. It feels like when we tried summonings in my youth. It was different then, but the gist is here."

Eger stared at him. "So... someone is trying to ruin us? Is that so?"

"That's one possibility."

"Damn!" Eger exhaled. "I'm sorry... The theater is under a lot of pressure lately. Can you find the culprit?"

Leppin shook his head. "Not unless they try again, I'm afraid."

"Well, can you stop them from doing that?"

"Jiří has shown me how to make wards a couple of times. I will set them up around the theater." Leppin's gaze fell to the old marks at the sides of the stage. "Perhaps I could also reinforce the old wards put here by Gustav."

"What about the people, can you make wards at least for the performers?" Eger inquired.

"I don't dare to, not yet. If I did it wrong, it could harm them rather than help. It's much easier with places than people; I see no risk in warding the building itself."

"All right. Thank you."

A fleeting trace of bitterness appeared on Leppin's face. "Don't thank me yet."

THEY COULD HARDLY MISS the presence of a strange old man going about the theater, muttering for himself and drawing shapes in the air. The stranger was tall, lean and stooped. His thin face was sharp, almost fierce. The sight of him gave Stefan the creeps. Suddenly, the man turned and their gazes met. Stefan shuddered. The man's piercing eyes seemed to cut through his flesh and bare his soul. He turned and hurried away.

Hanna looked up as he slipped into her sewing room.

"There is an… exorcist in the theater," Stefan started.

But Hanna just nodded. "I've heard. But he's not an exorcist, he's a writer whom the director invited to play one. Maria knows him, his plays were performed here before either of us joined the theater. His name is Paul Leppin."

Suddenly, a knock on the door interrupted them.

"Come in," Hanna said. Perhaps she expected the wardrobe master.

But Leppin stood in the door. "Good morning." He bowed his head politely. He looked around the tiny room as if searching for something. He seemed surprised at it.

"Can we help you?" Hanna added. Stefan had to admire her composure.

"Has this always been a sewing room?" Leppin asked.

"Yes, as far as I know."

"Times change," Leppin murmured under his breath.

Silence fell.

"Do you need anything?" Hanna spoke again. This time, a sting of impatience made it into her voice.

Leppin looked at them—again, that piercing stare. "Might I use this room when you're not here?"

"Why?"

He shrugged. "I don't have an office, and I might be required to spend some time here."

Hanna visibly hesitated. "All right," she allowed in the end.

Leppin bowed his head again and closed the door after himself.

"He knows," Stefan said in a deadpan tone.

"Nonsense," retorted Hanna. "If he did, the director would already be firing us, or worse."

Stefan scratched his head. "I keep thinking... what if we really did nothing wrong?"

"Just like I was telling you earlier."

"No, I mean—what if someone else saw us and then misused the ritual?"

Hanna stared at him. "You're serious?"

"It makes sense."

"No, it doesn't. Who would be in the theater at such an hour, watch us—and *remember* the ritual? I was sitting right opposite you, and I can't remember the words!"

"He speaks Greek. Or she. Grammar school education."

"You're just being paranoid."

Stefan looked hurt, and Hanna regretted her words immediately. "Look," she said calmingly, "I just don't think it's likely, that's all. And we can hardly ask around."

"No..." Something dawned on Stefan; his gaze changed. "But we *could* ask someone."

"Who?"

"A ghost."

LEPPIN LIKED the no one's hours between late night and early morning, when even the seediest pubs and bordellos grew quiet and the streets were dark and deserted. He'd loved to roam them in his youth. He could spend the whole night randomly wandering through the city—unless he took refuge in one of those pubs and bordellos.

But spending these strange hours in a former exorcist's room also had its charms. For now he was certain that what was a sewing room nowadays had previously belonged to the house's exorcist. He had the same feeling of being close to some invisible veil between worlds here as he had a long time ago in Gustav Meyrink's apartment.

He could recall the expensive engraved furniture, Buddha statues, ancient scrolls, eerie paintings, and vials full of the strangest substances, all crammed into the tiny little flat next to an abandoned factory. Meyrink's last refuge before he bid Prague farewell.

In that strange space, you couldn't resist the feeling that you were about to face a ghost any moment.

Leppin closed his eyes. *Who are you?* he thought. *Why now, after all those quiet years?*

And would you talk to a fraud like me at all? I'm no exorcist, I'm just a writer playing one.

Gustav and Jiří were equally talented in many disciplines. They exorcised; wrote; translated. He… wrote and translated.

If you were right and you can still be somewhere out there, I need your help now more than ever, Gustav Meyrink, Leppin pondered. He sighed and opened his eyes.

He had many wards to reinforce, and a ghost to catch.

EGER SAT opposite his opera dramaturge Frederick Weber, clutching a list densely covered in a neat handwriting.

"I just received a letter from Ernst Křenek. He won't be able to attend the premiere of his *Karl V*. He has fled to America," Eger stated. He was aware of the bitterness that had crept into his voice.

"That could be expected. I don't think it's wise for us to perform his opera at this time," Weber said.

"Not an option," Eger interrupted him, perhaps too fiercely. In a calmer tone, he added: "We mustn't give way to fear and prejudice. And to drop such a unique piece... no, it stays."

It was clear from Weber's face that he disagreed—but he knew when it was pointless to argue with the director.

Eger set his jaw. He'd heard some unwelcome rumors about Weber lately, even that the dramaturge had been seen talking to Henlein's pet Franz Höller.

At least the papers seemed to have praised the theater lately. He just didn't know whether to interpret it as a good sign, or consider it a bad omen.

"All right, let's look at—"

Suddenly, the door burst open. Eger was just about to chastise the stagehand who'd run in so rudely, but the look on his face made him stop.

"There was a... manifestation in the dressing rooms."

"Where's Leppin?"

"He's already there. I just thought you should know."

Eger strode in his wake—but he didn't run. There was morale to be upheld.

Leppin stood in the middle center of one of the soloists' dressing rooms and clutched something that looked like improvised divining rods. There were shards all over the room.

"It's gone," he said grimly. Eger guessed he didn't mean permanently.

"What happened here?" the director asked.

Actress Elsbeth Warnholtz looked up from the cup of tea someone had briskly fetched for her. "I just came in to prepare for the evening performance, looked in the mirror, and I saw some... dark shape behind me. I turned, but there was nothing. When I looked in the mirror again, it was there, and it leaped at me! I screamed and smashed the mirror with my brush. I'm afraid it's a mess here, and the theater has a mirror to replace…"

"Don't worry about that. What's most important is that you're safe."

Miss Warnholtz seemed shaken, but uninjured and more determined than ever. "I've almost become used to threats from living people, even if hidden behind pseudonyms, but this is new," she tried to joke. "I guess we can't beat a ghost with a petition, can we?"

"If it could be done, I'm sure you would achieve it." Eger smiled. Warnholtz was one of the most outspoken members of the Club of Czech and German Theater Employees and the informal Communist group in the theater, and she was never afraid of arguing even with Weber, Feistel, Götz, and other opponents within the theater. "I'm afraid the dressing room will be subject to Mr. Leppin's work for a while. Would you mind preparing in Mrs. Kunz's room—that is, if you're up to performing tonight?"

"Oh, it takes much more to stop me," Warnholtz assured him and strode out.

Eger and Leppin were left alone in the dressing room.

"This could have ended badly. We need to get rid of the ghost," Eger stated, overlooking the disarray and trying to imagine what could have happened if not for Warnholtz's quick wits.

"Damn well I'm working on that, aren't I?" Leppin lashed out at him.

Eger's theater experience allowed him to maintain a measured expression. He merely said, "I do hope so."

Leppin, on the other hand, looked aghast by his own outburst. "I'm sorry," he mumbled and turned his gaze away. His hands shook.

"If you're not well, we can try to manage otherwise. I don't want you to exhaust yourself…"

"I won't be well even if I'm sitting home. Here, I might at least be useful," the older man said.

Pain, tremors, mood swings… Eger didn't dare to ask about his suspicion. What could it change if he had it confirmed?

"Thank you." He nodded and left the improvised exorcist. But he was determined to try to reach Jiří Karásek as soon as possible. They clearly needed an experienced exorcist.

After returning to his office, Eger sank to his chair. Only then did his gaze fall upon the pristine white envelope on the table.

It hadn't been there when he'd left.

With an ominous feeling, he reached for it and pulled out a note. Written in an ornamental script in dark-red ink, it read: *If you value the theater and its safety, get rid of the Jewish and Communist filth. The next one won't be so lucky.*

Eger scarcely overcame the urge to crumble the note and toss it angrily. Instead, he laid it back on the table. Perhaps Leppin could learn something of use from it.

Paul Leppin appeared soon after. But he did not bear good news.

"It's gone for the moment, but it could return anytime."

"Then there's nothing to do?"

"I'll keep trying." Leppin looked Eger in the eye. *But I don't know whether it won't be in vain,* his gaze seemed to say.

"What about this?" Eger handed him the note.

Leppin read it, and his expression grew even grimmer. "I have never heard of a ghost who'd leave messages like that."

"So a human left it?"

"More likely."

"Well…" Eger sighed and leaned back. "At least that's a force I can reckon with."

A DOZEN distorted faces were looking sternly at Leppin.

Is it even still my own face? he wondered. He could hardly recognize those sunken eyes staring at him. Had he transformed into a ghost before he died?

Or, perhaps…

No!

It couldn't have been his son's eyes looking at him all of a sudden.

Leppin shivered and threw his jacket over the mirror shards on the table.

He'd hoped to learn something from them—but what was he thinking? He felt a fool; no, worse, a fraud.

There was a ghost haunting the theater, and nothing he could do.

The world was head over heels, and there was nothing he could do.

His son Paul was gone, and there was nothing he could do. Meyrink, perhaps, would have been capable of that. There were rumors that he'd contacted the soul of his son after the young man had killed himself. But Meyrink himself had died scarcely half a year later, and they hadn't been in contact with Leppin for some time then.

Meyrink, perhaps… But there is nothing I can do!

In one outburst of rage, Leppin swept the contents on the table angrily on the floor.

One shard landed on his leg, however.

In it, Leppin glimpsed his own face—for it *was* his own, there was no doubt—contorted in anger, and something recoiled in him. It felt prophetic; a vision of the future.

A future that only held fear for him, although he would never admit that.

"ARE YOU SERIOUS?" Hanna stressed.

"Yes."

"All right. Let's do it."

This time, they were cooped up in Hanna's sewing room. They saw the exorcist leave and the whole theater was deserted, but the stage still felt too exposed. Hanna didn't miss the strange expression in Stefan's face when she suggested they stay here in this room. She half-expected him to refuse, saying quite reasonably that the exorcist came to this room, but he didn't.

She spent several evenings in the library, devouring everything related to ghosts and summonings. She looked up works of the famous exorcists of the old times, but to her disappointment, she only found fiction with precious little specifics in these piles of books.

Many of them could no longer be found in her homeland.

Not that she would be able to enter a library there.

Hanna wondered grimly just how long she'd remain allowed in libraries here.

"Sit next to me."

"Not across like the last time?"

"We'll try a variation of the ritual."

The Athanasius variety? she thought, but kept silent. After much searching, she'd found what she'd been looking for. Now she felt like she understood what each piece of preparation Stefan had made the last time meant. She watched him draw a slightly different set of ornaments on the floor, and she recalled seeing those symbols.

It takes two to perform this ritual, she remembered. *Good. It would give me more power over the ghost.*

"This time, I'll need you to say a few words." Stefan looked her in the eye. "You'll be repeating after me. Can you do it?"

Hanna suppressed a wry grin. *"Can a girl repeat a few words"—coming even from you?*

"Of course," she smiled instead.

Stefan lit the only candle and Hanna switched off the electric light. They sat inside their part of the ornament.

Hanna had to admit she wouldn't have remembered all the words of the ritual—but as Stefan incanted them and gestured to her to repeat some parts, she could recall seeing them written somewhere in the stacks of books she'd gone through.

They uttered the last words. Hanna felt as if something brushed against her shoulder lightly, and almost gave a start.

It was just draft, it must have been. It's coming.

The air before them shimmered faintly—and then an outline could be recognized.

This time, they could see the ghost's features more clearly. It may have been the same one; may not have. But it was—or rather had been in life—a young woman. Hanna caught herself wondering whether the ghost's look depicted the person when they died, and if so, why this girl had died at such young age.

"Don't be afraid," Stefan spoke softly. "We won't hold you here for long. Do you understand?"

The translucent girl nodded.

"We'll just ask you a few questions and then let you go. Do you know what's causing the recent apparitions in this theater?"

The ghost seemed to consider Stefan's words, and again gave a slow nod.

"Tell us."

Hanna could see the apparition's face move, as if it tried to speak—but no sound came.

"Write it down," she compelled it.

Stefan gave her a surprised look, but nodded.

The girl's face looked blank. When Stefan made a gesture of writing, she shook her head.

"She can't write," Hanna realized.

"Has anyone from the theater summoned a ghost to haunt this place?"

A nod, this time.

"Do you know who did it?"

Another nod.

"Are they employed as an actor or singer?"

She shook her head.

"Technical crew?"

No.

"Management?"

No.

Stefan continued the list, but the ghost gave a negative answer for each. Exasperated, Stefan looked at Hanna. "I'm not sure we'll get anywhere. We should probably release..."

"No," Hanna said in a measured tone. She shifted her gaze back to the apparition.

It was now, or never.

She uttered the initial binding spell, and continued in German: "By the power of Hades and Persephone, by the darkness enshrouding the world of the dead, I bind you to serve us and obey our commands."

With her peripheral vision, she glimpsed Stefan's ashen face, his mouth forming a silent O. But she was looking at the ghost, whose shimmery face stayed blank. But something, perhaps, shifted in the dark eyes of the long-dead woman.

Hanna raised her head higher. "I thereby command you to protect this theater and its people. You shall above all else protect the lives and health of the people, guard the theater itself and its belongings, and fight any earthly or spiritual influences that seek to do us harm. Do you understand?"

The ghost's shape blurred. Then it shot toward Hanna.

"No!" shouted Stefan and threw himself in front of her. The spirit collided with him and seemed to have disappeared into his chest. Stefan gasped for air. His eyes rolled.

For a split second, Hanna froze, but then memories revolved in her mind. *Exorcisms. Banishings. First aid.*

She hastily muttered what she'd remembered of the words to end the ritual, and she held Stefan's shoulders to prevent his shaking body from getting injured. "Stefan!"

The tremors stopped as abruptly as they began. Hanna checked his breath. To her relief, he was breathing, albeit shallowly. She slapped his face gently. "Stefan, wake up."

Her grandmother would have had smelling salts on herself. Hanna never did.

Suddenly, Stefan blinked. "W-what... oh..."

Hanna laughed with relief. "Stefan! I'm so glad you're all right. I'm so sorry..." Her voice broke. "I never meant for this to happen."

But he wasn't looking at her, perhaps even listening to her. "S-so cold..." His teeth chattered.

Hanna took off her sweater and shawl and wrapped them around his chest. Now she felt cold just in her blouse, but the cold he was feeling was something else entirely. His face was ashen, the skin almost translucent.

She reached to touch his forehead, just to see whether he could have had fever, but Stefan's gaze shot toward her and he spoke coarsely: "Don't touch me!"

Hanna withdrew. "I'm sorry," she repeated hollowly.

Stefan sat up laboriously, leaning on the wall. "It could have killed me."

"But you deflected it."

"I didn't. Something else saved me." Stefan struggled to stand up. Hanna offered to help him, but he pushed her away. Leaning heavily on a chair, he stood.

He gave a bitter look to the ornaments on the floor. "I'd leave and let you clean this up, but I'm afraid you'd try something crazy again."

"It was a mistake. I'm sorry."

His expression, a mix of fear and disgust, tore at her heart—but she didn't allow it to show.

"I only meant to protect us and the whole theater. I know it was a bad idea now. Forgive me."

"Would you have forgiven yourself if you'd imprisoned the ghost in our world, forced it to fight our battles?" Stefan said quietly. "And—would you have forgiven yourself if it killed someone?"

Her facade of proud determination almost broke. "I would have released it when we were safe. And as for… No. I wouldn't. You know I wouldn't."

Stefan's face contorted. "I'm afraid I don't know that anymore."

***

THE EMPEROR WRITHED in pain on his deathbed. Paul Leppin could relate.

He had to muster all of his strength just to keep focused. The back pain was more severe today, he'd scarcely gotten any sleep, and he felt his mood swing disturbingly. On top of it, the little sewing room felt different today—somehow ominous.

A mirror shard rested in Leppin's lap now, reflecting only his thin worried face.

He'd tried to enchant it to show him in advance where the ghost was going to strike next. But to no avail, it seemed so far. If it was connected to the ghost at all, he didn't manage to make use of it. It only ever reflected his likeness.

At least it didn't show him his son again. It had been just an illusion back then, a product of his imagination... or a deteriorating mind? He dared not think about that.

"Leben: die helle Seite dort, erfüllt mit Tat und Hoffnung auf Vollbringen, hier das dunkle, tatenlose Nichts, die Nacht gebrochen Wahns," the excellent Pavel Ludikar as Charles V. lamented.

Leppin knew that the king too had outlived his child, infanta Isabel. But his other daughters and sons would live past his death.

He didn't have to live through the death of an only son.

Leppin's fingertips tingled. He sat up straighter. *Fatigue, ghost, or... hallucinations?*

Then came the almost intangible smell of metal, and Leppin felt icy cold deep in his arthritic joints. The divining rods in his pocket twitched, and he felt half-cautious, half-elated. It had actually worked! Something was happening to the shard too. Its surface dimmed, and then began to show an image of the deathbed onstage. But in the image, Ludikar wasn't gesturing and singing. He just lay there, menacingly motionless.

Leppin stood up. His joints protested, and he hissed from the back pain. Today was not a good day.

The rods led him backstage. There were a few technical workers and actors waiting for the start of their part. It was quiet.

But the divining rods still twitched, as if they wanted to point in two directions at once. They were trying to bend... up? Leppin looked there, but saw nothing unusual.

One of the actors headed onstage, a knight. The rods twitched again.

They pointed right toward the emperor.

Leppin cursed under his breath and walked onstage. "Pause the—" he started.

The knight's hand jerked, as if it didn't belong to him at all. He cried out, more in surprise than fear.

Leppin shouted the first thing that occurred to him, a spell he'd known from Jiří.

To no avail. The wooden sword—because it was the sword held in the actor's hand that was seized by another power —swung and bore down on the emperor, who didn't roll away in time—he barely managed to cover his head with an arm. The sword hit it hard. The singer shrieked in pain.

Leppin fumbled for holy water in his pocket. Suddenly, extreme pain shot from his back through his whole body. He gasped and fell to his arthritic knees. Was it the ghost's doing, or just his illness choosing the worst possible time?

Through the mist of pain, he saw the sword bearing down on Ludikar for the second time.

Despite the agony, pure undiluted fury grasped hold of him—fury against the ghost, against the world, against the odds that put him here instead of someone competent, such as Karásek or Meyrink. The divining rods snapped clean in his hand. Something changed in the air. It almost crackled with electricity.

Then everything seemed to go still for Leppin. He saw the sword descend as if in a slowed-down movie. All tension vanished. The pain was gone. Leppin felt warmth and serenity wash over him. *This is not right*, he thought vaguely, watching the sword.

The weapon changed its trajectory, gliding elegantly toward the edge of the bed instead of Ludikar's body. Leppin smiled a calm, satisfied smile as he watched it do so.

Cut—and the world was speeding past him again.

The sword hit the bed with considerable force, and the actor dropped it like something poisonous. It clattered onto the floor and stayed there, unmoving.

Leppin felt the otherworldly presence rapidly subside.

But before it was entirely gone, a torn part of the curtain fluttered down to the stage and descended onto the old floorboards slowly, neatly unfolding.

On it was written in large, gothicized letters: AWAY WITH THE FILTH IN THIS THEATER.

Paul Eger felt a disconcerting *déjà vu*, when the door burst open and a terrified man stood in it, while he'd been absorbed in a discussion of the matters of his theater with his dramaturge Weber.

"The ghost... the sword... Mr. Ludikar..."

Weber ran through the door, Eger just after him. They found the lead singer still on the emperor's deathbed—sitting and clutching his right arm.

"I think it's broken," he hissed when he saw the director. He was ashen and obviously in pain, but Eger felt a wave of relief that nothing worse than a broken arm had apparently occurred. He spoke with the singer, assured him he'd get a doctor—a stagehand had already been sent to fetch one—and some compensation. Then his gaze finally fell on the piece of curtain on the floor.

The black looming letters on the red velvet felt like a slap on the face of this theater, its history and people. Eger sucked in air.

"This cannot go on," he said so quietly that no one but Weber, standing right beside him, could hear him.

Eger went on to talk with Leppin. The exorcist had to admit that although he'd managed to stop the ghost this time, it wasn't a permanent solution. He had no idea how to banish it.

They dismissed the ensemble save for the evening's performance. The ghost never manifested during any play, and Eger still hoped for the best though he was reluctant to potentially risk lives. But what was he to do—shut down the whole theater?

"Cancel *Karl V.*," Weber suggested.

The casualness with which he made the suggestion stirred something inside Eger. He recalled the rumors about Weber's suspicious acquaintances, his embrace of a nationalist worldview... He had never tried to push it forward in the theater—but perhaps he was just plotting behind everyone's backs.

"Come with me. Now!" Eger snapped when he saw Weber's hesitation.

Eger strode to his office. Frederick Weber could barely keep up with his pace. He entered the director's office bearing a perplexed expression.

As soon as the door closed after them, Eger shouted: "Is this all your doing? Admit it!" He was shaking and deathly pale with fury. "I know what people you've been meeting with, what politics you prefer and that you disagree with my choice of repertoire. Now you're trying to make me drop an opera by an emigrant, in a style that doesn't suit the preferences of... your acquaintances. Just like last time, an incident occurred when you've been in my office. Seems like you set it all up before and were trying to have the best alibi, doesn't it?" The director gulped. "That disgusting letter, the words on the curtain—you wrote that, didn't you? Just finally admit it..."

"You're right that I'm not trying to hide what I think," Weber said slowly. "Even if it gets me the sneers and frowns of other people. Doesn't that at least make me more honest than those people who pretend they're against nationalism, while they would leap at the first chance to embrace it if it could get them higher? I'm not a hypocrite."

"The ghost—is it your doing?" Eger pressed on.

"No." Weber's gaze fell upon the director's desk where they sat just half an hour ago. His eyes first widened with surprise. Then he produced a sad little smile. "And I think I see a proof of that."

A pristine envelope rested on the papers they had been going through before the incident. Eger walked to it slowly, as if in a dream, and took out the folded letter inside.

It bore the same ancient-like handwriting. The same hate-spewing kind of message.

We have warned you before. Stop filling this theater with this truculent Emigrantenkunst. Unless you do, it will be done for you.

"I couldn't have left this, I was with you all this time," Weber remarked into the ensued silence. "Unless you think I can be at two places at once or the theater is teeming with accomplices."

Eger stared at the letter. "I'm sorry."

"It's a little late for that."

"No, I have been wrong to suspect you and made a terrible mistake in not trusting you. Please forgive me." Eger set aside the awful paper.

"I... I'd be honored if you stayed, despite what I'd said. This theater needs you."

"And how can I know that you won't leap to the same conclusion if something else happens?" Bitterness permeated Weber's voice. He stuck out his chin. "No matter. I didn't want to tell you, but I've received a good offer from Ostrau. I was inclined to refuse, but given how little you value me here..."

"You'll be the first in line in Ostrau."

"There's one thing in which you were right. I don't really mind the possibility of that." Weber raised the corners of his lips in a bitter smile. "Good luck finding another dramaturge right now."

Eger watched him leave without another word.

The feeling of control inevitably slipping away from him grasped him especially strongly now. God, he needed some good news. The premiere of *Karl V.* was supposed to be in less than a month, but their lead singer had a fractured arm and Eger wouldn't be surprised if he refused to step into this house ever again, and he wouldn't be able to persuade the singer without giving up his honesty and principles.

Is this the end? occurred to him. *Or just a prelude to it?*

HANNA PONDERED her fate long and hard. But there was only one conclusion she seemed to reach every time: no matter what happened to her later, she had to come clean. But she also had to protect Stefan. After all, the "Let's get another ghost on our side" was her own stupid idea, and might have turned out to be a far too costly one.

That was why she turned up at the doorstep of a ground-floor flat scarcely after dawn.

Her hand stopped short almost touching the door.

She was going to throw away a job, perhaps a future...

No. She wouldn't turn her back.

Hanna knocked strongly, perhaps too strongly. The older woman who opened the door didn't seem pleased. "Yes?"

"I'm sorry for intruding so early, but I need to speak with Mr. Leppin. My name is Hanna Weisz. I work in the theater."

"Another one?" The woman raised a brow. Her lips were pressed tightly. "Come in, then."

Another one? Hanna wondered before she entered the tiny living room. There sat Leppin in a huge recliner chair—and opposite him sat Stefan. He looked at her with utter astonishment.

Leppin looked her up and down and said: "I suppose you're here about the ghost too?"

Hanna collected herself enough to nod. She sat in the remaining empty chair. A cup of tea landed before her the next thing, even though she hadn't asked for any. She glimpsed the woman, probably Leppin's wife, leaving the room with a stern, disapproving expression.

"It's my fault—" Hanna started at the same time as Stefan, uttering the exact same words.

They looked at each other in disbelief.

"I summoned it," Stefan said firmly and turned to Leppin again. "Let me tell you what happened."

"Pray continue. And be so kind as to tell me the truth. You're obviously both implicated, so don't keep up this charade of *my fault, your fault.*"

Leppin listened to their account without interruption. The expression on his thin long face was stern.

Heavy silence fell when they finished. The tea had grown cold; none of them touched it during their conversation.

Finally, Leppin spoke: "That's quite a tale. I should tell you that you made a horrible mistake and meddled in something that must be left alone. That you endangered not just your lives, but the lives of everyone in the theater, and that you should have told me right away." A melancholic smile played on the old man's lips. "But I won't, since you already know that and since I used to be the same fool like you two are."

He absently picked up the cold teacup. "Let's focus on ridding ourselves of the current ghost. You've mentioned that you might have given someone the idea to summon a ghost if they saw you performing the ritual. Any idea who might that be?"

"The actors tend to be superstitious, and might know more about old theater rumors and rituals. As to motive… Trabauer doesn't seem to mind the hakenkreuzers," Stefan said after a momentary hesitation. "He plays Frundsberg in *Karl V*. Or perhaps Grahl, who plays Francisco Borgia."

"Do you think either would have stayed late in the theater and seen your ritual?"

"No… I don't see how."

"Anyone stays there late habitually?"

"Apart from the director, the cleaners, of course," Stefan said. "Sometimes carpenters if there's scenery left to work on, but not that night."

"It might have been Götz," Hanna added. "He's an actor and stage director, and he's started openly sympathizing with Hitler."

Stefan nodded reluctantly. "I've seen him here late a few times when there was work to be done shortly before premieres he was involved in, but that wasn't the case that night."

"We're forgetting one thing," Hanna reminded him. "Whoever saw us couldn't memorize the ritual, unless they had some previous interest or experience, or knew where to look it up. It could have been someone whose friends or relatives were involved in spiritism or exorcism earlier."

"Like you two?" Leppin suggested dryly. He shook his head. "This way of making a… list of suspects… reminds me of the way other lists are being put together. I don't like the notion."

"What else can we do?"

Leppin laid aside his empty cup. "When the ghost you summoned attacked you, what did you feel?"

Stefan seemed taken aback by the sudden change of topic. Hanna lowered her eyes.

"Well… cold, *hollowness*… I couldn't move when it was already next to me, reaching *into* me—but then something stopped it. I didn't do anything. I felt the presence of something or someone else. Then it vanished, just like the ghost."

"Interesting," Leppin mumbled under his breath. For a moment, he seemed utterly lost in thought. Then he looked up sharply. "Do you realize I have to tell Director Eger sooner or later?"

"Do what you must." Hanna set her jaw.

"But I ask you to let us stay until this trouble is over," Stefan added. "If we can be of some help…"

"Perhaps, perhaps you can…"

Hanna watched the old writer and new exorcist's thin wrinkled face and sunken eyes with a sting of pity. They were the ones who'd turned this frail, ill man's life upside down, and the theater's life as well. She really hoped they could help.

Suddenly, he looked up with a strange gleam in his eyes. "Speaking of the ritual you performed, I suppose you can't summon some ghost in particular, can you?" he asked. "If you, for instance, wanted to summon the spirit of let's say… Mozart, could you?"

"It would be difficult, but not impossible, I think," Stefan said hesitantly.

Hanna frowned at seeing the distant pensive expression that set in Leppin's face.

It was the look of someone contemplating a grave mistake. Perhaps she'd looked like that when it had occurred to her to bind another ghost to help them prevail over the previous one.

"Ghosts…" Leppin mumbled. Then, he raised his gaze to meet Hanna's. "What did you say that young woman's ghost told you?"

"Well, at first she said that someone from the theater summoned the other ghost, but when we asked about that person's profession, she told us nothing."

"How did you ask again?"

"If they were employed as an actor, singer, technical crew… The answer was no to everything."

"Ha!" Leppin chuckled all of a sudden, making Hanna and Stefan look at him in surprise. "I think I know the answer to this little riddle —and hopefully to our summoner as well."

"PRESIDENT CALLS for caution and unity! Sudetendeutsche Partei celebrates victory in the regions that voted yesterday, remains at low in Prague! Temporary ban of public gatherings and marches!"

The newsboys were getting a lot of attention this Monday morning. Eger himself bought *Prager Tagblatt*, like he did regularly every morning on his way to work.

This particular late May morning was warm and sunny, and had all the charm of spring at its peak. It was in sharp contrast to the overall mood. Nature didn't play by dramatic rules; it would be doing whatever it pleased no matter what feuds people waged with each other.

Later, in his office, Eger got several calls and telegrams from his contacts about news in German newspapers. They referred to a Czechoslovakian military airplane that had supposedly crossed German borders without permission; should peace be risked because of this provocation; powerful victory of the righteous Sudetendeutsche Partei; armed Czech Sokols had caused incidents at Polish borders...

He didn't know whether there was truth in any of that, apart from the election results, but he knew with grim certainty that it would be well-used by Germany regardless of it all.

A glance at his watch told him that he should get to the auditorium to manage another rehearsal of *Karl V*. He didn't have to, but wanted to oversee this performance personally, especially after his opera dramaturge had left.

What should he tell the ensemble?

Eger took one final look at Angelo Neumann's picture on the wall. *Showtime.*

Conversations were dying down when he passed by. Whispers quieted.

The silence that fell when he stopped center stage couldn't have been any heavier.

"I don't have any clever quote or sure advice for you," Eger began. "I won't lie to you. The future is uncertain and looks darker with each passing day. What place does theater have in a world where we're witnessing atrocities and where many of you worry about your loved ones who have remained behind our borders? I have no the answer for that. I know only one thing for sure: people who fear and worry during the day burst into laughter here in the evening, hold their breath with expectation and feel hope. I don't know what awaits us and when, but we cannot take this away from them—or ourselves."

He felt strange, seeing their tense faces. They held onto his words, cradled them in their souls like prayer. The crowning achievement of his acting career might be… a speech for the ensemble.

He really was good. He'd managed to persuade even himself that they should persist.

Strangely elated, in a dream-like state, Eger shivered. But the cold he felt was dream-like too.

"Oh no," he breathed. A little cloud of vapor formed by his mouth.

He wanted to move. But he couldn't.

So this is what it's like to be touched by death, he thought. He failed to feel fear, but was sure that it would come sooner or later.

***

PAUL LEPPIN'S eyes widened with consternation—and fear, which he didn't fail to feel.

Director Eger stood motionless center stage, mist condensing around him and needles of frost forming on his fingertips.

Almost unconsciously, Leppin started reciting the spell that would reinforce the wards around the stage. His joints hurt more with every word. He uttered the final syllables in pain and almost collapsed, but a pair of strong arms caught him in time.

"What do we do?" Stefan asked.

Many possibilities flew through Leppin's mind. Spells; amulets; holy water… But he instinctively knew that none would work, not even with Stefan's and Hanna's help.

Hanna… The girl stared at Director Eger, just like everyone else, but she alone wasn't standing stiff with fear or disbelief. Her expression was one of grim determination. She stepped toward the stage. In this instant, she reminded Leppin of Milada, a character from one of his old stories. The stage light created a halo around her head for a passing moment, but she was far from a saint. She was bold, stubborn, alluring.

"What do we do?" echoed in Leppin's ears—but no, Stefan was just repeating those words.

In that moment, a shout overcame all the murmur. "You coward! Hiding behind a dead soul!" Hanna screamed at the whole theater. "If you want to fight, at least face us!"

She jumped onstage and walked toward Eger. This time, fear was very much apparent in her face, but she didn't falter. She extended her arm and touched the director's shoulder. She gasped.

Some of the needles of frost on the director's fingertips melted, but others formed on her body.

Leppin awoke. He muttered a spell to reinforce the wards, but it did nothing at all. He tried *seeing* the spirit, but that failed too.

A cloud of vapor formed in front of Hanna's face, and she was shivering, but she breathed out some words and the frost on Eger's body thawed slightly. But it grew on hers.

"Come back!" Stefan called out. "You'll hurt yourself!"

"I—don't—care," Hanna uttered through her clattering teeth. Somehow, she managed to raise both her head and her voice, and called out: "Whoever the hell you are, try to take me first! I am what you most despise, no? A Jew who ran from those bastards across the border, begging for work here! So—do you have the courage to face me?"

No one responded.

Eger and Hanna were past shivering. Frost was crawling up their bodies, forming a translucent mosaic on their faces.

It must be someone here. Someone from the theater. But not employed as… anything. Leppin looked around. He tried to remember what he'd seen in the documentation Director Eger had reluctantly agreed for him to glance through. His memory wasn't what it used to be lately, but he could still recall Eger's "creative handling of contracts." Among other things, it meant that some of the people working here weren't technically employed by the theater.

He drew a sharp breath. *But who?*

Suddenly, he noticed an empty space where someone had been just a moment ago.

Horst Feistel. Of course. But where has he gone?

With the rods broken, Leppin resorted to throwing pinches of sand into the air, as Meyrink had shown him ages ago. To his own amazement, it worked. Even to his old eyes, the direction was clear. Movement became difficult, as if he were trying to walk through water, but both he and Stefan got backstage. There sat a man hunched over a chalk ornament.

It really was Feistel, the scenographer. Formally employed by a film company where Eger had some friends, Leppin realized.

Feistel opened and closed his mouth, much like a shored fish. "I'm trying to stop it," he blurted out.

"So do it," Leppin said coldly.

"I... don't know how."

Stefan looked as if he were about to punch the scenographer, but both he and Leppin could see that he was telling the truth. He really had no idea how to control the spirit he'd unleashed.

Precious seconds were running by.

Leppin took the surprised man by the collar and nearly dragged him the shortest way to the stage. Eger and Hanna were both covered in a thin layer of frost. Such beautiful patterns...

Leppin threw the man toward them. "Stop it or join them," he stated.

Feistel straightened himself and looked at the shocked audience. "No," he said. His voice carried through the hall. "Not until I'm convinced the theater will change for good."

Stefan could no longer control himself and lurched at him, but he froze mid-motion. He looked at Hanna with desperation. Her chest rose with shallow breaths, but otherwise she resembled a ghost more than a living person.

Leppin couldn't miss the strange gleam in Feistel's eyes, and it occurred to him how much of the man and how much of the ghost was in charge. He wanted to take a step toward him, but found that he couldn't. Each attempt to move led to unspeakable pain in his joints, and it was no longer like trying to walk through water, but through treacle. Taking a step would mean passing out from the agony.

"We'll no longer suffer the current direction of the theater!" Feistel continued. "So why delay the inevitable?" He looked around at his colleagues. "We haven't been a truly German theater for some time, but we can become one again! We *will*. It's just a matter of time. Why wait?" The scenographer raised his voice: "Just look at us! We've been losing audience for *decades*! We were being ridiculed and mocked."

"That is not true," Leppin managed to croak.

"It is, and you've enabled it, just like the director! Not out of malice, I hope, but you're being myopic!" The scenographer burst into a sad, desperate laughter. "Even bloody Czech journalists see it! And it's time something was done. Something that should have been done a long time ago."

Leppin's desperation could be matched only by his rising anger.

It would kill him, Henriette had feared back then, when Eger came calling for help.

So be it. He had one foot in the grave anyway.

Unless I'm mistaken, if it's truly you, my friend... listen to me. You know it could kill me, but you must also know it's worth it. We must stop this, he thought.

Back home, he'd hesitated whether to reveal his suspicion to the two youngsters. In the end, he'd kept it to himself. Perhaps he was just an old fool when it occurred to him that Stefan's rescue and his success with temporarily driving the ghost away could have been caused by another ghost—of someone who'd had lots of experience with exorcism in his own life.

"I call you, ghost of Gustav Meyrink," he whispered. "I offer you this old body as your shell in our world. I will pay the price gladly. If you're here, don't wait anymore."

A scent of something smoky and sweet, and something warm on his chest.

Of course…

On a chain tucked under his vest hung a small vial containing blue crystals.

Gustav had given it to him. Leppin couldn't resist and had immortalized the scene, with some little changes, in his *Severin's Journey into Darkness*. After all, the novel's Nicolas was a quite accurate copy of Meyrink after his life had fallen apart, and before his departure for Vienna.

"What is it?" Severin asks in the novel.

"Chinese poison," Nicolas replies.

"And you're giving it to me?"

"I have more where it came from."

It's poison. My way out, my escape if I feel I'm losing myself too much… that I'm losing against the disease eating me away, Leppin thought grimly. Should he depart on his final journey now?

With as much effort as he could muster, in spite of the agonizing pain, he raised his arm, took out the vial, and pressed it to his lips.

The poison tasted bittersweet. But before he could empty the vial in his mouth, it turned strongly bitter. Leppin pulled the vial from his lips. More than a half its contents still remained.

His gaze unfocused. His legs felt even heavier than before. His own body felt strange, almost alien to him, like a robot he was controlling from somewhere else.

He recalled having shared his body for a few eternal seconds with a restless ghost, whom no one had believed when she'd been alive. But that wasn't *his* memory, was it?

Leppin felt his lips widen into an insane smile.

So you've made it! I'd love to talk with you about everything… but we've got work.

Suddenly, he clearly saw the silvery net surrounding the whole room. The employees were trapped in it like caught fish. Icy mist swirled around Eger and Hanna.

Feistel's eyes shone with unearthly light. Did he control the specter without even realizing it, or had the ghost gained control over him?

It didn't matter. He could recall all the ghosts whom he'd ever sent back behind the veil, and knew that he hadn't got his faithful tarot cards, divining rods, holy water, Ganges or Nile water, dried herbs, amulets... he had nothing but his own experience.

But that was enough.

Leppin felt pain shoot through his whole body as he stepped toward Feistel, but he regarded it as something distant, unimportant. The scenographer's face betrayed consternation. He was within reach now. Leppin touched Feistel's forehead and felt power flowing like water in a well. Feistel didn't control it, not consciously at least.

Leppin spoke something he wouldn't understand, but somehow he *knew* what the ancient Arabic spell meant.

He felt the power flowing from Feistel into his palm, but it put up a fight. It threatened to take him down with it if he banished it. Leppin wouldn't struggle if it meant the theater would be safe.

However, his old friend would never allow such a thing.

He touched the invisible threads with his other hand and pulled. He heard dozens of relieved and terrified breaths being released.

But Feistel didn't give up, and neither did the ghost within.

"Stop!" Feistel screamed. "You're just sinking this theater! I want to save it, whatever the price!"

Leppin glimpsed Stefan leaning above Eger and Hanna, both trembling, but alive.

It was just between him and Feistel now.

Leppin caught Eger's gaze and something in him, perhaps his old friend, spoke: "This theater doesn't need saving—not now. Perhaps soon... not by the likes of you, but from them. It will put up a fight, because it lives in the dreams and memories of people who won't let you take it from them, not without defending it."

He grasped Feistel's temples with both hands. It felt like being struck by lightning. Something shot through him, flowed inside him alongside the poison in his veins. He feared that his heart wouldn't stand it, that the ghost would escape and he'd die without stopping it—but something else managed to do just that. Leppin felt the ghost losing the battle taking place within him.

Paul Leppin's life flashed in front of his eyes. The smiles of women, the rustling of dresses and light of lanterns. Blue dusk, and a cold morning breeze just before the golden dawn. Melancholic waves upon the river while he walked the deserted riverbank. Laughter, cries, biting frost, scorching flames, love, betrayal. The intoxicating scents of churches and brothels. Empty pockets and halos of cigarette smoke. Eager faces of students and specters in the eyes of old women. Cobblestones under tired feet, and the endless arch of heaven above disheveled hair. Grotesques and tragedies. Births. Funerals. Sorrow…

And among all that, he caught glimpses of another life…

…before they vanished like fine mist above the river at dawn, and he suspected it was the last time they would meet—at least in this world.

"Thank you, my friend," Leppin whispered, barely audibly.

The presence of something otherworldly had passed and he stumbled, but someone caught him. It was Stefan, who gave him an encouraging smile and helped him to a chair.

Horst Feistel trembled and fell on his knees, his face distorted in defeat.

"I only wanted to save this theater," he whispered. Tears ran down his cheeks.

Leppin despised him—but at the same time, he believed him.

MIDNIGHT SOUNDED. Then one a.m. Two.

Paul Leppin stared at a picture of his son, taken just months before his death.

He'd never gotten to say goodbye.

On one hand, I'm glad you didn't get to see how the world crumbles further around us. But on the other hand… you had your life ahead of you. You should have lived, not me. Not me.

How easy it would be to perform a summoning ritual, and try to call for this particular soul…

"No," he sighed, and laid down the photograph. "I trust you're in a good place, wherever that may be. Rest in peace."

THE EMPEROR HAD DIED. He'd left behind an empire on which the sun never set.

It would soon crumble. But history would remember it… Paul Eger wondered if it would too remember something as small as a theater after it was gone. His gaze traveled from Charles V.'s deathbed to the empty place in the box next to the stage. But the young Stefan and Hanna sat beside the empty chair, prepared to intervene if needed. Eger doubted it would ever be necessary again. The time of ghosts seemed to be over. Something much more sinister haunted the world now.

"Unfinished is his work," stated Juan de Regla, and Eger focused on the stage again.

"But we are eternally grateful to him, for he tried heroically," said Francisco Borgia.

Eleonore finished hoarsely: "Peace be with him."

A moment of silence.

Then, a round of ground-shattering applause.

Paul Eger watched it with the same mix of joy, pride, satisfaction, and melancholy as always. It was a marvelous ending for this operatic season.

Later, when congratulations for the performers were over and the backstage grew silent, he retreated back into his office. There was still work to do.

He shouldn't spend time with financial overviews and contracts so late and after a successful premiere, but he would have peace at this time. Tomorrow, all the crazy wheel of fortune that was theater would start spinning anew.

As he unlocked the office, his gaze fell upon a folded piece of paper on the floor. Someone must have slid it under the door. Eger reached for it with a tightening feeling in his gut.

The spiteful, threatening contents confirmed his expectation. Anonymous, of course, and typed. It wasn't the first such note, nor would it be the last, Eger was sure. Ever since the May election, he felt like they were all living on borrowed time.

Eger sank into the chair and buried his face in his palms. The sensation of his cold thin fingers on his forehead felt ghost-like. He would never let others see it, but he was impossibly tired. Sometimes he wondered what he was still doing here. He could quit. Leave, and never return. Find another job. Maybe another place to live.

But he could never bring himself to actually do it.

"You knew how it is, didn't you?" he spoke toward the picture of Angelo Neumann. "No matter how much it drains you, how many obstacles you must face, you can't simply leave. Not when the reward is seeing a masterpiece come alive. Not when it sends shivers through your body. Not when you see the faces full of awe, anguish, joy— whatever you want to make them feel. It's impossible to just leave this behind, isn't it?"

He knew the answer.

The show must go on, all the way to the bitter end.

If only it did not loom so close.

THE SHOW IS OVER, *the German theater in Prague has stopped existing. A precious treasure to which many people clung with their very hearts... Something great and unspeakably beautiful has ended...*

—translated from a *Bohemia* editorial, November 2, 1938.

AUTHOR'S NOTE: *The story and its take on real historical figures are fictitious, but when portraying people who've really existed, I've tried to adhere to their actual lives as much as the story allowed. Here are the fates of some of them.*

Paul Eger with his family left Prague on September 29, 1938, the day of the Munich Agreement. He died in 1947 in Switzerland, aged sixty-six. Many other employees of the Neue Deutsche Theater fled. The remaining ensemble tried to keep it working, but in vain. Karl V. had no reprise after the June premiere. On November 2, 1938, the theater shut down after more than half a century.

Max Brod, with his wife and a handful of friends, left Prague on a visa to Palestine at the last minute—less than a day after they'd fled, in March 1939, Czechoslovakia ceased to exist. His fate, at least, was quite happy. Though his life in Israel was hardly easy, he continued to produce influential work in journalism, fiction, drama, music, and translation up to his death in 1968.

Paul Leppin was arrested by the Nazi regime in March 1939. He was set free after he suffered a stroke while in jail, and he was forced to sign an allegiance to the NSDAP. His health declined rapidly and he was confined to a wheelchair. He died on April 10, 1945. His wife Henriette lived to see Prague liberated—and then was forced to leave Czechoslovakia along with other Germans by the Beneš decrees. She died a year later.

THIS STORY originally appeared in *Samovar*.

JULIE NOVÁKOVÁ (1991-) IS A SCIENTIST, educator and award-winning Czech author, editor and translator of science fiction, fantasy and detective stories. She has published seven novels, one anthology, one story collection and over thirty short pieces in Czech. Her work in English has appeared in *Clarkesworld, Asimov's, Analog* and elsewhere. Her works have been translated into eight languages so far, and she translates Czech stories into English (in *Tor.com, Strange Horizons, F&SF, Clarkesworld, Welkin Magazine*). She has edited or co-edited an anthology of Czech speculative fiction in translation, *Dreams From Beyond,* a book of European SF in Filipino translation, *Haka,* an outreach e-book of astrobiological SF, *Strangest of All,* and its more ambitious follow-up print and e-book anthology *Life Beyond Us* (Laksa Media, upcoming in late 2022). Julie's newest book is a story collection titled *The Ship Whisperer* (Arbiter Press, 2020). She is a recipient of the European fandom's Encouragement Award and multiple Czech genre awards. She's active in science outreach, education and nonfiction writing, and co-leads the outreach group of the European Astrobiology Institute. She's a member of the XPRIZE Sci-fi Advisory Council.

Find Julie Nováková on the web at www.julienovakova.com, and on Twitter @Julianne_SF.

ABOUT THE EDITORS

ALEX SHVARTSMAN

Alex Shvartsman is a writer, translator, game designer, and anthologist from Brooklyn, NY. His adventures so far have included traveling to over thirty countries, playing a card game for a living, and building a successful business.

Alex is the author of *The Middling Affliction* (2022) and *Eridani's Crown* (2019) fantasy novels. Over 120 of his short stories have appeared in *Analog, Nature, Strange Horizons, Fireside, Weird Tales, Galaxy's Edge*, and many other venues. He won the WSFA Small Press Award for Short Fiction in 2014 and was a two-time finalist (2015 & 2017) for the Canopus Award for Excellence in Interstellar Fiction.

Alex's translations from Russian have appeared in *The Magazine of Fantasy & Science Fiction, Tor.com, Clarkesworld, Asimov's, Apex, Strange Horizons*, and elsewhere.

He's the editor of the Unidentified Funny Objects series of humorous SF/F, as well as a variety of other anthologies, including *The Cackle of Cthulhu* (Baen), *Humanity 2.0* (Arc Manor), and *Funny Science Fiction* (UFO). He's the editor and publisher of *Future Science Fiction Digest*, a magazine that focuses on international fiction.

His website is www.alexshvartsman.com and his Twitter handle is @AShvartsman.

TARRYN THOMAS

Tarryn Thomas is a freelance editor and proofreader from the Eastern Cape Province of South Africa. She has a Humanities degree from Rhodes University and a die-hard love of science fiction. She started reading fantasy stories as a child and soon graduated to McCaffrey, Cherryh, Asimov, Eddings, and Feist.

Lately she is realizing her dream of working in the publishing industry, as a slush reader for Flash Fiction Online, managing editor for Nightshade and Moonlight, and as an associate editor at UFO.

She spends most of her time behind a keyboard, drinking coffee and wrangling commas. The beach will have to wait. She is owned by three cats.

You can find her on the web at tarrynthomas.com.

www.ingramcontent.com/pod-product-compliance
Lightning Source LLC
Chambersburg PA
CBHW070828190726
48292CB00006B/2143